BLESSED POISON

DONNY HUNT

World Castle Publishing, LLC
Pensacola, Florida
Copyright © Donny Hunt 2016
Paperback ISBN: 9781629894409
eBook ISBN: 9781629894416
First Edition World Castle Publishing, LLC
http://www.worldcastlepublishing.com
Licensing Notes
Cover: Karen Fuller
Editor: Maxine Bringenberg

BLESSED POISON

Another hard day and you're running for the shelf
For that little bottle of pills that makes you feel like yourself.
Whatever it takes to dull the pain, whatever it takes to kill the
shame.
I've watched you circle the drain for so long.
I've got no love left though I know that it's wrong.
Disgusted by your sight and sick of your presence,
I'm thinking of the future while you're dying in the present.

Everybody tells me I'm blessed
But my blessings have all been poisoned.
Behind my smile they can't see how I'm stressed,
Because my blessings have all been poisoned.

Those same demons that haunt you chase after me,
Inside of my head, tormenting constantly.
I don't reach for a bottle or vial to make myself right;
I deal with the voices that bombard me at night.

All around me strangers offer easy solutions,
A simple way to escape the strife,
To kill my spirit in order to save my life.
Just a taste of sweet, blessed poison.
If I take that escape then I become like you.
That's one thing I swear I'll never do;
I don't want your sweet, blessed poison.

Every night I lie awake in bed.
I console myself from those things that I dread.
A daily battle to keep myself sane,
Because you're the poison I can't get out of my veins.

Everyone tells me that I've been blessed
But my blessings have all been poisoned.
Sweet, blessed poison.
One day I know that I will fail the test
Because my blessings have all been poisoned.
Sweet, blessed poison.

PROLOGUE

For all of Danielle Regan's young life, there was music. Music and people. Music and laughter. Music and yelling, but always music. Always.

It all seemed to revolve around her parents. There was her dad, Big Rick Regan. Nobody ever called him Rick...it was always Big Rick. He was tall and stocky, quick with a joke, and a constant flirt, with a laugh and a temper as big as he was. He was a giant to little Dani, and she cherished the few times that they had alone together.

Dorothy was her mom and she was the hostess, roaming from person to person, filling glasses and plates and scurrying Dani off to bed when it became "adult time." She was always cold and distant.

When the music stopped and the people went home, her parents would fight and Danielle would retreat to the solace of her room and her collection of blues records to drown out the screams.

Luckily for Dani, that wasn't often. There was always somebody at the house, usually musicians. Jam sessions would break out at all times of the day or night, and people would usually play and drink and whatever else they did until they finally passed out where they sat.

That was Big Rick's job, as she recalled; taking care of musicians. It seemed to little Dani that it was a tough job, and one that required a lot of his time.

They lived in a big house at first, with plenty of room for everyone. It seemed that every night somebody new would put her to sleep by singing or playing an instrument. Later she would see them on TV, but back then she only knew them by appearance.

Her favorite was The Funny Looking Man. He was soft spoken with a nice smile, and never seemed to be mad at anybody. She liked to hear him sing, and would often have his voice in her head for days. She wished that he would trade places with Mom, but he never stayed long; he liked to be with the adults.

In the beginning, it was fun. She would sneak out of bed and watch the adults laugh and drink and smoke and do other things that she knew she shouldn't see. Someone would start singing and soon everyone else joined in. It seemed like the perfect life.

Soon though, they had to move to a smaller house, and then another and another. The neighborhoods got rougher and the people stopped coming around. Eventually, the music stopped and left only the yelling. Big Rick started staying away, although Dani never blamed him.

Mom started dragging her to church and talking about the devil. Big Rick had the devil. Dani wondered if he was the one who took the music and the house and the people away. Mom said the devil was in the music and took all of Dani's records away.

Dani cried for days. Now when Big Rick did come home, nothing could drown out the screams and the breaking dishes and the nasty names. She would just climb into bed and pull the covers up over her head and imagine that the people still came around, but no one never came.

By the time she was eight she knew what all of the boxes in the hall meant when she came home from school. It was time to move, but if their house got much smaller, someone would have to start sleeping outside. Mom told her that they were leaving for good this time, and were going to live with Grandma and Grandpa in some town she could barely pronounce.

She didn't want to leave. Austin had always been her home, but Mom wouldn't listen. The devil was in Austin. Secretly, Dani wondered if the devil was in Mom, but she would never dare say that.

On her last night in Austin, Big Rick knocked softly on her window so as not to wake Mom. Dani went to the window and found him in tears. He didn't seem like Big Rick anymore. He was skinny and looked sick. He didn't laugh anymore. She didn't like to see him like this.

He pulled her out of the window and sat her on the grass. It was cool from an evening rain and the smell still hung in the heavy air. He held her and hugged her for the longest time, never saying anything.

Finally, he put her back in the window. He put a hand on her cheek and said "I'm sorry." She never knew why, but Dani started crying. All Big Rick could say was "I'm sorry," and then he left, and Dani knew he wasn't coming back.

She never told Mom because she didn't want to risk Mom's anger. In the morning, they loaded up the car and drove away. Dani sat in the backseat and watched until the very last images of Austin vanished on the horizon. Mom kept telling her that everything was going to be better now. Dani didn't believe her. Nothing would ever be better.

Mom drove on regardless of how badly Dani wanted to stop. Soon the red and blue and yellow wildflowers on the side of the road quit following and the hills flattened out. Then the grass stopped too, and there was nothing but dirt and twisted sticks for trees that Mom called mesquite.

Dani began to wonder if Mom was going to drive all the way to the ocean, or maybe to the end of the earth itself. But finally, she stopped driving. They had reached Grandma and Grandpa's house, in a town called Chaparral.

CHAPTER ONE

Chaparral, Texas sat where the rolling South Plains butted up against the desert of the Permian Basin. Danielle's grandpa described it as being "a spit's distance" from New Mexico. Mom described it as a shithole.

Chaparral was an old oil field town clinging to life now that the oil boom had gone bust. As a result, many of the town's stores were closing and people had begun leaving for the city. It got so bad the town even lost its Dairy Queen, a staple of life in small Texas towns.

Danielle had never seen Grandma and Grandpa in person because they refused to go to Austin to see their daughter. The devil was in Austin, as she well understood by now. It didn't take long for Dani to realize that they didn't get along with Mom that well either, so maybe it didn't have anything to do with Austin. The devil, however…that was a different story.

Grandma was short and plump, with gray hair that she kept in a constant perm. She waddled a little when she walked, and her chin folded in a way that made it obvious that she had false teeth. She wore thick glasses and had a flighty voice. She made sure to never be seen without her hair and makeup done, and she always smelled of perfume and lipstick.

Grandpa was tall and lean with thinning gray hair. He tried to look serious, but his blue eyes gave away a mischievous character. He was a sloppy dresser who didn't give a damn what anybody thought. He was also friendly and generous and almost universally liked about town.

Danielle took immediately to them both and they both fawned over her, albeit in very different ways. Grandma liked to dress Dani up in pretty dresses and makeup and style her long brown hair. Then she would go to the beauty shop and stay there all day while all the other old ladies, of which Chaparral had a large supply, would fawn over her as well.

Grandpa liked to take her in the garden with him, where they would eat ripened tomatoes off the vine. Sometimes he would take her out in the field across the way to teach her how to shoot and she got pretty good at shooting jackrabbits with Grandpa's old .22 rifle. She also learned how to keep his old Ford pickup running, and Grandpa took advantage of her skinny, nimble fingers to retrieve dropped bolts from tight spaces.

In the early days things were great. Mom was working two jobs. When she wasn't working, she was usually asleep or out with a guy, so Dani seldom saw her. Instead she hung out with her grandparents or rode Mom's old bicycle all over town.

As summer ended a new family with a girl Dani's age moved into town three streets over. Grandma arranged a meeting between the two girls. It didn't take long for them to become friends.

Brooke Farmer was the opposite of Dani in every way. Brooke was slightly heavy with golden hair, pale blue eyes, and fair skin. She was sunny and fun loving and talked a mile a minute. Brooke helped bring Dani out of her shell, and soon they were tearing up the town on their bicycles, running through people's sprinklers, or darting from one piece of playground equipment to the other in the city park.

On Sundays, they both sang in the church choir. Brooke imagined herself a singer and she would belt it out loud and proud. However, it was Danielle who caught the attention of the choir director. Getting Dani to loosen up enough to sing a solo in front of the congregation was an almost impossible task. Once she did, Danielle felt a thrill at performing that would change her life.

After church both families would congregate at Grandma and Grandpa's for a big lunch. Everyone except for Mom, who would go off with her latest boyfriend and stay gone until it was time for work. Nobody missed her. Everyone feared her razor tongue and her mad ravings.

#

Dani would learn that things never stayed the same for long. Her grandparents were spry and fun-loving, but they were old and age caught up fast. One day Grandma didn't feel well enough to get out of bed. Soon, she couldn't. Grandpa had to take care of her, and the strain began to wear on him.

Word soon spread through the town. People would tell her that they were praying for her grandparents. Dani decided that it couldn't hurt. She stopped by the church at least once a day, hoping God would hear her better from there.

Winter came and it brought bitter, icy cold north winds that Dani had never experienced in Austin. By now, the stress of taking care for Grandma had become too much, and Grandpa was also ailing. Mom had to stay home more to care for them, and the stress brought the devil out in her. Danielle and Brooke now played almost exclusively at Brooke's to avoid bothering Dani's grandparents.

As Grandma got sicker, the only thing that soothed her was Danielle's singing. So she would sit on the end of Grandma's bed and sing church hymns, singing louder to overcome the coughing spells until Grandma fell asleep. She slept a lot now, and Dani knew what that meant.

Grandpa still had a little fire in him. He sat her on the bed and taught her how to play his harmonica. He would tell her stories of growing up in the Depression and fighting in World War II. She tried the best she could to tend to his tomatoes and keep the lawn watered, but she didn't have his green thumb. The tomatoes never came up and the grass quickly turned brown in the late spring heat.

Surprisingly they both made it to her ninth birthday. Grandpa arranged for a friend to buy her a new bike, and he forced himself out of bed long enough to watch her ride it. He was doing fine until Mom yelled at him and forced him back to bed. Sometimes, Dani thought, she really hated her mother.

#

The first time death touched Danielle, she was on her way home from school. She and Brooke saw the ambulance go blazing by them. By the time they ran home, Grandma was gone.

The church was packed with mourners for the funeral. Danielle wasn't among them; she was in the choir. She didn't want to sing...she wanted to be there with Grandpa to hold his hand and

13

reassure him. Instead, Mom sat next to him and ignored him the whole time.

Dani's heart broke as she watched him, his body racking with the sobs and coughs. Like her father a year earlier, he didn't seem so big now. He was shrunken and frail. She started to get down from the stage and go to him, but a glare from Mom broke that urge.

It came time to end the service with Grandma's favorite song, "Amazing Grace." Danielle hated the song, but she would sing it for Grandma. Only when the music started and it came time, her voice wasn't there. It was overcome by the sadness. Luckily, Brooke quickly jumped to the rescue, taking the solo while Danielle darted off the risers so no one would see her cry.

Music. It had always made things seem better, but it had failed her this time.

#

Mom put Grandpa to bed and left for work. Danielle sat on the porch and stared intently into the distance. She was looking southeast, towards Austin, towards home. Only it wasn't home anymore. This tiny town in the middle of nowhere was home, and in a way she was fine with that.

She was suddenly aware of a presence beside her.

"That's a long old prairie out there," Grandpa said. His voice was shaky and his breathing labored. "Long way from Austin."

Danielle jumped up and helped him to the porch swing, and when he sat, he grabbed her arm and pulled her down beside him. His arm wrapped around her shoulders and pulled her in close. She kept her head down, not wanting to look into his fading eyes.

"You had a little letdown today. Grandma would be mighty disappointed in you."

She couldn't help but look up at him then. The thought of disappointing Grandma made the tears come again. He wiped them away with a wrinkled finger.

"Now there," he said, pulling her even tighter. "Life beats on everybody, young 'un. When life starts beating you down, you've got two choices. Your mom, she runs away. She always has. That's why she's so miserable."

Danielle didn't quite get what he was saying, but she nodded slightly. Grandpa pointed at her. "Now, you're gonna run into

14

trouble in your life. Everybody does. You promise me that you're not gonna run away like she does. You've got to stand your ground and fight, no matter how bad it seems. You think that I got to run away when we were fighting those Japs in WWII?"

"No sir," she whispered.

"Soon I'm going to go to be with Grandma. You know that, right?" She nodded yes. "Now, you're gonna have to stand in that choir and sing that song. And you're gonna want to cry like you did today." He put his finger under her chin and brought her gaze back up into his. For a moment, those eyes were alive again, full of fire and mischief. "When that happens, you stand your ground and you sing. You sing louder and prettier and better than you ever have. You sing right straight to heaven, and I promise you, we will hear you. You do that for me."

"I will," she whispered. "I promise." Three weeks later, she did just that.

#

With Grandma and Grandpa gone, things got worse around the house. Mom's temper got shorter, and instead of running off to spend time with her boyfriends, she started bringing them around the house. In order to stay gone as much as possible, Dani started spending more time at Brooke's house.

When summer came the Farmer family loaded up their van and headed for Florida where Brooke's grandparents lived. Brooke was going to spend the entire summer there and they invited Danielle to go along. She begged and pleaded with Mom to let her, but it was no use.

Mom had a new job now; a steady eight to five job that left Danielle at home with plenty of time to explore. One day while digging around in a closet, Dani discovered a box of old records. Curious, she took them down to the den, where Grandpa's record player sat neglected in the corner.

She didn't recognize any of the names but she didn't care. Dani just wanted hear some music. She would spend hours spinning those records. She didn't like them all but she enjoyed having music around the house again. She would dance and sing without a care in the world all day. At least until five o'clock started creeping around. That was when Danielle had to put them up and make herself scarce.

Until the day she lost track of time. Danielle was dancing and didn't hear Mom pull into the driveway. She came in the door and went ballistic immediately. "What the hell is this?" she screamed.

Dani, caught red-handed, stammered to come up with an answer. "It's just...." She was out of breath and scared, desperately searching for the words that would get her out of trouble. "They're Grandma and Grandpa's. I found them in the closet."

Mom stormed over and ripped the record off the turntable, then marched over and slapped Dani across the face with it. The record broke in half and a jagged edge cut Dani's cheek, drawing blood.

"This is devil music and I won't have it in my house."

Dani put a hand to her cheek and felt the blood. Tears began to well up in her eyes. In that moment her knees felt weak, and all she wanted to do was to melt away. Then she remembered what Grandpa had told her, and a surge of anger raced through her.

"If that's devil music, then why did Grandma and Grandpa have it? Were they devil worshippers?"

Mom pointed half of the broken record at Danielle's face. "Don't get smart with me, girl. These records are going in the trash."

"Don't do that," Danielle answered. "Give them away, don't throw them out."

"I won't pass this scourge on to someone else. Now gather up these records and throw them out. Then clean yourself up...you're getting blood everywhere."

"No," Danielle answered. "There's nothing wrong with this music."

Mom's rage was barely contained. She leaned down until she was nose to nose with Dani. Her voice was a razor. "Don't question me again, little girl. Do as I say. Get that devil music out of my house." She turned and started to storm out of the room.

"There's only one devil in this house," Danielle blurted out. "And it's not in the music."

Mom stopped in her tracks. "What did you just say?" she asked without turning around.

Dani shook all over, but she also felt exhilaration sweeping through her. "I think you heard me."

Mom beat her mercilessly after their little exchange. It was the first time she had felt her mother's full wrath, and it was terrible.

16

Danielle, though, felt she had earned a small victory. She had stared down the wicked witch and lived to tell the tale.

#

Once they hit high school, Brooke and Danielle began to drift apart. Brooke had lost weight and gotten contacts. She started hanging out with older girls and wearing revealing clothes. She was a natural flirt anyway, but with a better body she began to enjoy all kinds of attention from the boys.

Dani did everything she could to hide herself and her body. She immersed herself in the school choir, where she could escape in the music. Her talent was undeniable and she soon became the star of the choir.

Shortly after her sophomore year started, Mom began dating the manager of the local supermarket. His name was Sean McClain, and Dani took an immediate dislike to him. He was average by all measure, barely six foot and skinny, with dishwater blond hair and a sorry attempt at a mustache. His skin was blotchy and his eyes bugged a little bit, but Mom was totally taken with him.

She began talking about the three of them being a family and how Sean would be the father Danielle had never had. He seemed like a nice enough guy, one of the few that didn't leer at her every chance he got. Still, there was something about him that Dani didn't like.

Later that fall, Brooke confided in Dani that she had taken the ultimate step and lost her virginity to her new boyfriend, a preppy senior named Trent. Brooke believed that they were in love. He was going to Stanford and was going to take her with him. He was going to be a big shot lawyer and she would be his trophy wife. Danielle thought she was being naive.

#

On an unusually hot October afternoon, Danielle was walking home when she noticed a group of five older boys congregating around the mailbox of an older black man. The old man stood just inside his fence, begging for the boys to give him his mail.

They stood there shouting insults and taunting the old man. Finally, they started slinging his mail at him like Frisbees, laughing each time one of the envelopes smacked into the old man.

"Why don't you dickheads leave him alone?" she yelled out. She dropped her backpack off her shoulder so that she could swing if she had to.

"Are you gonna stop us?" one of them asked. Another started to size her up. "I bet she would be more fun."

"I bet if you try I'll kick you in the nuts so hard that they'll tickle your tonsils."

The boys started to laugh and walk towards her. Dani realized that she may have bitten off more than she could chew. At least they were ignoring the old man, who stood in his yard holding onto his fence and shaking.

The boys were getting closer to Danielle, taunting her. "Little girl wants to play with the big boys. Let's have some fun."

Danielle tightened her grip on the strap of her backpack and got ready to swing. She was ready for whatever happened next, but instead the boys turned and ran away.

She looked over her shoulder. The sheriff was driving up the street towards them. He pulled up next to her and rolled down his window.

"What's going on here?"

"Those assholes were messing with that old man. They took his mail and were throwing it at him and calling him names."

"And you decided to take them on?"

"I had to do something to get them to leave him alone."

He started laughing, a deep belly laugh that made her think of her dad. "You best be careful picking fights like that. I know those kids. I'll have a little talk with their parents, and I bet we don't have another problem." Then he leaned over into the passenger seat and pointed a finger at her. "But you had better watch yourself, jumping into the middle of something like that. Those boys could have hurt you. Or worse."

"I've taken worse than they can give."

"I'm sure you have," he answered. They both knew what she was talking about. "Those boys may not have been satisfied just to beat you up. Watch yourself." He rolled up his window and drove away.

She walked up to the house and into the man's yard. His mail was scattered everywhere, and it was clear that he wasn't going to be able to pick it up. She quickly gathered the envelopes and presented them to him.

"Thank ya, sugar," he said in a raspy voice. "Thank ya so much."

"You're welcome."

He was a tiny man, bald and wrinkled, with a face that showed he had seen a lot life. His eyes still had the crackle of life in them. In that way, he reminded her of Grandpa.

"Why don't you let me get you in the house?"

He chuckled and patted her arm. "I'd be pleased. Ain't had a pretty girl pay no attention to me in a long time."

His house was small and dusty and full of junk. She didn't want to touch anything, and stepped lightly to avoid stepping on anything.

"Sorry 'bout the mess," he said, sounding embarrassed. "Don't ever have company, and not in much shape to clean. Get my meals from the church every evening, so I don't need to cook."

It's okay," she said, trying not to show her disgust. She knew that he couldn't help it, but it was still gross. He pulled away from her grasp and headed down a short hall. "I'll be right back. Don't go nowhere."

She didn't want to stay any longer than necessary, but it would be rude to bolt now, so she stood in the living room and looked around. There was one corner that was clean. In that corner, sitting on a stand with a wide berth, was a red and white guitar. She had seen guitars like that before. She had seen The Funny Looking Man play one like it.

She strolled over and looked at it more carefully. The name was branded on the head of the guitar: Stratocaster. She took her index finger and strummed the strings along the neck.

"I see you found Ole Red," he laughed, plopping down into his dusty green recliner. "Me and Ole Red go back a long way. What's your name, darlin'?"

She dropped her fingers away from the guitar and turned. "Danielle Regan. I live over on Roadrunner."

"Kel Shepard, nice to meet you." He held out a wrinkled hand and she took it. "Regan, huh? Like Ronald Regan, the president?"

"I guess," she said uncomfortably. "It's spelled different though. I'm sorry about those guys today."

He waved her off. "Don't worry 'bout them fools. They don't even know why they do what they do. They just think they bein' cool. Not like in the old days. Back then, fellas really hated and they came real. You had to be scared back then. Now people just like to be bullies. They don't bother me none."

"I guess you've seen some pretty bad times in your life."

"Seen my share," he nodded. "Seen some bad things, met some bad people." He made a motion with his hands like he was brushing himself off. "I let it roll off. Prefer to think 'bout the good times. Lots of good people too." He leaned forward. "Let me tell ya a secret."

She found herself leaning in closer, like she was about to receive some vital piece of information.

"Some of 'em is white!" He laughed and leaned back in his chair. He was clearly pleased with his ability to hook the girl. "Some black folk won't say that. I will. Lots of good people out there, you just can't tell by lookin'. Gotta get to know people, ya know?"

"Yes I do."

He looked over her shoulder at the guitar. "You like Ole Red? Go get him and play him a bit. I don't mind."

Dani suddenly became very nervous. "I couldn't do that. I don't know the first thing about guitars."

"Well, you ain't gonna learn nothin' by sittin' there. Go get it."

"Sir, I really couldn't—"

"Sir," he laughed heartily. "I ain't no sir. You call me Kel." He leaned forward and patted her knee. "Let me tell you somethin' 'bout guitars. They got souls, just like people do. They need to be played. I can't do it no more. Old hands just can't. But Red there, he needs to be played. So go get him and give it a try."

She was curious, and felt a strange pull to the instrument. She remembered when she was a kid watching her parent's parties, she had always been drawn to the guitar players. The Funny Looking Man had played guitar. Of course, she knew his name now. He was a star.

She got up and retrieved the guitar, and was surprised by how heavy it was. She came back and plopped down on the couch. She was incredibly self-conscious. Kel just laughed at her.

"Quit bein' so shy. I can tell by lookin' that you're a hurricane. You got a whole 'nother you just dyin' to get out. Go on, let loose."

She let out a slow breath, wishing that she didn't feel so uncomfortable. She should have never come in here, she thought. But it was too late now. She put her fingers on the strings and strummed. A horrible noise came from Ole Red.

"Whoo boy, you don't know anything 'bout a guitar, do ya?" He struggled up out of the recliner and slid over to the couch beside her. Then he took her left hand in his and placed her fingers on the strings. "You gotta put 'em right above the frets there…make sure you're on 'em good. Like this. Now strum."

She did and it sounded much better. "There you go. Now all you gotta do is practice."

"I'm sure that there's more to it than that."

"Not really. First you learn the basic chords…that one there was an A. Once you learn your basic chords, you'll just kind of pick up the rest. It comes natural. I tell you what. You come by every day after school and practice, and when you get really good, I'll give him to ya."

"Sir…Kel, I couldn't take your guitar."

"Nope," he said, holding up his hand. "He's not mine. Not no more. He's done picked somebody else. He likes you. You can't argue with that. Some people are just destined."

Danielle began to stop by Kel's house every day on the way home from school to practice. He showed her all the tricks, starting with the basic chords. By the end of the third day she was playing her first twelve bar blues.

She also started cleaning his house and cooking for him. Spending so much time alone had forced her to fend for herself, and she was already turning into a fine cook. One day while she was cleaning, she came across a box of old blues records.

Kel smiled as he flipped through the box, reading off the names as he went. B.B. King, Muddy Waters, Howlin' Wolf, Albert King. "This is music, right here," he said. She was sitting on the arm of his recliner, looking over his shoulder. "Real American music. Real black music. Not that boom boom stuff the kids listen to now. Come right off the plantation. We took it out of the delta and to the cities, and the white kids fell in love with it."

21

Danielle smiled as she watched Kel trip back in time. "Man, I remember those days, in the early sixties, when the British kids got everybody interested in our music. Gigs were easy to come by back then. Every bar wanted its own black bluesman." He flipped through some more. "This guy, Buddy Guy. I played with him a few times. You ever heard of Jimi Hendrix?"

"Of course," she answered. "Who hasn't?"

"Buddy was Jimi before Jimi. Hendrix took his whole bit from Buddy. Notice I didn't say stole? We all borrowed from each other. The blues is a community. We all give and we all take. That's how it works."

She took the record from him and inspected it. "I recognize some of these. Stevie Ray plays some of these."

Kel shook his head. "Stevie who?"

"Stevie Ray Vaughan. He's a blues guitarist out of Austin. He used to hang out at my parents' house when I was little, before he made it big."

"Never heard of him. 'Course, I don't really listen to music anymore."

"If my bit...." She caught herself. "If my mother would let me have music in the house, I'd bring some over. She thinks music is the devil's tool."

Kel laughed hard at that. "I've seen lots of devils. They ain't in the music. Somethin' I learned a long time ago. We all got a devil. Some people control it, some can't." He put the records back in the box. "You got a way to play these?"

"Yeah. Mom hasn't thrown out Grandpa's old record player yet. She thinks that she can sell it and make some money. I can listen when she's not around."

"Then you take these and give them a listen. You'll hear what I'm tryin' to teach ya."

The guitar had reawakened her interest in music. Brooke's parents bought her a Walkman, and Brooke's mom set about the tedious task of recording all of Kel's blues albums onto cassettes. She would hide them all under a loose floorboard in her closet to avoid Mom's periodic inspections. She started doing odd jobs for other elderly people in the neighborhood, and used the money to buy cassettes at the local truck stop. She would buy anything that peaked her curiosity, and what she didn't like she would trade with the kids at school.

She brought her Walkman over to Kel's one day to introduce him to Stevie Ray Vaughan. Kel listened intently, nodding his head and moving his fingers like he was playing along. After a while he took off the headphones, smiled, and said, "That's the blackest damn white boy I ever heard."

At home, things were starting to improve. Sean was having a positive effect on Mom. Her temper flared less often, and she seemed to be happy for the first time in her life. There were still occasions when Mount Dorothy would erupt, but they were fewer and farther between. That had an unexpected downside for Danielle, as Mom started insisting on having more family time. Danielle had become used to coming and going as she pleased. She found dinner time and mandatory family nights strange.

For the first time in her life, things were calm. She had friends, a hobby, and some sort of family life at home. She even found herself taking a liking to Sean after a while. She confided in him about her secret stash, which he swore not to mention. Things were good.

#

Days before Thanksgiving, Brooke came over while Danielle helped Mom put away groceries and asked Danielle if they could talk. She could barely control her excitement. Danielle excused herself from her chore and took Brooke to the bedroom.

"What's going on?" she asked as she closed the door. Brooke was beaming from ear to ear, and just short of actually bouncing as she stood there.

"Trent and I are going to have a baby," she announced. "Isn't that great?" She bounded over to Danielle and hugged her more fiercely than ever. She pulled away when she realized that Danielle wasn't returning the hug. "Aren't you happy for me?"

"No," Danielle replied. "You're sixteen. You can't even drive yet. What about college?"

"Who cares?" she spat back. "All I want is Trent, and now I've got him. We'll be together forever."

Stunned, Danielle pushed past Brooke and sat down on her bed. "Did you get pregnant on purpose?"

Brooke shrugged with a faint smile. "Maybe I didn't take all of the precautions I should have."

"Oh my God," Danielle answered, burying her face in her hands. After a long silence, she looked up at her best friend. "And what does Trent think of all of this?"

Brooke sat down on the bed next to Dani. "He's in a little bit of shock right now. He didn't have much to say, but he'll come around. You'll see."

"What about your parents?"

Brooke shrugged. "They don't want to admit that their little girl is a woman now. They'll just have to live with it." She rubbed her belly and smiled again. "Mrs. Trent West. I like the sound of that."

The next few weeks became a struggle for Danielle. Word of Brooke's pregnancy got around quickly. Chaparral was a conservative town with few cases of teen pregnancy. Brooke became infamous.

Danielle wanted to stick up for her friend when people said nasty things about her. On the other hand, she felt that Brooke was making a huge mistake and that she deserved to be derided for getting pregnant on purpose.

She was thankful for the Christmas break. She hoped that the time off would allow things to cool down. Mom and Sean decided to go all out for Christmas. Danielle hadn't had a real Christmas since her first year with Grandma and Grandpa. She looked forward to having a Christmas like the ones she heard about from the kids at school.

It was a nice Christmas, even if the temperatures hovered in the low 50s and the closest snow was a hundred miles away. She loved decorating the house, and Sean took them all caroling at a local retirement home. For the first time, Mom actually complimented her on her voice. Danielle was getting used to having a real family.

Sean was a devout Christian and suggested that they attend a midnight church service. Danielle didn't object, despite her own religious doubts. The Baptist church was filled with people when they got there and seats were going fast. Danielle stood beside her mother, both of them wearing fancy Christmas dresses, when she heard a commotion. She started picking her way through the crowd, standing in the main aisle until she found the source.

It was Brooke, dressed in her Christmas best, her belly starting to pooch ever so slightly. She went from row to row, trying to find a seat, only to have people in each row dismiss her.

Danielle watched the scene with sadness, her heart breaking as Brooke's tears began to flow more with each rejection. Sean finally found them a space in the very last pew. Brooke saw Danielle and they locked eyes. Mom was pulling on her arm to get her to sit down as the service was about to start.

"I'm going to get Brooke," she whispered.

"No you're not," Mom said adamantly. "We won't have that tramp sitting beside us in church."

Dani pulled her arm away from her mother. "Yes, I am. Nobody else will let her sit." Brooke stood feet away watching the drama unfold with hope in her eyes. Danielle took another step away when she felt another hand on her shoulder. She looked back at Sean, who shook his head.

"Not tonight, Dani. Don't do this tonight. For me, for your mother, for God; don't do this tonight."

"Don't you think that God would want someone to let her sit down?"

"If he does, then someone else will let her sit. Now please, stop."

Danielle looked back at her friend. As the realization that she wasn't going to get a seat set in, Brooke rushed out the back doors, crying hysterically. Danielle kept waiting, hoping that Brooke would come back. She never did.

Dani didn't talk on the way home, choosing to go straight to bed. She tried to enjoy herself the next morning, but her thoughts kept drifting back to Brooke. She was kicking herself for not standing up for her friend.

She would have gone to her that night, but Mom insisted that she help with dinner and then it was straight off to bed. She went to Brooke's the next day only to be told very rudely by her parents that she was gone for the day. Over the next several days, she tried to call, but Brooke never answered.

Dani woke up early on New Year's Day. She had always liked New Year's; it gave her hope of better things on the horizon. She went outside to breathe in her first breath of the New Year. She decided to go to Brooke again.

After getting dressed, Dani jumped on her bike and rode to Brooke's. The sun was shining bright and it almost felt like spring. She was confident that she could repair things with Brooke, and she swore to herself that she would never again let a friend down.

As she turned the last corner to Brooke's house, her heart dropped. There was a For Sale sign in the front yard by the curb, and the house was clearly deserted.

The man next door was standing on a ladder removing his Christmas lights. "They're gone. Just packed up and moved in the middle of the night."

Danielle stood stunned, staring at the house that had been more of a home to her than her own. She couldn't believe that Brooke was gone.

It's my fault, she thought. *If I had stood up for her, fought for her, they wouldn't have left.*

By the time she got home, Mom and Sean were sitting anxiously. Dani walked into the house emotionally exhausted. Mom stood just inside the door. Sympathy wasn't her strong suit.

"That's what happens to girls who—"

Dani wheeled and stuck a finger in her mother's face. "Don't you dare finish that sentence. Don't dare."

The old Mom started to rise up and Dani was ready for a fight, but Sean interceded.

"Dorothy, sit down. This isn't the time." He put a hand on each of them and pushed them away from each other. Dani looked down to see his hand on her breast.

He caught it and pulled his hand away with a blush. "I think that your mom is trying to say that God has a way that he wants us to live, and if we don't follow God's plan—"

"Doesn't God also talk about not judging people? About love and forgiveness? Where is all of that?" Sean dropped his eyes to the floor. She stepped closer to him, but her eyes were locked on her mother's. "It's funny. People like you always want to thump on that damn book and tell people how to live their lives, but the most important lessons in there are the ones nobody ever seems to learn."

She stormed off and thankfully, nobody followed.

#

Kel could tell the second she walked in that Dani was upset. She started cleaning immediately, not bothering to talk to him. He didn't say anything, just sat and watched TV and let her work. Then she fixed him his favorite dinner, soup and grilled cheese sandwiches with iced tea. She set the TV tray in front of him with a thud, put the food down, and started for the door.

"Sit down, young 'un," he called out sternly. He'd never taken a tone with her before. "You can't come in this house and ignore me. Sit down."

She stood at the door with her back to him, fuming, then slowly turned around. "I'm not really in the mood today."

"You got problems? So what? That make it okay to be rude to me?"

"No," she answered like a scolded child.

"Now grab that guitar, sit down, and do your practice."

"I'm not in the mood," she said, drawing out each word for effect.

"I don't care," he shot back. "My daddy didn't want to be no sharecropper, but he did it. Just 'cause you got problems doesn't mean that you get to shirk your responsibilities. It doesn't give you a reason to quit."

"I'm not quitting," she said with exasperation. "I just need a couple of days off."

"No," he answered firmly. He pushed his TV tray aside and struggled to his feet. "You walk out that door like this and I'll never see you again."

"That's not true."

"Yeah it is. You got an important lesson to learn right now. It's not about the guitar, it's about life. You got a problem and you're tryin' to run away from it. Once you start runnin' you'll spend your whole life runnin'."

Dani was getting more frustrated by the minute. "It's just a guitar lesson."

"No it's not. Sit down."

She saw that she was fighting a losing battle. She trudged over to where Ole Red sat on his stand, still hooked up to an old amp she had dug out of a back room. She sat down and got ready to play.

Kel reached out and grabbed her hands to stop her. "Now," he said as he sat back down. "My daddy didn't want me growin' up to be no sharecropper like him. So he made me learn the guitar. He told me that when you got problems, that's the best friend to have 'cause it won't judge ya, and when you don't wanna talk, it'll talk for ya. So you got problems, right?"

"Yeah," she muttered.

"Don't tell me. Don't talk about it. Play it."

Dani shook her head. "What do you mean?"

He leaned over to her. "I mean, let the guitar do the talkin' for ya. You set your fingers and just let go. Quit thinkin' about it, quit feelin' sorry about it, and let go. Play with your heart, let all your anger and sadness out through the guitar."

Danielle began to play, concentrating more than ever, still not understanding what he wanted.

"No, no, no. You're trying. Close your eyes and play."

"I am playing."

"No, you're trying. Forget about lessons and technique and all of that garbage. Don't worry if it's good. Just play. Talk through the guitar, pray through it, cry through it. Get all of those bad feelings out. If you don't, they'll poison you. I've seen it happen. You've got to learn to let go."

She took a deep breath and closed her eyes. It was odd at first, but as she thought about her friend starting over somewhere else, spurned by the one person who should have had her back, she began to drift away from everything else. Her fingers took on a life of their own and danced along the strings. She wasn't even listening; she was just playing.

She drifted along that way like she was in a trance, losing all track of time. By the time she opened her eyes and stopped playing, darkness had fallen outside. Kel sat in his chair, eyes closed, nodding gently. "Child, child," he finally said. "You are something else. I don't think I've ever heard nothin' like that before. You have got a talent as sure as you're sittin' here today."

She got up and put Ole Red back. Her hands and fingers burned, but she felt as though a thousand pounds had been lifted off of her shoulders. "Thanks," she said shyly. She headed to the kitchen, got a Coke out of the fridge, and plopped down on the couch.

"What was all that 'bout anyway? I ain't never seen you mad like that before. You're kinda scary when you get like that."

She grimaced at the thought. "Sorry. Controlling emotions isn't something my family is good at." She stood and paced, the whole sorry affair clouding her mind again. "My best friend moved away. She got in trouble and I didn't stand up for her. The goddamn town turned on her and I just stood by and let it happen."

Kel sat and nodded, thinking it all over. "Thing about small towns, people are pretty small minded. What'd she do?"

"She was pregnant, her boyfriend dumped her, all the kids at school were making fun of her. Even the people at the church turned their backs on her."

"And you?"

Dani took a long drink. "She knew that I didn't agree with what she'd done." Then she paused. Kel let her sit there and think about it. "I didn't do what I should have done," she finally said. "I didn't stick up for her. I should've had her back."

"Ain't nothin' you can do 'bout it now," he answered. "You just gotta learn from your mistakes. Be there the next time a friend needs you."

"I guess so."

He started chuckling. "You kids, always wantin' to grow up so fast. I learned a long time ago 'bout that sex. It'll get ya in trouble quicker'n anything." He took a drink of his tea. "Back when I was younger, I had me a band with this boy named Johnny Dale. We were livin' in Baton Rouge at the time. Johnny was a real good lookin' boy and he didn't have to work too hard to get him girls. He'd set his sights on a couple and he'd take the first one willin' to go and I'd get the leftovers. Johnny, he didn't think too much of girls, just thought they were there for him to have fun with. He wound up gettin' this little gal pregnant, and her daddy didn't take too good to it. One night we were in our apartment; I was asleep in my room and he was with this new girl in his. The first girl's daddy broke into our place and took to beatin' Johnny with a Louisville Slugger. You know what that is?"

"A baseball bat," she responded.

"Finest baseball bat they make," he corrected. "Well, he was beatin' Johnny, who couldn't really defend himself too good, and that fella broke that bat off at the handle. So he took it and jammed the jagged edge right into Johnny's heart and killed him. I came in there and saw all that blood, and right then I decided that my sexin' days were over. And sure enough, I didn't touch 'nother woman 'till I got married, and ain't touched another one since."

Danielle shook her head in disbelief. "You've got a story for every occasion, don't you?"

"They're all true," he defended. "Ain't got the smarts to make stuff like this up."

They sat in silence for a while. Danielle was thinking about Kel's story and Brooke and her mom. It all added up to one ugly picture. She finally decided to change the subject. "I don't guess that I knew that you were married."

"Yep," he said between sips of tea. "Near thirty years. That's how I stayed here all of these years."

She leaned forward, put her elbow on the arm of the couch, and rested her chin in her hand. "How did you wind up here?"

"That's a good story. I had me a blues band, and after the Brits came over here 'round '64, they got people interested in the blues again. Every club had to have a real life Negro blues band. Times were good. Then it all just dried up. People lost interest and it got real hard to find a place to play.

"About '71 we had us a regular spot in this ratty little Austin club. Then it burned down and we was out of luck...no job, no money. A friend of mine said he knew 'bout this club in Las Cruces that needed a band, and he made a call and got us the gig. So we piled in my old station wagon and headed west. Damn thing overheated just outside of town here. I was able to get it into town, and that's as far as that thing ever went again. So we were stuck, had no money at all, no way out. This fella ran an oil field outside of town and he needed a reliable hand. He had a couple of guys more interested in drinkin' and fightin' than workin'. He said if I'd show up every day and work hard, I could have the job.

"I was only gonna do it for a little while, but I met this girl working in a coffee shop over on Sagebrush Trail, and that was it for me. Married her as soon as she'd have me, and we settled right here in this very house and I never thought 'bout leaving' again."

30

"That's sweet," she said, and drained the last drink of Coke. "How did she die?"

He waved her off. "Doesn't matter how or why. I figure God needed her back and that was all that mattered. I figure that one day soon, God willin' and if I've been a good enough person, he'll need me back and then we'll be together again. Till then, I just do the best I can."

Danielle got up and walked over to him. "I hope he doesn't need you any time soon, because I need you." She leaned over and gave him a peck on the cheek. She tasted the tears that were wetting his cheeks.

"You see what you made me go and do?" he said, wiping at his eyes. "You get out of here and go home." Danielle chuckled and headed for the door. Just before she left, Kel called out.

"Danielle."

She turned to look at him. He paused, searching for the words. "I love you, gal."

She smiled back at him. "I love you too."

#

Things returned to normal after that. Spring brought her sixteenth birthday. Kel gave her his old pickup to drive, although she had to put in a lot of work to get it running again. The thing was almost as old as she was and all the paint had rusted away, but it was a set of wheels. In order to afford the upkeep, she had started working at a local greasy spoon called Hud's Hut.

By now, months of practice had made Danielle solid on the guitar, and she would spend much of her free time in school writing her own lyrics, then would race to Kel's to work out the music. He loved to sit out on the porch in the evenings and listen to Danielle play while he rocked in his swing.

By late May, the heat was getting oppressive. Her truck didn't like the heat and it took a lot of work to keep it running. One Saturday, after spending the better part of the afternoon working on the truck, she came inside the house to get a snack and cool off.

She stood in front of the open refrigerator, enjoying the cold air as much as anything else, when she was aware of someone behind her. She turned to find Sean standing behind her, close. Uncomfortably close.

She was wearing a stained white tank top, which clung to her tightly, and a pair of cutoff jeans that showed plenty of leg...and she had plenty to show.

Sean looked her over like a lion eyeing a piece of meat.

"You know," he said quietly, edging even closer to her. "I've been thinking about you a lot since Christmas. You know that was an accident, but I believe we both felt something then."

Danielle backed up until her back was against the fridge. His arms went on either side of her, boxing her in. "You're sixteen now, seventeen in a year. That'll make you an adult in Texas."

"Yeah, I'm aware of that," she said. Her eyes darted around the kitchen, looking for something she could use if this went too far.

He began to stroke her hair with his right hand. "Your mother is a fine woman, but nothing like you. You're so young and sweet and innocent." He moved his hand down to her shoulder, then down her arm. He closed his fingers around her wrist. "I could teach you a lot of things. I would treat you right, not like your mother has done."

She tried to work her arm free of his grasp. "I'm really not interested, Sean. That would be creepy. You're...." She had to swallow hard to force herself to say it, but she did. "You're like a father to me"

"I'm glad of that," he said. He was face to face with her now, his grip on her tightening. "But I could be so much more."

Quickly, he let go, grabbed her face with his hands, and brought his lips to hers. He moved his hands down and began to fondle her, keeping the kiss locked. She strained to push him away, but he was stronger than she gave him credit for. She pushed away enough to tell him to get off, but he wouldn't listen. He began trying to tear away her shirt as he kissed her again. It was sloppy and wet, and she could feel his spit on her lips and chin.

"What the hell is this?"

He broke the contact and spun around. Danielle slumped against the fridge, gasping for breath and staring daggers at him. Mom had come in from a day of shopping and caught him. Now he was done for sure. Danielle thought that, for the first time, Mom's temper was going to work to her advantage.

She stormed into the kitchen towards them. Sean put up his hands and began to back away, looking terrified. She drew back her open hand and brought it down across Danielle's face, screaming.

"You little tramp! How dare you?!"

The force of the blow sent Dani to her knees. She looked up just as her mother brought another wicked hand down on her. The tears came instantly from the pain. All she could blurt out was "Me?" before another slap came down.

"You just can't stand it, can you? You trifling whore! You can't stand for me to be happy!"

Danielle grabbed the kitchen counter and pulled herself up. Sean stood over to the side, frozen in disbelief. Dani felt hurt, violated, and angry. Mom loaded up another slap.

Danielle lunged forward, wrapping her hands around her mother's neck and driving her back into the door jamb on the other side of the room. Her mother's last slap died weakly on Danielle's back.

Dani looked down into the face of her mother. She was so old, wrinkled, and gray before her eyes. Her eyes lost that fire and rage now. She was short and prone as Danielle held her there, plastered against the door frame. She could squeeze the life out of her mother so easily, and they both knew it. Dani leaned in until the tips of their noses touched.

"If you hit me again, so help me God, I will kill you where you stand." This was no threat, and Dorothy Regan knew it. She slumped in her daughter's hands and Dani let go, watching her slide all the way to the floor.

The devil was dead. She was just a tired old woman after all. Yet, she still had a bit of fire in her. She looked up at her daughter, with torn clothes and red cheeks and eyes still filled with tears, and managed a snarl. "Get out of my house. Get out and never come back."

"Gladly," Danielle spat back. Sean was on all fours now, crawling over to Mom like a lost puppy. She didn't feel anything, no shame or regret. There was nothing left in Danielle's heart for her mother. "You two losers deserve each other."

Dani moved in with Kel, sleeping on his couch because she refused to kick him out of his bed. A week later, she went back when she knew they would both be at work to get her things. She found the house boarded up, with a For Sale sign in the yard, and Danielle's things in boxes by the dumpster in back. Her mom was gone, and Danielle couldn't have cared less.

At sixteen and soon to be a junior in high school, Danielle Regan was, for the most part, on her own. She worked two jobs in the summer, at the restaurant and at the local pool as a lifeguard. When school started she dropped the lifeguard bit, but picked up double shifts at the restaurant on the weekends.

She quit going to church completely and dropped out of the choir. She played volleyball and basketball and made varsity. Late in her junior year, the straight A student assumed the lead in the race for valedictorian.

In her free time, she played guitar and wrote songs. She shuttled Kel to his doctor's appointments and kept the house in order. He warned her that she was pushing too hard, that she would burn out, but she kept on. That's what strong people did, she told herself…they kept going.

#

When her senior year began, Danielle was ready to finish it strong. She felt that she owed it to Kel and Grandma and Grandpa. She was going to be valedictorian. She was going to rule the school. She would leave an impression that no one in Chaparral would ever forget.

Early in the year, Chaparral High had a big volleyball game against one of the best teams in the state. A win would be huge for the program and Danielle wanted to deliver it.

She hurriedly fixed Kel a snack and set it on his tray before she left. He wished her luck and she rushed out the door. As she drove to the court, she couldn't believe how good she felt. Finally, it seemed that everything had come together for her.

She was a monster on the court that night and the Lady Chaps rolled. Afterwards, she joined her teammates for a celebration dinner of burgers and shakes at Hud's Hut.

She came home late, but she was sure Kel would understand. As she walked in the door, she dropped her gym bag on the floor. Kel was sound asleep in his chair. She looked at him in his recliner

34

and thought about how lucky she was to have met him. He hadn't touched his snack she had fixed him.

She started to take the tray away when she realized that something wasn't right. Danielle instantly recognized that feeling welling up inside of her. Hesitantly, she reached out to touch Kel.

She pulled back instantly. Despite her best efforts, tears began to flow. "I guess God finally wanted you back." She didn't know what to. She wanted to scream and throw things...she wanted to cry. Then, in a moment of clarity, she knew what she must do.

She retrieved Ole Red from his stand and plugged in. She sat at Kel's feet and took a moment to wipe the tears from her face. Then she and Ole Red played the blues for their departed friend one last time.

#

Completely on her own, Danielle drove herself even harder. She continued to live in Kel's house, which he had willed to her, though she was rarely there. She was a gym rat after school, worked every night at the restaurant, and stayed up into the late hours doing her homework.

A couple of small colleges in the area were interested in her as a volleyball player, but Danielle knew that her future didn't lie in athletics. Her future was intertwined with her past. Her future was Austin.

In late May, the graduating class of Chaparral High School 1993, gathered in the school gymnasium one last time. It was over a hundred degrees outside, and the air conditioning in the old building couldn't handle the heat or the crowd, making it a sauna for the graduates and the audience. Danielle, as valedictorian, led them in. She sat strong and steady throughout the festivities, waiting for the moment when she would conclude the ceremony with her commencement speech. When that moment finally came, she walked slowly to the podium. These were her last moments in Chaparral.

"When I first came here ten years ago...," she started. Her voice was strong and clear. "I might as well have landed on a different planet. It was small and hot and dusty, and everything that my previous hometown wasn't. I thought that I could never be happy in such a desolate place. Now, I stand here, and I wonder if I can truly

35

be happy anywhere else. That's how much I've come to love this town and the people in it. I've had some rough times since I moved here and I've said goodbye to a lot of people I've loved. I'm thankful for the times I've had, good and bad, because they've taught me a valuable lesson. I've learned perseverance. In a few moments, each of us here will conclude this portion of our lives and start on a new journey. We will each be faced with new and unique challenges. Some of us will stay here while others will venture away, and no one knows if the road will ever bring us back. There is one thing that I am sure of. We will be faced with the toughest days, the toughest choices of our lives. It won't always go the way we want. There will be pain and there will be loss. There will be times when it seems that the best answer is to just give up. The secret of life is to never give up, no matter how bad things get. My grandfather taught me that. Graduates, we are about to be challenged. I hope that each of you finds what you are looking for. I hope that each of you will remain unmoved and unbroken when life challenges you. Ladies and gentleman, we are the class of 1993, and we are ready for the road ahead."

After the ceremony, the delighted graduates posed for pictures with family and friends. Most lingered, holding on to the last vestiges of their old lives. Many were secretly afraid of what was ahead. While the flashbulbs popped and the laughter filled the air, Danielle Regan was already on the road. Chaparral, her home for the last ten years, was disappearing fast in her rearview mirror.

Ahead, Austin beckoned.

Chapter Two

When Danielle Regan rolled into Austin in late May, 1993, Austin had never seen anything like her. She was an exotic beauty with big, soft green eyes, long brown hair, and a complexion that revealed the hint of Cherokee blood that flowed through her. She was a six-foot-tall wildcat with a lean, athletic body and all the right curves.

For all of her exotic looks, Danielle was very much a small town girl, with her roots buried deep in the West Texas sand. She was raised on her own and reared in the church, with a blue collar work ethic and a conservative viewpoint. She was mature beyond her years, steeled by a life of trial by fire, and was determined to bend the world to her will.

She was a walking contradiction; a fresh face with an old soul; an angel's voice with a rough edge; tough as nails but with a delicate touch. She drove into Austin with a chip on her shoulder and a guitar on her back. That was all she had, and it was all she needed.

The money she'd gotten from selling Kel's estate wouldn't last long, so Danielle worked quickly. She found an apartment on the east side that wasn't too disgusting. The neighborhood was a rough one, and she slept every night with one of her Grandpa's pistols under her pillow.

She quickly found work at a Mexican restaurant just blocks from her apartment. That was a stroke of luck, because Kel's pickup finally gave up the ghost shortly after arriving. For better or for worse, she was stuck now.

She was constantly on the lookout for an opportunity to break into music. Austin was the Live Music Capital of the World, but it was also the out of work band capitol of the world. There seemed to be musicians on every corner, ads plastered to every wall. Danielle was confident she had the skill and talent to stand out, but she needed the right group. She was going to have to be patient.

She had another reason to go to the clubs at night, though. She was looking for Big Rick Regan. She had little to go on. She had no pictures and couldn't describe him because it had been ten years since she'd seen him. She knew that he used to work in the music industry, but she didn't know in what capacity. He may have been Big Rick, but he was a small needle in a big haystack.

Danielle quickly learned that the old order had been wiped away. None of the current club owners or talent scouts or bookers were around ten years ago. Every door she knocked on proved to be a dead end. Except one. The one door she couldn't get access to. Clifford Antone.

The music scene in Austin was Clifford Antone. His club was the club of clubs. If you played Antone's, you were legit. Danielle wasn't interested in playing there yet. She just wanted to talk to the man. If anyone in Austin would know what happened to Big Rick Regan, it would be Clifford Antone.

She started going to Antone's every night, hoping to catch him coming or going. She couldn't get inside because she was too young. Even a group of frat boys couldn't get her past security.

She started waiting by his home, recognizing that she was a hair away from becoming a stalker. Her mind was clear though. It was not Clifford Antone she was after. He was just a means to an end.

It went on for weeks. She just couldn't find the right time or way to approach him…until he approached her. After arriving at the club one night, he got out of the car and they locked eyes. He immediately pushed his way through onlookers and started across the street towards her.

Danielle was caught off guard and Antone was on her in an instant. He was a big guy with short brown hair. He wore a Texas Longhorns baseball cap, a bluish gray suit with white tennis shoes, and a scowl on his face.

"Is there something I can help you with?"

Danielle froze up. She couldn't get the words out of her mouth. Antone got more annoyed.

"I've been seeing you everywhere I go. Now unless you tell me what you want, I'm gonna call the cops on you."

"My father," she whispered. "I thought you might be able to help me find him."

He looked down at her for a minute, then his features got softer. "You shoulda just said so. Come on."

Antone's wasn't what she had imagined. It wasn't flashy at all. A simple stage, a bar, some tables, and plenty of room in front to dance or drink. That was Austin. It wasn't about glitz or glamour. It was about music.

Clifford Antone's office was much the same. There was a desk, some chairs, and lots of pictures on the wall of Antone and the musicians he had hosted. She thought to herself that one day her picture would be on that wall.

She took a seat on the other side of the desk in front of him. He tossed his hat down on the desk and sat. "Why do you think I can help you find your father?"

She leaned forward, rested her elbows on the desk, and looked him straight in the eye. She was no longer nervous.

"I know that he used to do something in the music scene. I remember when I was a kid that he was always hanging out with musicians and hosting parties for them. I think he worked in a club, but I don't know for sure. I haven't seen or heard from him in ten years, so my memories are pretty vague."

"I'll say they are," he laughed. "He could have been a drug dealer, or a hanger on."

"No, he was somebody. We used to have a big, nice house. My mom threw these real lavish parties and all of the big artists of the time were there. My God, I remember Stevie Ray singing me to sleep sometimes."

"Darlin'," he said with a chuckle. "Back in those days Stevie Ray went any place there was music or drugs. That doesn't say much."

She threw herself back into her chair and exhaled. "I'm never going to find him."

"I'll tell you what," he said. "You give me your name and number and I'll ask around. If I find anything, I'll let you know. What was his name?"

She kept her eyes on the ceiling. "Rick Regan. Everybody called him Big Rick."

Antone threw his pen down. "Big Rick Regan. I remember him. Big, jovial guy, always flirting with the girls. Drank like a fish. He used to help me book acts. Had a great eye for talent."

"Do you know where he is now?" she asked excitedly.

Antone shook his head. "Nope. Hadn't even thought of him in years. I remember that he used to work with this guy, Randy Holder. They were the two biggest bookers in Austin for a while. Randy's still around. He's got a used guitar shop on Lamar. You look him up, and I bet he can point you in the right direction."

#

Randy's Reeds and Strings was the name of the place. It wasn't just a guitar shop. In fact, the entire front of the store was dedicated to band instruments and pianos. The guitar section was in the back behind a glass door. It was a big store, the last remaining inhabitant of an old strip mall.

The front of the store was empty except for a pimple faced kid behind the counter. He was tall and lanky with sandy blond hair. He checked her out from head to toe when she walked in, and seemed to like what he saw. "What can I help you with, gorgeous?"

She walked up to the counter. "I have an appointment to meet with Mr. Holder." The kid's face showed his disappointment. "In the back," he said, and turned his attention back to the issue of *Guitar Player* that he had been reading when she walked in.

Through the glass door she could see three older men. One was tall and skinny and very professional looking, with short, well-trimmed gray hair. He wore khakis and a navy blue polo shirt. The second was short and squat with a cleanly shaved head. He also wore khakis and a polo shirt, but his didn't seem to fit as well and were slightly wrinkled.

The third guy was her guy; she was sure of it. He sat on a bar stool slumped over a black and white Stratocaster. He was a fat man with long brown hair shot through with streaks of gray. He had a full beard and thick glasses, and wore jeans with a short sleeved button up shirt that was only partially buttoned up, showing off a chest full of gray hair. His thick arms were covered in tattoos and looked ready to burst out of the tight sleeves at any moment. But when he looked at the other men he did so with a big smile and a hearty laugh. She took a deep breath and straightened out her clothes, then started for the back room.

All three men turned to look at her when she entered the room. It was guitar heaven. Guitars of every kind hung on the walls from ceiling to floor. Dozens of amps were stacked up in the middle, and a side room housed effect pedals, cases, and all the other essentials. A glass counter to her right was filled with packs upon packs of strings locked inside, and plastic bubble gum tubs sat on the counter, filled with various types of picks. It was like walking into Willy Wonka's Chocolate Factory, if you were a guitar junkie.

The man on the bar stool looked her over carefully. "Are you the girl I'm supposed to meet?"

His friends laughed at him. The bald guy spoke first. "You're stepping up in the world, big man," he said, and he slapped the big man's arm.

The other one shrugged him off. "Nah, he just needs someone to change his diapers for him."

She could tell that they were all lifelong friends, and she liked the warmth that she felt between them. She stepped between the two men who were standing and offered her hand to Randy Holder. "My name is Danielle Regan."

He shook her hand with a strange expression. "Danielle Regan. You wouldn't be related to old Big Rick Regan?"

She could feel her face light up. At last, she had found a trail. "I'm his daughter."

Randy jumped off his stool and was on her in an instant. He picked her up in a bear hug so tight she was sure that she felt a rib break. He laughed that hearty laugh, and his eyes beamed with delight. "Little Dani," he said as he put her back down. He held her at arm's length to get a good look at her. "My God, I haven't seen you since you were a little one. You sure have grown up."

"I've been gone ten years."

"Hell, ten years…seems like twenty. Damn, it's good to see you. I used to give you piggy back rides. You'd just laugh your damn head off. That was back in the good old days."

"That's kind of why I'm here," she said. "I came to town to find him." She could tell by the way the energy went out of the room that it wasn't likely to happen.

He patted her on both shoulders. "Fellas, if you can excuse me. I've got some business to attend to."

Randy's office was off of the main room and wasn't much bigger than a broom closet. His desk was cluttered with papers. There were no personal pictures there, but autographed posters covered the walls. Billy Gibbons was on one wall, Steve Miller on the other. Bonnie Raitt, The Fabulous Thunderbirds, BB King, Buddy Guy…they were all hanging there. Some others she didn't know. Right there across from his desk, where it could be seen easily by Randy at any time, hung an autographed Stevie Ray Vaughn poster. She let out a long whistle.

"You've met most of these people, Dani. They used to hang out at your parents' house in the good days. Of course, they were nobody outside of Austin back then. Just a bunch of kids who loved the blues. Austin…man, it was wild back then. It was fun, real fun."

She sat down in an old leather chair on the other side of the desk from Randy. It buckled, but held.

"Yeah, be careful with that old thing. It'll throw you quick if you don't watch it."

"I will," she said. "Now what about my father? Do you know where he is?"

Randy rested his elbows on the desk and locked his fingers. He didn't want to look at her, but he did. "Yeah, I do." Then he leaned closer. "Do you remember your dad?"

Danielle shrugged. "Some. I remember that he seemed like a giant. I remember he was hairy, like a grizzly bear. Laughed a lot, yelled a lot, drank a lot. I remember that I was never scared of him." As the memories came back, her voice started to trail off. "I remember he wasn't home a lot. I know that he and Mom fought all the time. And I remember how sad he was the last time I saw him."

Randy exhaled and leaned back in his chair. "I'm glad you have some memories of him. That's why I'm going to tell you this. Drop it."

"Drop what?" she asked, her voice rising. "I deserve to know where my father is."

"Deserve it? Yeah, you deserve it. I figure you deserve a whole lot. What I'm telling you is, you would be better off not knowing."

She stood up and leaned over the desk. "If you're trying to protect me, don't. I'm not some sweet little innocent girl who just rode in on the turnip truck. There's nothing that you can tell me that would be any worse than what I've already lived through. So please don't insult me. Just tell me what happened to my father."

A thin, sad smile spread across Randy's face. "You are a firebrand. You get that from your mom." He paused for a long moment, and Danielle could tell that he was trying to find a way out of it. He finally gave up. "Okay, you want to know, I'll tell you. You do deserve that. But if I'm going to tell you about your dad, I've got to go back to the beginning. I'm going to tell you the whole story, warts and all. You think you can handle it?"

Danielle sat on the edge of the desk, knocking some papers onto the floor. "Hell yes."

"Your dad was crazy about music. See, we go way back, me and your dad. We went to college together. When the music scene kicked off in the seventies, we dropped out and started hanging out in the clubs, with the bands and the managers. Well, there was this guy we both knew named Clifford Antone, and he started up his own club in the mid-70s. Your dad talked Cliff into hiring him to book the acts. Your dad could spot a great act a mile away. Eventually, he moved on and started working freelance. Even managed a couple of bands, but nobody you would know."

"So he was successful," Danielle asked. She was listening intently, trying to piece this information together with what little she remembered about her dad.

"He was successful, but he didn't make much money. You probably remember the house out in Westlake. He didn't get that working in the clubs. Your dad came from old Austin banking money. He was a trust fund kid. Anyway, he met your mother along those lines. She had come to Austin to go to UT, but started hanging out in the clubs. She was a groupie, looking to hitch her wagon to whatever star seemed to be on the way up. Here's your dad riding around town in a Caddy and wearing the newest clothes, playing the big shot. It was a match made in hell."

"You must have known my mom pretty well to say something like that," she joked.

Randy chuckled. "Yeah, she was a piece of work. Of course, it helped that she was hotter than hell back then. Pretty girls can get away with a lot." Then he took another look at Danielle. "You probably know a lot about that."

Danielle was offended. "I do not. I have never used my looks to get something I wanted. Hell, most of the time, guys never even bother to look at me." She could tell by his look that he didn't believe her. "I usually don't dress like this. I'm a bit of a tomboy."

"Nothing wrong with that, honey," he said. "So, to get back to the story. Your mom convinced your dad to open his own club and to buy a big house in Westlake. She always pictured herself as the proper southern hostess, and they would throw these lavish parties. He would invite all of these undiscovered bands, really anybody in the music industry. He was trying to impress them, thought it was good for business. Any musician worth his salt went to Big Rick's parties. Of course, it didn't take long for the drug dealers to find their way in. That's how you networked back then. You didn't take somebody golfing or to some snooty French restaurant, you downed a bottle of vodka and snorted a couple of lines. And musicians, being what they were, judged people by how much poison they could ingest without passing out or dying. It didn't take long for your parents to get addicted. That's when things went south. The club failed and they snorted their way through your dad's trust fund. So they sold the house and found a smaller one. Eventually, they had to sell that one, and so on it went. They fought all the time, sometimes physically. My wife and I would have to take you out of the house sometimes when things got too bad."

"I'm sorry," Danielle said, shaking her head. "I don't remember that. I remember some fighting, but that's all."

"You probably blocked it out, which is a good thing if you ask me. They were crazy, those two. Then your mom was saved by the glory of the good Reverend Jimmy Swaggart, right there on her TV. She got clean and decided that if your dad couldn't do the same, she was going to leave. When he couldn't do it, she packed the two of you up and moved to Buttfuck, Texas, or wherever the hell y'all moved to."

"Chaparral. That's where we moved."

"Whatever. Anyway, you were the only good thing in his life then. He begged your mom not to take you, but she did. He about died after that, went on a serious binge. I was always having to go get him, bail him out, whatever. Bad, bad days. On the good side, though, watching them scared my wife Teri and me straight. Anyway, I knew your dad wasn't going to make it unless something changed. So I gave him you. I convinced him that if he cleaned up and got a job and proved he had changed, he could go out there and ask for partial custody, or at least visitation. It motivated him. He got clean and got a job and a place of his own, and held it for over a year. So the two of us drove out there to see your mom. We made a case for him and your mom laughed in his face. She told him he was a loser. Then she told him that you hated him and never wanted to see him again."

Danielle tightened her grip on the arms of the chair and squeezed with all she had. "That bitch," she spat out. "I can't believe she did that. That horrible, awful woman."

"Yeah," he said, shaking his head sadly. "About that time, you came running in with this chubby little blonde girl. He smiled at you, but you ran by him and gave him this dirty look. It broke his heart."

"Oh my god," Danielle cried out. She buried her face in her hands and started to cry.

"Do you remember that day?"

"No," she said between sobs. "Not specifically. But Mom always had guys coming around, and they were always creepy and I didn't like them. I probably thought he was another one of them."

Randy came around the desk and stood behind her, rubbing her neck and shoulders with big, soft hands. "Don't worry about it. You probably wouldn't have recognized him. Life had been hard on him and he didn't look the same. He didn't blame you. I want you to know that. He blamed your mom."

"Crazy old wench," she spat out. "She never told me anything about him. If I asked, she would just yell at me. I never knew anything about him after we left." Then she looked back over her shoulder at him. "Where is he now?"

Randy's long pause told her everything she needed to know. "He's in lot 3210 of the city cemetery. After we got back to Austin, he just fell off. OD'ed in some back alley. I had to identify him. Nobody else cared…they had all forgotten about him."

They sat there for a long time in silence, both paying their own silent tribute to a deeply loved and deeply flawed man.

"Well," Danielle finally said, her emotions under control. "I can't say I'm entirely surprised. But I got what I came for." She stood and faced Randy and held out her hand. He shook it firmly. "I thank you for your time."

She was almost to the door when he called out. "Hey, wait. How long are you in Austin for?"

She turned, a slight smile on her face. "For good. I've got a job and an apartment east of I-35."

"Where are you working?"

"A little Mexican place called El Mariachi. It's just a couple of blocks from my apartment."

"Jesus Christ, girl," he spat out. "What are you doing over there? That's dangerous territory. Especially for a pretty little thing like you."

"I can take care of myself," she said confidently.

"I'm sure you can, but there are places in that part of town the cops don't even go in. A lot of bad things happen over there."

"I'll be careful."

"No, no, no," he called out, stopping her from trying to leave. "Come sit down, please."

She did as she was asked. He used one of his big arms to brush a ton of papers and other items off one corner of his desk and sat down. "Now, I want you to listen to me on this, okay? My wife and I have this little place, not far from the university. It's an older house and it's got an apartment over the garage. You can stay there, rent free, as long as you keep the place clean and keep the noise down. And as far as a job, I've got an urgent need for a sales person up front. Ty, the guy who works there now, he hates it and wants to move to guitars. It's a full time job, salary plus a small commission. It's not much, but it's safer than living and working over there. In a few months, you could probably save up for a better place and find a better job."

"I'm thankful for the offer, Mr. Holder, but I couldn't do that. I will be fine on my own."

"Please do. I hate the thought of you living over there. Now, I couldn't save your father, at least let me help you out."

Danielle wanted to, but she was reluctant to take his help. She wanted to stand on her own two feet, but the neighborhood she lived in did border a much rougher neighborhood and she was terrified every time she stepped foot out of the house.

"Don't you think that you should ask your wife?"

"Are you kidding?" he said with a grin. "Once she finds out who you are...well, she'll skin me alive if you don't come."

Randy called home and his wife ordered them home at once. Home was in an older middle class neighborhood west of the University of Texas on a narrow tree lined street. The house sat back from the road, with a long driveway on the side and a detached garage. It was painted sea green with white shutters, although the paint was fading. The lawn was scraggly and needed a mowing, and flowerbeds along both sides of the walk were filled with tulips.

A small porch was two steps up from the walk, and that was where Teri Holder stood anxiously, bouncing on her feet like a nervous schoolgirl. Randy pulled into the driveway and shut off the engine. He looked over at Danielle, who was doing a bad job of hiding her nervousness. "We never had any kids, so don't be surprised if she takes that out on you," he said with a smile.

"Okay," Danielle said as she opened the passenger side door. She slowly rounded the front of the truck and found Teri was right there, nearly running towards her. She swept Danielle up in a hug that was eerily similar in type and strength to the one Randy had given her. *She may be short,* Danielle thought, *but she is strong.*

"I can't believe after all of these years," she said, her voice thick with her East Texas twang. "When Dorothy took you away, I never...." Tears started to come, so she hid them by crushing Danielle with another hug. When she released, she took Danielle's right hand in her left and stepped back, looking her over. "My, aren't you just the most beautiful thing? Not an ounce of fat on you. You look like a movie star from the '40s, but I can't think of which one."

Randy playfully punched her in the arm. "It's not one in particular, it's just her type. The curves, the hourglass." His eyes went up to Danielle's. "Actually, I think she kind of looks like that one girl in the movie about the kid with the jet pack."

"That fought the Nazis," Teri responded. She looked Danielle over once again. "Yeah, she does kind of look like that girl. But she's more muscular. You were an athlete, I bet."

Danielle was starting to feel like a prized heifer at the auction house. After another long look over, Teri looked up into Danielle's face and smiled. "We are going to have so much fun. I'm going to go get my purse and you and I are going shopping. You're going to need a wardrobe for work, and God only knows what kind of hideous things your mother sent along with you."

Danielle gently pulled her hand away and stepped back. "I've got plenty of clothes, really."

"But do you have clothes suitable for a professional saleswoman?" Danielle delayed just a heartbeat. "I knew it. You can't wear T-shirts and jeans to work, you know."

Danielle looked over at Randy. "Ty was."

"Ty's a slacker," Teri answered first. "Boy couldn't find his junk with both hands and a map. You want to sell? You have to dress the part." Then she turned to Randy. "Will you back out so that I can get my car out? And then start straightening up the apartment over the garage, will you? I figure tomorrow I can start hitting thrift stores and garage sales for furniture."

"You got it," Randy said without question, and walked past them to the truck.

Teri turned back to Danielle. "You can sleep on our couch until we get the apartment ready. It folds out. I've already vacuumed it off and got some sheets out. Then we'll move you into the apartment when it's done. We've been using it for storage."

Randy pulled the pickup into the street and parked it in front of the house. As he walked up the cement walkway, he called out, "What should I do with all that shit in the garage?"

"Call the Salvation Army, they'll come take it away. Just leave it in the driveway till they come get it."

Danielle finally saw a chance to get a word in. "I really don't mean to intrude. I have my own place—"

"Over there in the ghetto? Dear, you stay over there and you're a rape victim waiting to happen. Now, no more arguing. Tomorrow after work, we'll both go over there and help you empty out that apartment of yours. You'll be much happier here. You'll see." Then she gave Danielle another bear hug. "Come on," she said, taking Danielle's hand and virtually pulling her toward the garage.

Teri took Danielle around to various low rent used and vintage clothing stores around town, putting together a look that would play on Danielle's "classic looks and killer figure." Teri explained, "You get some forty-five-year-old father of two coming into the store to buy his daughter her first clarinet. He doesn't want to be there. He just wants to get it over with so he can go home, drink a beer, and watch the game. But now, here's this nineteen-year-old woman in front of him with more curves than a mountain road, and she's talking to him and him alone. He's going to stay and he's going to buy. He'll even buy something more expensive just because he's hoping in some strange way to impress you. That's how you sell."

Teri, as Danielle found out, had employed the same tactic for many years before middle age spread had decimated her figure, and a bout with uterine cancer had weakened her and scarred her to the point that she no longer wanted to work.

Danielle soon learned that Teri was an open book; there was no subject that she wouldn't readily address, even if she didn't need to. The all-day shopping trip reminded her of the kind Grandma used to take her on. Her immediate uneasiness soon dissolved.

That night they cooked steaks on a grill out back. The back yard was surrounded by a high privacy fence. The lawn was greener and more trimmed back here, and there was a smooth cement slab for a patio, with a swing facing the house and a pair of patio chairs set against the wall. Teri pulled a folding table outside so they could eat.

Over dinner Danielle watched as they needled each other, but it was always clear that there was true love behind the snide remarks. She found herself wishing that they had been her parents all along. This was the way life was supposed to be, not the constant struggle of the past ten years.

When dinner was over, they stayed out there, listening to the blues on KABJ. They drank Coors Light longnecks, while Danielle stuck to Coke.

"So," Teri started. "What are your long range plans in Austin? Are you going to go to school?"

Danielle laughed, although she hadn't intended to. "No. Not that I don't have the grades, but that's not why I came here. I came to be a musician."

"Oh really," Teri answered with a nervous edge to her voice. "Why?"

"I've always loved music. I remember a little bit of the parties my parents used to throw...." She saw immediately that the subject made them uncomfortable, and decided to pass it by. "But I really was inspired by a friend I had back home who taught me to play guitar. I promised him before he died that I wouldn't waste my talent."

"She's a guitar player." Teri nodded at Randy. "How original."

"Sssh," he chided back. "Let's see how good she is." He got up and trudged into the house.

"I don't mean to be rude," Teri started once Randy was gone. "But it's such a cliche. Young kids come to Austin with a guitar slung across their chests, all wanting to be the next Stevie Ray. Most of them never amount to anything. It's just hard to take anybody seriously anymore."

Danielle felt herself go hard. She stared across at Teri intently, and the older woman saw it. "Believe me, I'm not like that."

If Danielle's sudden hostility stunned Teri, she didn't show it. "I hope not, Dani. But I knew both of your parents, and they were weak. They couldn't handle the lifestyle. I hope you're stronger than they were."

"By leaps and bounds."

Randy came lumbering out of the house carrying a small amp and a blue and white Stratocaster. He held it up for her to see. "Fender Strat...don't accept anything less." He set her up, running a thick orange extension cord back into the house. He handed the guitar to Danielle. "Show us what you got."

Feeling challenged, she stood and slipped the strap over her head. She took a few moments to familiarize herself with the new guitar and fiddle with the tunings. Then she began to play, letting her fingers take over, and she let her mind drift away.

Her father was gone, a victim of a dangerous lifestyle and an evil woman. She had expected it. She'd lost her chance to reclaim her family, but had made two new friends who could be a link to her past. There was a new job, a new place to stay, and there was now opportunity. She could once and for all bury her past with her long dead father and concentrate fully on her future.

When she finally stopped playing, Teri and Randy sat in stunned silence. Feeling vindicated and a bit cocky, she smirked at them. "How was that?"

Randy cleared his throat and rose to take the guitar back from her. "There's some people I want you to meet."

#

The next day, instead of going to her job at the Mexican food restaurant, Danielle reported for duty at Randy's place. There she officially made the acquaintance of Ty Woods. He was just a tick shorter than she was, with a bushy blond hair and blue-gray eyes. If it weren't for his acne, he would have been a good looking kid, she thought. He was very well spoken and very confident.

He was instantly grateful for Danielle's hiring. With her on board, he could move to the back and sell guitars instead of the "band geek" instruments. Ty admitted that he didn't relate well to those customers, and that the store was suffering for it.

Danielle also learned that Ty was an aspiring guitar player and songwriter as well, and had his own garage band. She was intrigued, and they talked about getting together to jam some time.

Things were slow during the week, giving them plenty of time to talk and get to know one another. She felt no attraction to him, but it was nice to find a friend.

On Friday of that week, they took advantage of an especially slow day and spent most of their time jamming in the back. Danielle arranged herself where she could see if someone came in, since there was no way she would hear the bell that chimed when the door opened. Ty was good, but not as good as she was. He loved what he called "riff and roll," and promised her that he would make her a tape.

That night, Randy arrived about a half hour before closing. He headed for the storage room in back and emerged a short time later with some chairs. Ty started bringing gear in from the guitar room. When they had everything set up, Randy excused himself and left again. The store was set to close in ten minutes.

"What's going on?" she asked as she watched Randy leave.

Ty walked to the front of the store and turned off the neon OPEN sign. He turned around with a smirk on his face. "Friday night jam session. Randy gets all of his old buddies together, and they sit around drinking beer and eating and jamming. I've heard it can go on all night when it's really good. I've been trying to get him to let me in for months and he won't do it. Says it's for old timers only. So we get to go home early on Fridays."

"That sounds like fun," she answered, her mind drifting back to the parties her parents used to throw. "Maybe we ought to start our own jam sessions."

"You can always join my band."

Danielle laughed. "I'm not interested in playing skating rinks and high school dances, but thanks anyway."

"It's an open invitation. We may not be good, but it is fun."

Two cars pulled in to the parking lot outside, and soon the two other men she had seen with Randy on her first day walked in. They were still dressed like they had just come in from the golf course, with the taller man wearing it much better. They both carried instruments. The bald man was carting a drum kit, while the tall man was carrying a standing bass.

She rushed over to help the bald man with his drums. "Thank you, darling," he said. "Appreciate it."

The taller man looked at them with scorn. "I remember when you used to take pride in the fact that you never needed help with your drums."

The bald man looked up in annoyance. "I wasn't knocking on sixty then." Then he cast a mischievous glance at Danielle and winked. "And I didn't have pretty girls offering to help me then, either."

"Al," the tall man said. "Nobody could help you enough to know what to do with a girl like that."

"That may be true, Jimmy," Al said, his grin getting bigger. "But I sure wouldn't mind giving it a try."

"Quit hitting on the new girl," Randy called from behind them. He was carrying a cooler that obviously weighed a ton. Ty jumped to help him. "Dani," Randy said with strain. "There's snacks in my car. Can you please grab them?"

"Sure thing, boss," she answered. She found several plastic bags filled with snacks in the back seat and brought them in.

Randy had set up a long folding table off to one side, and Danielle set out the snacks. Randy was busy arranging folding chairs and mismatched bar stools in a circle. Al, the bald drummer, set up his drums between the outside of the circle and the guitar room so he could see everything. They both got a longneck out of the cooler and began drinking. Jimmy, the tall one, lit a cigarette.

"Well, I guess it's time for us to bolt," Ty said, taking Danielle by the arm. "We'll see you on Monday."

Randy dismissed them with a wave as they headed for the door. Ty had one foot out the door when Randy called, "Wait. Dani, I want you to stay."

"What?" Ty yelled out, spinning around. "Why does she get to stay? I've been asking you for months to let me stay. She's here one week—"

"Ty," Randy said with exasperation, "go home. This isn't for you. This is for us old timers."

"You're letting the new girl stay."

Randy chuckled. "She's not as new as you think."

"Actually, I am," Danielle interjected. "Just because you knew my dad doesn't mean that I'm a part of your group. Ty's right. It's not fair for me to stay and him not."

"It's my group; I decide who stays."

"That's fine," Danielle said firmly. ""Then I will see you when you get home. Have fun." She started out the door, pulling Ty after her.

"Danielle, you can't do that. I've got people expecting you. You can't leave."

She didn't look back. "Let Ty stay."

"No. Absolutely not."

"Good night," she answered, and stepped out the door.

She heard Randy call out, and she stopped and looked back. A second later, Randy pushed through the door, huffing and puffing from the exertion of running to the door.

"Are you really going to do this? I called people and set this up for you to help you. Is this how you're going to thank me?"

She squared up to Randy. "It's not that I don't appreciate it, but Ty has been wanting to get in on this for months and you won't let him. It's not fair that I just sweep in like this."

Randy reached out and brushed some of her dark hair out of her face. "Life's not fair, Dani. You gotta understand that. You are an exceptional talent and I'm trying to help you out. Ty is just a kid with a guitar." He realized that Ty was standing right beside him and blushed slightly. "Sorry, no offense." Then back to Danielle. "Dani, please."

She crossed her arms in front of her. "What is it going to hurt?"

Randy looked from the defiant Danielle to the hopeful Ty and back. His shoulders slumped and he sighed. "Fine." He turned back to Ty, lifting himself back to full height. "But you stay out of the way and keep your mouth shut."

"But he gets to play, right?"

"Hell no. He can watch."

"Bye." She turned. Randy reached out and grabbed her shoulder, spinning her back around.

"Wait. I guess he can play some rhythm as long as he doesn't make an ass out of himself."

Danielle looked over to Ty. "Are you agreeable?"

"Hell yeah," Ty answered.

"Then we have ourselves a deal," she said with a smile.

"Well, I can tell you this," Randy huffed as they walked back into the store. "I ain't never seen nothing like you before. You're a hell of a lot more strong-willed than either one of your folks."

She gave him her biggest and brightest smile. "I'll take that as a compliment."

"You should," he smiled back at her as he reached into the cooler and pulled out a twenty ounce Coke, then tossed it to Danielle. "I bought these for you."

She tipped her bottle at him in salute. Ty leaned over and said, "I'll have one of those Coors Lights."

Randy shoved a Coke in his hand. "My ass you will."

There were ten old-schoolers altogether and they made a motley collection. Some were well dressed and sharp, while others looked like Hell's Angel rejects. Some looked healthy, and others showed the signs of years of hard living. There were three guitar players, two bass players, a drummer, a percussionist, a fiddler, a steel guitar player, and a harmonica player.

Danielle and Ty set their equipment up outside the main circle. It was a disorganized situation. Someone would just start playing something, an old song they knew, one they made up, or sometimes just gibberish. Then everyone else would join in. Yet, somehow, through all the chaos, they would have it sounding like a real song in short order. Danielle watched and played along, trying not to screw up and draw attention to herself. She also developed a quick appreciation for how well a cohesive group could come together.

It went on like that for over an hour before Randy called an intermission. They all headed off to the bathroom and to refresh their beers and snacks. When everyone came back, Randy grabbed their attention.

"Okay, folks, listen up. That beautiful young lady over in the corner is old Rick Regan's kid. She just blew back into town, and you have got to hear this girl play." All heads turned her way.

Suddenly self-conscious, she nodded at the group in recognition. "Thanks for having me," she said. "It's an honor."

The guy playing the steel guitar yelled out. "Quit kissing our ass and play something."

Danielle was taken aback by the rudeness of the comment, and Randy stepped in with encouragement, asking her to play the same song she had played for them earlier. She did as he asked, playing the same soft, slow, almost jazzy solo she had played on the porch a few days earlier.

Getting antsy beside her, Ty waited for an opening. As Danielle started to wind her song down, he launched into a quick, upbeat rock number. Danielle was momentarily taken by surprise, but seeing the smile on his face knew that it was meant as a friendly challenge. It was time for the young lions to strut their stuff.

The two sat side by side, trading turns as they showed off their skills. Soon they fell into their own rhythm, with Ty playing the riffs while Danielle improvised over the top. Al, the bald drummer, began to drum a quick beat and the other bass player began to add a throbbing bass line to the jam. The harmonica player was a short, balding man with a porn-star moustache, but he could play a mean harmonica and he began to add his own pieces to the mix. Danielle risked a quick look up at Randy, who was standing silently, smiling like a proud parent. Infused with confidence, she really let go, starting on a loud, wailing solo that would have made Stevie Ray smile.

Everyone eventually got into the act, except for Jimmy, the tall bass player, and Randy. They stood beside each other and whispered back and forth. After another hour of continual jamming, in which everyone took their turn leading, it finally ground to a halt and one by one the old guys started to leave.

The harmonica player took a moment to introduce himself on the way out. Danielle already knew who he was. She remembered him as the lead singer of the Fabulous Thunderbirds. Now, however, she was on a first name basis with Kim Wilson.

In the end, even Ty left, leaving Danielle alone with Randy, Al, and Jimmy. She liked Al; he seemed very nice, and they traded barbs throughout the evening. Jimmy, though, was stand-offish and had spent most of the evening glaring at her.

She started putting up when Randy finally spoke up. "So, what do you boys think?"

Danielle quit what she was doing to look at them. Al winked at her and said, "I think that little girl kicks ass, and she'll go as far as she wants to go."

She smiled at him and then turned her attention to Jimmy, who was still glaring.

"I wouldn't put my faith in anybody that came from Dorothy and Rick Regan. No matter how flashy she may be."

Danielle wasn't sure exactly what Jimmy had against her, but she was sure fed up with it. She strode up to him with all the cockiness she possessed. "Listen, pal, you can say whatever you want about my parents...I know who and what they were. But don't hold that against me. I'm nothing like them."

He stared back at her with cold blue eyes. "The apple doesn't fall far from the tree, sweetheart."

"This one did," she answered coolly.

Randy stepped between them. "Easy now, just calm down. I can attest to the fact that Dani here is nothing like her parents."

"Bullshit," Jimmy shot back. "You've known her a week. You can't say something like that. You don't know anything about this girl."

"I know enough," he answered. "I put my faith in her, and I'm comfortable doing that."

Jimmy turned his blue eyes back on Danielle. "It's coming too easy. I want to know she's strong enough. That she'll be able to handle it. I want her to pay some dues."

Danielle didn't like the fact that she was the center of attention, but knew nothing about what was going on. Before she could interject, though, Randy was talking again.

"What do you want her to do?"

Jimmy stepped past Randy so he could be face to face with Danielle. "I want her to lose that chip on her shoulder. I want her to play the street corners for a while, learn some humility. Then we'll talk."

Danielle didn't know what they were talking about, but she wasn't going to back down. "You think I'm scared? You pick the corner, I'll play it."

#

"What the hell was that little exchange about?" Danielle asked as she and Randy got in his truck for the ride home.

Randy looked a bit sheepish. "I've been pulling some strings for you, trying to help you out. I don't want to see you fail like your folks did."

"What kind of strings are you pulling?"

"Those two guys, the tall guy and the bald guy, they are long time professional musicians, real hard core guys. Jimmy Silver and Albert Barber. They've been playing together since high school. They've done sessions with some of the best, toured the country...they've done it all. They're pretty much retired, but they are thinking about coming out of retirement, as a favor to me, to help you."

"Well, thank you, Randy, but I think I can do it on my own."

He dismissed her with a laugh. "Dani, you've got a good head on your shoulders and plenty of attitude, but you have no idea what you're getting into. I've seen a lot of really talented musicians, some more talented than you, wash out. There are so many traps, so many turns to take. You need experience like Jim and Al have. They can help steer you in the right direction. They are consummate professionals, and I trust their judgment. That's why I wanted you to stay and play tonight. And I must say that you availed yourself very well."

"Thank you," she said. "So what's the deal with the street corner thing?"

"Jimmy thinks you're too cocky and that I'm making a mistake taking it easy on you. He wants you to get out there with people. Being an Austin street musician is something every aspiring musician should do. We love our music down here and a phony will be spotted quickly. But if you're legit, if you can make the crowds love you, then you'll be ready to form a band and start playing clubs."

"Isn't it dangerous?" she asked.

"Not if you know where to go. Besides, the cops do a much better job of watching 6th now. You'll be fine."

The next night Danielle found herself on a street corner in front of a boarded-up tattoo parlor on 6th Street. 6th Street was quite a sight for the kid from Chaparral, Texas. Dozens of clubs lined the street, with virtually every type of music spilling out of them. There were tattoo parlors, adult novelty stores, and a walk-in pizzeria that smelled heavenly. On the weekends, traffic was shut down so that the crowds could walk the street without fear. It was a wild mix of people; bikers and preps, grizzled old timers, and fresh faced college kids. Danielle even saw an old homeless guy wearing nothing but a hot pink bikini and cowboy boots. It was a motley collection of humanity, and Danielle was right in the middle of it.

For her first trip down Randy allowed her to take Ole Red, although he told her that he would eventually want her to come down here with an acoustic and do it unplugged. The owner of the adult bookstore was kind enough to let her run an extension cord for her amp. She sat on an old milk crate, left her guitar case open in front of her for tips, and began to play anything that came to mind, most of which were songs that she had written herself.

Randy was right, this was a quick core for cockiness. She struggled early, her voice quivering with nervousness and her palms sweating. The crowds that walked by let their displeasure be known.

Doubt began to creep in. She had to stifle the urge to pack up and leave.

Yet, not everyone was unsupportive. The owner of the adult bookstore came out when his store was empty and offered her some vodka to calm her nerves. She politely declined, telling him she didn't drink.

There was also a kid, not much older than Danielle, who stood in front of her the whole time, completely into her performance. He was a gangly kid, but she thought that he was cute, nonetheless. He was taller than Danielle, with long, wild, strawberry blond hair, piercing blue eyes, and two day's growth on his baby face. Despite his goofy appearance he had a warm smile and a gentle air about him. Danielle knew she wasn't performing up to her abilities, but he seemed to genuinely enjoy the show, swaying to the music, tapping his feet to the beat, and even spontaneously dancing with a passing girl on occasion. She chalked it up to just one more of Austin's kooky inhabitants.

She spent the following week working hard in the store and earning praise from Randy for improving business up front. He loved her professionalism and her knowledge of the instruments she was selling. In the evenings, she took to jamming with Ty's band, First Glance, in his parents' garage. They weren't half bad and she liked the loose, riff-oriented music they played; it gave her a great deal of freedom to improvise. Yet she again turned down an offer to join the band.

The next Friday night, she and Ole Red were back on their same corner. Danielle was determined to do better. This time she stood, guitar slung low, and let it all hang loose. Her first visitor was the blond kid from the first night. He was wearing baggy denim shorts and had his T-shirt tied around his waist, showing a better body than she expected from such a scrawny kid. He also had a backpack over one shoulder. He did his same routine early every evening, but as the crowd around her started to get bigger, he got less demonstrative.

The oppressive heat and humidity began to get to her, so she finally sat down on the milk crate. When she did, the scrawny kid unzipped his backpack and pulled out a pair of bongos. He then proceeded to sit down beside her and beat out a beat. He wasn't a great drummer, but it made her laugh and rejuvenated her. She spent the rest of the evening playing her heart out and smiling at the scrawny kid who kept the beat the rest of the way.

As she put up at the end of the night, he approached her. He stuck out his hand, which she took. His grip was stronger than she anticipated, but he didn't crush her hand. "Thanks for letting me sit in with you. That's one more experience I can cross off my list."

"Glad I could be of service," she answered as she picked up her guitar and amp and headed for where she had parked Randy's truck.

"You see," he said, ignoring her comment. "I figure life is short, so I want to have every experience I can before I die. And to play with an Austin street musician is one of them." As Danielle started lugging her gear down the street, he interrupted himself. "Do you need any help with that?''

"Nah, I got it. Do you need a ride somewhere?"

He shrugged. "I don't guess so, unless you're going somewhere really cool."

Danielle chuckled. "Not unless you count the Denny's across the interstate as really cool."

"I consider food really cool. I could go for a bite, but I don't have any money, so I'll have to take a rain check."

Danielle knew he was angling for a free meal, but it didn't matter to her. She was curious to know more about this strange boy. "Come with me. I made enough to buy us both a burger. You do eat meat, don't you?"

"It's what's for dinner," he said with a huge smile. "My name is Adam Quisenberry."

"Pleased to meet you, Adam Quisenberry...I'm Danielle Regan."

Over burgers and Cokes at Denny's, Danielle learned more about her admirer. He was from a tiny town deep in the Piney Woods of East Texas and was attending St. Edwards on a drama scholarship. His long term goal was to become a movie director. He was raised by relatives after his parents both died when he was young, thus explaining his desire to live life to the fullest at all times. He was intelligent, rounded, witty, and charming, and he hadn't lost his small town nature.

She found herself thinking of him often over the next week, something she hadn't done over a boy before. She found it hard to concentrate during the week, and was nearly worthless on the next Friday as she got ready to go back out.

On the third Friday, she took only an acoustic guitar that Randy loaned her. It was going to be a new experience for Danielle, since she had always played an electric, but she was ready for the challenge. Sure enough, her film student showed up, wearing loose denim jeans and sandals. He didn't join in this time, but the two of them traded smiles during her performance.

There was another notable member of the audience that night. As she put up, Clifford Antone approached her. "I heard that there was this hotshot young guitarist down here I needed to see." He offered his hand and she took it. "Did you find your dad?"

"He's dead," she said directly. "But I found a good friend in Mr. Holder. He's helping me set up a band."

"Well," he answered. "You keep that up and I bet I can find a place for you at my club."

"That would be an honor, Mr. Antone," she said with a big grin. "Thank you."

"Keep playing and the rest will take care of itself." He patted her on the back and moved on down the street.

"Who was that guy?"

She looked at Adam incredulously. "That was Clifford Antone."

"Who's that?"

"He's the man on the scene around here. His club is the summit. You make the stage at Antone's and you're somebody. I can't believe you've been here this long and you don't know who Clifford Antone is."

"My passion is movies, not music. What's the deal with your dad?"

"That's a long story," she said. "But if you want to go to dinner with me, I'll tell you all about it."

"You buying?"

"Of course."

Adam sat quietly, intently listening as she laid out the story of her life over greasy burgers with neon orange cheese and watered down Cokes at Denny's. "That explains a lot," he said when she was done.

"A lot of what?" she asked.

"Of why you are so aloof."

"I'm not aloof."

"Yeah, you are. It's okay, it actually works for you. It gives you a hint of mystery. I'd love to put you in one of my movies. I bet you would light up the screen."

"Stop it," she said, blushing. "I'm not an actress. I'm a guitar player. Besides, there's no mystery to me."

Adam jumped up so the he was kneeling in the booth instead of sitting, and he put his fingers together like a movie screen. "That's not true," he said excitedly. "You've got these smoky green eyes. They're stormy, like the ocean in a hurricane. Your smile is so pure and sweet and innocent, and your face is like an Indian princess...but then there are those eyes. Those eyes speak of unbelievable sadness; they show unbridled emotion. You keep yourself in such tight check all of the time, but those eyes give you away. Your eyes show everything that you try to keep hidden. That's where all of your pain and vulnerability is. Those eyes could make you a star."

Danielle realized that everyone in the restaurant was looking at them. "Sit down," she whispered, hiding her face in her hands. "You're embarrassing me."

He bounded over beside her. "Don't be embarrassed, Dani. Life's too short. I never worry about how people look at me because it won't matter in ten minutes. The only thing that matters is how you feel about yourself. If you could see you like I see you, you'd understand."

"Understand what?" She was staring deep into those blue eyes now and she was getting lost in them. No one had ever spoken to her like this before.

"How unbelievably beautiful you are." There were no false dramatics in what he said. She felt like she was floating. She had the urge to reach out and grab him and kiss him, but she resisted. He looked like he would come in for the kiss anyway, but their waitress started beating on the table, ending the moment.

"Hey, drama geek," the harsh woman said, "sit down or get out. This ain't no playground."

Adam saluted as she walked away, and they both shared a laugh as they finished their meal.

When they were done, Dani drove him back to his dorm on the campus of St. Edwards University. St. Edwards was a historic campus that sat on a hill overlooking downtown Austin. Danielle looked in awe at the Gothic buildings as she drove through the campus. Being on a college campus made Danielle wonder if she had made a mistake. Maybe, she thought, she should have gone to college first and gotten a degree. After all, what would she do if she didn't make it?

"Don't worry about it," Adam said as if he was reading her mind. "College is overrated. You don't need a degree to be smart. You're not missing that much."

"Yeah, right," she answered as she pulled up in front of his dorm. "Last stop."

He didn't say anything. She barely had a chance to react before her face was in his hands and his lips were on hers. She felt like an electric charge had been sent up her spine. They quickly fell into a deep, passionate kiss; the first real kiss she had ever had. When he finally broke the embrace, all he said was goodnight before quickly slipping out of the truck and into the dorm.

Danielle exhaled slowly as he disappeared from sight. That was one life experience she would love to repeat.

#

The summer rolled on like that. She worked during the week, jammed with Ty at night, and spent Friday and Saturday nights on 6th. As her playing got sharper her tips improved, and Danielle was proving to everyone just how serious she was.

It did turn serious with Adam. They spent as much time together as possible. He loved to film her as they scurried about town or as she wrote a new song. Their first kiss turned into more serious make out sessions, which Danielle loved. But no matter what he said or did, she wouldn't let it go farther. There was a future to think about, and people were counting on her.

At the end of August, Danielle was invited to attend another of Randy's jam sessions. This time, she took charge from the start. The summer full of playing had sharpened both her skills and her focus. When it was over, there was no doubt in anyone's mind. She had the skill, she had the desire, and she had already started building an audience.

All she needed was a band. In Jim Silver and Albert Barber, two old-school Austin blues veterans, she found a damn good one. Randy called in some more favors and Danielle had her first official paying gig, at an east side blues club called Sliders. The time was now.

CHAPTER THREE

With one week to go before her big debut at Sliders, Danielle was beginning to doubt herself. She, Al, and Jim had been rehearsing every night for a week in an abandoned warehouse in Austin's industrial park, but it wasn't coming together the way they planned. The band just wasn't clicking.

Serving as an audience, Ty, Randy, Teri, and Adam were trying to be supportive, but it was clear to all that the chemistry was not there. As each pass went sour, Danielle began to get more down on herself.

The rehearsals began to devolve into a tug of war between Danielle and Jim. Jim wanted to concentrate on blues standards, songs the audience already knew. Danielle wanted to focus on her original songs. Randy was trying the best he could to be the peacemaker, but both were getting frustrated.

After a particularly horrid run through of a Danielle song titled "Someday Baby," Jim became so disgusted that he stormed out of the building. Danielle, exhausted, collapsed in a heap on the floor.

"Hey, keep your head up, kid," Randy consoled her. "This is why you rehearse before you play a real show. You'll get it straightened out."

She looked up at him with disbelief. "There's no straightening out this mess. It's awful."

He walked around behind her and started to rub her neck and back. "You're too tight, Dani. You've got to loosen up and do what you do. You're trying. When you're at your best, it just flows out of you. Nothing's flowing."

"Yeah, I know that. I just can't seem to make it happen."

"You will when you relax," Randy assured her. "You've got to loosen up. Quit playing everything so close to the vest. This should be fun. There are no recording contracts to honor, no one expects anything out of you. Just play."

"I can't," she responded. "I expect something out of me."

"What? What do you expect?"

"Perfection," she said coldly. "Nothing else will do."

"That's not true," Randy answered.

Danielle shot to her feet and turned with a catlike quickness that took Randy's breath away. "It is true. I have to be three times as good as anybody else in order for people to take me seriously. Nobody's going to take a chick guitar player seriously any other way."

Randy shook his head sadly. "Where did you get that idea?"

She rolled her eyes in the direction of the front door, where Jim was stubbing out his cigarette. Randy got her point.

"Listen to me," he said, taking her shoulders in his big hands. "You are already better than ninety percent of the guitarists out there. You don't have to be perfect; you just have to be you. Don't let that grumpy old man get in your head. He's mad at the world because he never made it big. He's jealous of your talent. Don't let him drag you down."

She nodded her head in acknowledgment as Jim passed by them both and mounted the makeshift stage they had constructed. Danielle followed, strapping Ole Red on again and getting ready for another pass. Only this time, she had another idea.

"Give me a second guys," she implored her band mates. She began to play her solo, the one she had played at the first jam session, which she had named "Small Town Life." She closed her eyes and blocked out everything else around her, feeling the music for the first time in a week.

As she began to wind the song down, she opened her eyes and caught sight of Ty sitting in the audience. She remembered the night of the jam session, how he had taken her original riff and turned it around, rocking it up and making an entirely new song out of it. She gave him a sly smile and then turned to Al, waiting patiently at the drums. She gave him a slight nod and then kicked the song into overdrive. A big smile spread across Al's face as he began assaulting the drum kit with vigor. She turned to Jim, who disgustedly took off his bass and left the stage.

The song screeched to a halt and Danielle half threw Ole Red to the ground as she followed Jim off the stage. "What the hell are you doing? We were starting to get a groove going."

Jim lit another cigarette. Holding it in his fingers, he pointed it at Randy. "You said this was going to be a blues band. This isn't the blues."

Danielle reached out and grabbed him by the arm and spun him around. "Talk to me, not him."

"Fine. I didn't sign on to be in some teeny bopper rock band. I play the blues."

"Who the hell cares as long as it's good?" she responded in frustration. "How is that any different from anything Stevie Ray ever did?"

"Stevie Ray, darling, was a thief. He didn't play the blues, he stole them and twisted them. I play the blues."

"Maybe that's why he was a star and you're a washed up loser with a bad attitude."

Randy tried to step between them, but there was no separating them now. Jim pointed his cigarette at Danielle, the lit end centimeters from her face. "And I damn sure didn't sign on to be disrespected by a snot nosed teenager," he sneered.

"Nobody's making you stay," she shot back.

"Guys, please," Randy begged, finally muscling his way between the two. "We all want the same thing here." He turned his attention to Jim. "Come on, man. This is your shot too. Nobody wants to hear Muddy Waters anymore, dude. You know that. You provide the blues and let Danielle provide the sizzle. Y'all gotta get on the same page."

Jim was seething, but Randy's words were getting through. He finally huffed and turned away. "Shit, man. This isn't my music."

"It's not your shot," Randy said with compassion. "Your time is gone, man. You want to keep playing golf and wondering what might have been, or do you want to give it one last shot?"

Jim nodded, stubbed out his cigarette, and blew his last lungful of smoke into the air. Then he forced himself to look Danielle in the eyes. "Do you think you could pull back on the Stevie Ray impression just a little?"

"I'll do whatever I need to," she said, still glaring past Randy at him. "If you'll quit being such a pain in my ass."

Randy turned back to Jim. "There, see? She can be reasonable. We'd talked that this was going to take some sacrifice, remember? What do you say?"

He didn't want to, but something swayed Jim in that moment. Danielle would spend a lot of sleepless nights wondering what it was that played across his face in those fleeting moments before he finally relented. In the end, though, she got what she wanted. For the moment at least, she had won the battle.

A fierce thunderstorm moved through Austin that night. Danielle sat in the dark, wearing nothing but a Texas Longhorn nightshirt, absentmindedly fiddling with Ole Red as she watched the rain lash against the window and the lightning dance across the sky.

She thought about the day's events and about the show ahead. She felt stifled by Jim's insistence on their being a blues band. She didn't like anyone else having control of her creativity. She couldn't get the look of Jim's face out of her head. Something had changed his mind. Randy had set this all up behind her back. Was there some sort of back-office deal between the two of them?

She didn't want to doubt her friends, but it was curious. She hated the thought that people could be using her and she not know it. Were they really helping her, or taking advantage of her naiveté? She began to feel sick to her stomach trying to comprehend it all.

She was snapped out of her thoughts by the sight of a gangly kid skateboarding up the driveway. By the time she got to the door, Adam was already there, drenched from head to toe.

"What are you doing skateboarding in weather like this?" She laughed as she invited him in.

He immediately peeled of his rain-soaked clothes. She edged by him, trying not to look at him as she did. She grabbed a towel out of the bathroom and tossed it to him.

"I don't need it. I like being naked."

"I would feel better if you would cover up," she said, never having felt more awkward than she did right then. "I can't carry on a conversation with you like this."

He got a mischievous smile on his face and approached her. Quickly she was wrapped up in his arms. She could feel him rising up against her. "Who says I want to talk?"

She pushed away easily. "Please put the towel on."

"Okay," he said, sounding a bit annoyed. "What are you so afraid of?"

She plopped down on her bed. "I'm not afraid of anything. I'm just not ready for this. I feel like you're pushing me."

Adam sat down on the bench with his back to the window. "I don't mean to push, but we've been dating for six weeks."

"Six whole weeks. Yeah, that's such a long time," she said with a sneer. "It's too soon."

"I think you're too old fashioned. What if you were to die tomorrow? Would you want to go to your grave never having made love?"

"If I died tomorrow it wouldn't matter, would it?"

Adam spread his arms wide with a smile. "Right. So if it doesn't matter anyway, let's get to it."

Danielle threw a pillow at him in response. "Stop it. Sometimes I think that's the only reason you're with me."

"That's not the only reason," Adam said defensively. "But sex is a part of a healthy relationship between two consenting adults."

"If you haven't noticed," she responded, "I'm not consenting."

"Yeah, I know."

"Is that the only reason you came here?"

"Oh no," he said. "I almost forgot. I'm going to be leaving for a little bit."

"Leaving?" she asked. "Where to?"

"Houston. My drama professor has a friend who's a filmmaker, nobody you would have heard of. Anyway, this guy is from Houston and he's going back there to shoot a movie, and my professor got me a small part."

"That's great," Danielle said. She was glad to see him get a break. "But I thought you wanted to be a director, not an actor."

"I don't really want to be an actor," he said, barely containing his excitement. "But this is a step in that direction. It gets me on a real movie set around a real director and real actors. I figure that will be a great experience for me, and maybe I can make some contacts. It's a step up the ladder."

Danielle got off the bed and strolled over to Adam. Taking his face in her hands, she gave him a soft kiss. "I'm proud of you. I think we're both on the way to better things."

He wrapped his arms around her and yanked her down. They both tumbled to the floor and his towel fell off. "I'd like to get to better things right now."

Danielle rolled her eyes. "Would you please stop?"

Adam sat up, flustered. "Why are doing this to me? Can't you see what you're doing to me?"

Danielle sat up and scooted out of his reach. "I can see quite well. But I'm not doing this to you. You're doing this to yourself."

"That's the problem," he said as he retrieved the towel. "You don't have to do anything. You just have this natural sexiness. I guess that's why you always dress yourself down."

She scooted back over until she was next to him and wrapped her arms around him, resting her head on his shoulder. "I don't know if you will understand, but sex terrifies me. I've seen lives destroyed because of it. I'm just not ready. I've got too much at stake, too much I want to accomplish. If you love me, any at all, just be patient. I won't leave you. You just have to wait for me. I'll know when I'm ready."

He sighed loudly. "Okay, I won't push you anymore. Just know that it's not because I want to conquer you. I only want to love you. Please know that."

"I do," she whispered.

"Any chance for another make out session?"

She looked up at him with a smirk. "I don't think that's a good idea in your present condition."

#

On a sultry, mid-September Saturday night in Austin, Danielle Regan took the stage for real. The marquee out front read "Danielle Regan and Texas Pride." She had never agreed to the name, but Randy informed her that Jim and Al had been calling themselves Texas Pride since the late '70s, so it came with the territory. He also insisted that having their name on the bill would ensure a better caliber of audience. Danielle wasn't thrilled but she relented.

Sliders was a dingy, cramped rat trap on the east side of I-35. The stage was barely big enough for the band and all of their gear. As she waited backstage for her time, she peeked out into the bar. The place was filling up nicely and the beer was flowing freely. All she had to do was deliver.

Randy gave the introduction and she bounded onto the stage, Ole Red primed and ready in her hands. It was totally different up there on the stage. There were a hundred or more strange faces staring back at her. The lights were bright and hot, making her regret her choice of a long sleeved white shirt and blue jeans for wardrobe. She was already beginning to sweat and her hair was beginning to stick to her face.

She glared out into that crowd and wondered how she would do this. It was so hot. The crowd began to get antsy. She reached for Ole Red, but the neck slipped from her grasp thanks to sweaty hands. She rubbed them on her jeans and pushed the hair back from her face.

"Come on," Jim urged at her side. "Don't make us look stupid."

The crowd began to jeer. She couldn't even remember what song they were going to start with. Her head began to swim and her stomach began to flip. This was it, this was where the dream died.

"Come on, darlin'," Albert begged. "You can do it."

Her hair wouldn't stay out of her face and her shirt was clinging to her. It was terribly hot. There was a rubber band wrapped around her microphone stand. Trying to block out the jeers and the catcalls, she took the rubber band off and threw her hair back in a quick ponytail. She turned her back to the crowd and unbuttoned her shirt. It didn't matter that all she had on underneath was a bra, she had to cool off. She threw the shirt to the stage and the crowd cheered their approval. She looked back over her shoulder. She had their attention for sure now. A sly smile slowly spread across her face.

"Come on," Jim said more forcefully.

She closed her eyes and took a deep breath. It had to be now. She reached for Ole Red one more time and wrapped her hands around the neck. Her fingers automatically found her first chord. She poised her right hand, ready to strike. Around her, Jim and Al waited for their cue. With one more deep breath, she started....

Exhausted, bordering on delirious, sweat-soaked and shaking, Danielle stumbled off stage three hours later. Her voice was nothing more than a hoarse croak by the end. No one had planned on her playing that long, but the crowd kept cheering and the more they cheered, the harder she pushed. Her ears were ringing so badly that she could barely hear the congratulations of her friends as they greeted her. Even Jim had to pat her on the back after her performance. The owner of the club offered them a weekly spot, which they gladly accepted.

After an impromptu celebration dinner, Danielle, Randy, and Teri returned home, where Danielle finally collapsed on their couch. Teri came up to her and rubbed her arm. "Whatever made you think to play in your bra?"

"I was just trying to keep from passing out."

"Well it was genius," Randy called from the kitchen, where he was fetching beer and Cokes from the fridge. "You had them all in the palm of your hands. It was brilliant."

"Don't expect me to do that again," she called tiredly. "It was a one-time deal."

"No," Randy responded as he put an ice cold Coke in her hand. He knelt beside the couch. "Don't do that. Sex appeal is a big thing in this business. Your sex appeal can set you apart from all the rest. Use it, make it a tool. You can control it. I think it would be fantastic."

"I want to be judged on my music, not my body." She took a long, delicious drink from the bottle. It had never tasted so good before. "That was a cheap stunt tonight."

"Millions have been made with cheap stunts. Look, you don't have to show your goods, just a little teaser. A little leg, a little shoulder. That's all you need to do. I bet we could find somebody around here to design you a wardrobe. It would be tasteful, yet revealing at the same time. Cowgirl chic. What do you say?"

Teri scolded her over-excited husband. "Let the girl rest. Don't you see how tired she is? And if she's not comfortable doing that, then she shouldn't have to."

"I don't know," Danielle whispered. "I was pretty comfortable up there. It gets so hot under those lights."

"Well, you do what you want to do and nothing more," Teri advised. Danielle did just that. She went to sleep.

Sliders became the club to be at on Friday nights. Every week, the band got tighter and Danielle began to introduce more of her original songs into a set packed full of Texas blues standards Austin audiences had been loving for years. The *Austin Chronicle* gave the band a glowing review.

Their success led to better gigs at better clubs, and soon Danielle Regan and Texas Pride outgrew Sliders. By early November, they were regulars on Sixth. Danielle could almost see herself on stage at Antone's.

In the midst of her early success, things were changing for Danielle. Ty quit the music store when school started. Randy thought that he was jealous of her success. She missed the days of jamming with his band in the garage, but she was on to better things.

Adam left for Houston and his big movie role. It was supposed to be a three-week thing, but when he never returned to school, Danielle knew he was gone. Austin had called to her and Hollywood had called to Adam.

Business at the store was booming because of people flooding in to see Austin's newest club sensation. Randy even started charging admission for people to come see the Friday night jam sessions, now moved to Tuesday night so Danielle could attend. She was beginning to feel like a sideshow attraction, but she was making money and making friends. She began getting invitations to sit in with more accomplished musicians when they came through town.

Then came the moment she had dreamed about. Danielle spent her nineteenth birthday on stage at Antone's, playing to an adoring crowd on a Wednesday night. At that moment, she decided that if all she ever did was play the Austin blues scene, she could be happy.

As the final note of her last song lingered in the air, Danielle ducked off the stage, through the arms of the fans, and into a side door, where her friends had a birthday cake waiting for her. Clifford Antone himself was there to congratulate her on another fine performance.

The group sat and ate and talked as the music from the jukebox filtered through the thin walls.

Then they were approached by a strange man. He was tall and powerfully built, with a shaved head and a thick brown mustache. He wore an emerald green button up shirt, black slacks, and a black sports coat, and carried a Coors longneck loosely in his big right hand. In his left hand, he carried a brown leather briefcase. He looked to be in his mid to late thirties, and had a confident, almost cocky air about him.

"Great show tonight, Ms. Regan," he said in a strong, clear voice. There was no hint of an accent at all. "I'm very impressed."

Danielle was slightly annoyed by the intrusion. "Thanks. I appreciate the kind words." She shot a quick glance at Randy, but he didn't seem to know who he was either.

The man was undeterred. He put his longneck on the table and reached a hand out to her. "My name is Steve Redus, Ms. Regan. I would like to have a word with you."

She took his hand and was impressed by his strong grip. He had a real man's handshake. "Well, we're kind of in the middle of a little party here. Is there another time we could talk? Maybe tomorrow?"

"I would really like to talk to you now, if you don't mind."

Danielle rolled her eyes, excused herself, and pushed away from the table. She walked to a quiet corner where they could speak undisturbed. "What can I do for you, Mr. Redus?"

"It's what I can do for you, Ms. Regan," he responded. "I would like to be your manager."

She looked around him at Randy, who was busy telling one of his many lame jokes to the rest of the table. He was having the time of his life. "I already have a manager, Mr. Redus. Right over there."

He nodded once in understanding. "I am aware of that, Ms. Regan, but how far will he be able to take you? How far do his connections travel? If all you want to do is bounce around the Austin bar scene, then by all means, stay with him. I want to take you further."

Danielle felt the emotion swirling inside her. She wanted to be loyal to Randy, but how much further could this new man take her?

"How far?" she asked, feeling dirty as she did.

"How far do you want to go?" She detected no cockiness in him, just supreme confidence. "I can take you anywhere you want to go. I've been watching you for a couple of weeks now, and I think that the only limit to your potential is you."

"What makes you think that you can do this for me?"

That big smile spread across his face again. He opened his briefcase and took out a thin red folder. "This is my resume. Look it over. There's a card in there with my number. I'll be in town until the end of the week. That's how long my offer to you is good for. The minute my feet hit the plane, the offer is rescinded. Have a nice night."

That night after Teri went to bed, Danielle and Randy sat around the kitchen table and reviewed the file Steve Redus had given her. He was thirty-nine and single, no kids, and was originally from Portland, Oregon. He now lived in Los Angeles, where he was starting his management business. Before that he had gotten his MBA from Stanford, and then a job with A&M Records. He had stayed with that label as an A&R man until the label was bought by PolyGram in 1989. He then moved to an executive level job at Columbia Records until late 1993. That was when he decided that he wanted to be a manager instead. According to his resume, he was supremely qualified to manage musical artists because he had an in-depth knowledge of record labels and how they operated, and a wealth of contacts inside the industry at both the talent and corporate levels. There were even letters of recommendation with former A&M talents Janet Jackson and Bryan Adams.

Randy whistled as he read over the resume. "He's certainly got his stuff in order. It's very impressive."

Danielle agreed, but was still uneasy about it. "Why do you think that he just suddenly decided to quit and start managing acts? The money is with the label."

"Maybe it's not about money to him," Randy opined. "He seems to be doing very well for himself. Maybe he just wanted a change. Maybe he didn't like the corporate side of things."

"Or," Danielle responded, "Maybe he got fired. Maybe he's a loser; or worse, maybe he got into drugs and lost his job."

"I guess you'll have to ask him."

She shook her head. "No. I already have a manager. I don't need him."

Randy chuckled and laid a big hand on her back. "Darlin', you're outgrowing me. You're too good to spend your life playing dinky blues clubs. If he can help you achieve more, then you need to do it."

"I won't turn my back on my friends."

"You won't be," he assured her. "Go with my blessing. I kind of miss the quiet life, and I couldn't live with myself if I was the reason you held yourself back. Please, meet with the man and see what he has to say."

Danielle was grappling with a sick feeling in her stomach. "I don't know if I can. Things are so good right now. I don't know that I want anything to change."

"Dani, baby," he said, patting her on the back. "There are much better things on the horizon."

Steve Redus was staying in the Hilton overlooking Town Lake. She agreed to meet him in the lobby, but he quickly decided to take advantage of the beautiful day and moved their meeting outside.

She declined his offer to buy her lunch, but he went ahead and ordered a salad and bottled water. She bought herself a Coke. After the waitress left to fill their order, Danielle got direct. "Why did you leave Columbia?"

He laughed. "That's the first question I always get asked. If you must know, I got downsized. Sony bought us in '91 and by '93 I was gone. I got fed up with all the corporate nonsense, all the buyouts and the turnover. I got tired of seeing good, hard-working musicians get screwed by their labels for a few bucks. So I decided to get into management."

It was a good answer. Maybe too good. "Who else do you represent?"

With that question, he sighed and took off his wraparound sunglasses. He leaned forward and rested his elbows on the glass patio table. He had beautiful deep brown eyes that she could almost see herself in.

"Honestly, no one. I've been traveling to all the hotspots: Nashville, New York, Seattle. I'm looking for the right kinds of clients, the diamonds in the rough if you will. So far, the few that I've found that I really believe in have rejected me. Nobody wants to take a chance on me."

"Why should I?"

"Maybe you shouldn't," he said as he put his sunglasses back on and leaned back. "I think I'm wasting my time trying to do this." Then he leaned forward again, nearly smashing his forearms into the glass tabletop. "All I want to do is help you people. I want to put all of my years of experience and knowledge to use, to look out for people who don't know all the slimy tricks record labels and concert promoters pull. That's all I want to do, but nobody believes in me."

He sat back again as the waitress delivered their order. He took a deep breath. "But I don't guess I can blame you. We suits have earned our bad reputation over the years." He stood up and offered his hand. "I do thank you for taking the time to review my resume and to listen."

Danielle stayed seated. "Do you always give up so easily?"

Steve sat back down slowly. "I'm just frustrated. I thought this would be so easy, but I keep getting rejected." He was showing some vulnerability now and Danielle liked it much better. "I've burned through my savings, borrowed all that I can, called in all my favors. I'll be lucky if I can make it home."

"Then why are you staying at such a fancy hotel?"

"You've got to impress people," he said with a sight. "Show them success. That's what people respect."

She shook her head. "Do you know what I respect? Honesty. This is the first time I've felt real sincerity from you. You should try that more often."

"Duly noted," he responded.

"So what's your big plan? How are you going to take me to the next level?"

Sensing that he was close to winning her over, Steve began to smile again.

"First thing we do is get you some paying gigs at some top-notch clubs. We'll start regionally and then work outward. Then we get you in a recording studio and get an album to sell. It can be on an independent label, that's fine. We hit the clubs and the radio stations hard, and let your music radiate out from there. With a little work, we can sharpen your stage persona and tighten your sound. You can do the rest."

Danielle sat and assessed him for a long moment. Her instincts were telling her to take the leap. "You have to understand something," she said. "I've been feeling like everyone has been controlling things but me up until now. I don't care for that. I love Randy, but sometimes I wonder who he's really looking out for, me or his buddies. If I agree to this, you will work for me, not the other way around. I want to be in on everything."

"That's how it is supposed to be," Steve answered. He was winning her over. Or was she winning him?

"Then I think we have ourselves a deal," Danielle said with a smile. "But please drop the power-broker act and just be yourself. I like you much better that way."

That weekend, Steve Redus watched from backstage as Danielle blistered her way through a monster show at an ultra-popular barbeque restaurant outside of town. The California cool manager got his first taste of Texas BBQ to go along with the Texas blues. He was a convert.

"That was a fantastic show tonight, Danielle," Steve told her as they drove back to Randy's. "You're going to kill once I can get you out of Austin."

Danielle, as always, was exhausted at the end of the show. She kept her eyes closed as he drove. "I hope so."

"But we need to spice up your stage show a little bit. People don't want to go to a concert to see you stand at the mike for three hours. You've got to move, interact with the crowd more. You need to use a little more sex appeal."

"No," she answered firmly. "I won't do that. I want people to pay attention to me for my music, not my looks. I've already had this discussion with Randy."

"Dani, I'm not asking you to do a strip tease or anything," he started. There was a long pause, causing Danielle to open her eyes and look at him wearily. He caught the movement and looked over at her with a smirk. "I just mean, strut a little more. Half of rock'n'roll is sex. It's a primitive thing, a tribal thing. Just keep an open mind. Next week I will pick you up and we'll discuss some things further. I have an idea. Okay?"

Danielle closed her eyes again. "Whatever."

The next Monday he drove her to an upper-tier strip club on South Congress called Honey's. Danielle had heard about strip clubs her whole life, but now she was in one. It wasn't what she expected. It was very clean, with thick, luxurious carpet. Everywhere she looked was shiny chrome and spotless glass. It was a big place with an elongated stage and the obligatory stripper's pole at one end.

Sitting on the edge of the stage was a woman that Danielle believed to be the most beautiful woman she had ever seen. The woman stood as they approached. She was as tall as Danielle but with longer, golden blonde hair and crystal clear blue eyes. She had full, pink lips, clear skin, and a body that was all natural and hard not to look at.

"Danielle," Steve said, his voice shaking slightly with nerves. "Meet Alex Starr."

The other woman, who didn't look like she was much older than Danielle, held out her hand. Danielle took it and was secretly surprised at how soft her skin was. Danielle realized at that moment just how much of a tomboy she really was.

"Sarah," the woman said in a soft voice with a thick Texas twang. "Call me Sarah, please."

"Okay," Danielle answered. "Sarah, not Alex."

"Alex is my stage name. I don't answer to it any other time."

"Gotcha," Danielle nodded. Then she turned her attention to Steve. "Why exactly am I here?"

"Because you need to liven up your stage show, and Alex — excuse me, Sarah — is going to show you some moves."

"Wait a second," Danielle answered angrily. "You said that you didn't want me to do a striptease, but you're having a stripper teach me moves?"

Sarah put a soft hand on her shoulder. "I'm an exotic dancer, and what I'm going to be showing you are dance moves. Steve here asked me to come up with something that you could do while performing, while playing your guitar, to make your shows more interesting. And honey, you really do need it. I've seen the tape."

"I don't like this at all. This is not me."

"So make it somebody else," Sarah answered. "Where do you think Alex Starr comes from? Little ole Sarah Wilson would never get up on stage in front of a bunch of horny, drunk old men and take all her clothes off. That's the entire point of having a stage persona."

"Again, Danielle," Steve stepped in, trying to assure her. "We're not asking you to take your clothes off. Just add some moves, some interaction. If you want, you can even take a stage name. I've been working on some for you, some that kind of relate your power. Like Gayle Force."

"It's a stripper name," Danielle shot back. "I'm not hiding behind some fake name, especially not a stupid one like that. Gayle Force? Are you kidding me?"

Sarah took Danielle's arm and gently guided her away from Steve. She leaned in close so that she could whisper in Danielle's ear.

"Listen, I understand why you're upset, but I really need this. I have a dream of being a choreographer so that I can quit doing this. Steve promised me that if I did a good job with you he would introduce me to some people who can help me. I promise you, I'm not going to make you look like a slut."

Danielle turned to look at her. She saw in the girl a desperation she had never seen before. She tried to imagine what it must be like to do what she did every night. Danielle thought that she would probably do anything to get out of a life like this.

"All right," she said quietly. "But please don't make me look stupid."

"I promise you, I won't. I like your music…I just want to help you make your show better."

"Okay," Danielle said with a sigh. "I'll put myself in your hands."

After a week of working with Sarah every morning before the club opened, Danielle was ready to debut her new stage show at a Saturday night show at a club called The Ledge. She stood backstage, waiting for the call, desperately trying to calm her nerves. Sarah had even come to get her ready, bringing a special outfit for the occasion; a strapless black leather dress that was almost embarrassingly short, and tall black boots. It was completely out of character for Danielle, but she was willing to give it a try.

When Jim saw her, he broke into wild laughter. It took all Steve could do to keep her from backing out, but he and Sarah managed to keep her in the outfit long enough to get her onstage. From the moment her boots hit the stage, it was magic. The crowd roared its approval, song after song, as Danielle prowled the edge of the stage like a hungry cat, toying with the audience. She moved to the beat of the song, slithered up next to the other band members, and even broke out some guitar acrobatics of her own, playing it from her knees or behind her back.

#

"Last Saturday, Danielle Regan took her performance to an entirely new level," Steve read aloud from the *Austin Chronicle* as he, Teri, Randy, and Danielle sat around the Holder's kitchen table. "Decked out in a black leather ensemble that would make Catwoman blush, Danielle finally came out of her shell in a big way. No doubt the girl's got all the chops on the guitar, but last night she proved that she can be a performer as well. She slithered and danced across the stage, putting on a show that will be long remembered around Austin. If the only thing lacking in her repertoire was a stage presence, she is well on her way to remedying that. We can now safely say that Danielle is Austin's hottest new commodity."

Randy and Teri applauded as Steve finished reading the review. Danielle sat with her head down on the kitchen table, embarrassed by the memories of her earlier act. When she finally did lift her head, she was red-faced.

"Well, it's not happening again. I'll tell you that right now."

"Why?" Steve asked, waving the newspaper in the air. "They loved it. The crowd ate it up. You are now the must-see act in town."

"I felt like a dominatrix out there. I felt dirty."

"You shouldn't feel that way," Randy interjected. "It's just a show. You shouldn't let it reflect on how you feel about yourself."

"But I do. You can say that it's just a performance, but people are going to form their opinions of me based on what they see up there. If I go onstage and play the slut, I can't expect people not to treat me like one."

Steve got up and walked over to her, crouching beside her chair. "If people can't tell the difference between an onstage performance and real life, then that's their problem."

Danielle stared back into his deep brown eyes. "Spoken like someone who never has to worry about it."

"Okay, enough, enough," Teri interrupted. "Dani, why don't you come with me? You boys go find something to entertain yourselves. I think it's time for a little girl talk."

Teri pushed away from the table and motioned for Danielle to join her, which she did. They didn't say a word to each other as they walked through the house and outside to the back porch, where they both plopped down on the top step.

"I can't imagine what you've been through and I don't expect you to tell me. But I want you to know that you're with people now who care about you and want the best for you. Steve and Randy are trying to help you achieve your dreams the best way that they know how. If you're not comfortable with this, maybe you should try something else."

Danielle turned her gaze to Teri. Teri was the mother Danielle had never had and she loved the older woman deeply, but at that moment she felt betrayed. "Why? Why does everyone feel that the only way I can succeed is by making myself a sex object?"

"Because, dear," Teri said softly. "That's the way the game is played. That is where your power lies."

"Bullshit," she spat back. She stood up and began to pace. "Did Stevie Ray have to do that? Eddie Van Halen? Eric Clapton?"

"No," Teri whispered. "They're men."

"What's the difference? Why do I have to and they didn't? Are they so much better than me?"

Teri stood up and took Danielle by the arms to stop her pacing. "Dani, you are a great guitar player, truly one of the best I've ever heard. But it takes more than that to make it. Great guitar players are a dime a dozen. You have to stand out to be noticed. That's the advantage you have over all the others, if you would only use it. You aren't a victim if you're in control."

"If I can't be noticed based on my talent, then I don't want to be noticed at all."

Teri shook her head sadly. "Then maybe you shouldn't. Baby, this has always been the way of the world. You're a beautiful young woman. You shouldn't be ashamed of your beauty. It's the one advantage that you have over men. Any guitarist can grab an audience's attention with some fancy moves. You're the only one that can make them stand at attention for a whole show, if you get my drift."

"I get the drift just fine," Danielle shot back. "But I'm not playing this stupid game. I'll make it on my terms or I won't make it at all. There is no other option. If y'all won't support me on that, then I guess I need to find some new friends."

She turned and stormed off, throwing the back gate open and stomping down the alley.

Danielle walked down the alley and turned right. Her thoughts raced. What would Grandma and Grandpa have thought of her last night? Or Kel? She could barely stand the thought of it. She was getting performance and wardrobe advice from a stripper. How far was she from becoming one?

She realized she had hit Guadalupe Street, or The Drag, as it was more commonly known. Across the street, the University of Texas stood proud in the spring sun. She leaned up against a building and watched all of the college kids whiz past. They all seemed so focused, so together. She'd had the grades to go there, she thought. Maybe there were grants or scholarships she could apply for. She could go for a real career, where something other than her looks could come into play. Something where she could earn respect.

But the only thing she had ever really wanted to do was play music. That was why she'd really come here. In her heart, she knew she could only be happy playing music; but to do that, apparently she had to sacrifice her dignity. She was beginning to understand the tortured-artist thing better than she ever thought possible.

She started walking again, turning her back to UT and heading back towards downtown, towards 6th street and the clubs. She was miles away, but she had nowhere else to go and nothing else to do. She felt more alone than before, and her old self-doubts began to creep back into her head.

At some point during her walk she became aware of a constant honking. She looked over her shoulder to see Adam Quisenberry, smiling and waving at her from the front seat of a brand new Mustang convertible. He looked different...in fact, he looked better. The strawberry blond hair was more blond now than strawberry, and it was cut short. The shorter cut made his five o'clock shadow look better, and he had filled out and muscled up. He looked much less like a beatnik now, but his smile was still a million watts.

Danielle felt her heart start to pound as he pulled the Mustang up to the curb. "Hey, beautiful, long time no see. Need a lift?"

She started for the car, then stopped herself. This was the guy who'd left her high and dry just a few months before. "No thanks," she said coldly, and started walking again.

She could hear the tires crunching the road behind her.

"Come on, Dani. We've got catching up to do."

She wheeled around quickly, her anger at a boiling point. "We wouldn't have to catch up if you hadn't forgotten about me."

Adam put the car in park and sat on the back of the driver's seat. "I didn't forget about you, but things started happening real fast and I couldn't take it all in. Man, there's been some crazy stuff happening."

"Well, at the risk of crazy stuff happening again, I will save you the trouble." She turned away again. She was trying to keep her cool, but she felt like a hurricane of emotions was swirling in her heart. So much of her wanted to jump into the car, into those arms. But she couldn't; this was a matter of pride.

She didn't even reach the end of the block before she felt his hand clamp down on her arm. He was stronger than she remembered. He didn't spin her around, though; he just stopped her and came around in front of her. Now face to face at this distance, she felt that anger slipping away. His eyes did that to her. She had to fight to hold onto it.

"I know that I should have called or written, and I really meant to. I thought about you every day. I let other things distract me, and when I realized what was happening, time had passed and I knew it was too late. I knew by then that the only way I could talk to you was in person, because a letter or a call wouldn't be good enough." He took her face in his hands; his touch could still be soft when it needed to be. "You know as much as I do that you wouldn't have accepted anything less."

Danielle let out a long, slow breath. He was right.

"Come on," he said, with a nudge. "Let's go get some lunch and catch up."

Nau's was an old school soda fountain located in the back of a pharmacy not far from campus. There, the burgers were always greasy, the shakes always thick, and the price always affordable. Adam insisted on buying since Danielle had always bought in the past, and she settled in a booth far from the counter. Adam came back a few moments later and slid in across from her.

He took her hands in his and gave her that smile again. "God, it's great to see you. You know, I fell in love with you the first time I saw you on that street corner last summer. I had forgotten all about

84

that feeling until I saw you on the street again today. One look brought it all back."

"You did not fall in love," Danielle answered back. "There's a difference between attraction and love. No one falls in love at first sight. You can't love someone until you know them."

Adam shook his head with a grin. "You are such a cynic. Maybe falling in love isn't the right term, but there is a feeling. It's more than attraction. And before you say it, it's not lust either. Because I could see a million girls I find attractive or that I might want to have sex with, but none of them would make me feel like I felt when I saw you that first night. Maybe its destiny or fate, I don't know. But there's something that two people can have in an instant, and we have it."

"Maybe we do," Danielle conceded. "But it doesn't take much to ruin it. You know, like, saying goodbye to someone for a couple of weeks and then not seeing them again for nine months."

Adam grimaced. "You've got me there, but I've got to tell you what happened. It was amazing."

Their number was called and Adam slid out of the booth to go get their food. He returned a few moments later with two greasy cheeseburgers and ice cold chocolate shakes.

Adam started right up like he was never interrupted. "So, I went to Houston to shoot this movie and it was only supposed to be a couple weeks, right? I got down there and the director liked the job I did so much that he expanded my role in the movie. When we were done shooting, he told me that he was about to start shooting another movie out in L.A. and he had a part for me in it, at double what I made for this one. Well, I couldn't pass that up. So I followed the guy to L.A. and shot this other role. Then he told another filmmaker friend about me, and that guy offered me a couple of small roles. Then, the first director, he came and said that he had a new movie he wanted to shoot, and he wanted me to co-star in it. He even gave me a bonus, like a signing bonus, for taking the part. It starts filming next month in Atlanta. So, since I had a little time, I came back here. I used my signing bonus to get a boss apartment downtown and my ride out there. Isn't that awesome?"

Danielle listened to his story with a mixture of guilt and jealousy. She knew she should be happy for Adam...he was talented and a hard worker, and deserved success. Still, she couldn't help but wonder why he had fallen into a great career and hers seemed to be an uphill battle. "That's great, Adam. I'm very happy for you."

"You don't sound like it," he answered as he chewed on a French fry. "What's wrong with you?"

She waved him off. "Nothing is wrong with me. Everything is great. Things are really great."

Adam wasn't buying it and she knew it. "Come on, Dani. I know you better than that. I can tell by looking at you. I don't think you've smiled once this whole time."

In response, she forced a weak smile, but her heart wasn't in it.

"You know, if you're worried about other girls, there weren't any," Adam explained. "I mean, I met others, even went on some dates, but nobody compared to you. Hollywood actresses aren't exactly the deepest people on earth."

"No, it's not that. Until today, I honestly never thought I'd see you again. So the fact that you dated other girls isn't a surprise."

"So, what's the problem?"

"I don't want to talk about it."

"Does it have anything to do with that performance last Saturday? I read all about it in the *Chronicle*."

Danielle felt herself blush, and lowered her head because she didn't want to look him in the eye.

"I'm assuming that wasn't your idea?"

She felt a fresh surge of anger. "No, it wasn't, but I went along with it. Now everybody is going nuts over it and they want me to be like that all the time. I hated it. I felt like a tramp."

He reached out and rubbed her arm. His touch felt good and it calmed her. His eyes were soft with understanding. "Can I tell you something?" he asked. She nodded affirmatively. "I was there that night. When I saw you were playing, I knew I had to be there. I can tell you that what I saw was, beyond a doubt, the sexiest performance I've ever seen."

"Great," Danielle whispered. Even Adam liked slutty Danielle better.

"But," he continued. "It wasn't you, and I didn't like it for that reason. I like you much better in some jeans and one of those nice little tank tops you wear. That's the real you; simple, down to earth, sexy without trying to be. That's how I like you."

She looked up with a sheepish grin. "That's kind of how I feel too."

"Then tell everybody else to fuck off. It's your name on the bill, it's you everybody is there to see. If you're not comfortable doing something, tell them to hit the road."

"Yeah. I guess. I don't know, Adam. I'm beginning to think I've picked the wrong profession. Maybe this isn't for me. My manager tells me that this is the way the game is played, and if I want to make it I have to play it."

"That's a bunch of bullshit. I think the only way you can be happy, as an artist, is to do things your way. Maybe I won't be a big star, but I'd rather be able to look at myself in the mirror anyway."

She took his hand, a genuine smile crossing her face for the first time. "Thank you," she whispered. "That's exactly what I needed to hear."

"Glad I could be of service, my lady," he answered in a bad British accent. "Hey, if you decide that you don't want to do this anymore, you could always come with me to Atlanta and watch me film my movie. I'd love to have you there."

"Maybe I will," she said firmly. "I'll think about it."

Two nights later, Danielle stood backstage at Antone's. Steve had brought her another skimpy outfit to wear, one that was far too low-cut for Danielle's taste. Still, she squeezed into it and got ready to take the stage. She could hear the crowd outside yelling in anticipation.

Jim and Al strolled by her and headed for the stage.

Jim called out, "Come on, Dominatrix Barbie, let's get this show on the road."

She started for the stage, then stopped. Instead of heading to the stage, she headed back to the dressing room. As Steve implored her to come out, she looked at herself in the mirror. Her hair was teased, her makeup plastered on, and the outfit was barely there. She hardly recognized herself. She thought about her conversation with Adam.

When she emerged minutes later, she was wearing the same UT T-shirt and blue jeans she had worn to the club that night. She had taken off her makeup, and as she made her way towards the stage, she threw her hair into a ponytail. Steve trailed behind at her heels, wanting to know why she had changed.

"It's not me, Steve. This is. That'll have to be good enough." With that, she took the stage. The crowd gave her a standing ovation.

Steve and Adam stood side by side as Danielle, sweaty and ecstatic, exited the stage. Adam had a big smile and applauded loudly, Steve glared and had his arms crossed over his chest. Danielle pushed her guitar behind her and walked straight up to Steve.

"The trampy thing is over. It's not an issue; don't bother bitching about it. I tried it, I didn't like it, and I'm not doing it again." Then she pointed back over her shoulder, toward the stage and the cheers still ringing in the rafters. "And I don't need it."

She then pushed past Steve to Adam, who immediately wrapped her up in his arms. "Let's go celebrate a great performance," he said.

"No," she laughed. "I'm all hot and sweaty. I need to go home and clean up."

"Then let me drive you. A fast ride in a convertible should cool you off nicely."

She agreed and the two left arm-in-arm. Only he didn't take her home, he took her out of town, racing along the highway. She recognized that he was heading toward Lake Travis, but she didn't object. The high speed thrilled her and the cool air felt good against her skin. She closed her eyes and let the sensations flow over her.

When he started to slow down, she opened her eyes. They were much farther out than she had ever gone before. It was an area out by the lake where there were few houses at all. He guided the Mustang up a steep slope and finally parked it on a bluff. Far below, the lake glittered in the moonlight.

"What are we doing here?"

Adam leaned over the middle console and wrapped his arms around her. "I'm going to build us a house, right here. I'm going to buy all the land for miles so that no one can get to us. We can get married here, raise our family here."

She looked at him. He was staring off into the distance intently. Or maybe he was staring at the future. Either way, it sounded good to her.

"If I really nail this next part, then I can start starring in movies. From there, all I need are a couple of big paydays and this can all be ours. It's going to happen."

Danielle turned in her seat so that she could face him and got up on her knees. "Do you think it will be that easy?"

He ran his hands up her arms and neck and cradled her face. "No. It's not going to be that easy. It's going to take some time and a lot of hard work. I've got to get better as an actor. But I'm dedicated to it. I'm dedicated to you. I'll make it happen."

Danielle reached for him and pulled him closer. Their lips locked together and they collapsed into the driver's seat with Danielle on top. They kissed with a passion completely unlike their previous make-out sessions. He ran his hands up her shirt and she responded by pulling it off completely. This was it, the moment was right…she was ready.

He pushed her away.

"What are you doing?"

Adam tried hard to catch his breath. "Stopping before this goes too far."

"No one told you to stop."

He looked at her hard for a minute, and then shook his head. "I made the mistake of pushing too hard once."

Danielle sat up next to him again, running her hands across his chest. "But I'm not telling you to stop this time. I'm ready."

"What happened to little Miss-I've-Got-Too-Much-To-Lose?"

She straddled him, crossing her arms around his neck. "Fuck it. I don't care about that anymore. I'm tired of running from a past I can't change or living for a future I can't control. All I've got in the world is the moment, and I don't want to waste this one."

Again, Adam pushed her back into the passenger seat. "Right now you are. This isn't what you really want. You're going through a bad time and you're not thinking straight."

"I can't believe you, of all people, are turning me down."

"I'm not turning you down," Adam shot back. "I'm being patient. I'll wait for the right time."

"And what if this is the only chance you ever get?"

He started the car and fastened his seatbelt. "I'd rather miss the chance than have to live with your regret."

"I wouldn't regret it," she said like a sulking child.

"Yes, you would."

#

When they got back to Randy's, Steve was anxiously pacing in the driveway. His mood brightened the second he saw Danielle get out of the car. Her mood was a different matter.

"Dani," Adam called out as Danielle started for her apartment. "I know you're stinging now, but you'll see that I was right about this."

Danielle turned away from him, right into Steve. "I've got great news Dani."

"What? Are you adding a stripper pole to the stage?

"No, I'm not."

She watched Adam pull out of the driveway and disappear down the street. "I'm sure whatever it is can wait until morning. I'm beat."

"You're going on tour," he said, ignoring her. "I've been working on some dates and they finally came through. Three weeks from now you'll be hitting the road. I've got dates lined up for you all through East Texas, Louisiana, and Arkansas, and I'm working on more. It's time to get out of Austin."

"Out of Austin," she chuckled. "That sounds like a good idea. I may not be going on tour though."

"What do you mean, you may not be going?" Steve asked in shock.

"I've been invited to go with Adam when he starts filming his new movie in a couple of weeks."

"Why would you do that? Things are starting to happen here. I may even be able to get you some studio time. If you go with him, that's all over. All of it, including me."

She looked at him coldly. "I guess I've got three weeks to decide."

#

Three weeks later Danielle sat by her window again. This time, the sun was shining, the trees were fully green, and all the flowers were in bloom. Her bags were packed, but she still didn't know where she was going.

In one part of town, Adam was packing his bags too. He was heading to Atlanta to film his new movie. He had bought an extra ticket and was going to leave it at the counter.

In another part of town, Steve was finalizing a deal to rent a used tour bus. It would take her to Louisiana and then Arkansas...closer to her dreams, but farther from her love.

Her heart said Atlanta. Everything else said Louisiana. She felt sick. She was a loser, either way. Why did everything in her life seemed to involve pain?

A cab pulled up in front of the house. Danielle closed her eyes and said a little prayer. Then she grabbed her bags and headed out. She didn't know when, or even if, she would ever be back in the little garage apartment. One way or another, she had reached another crossroads. She didn't know which road was the right one, but in that moment, she decided which one she had to take.

Chapter Four

Billy Ray's Blues Palace in Baton Rouge, Louisiana was barely more than a big, sweaty wooden box with a rickety stage. It was far removed from the A list Austin clubs that Danielle had been playing, but it was a new audience in a new city. It was a chance to win converts.

When she took the stage for the first show of her big tour, the crowd was rowdy and well on their way to being drunk. Still, from the first notes of her first song, they were a great crowd. They sang along to the more famous songs she did, and mumbled along to her originals. Every solo was met with a rebel yell, and she probably heard a dozen wedding proposals between songs.

It went better than she had expected, and no one cared that she didn't come out dressed like a porn star. Even cranky old Jim had nothing but nice things to say. The three of them shook hands with the handful of fans who waited by their bus, and then they climbed on board and took off for the next date.

Danielle had always heard that touring was tough, but she didn't know just how tough it could be. What had started as a quick trip through East Texas, Louisiana, and Arkansas began to grow as the band's reputation grew.

First, they dug deeper into Texas, then north to Oklahoma and Kansas. Following that, it was back down to Louisiana, where she was wildly popular, and a quick trip to Mississippi. From Jackson, Mississippi, they drove all the way to El Paso, and the trip to West Texas brought childhood memories flooding back.

There was no time for a quick trip back home, though. It was on to New Mexico and back across the Texas Panhandle and through

Oklahoma to Missouri. The towns and miles flew past. With each new town, Danielle wondered how she would summon up the energy to go on, but the excitement of a new stage and a new town would infuse the band all over again.

As the tour continued to expand and grow, so did the band's repertoire and Danielle's stage presence. The skimpy costumes were no more, but she found herself still using some of the moves she had learned, although now it was much more spontaneous. The crowds ate it up.

Finally, Steve took pity on his weary road warriors and turned down additional dates to give the musicians a chance to go home. Al and Jim missed their families and wanted off the ride, but Danielle, despite her exhaustion, could have stayed out there forever.

When the rented tour bus finally hit the Austin city limits, they had been gone five months. The club scene had gone on and new bands had filled the void left by Danielle's departure. However, when they announced a returning home show at Antone's, the tickets sold out in minutes.

On one of their first nights back, Danielle went down on 6th to check out a new band everyone was raving about. Later Gators was a new club, built in the remains of an old department store. The walls had been stripped bare to the piping to give the club an industrial feel. The lights were dim and the air was smoky, just like a good club should be.

Danielle awaited the appearance of Reckless Passions, Austin's newest darlings. When they hit the stage, she was stunned. Front and center was Ty Woods, her former coworker. This, however, was not the same band she had jammed with in his garage. This band was leaner and meaner. They ripped through an hour and a half set of original songs that sounded like they could have been taken from the archives of classic bands like Aerosmith. Ty as a singer wasn't that great, but he got the point across and the groove was tight.

She made her way backstage to congratulate him after the show. He had changed a lot in the year since she had last seen him. His blond hair was now long and curled up at the ends, and the acne was gone. He wasn't a knockout like Adam was, but he had a rugged look that fit him well.

He stood backstage talking earnestly with another, older man. The older man was paying him for the band's performance and berating him at the same time. She heard him tell Ty that without a better singer they would never be anything more than a bar band. Danielle started to intervene, but held back. This was Ty's battle and he would need to fight it the way she was fighting hers.

With the sermon finally delivered, Ty tucked the money into his faded, ripped up jeans and walked away. Danielle waved him over and a big smile spread across Ty's face.

"Hey, hotshot, where have you been?" he called out.

She hugged him like a lost brother. "I've been 'on tour,'" she said with fake seriousness. "I see what you've been up to."

"Yeah," Ty answered with a shrug. "I have you to thank for this. I probably never would have had the guts to actually pursue music as a living, but you inspired me. My parents were less than thrilled, but what the hell. College will always be there, right?"

"Right," she responded. "Well, I've got to say that I'm impressed. You've come a long way from the garage."

"Some people don't think so," Ty said, his eyes darting to the door that the club owner had ducked into. "It seems like the crowds like us fine, but all the club owners and managers think we need a new singer."

"To hell with them," Danielle responded. "You do what you're happy with. It took me a while to learn that. If it's your band, then it's your rules. If others don't like it, that's their problem, not yours."

"That's easier said than done when you're trying to fill dates. There are just so many good bands in this town; nobody really cares if one goes under or not."

"Don't give up," she warned. "I almost did. I came close to running off to Atlanta with an ex-boyfriend. I probably would have, but I knew I could never live with myself if I had quit. As a matter of fact, I may be able to help you out a little bit."

"How so?" he asked.

"We're going to do a big welcome home show in a couple of weeks at Antone's. I'll talk to our manager and see if he can get you a spot as an opening act. Maybe you and I could even get up on stage and jam together again. What do you think?"

"I would love you forever," he said.

Two weeks later, Reckless Passions opened for Danielle Regan and Texas Pride. The crowd was standing room only and they got their money's worth. Ty's band was tight and won the crowd over in their short set.

Then it was Danielle's turn. She pulled out all the stops in her triumphant return home. She started her show with a sultry rendition of "Texas Flood," taking the SRV traditional and turning it into a slow, sexy jam before surging into her normal set, which was almost all original songs by now. In the middle, Ty joined for some dueling guitar, despite Jim's obvious disgust. She then ended the show by bringing out jam session participant and former Thunderbird Kim Wilson for a duet of "Wrap It Up."

Steve locked the group into a series of dates at upper scale clubs stretching the I-35 corridor from Dallas to Corpus Christi to keep the group sharp without requiring too much travel. Onstage, things were clicking on all cylinders for the band. Offstage, however, Jim and Danielle clashed constantly over her insistence on adding more of her own songs. She was taking them further from their traditional blues roots, and Jim was resisting.

After a particularly intense performance in a Padre Island club called Beachcombers, Steve approached the band with new enthusiasm.

"All right, first the good news," Steve began. "We're going back out in mid-October for a month of shows in Tennessee and Mississippi. But don't worry, we will be back in Austin before Thanksgiving, and we won't go back on tour again until after New Year's so that you can spend time with your families. I'm already working on area dates for then. Now, for the great news. While on tour, I've arranged for us to get some studio time in Memphis. You'll be recording in the shadow of Beale Street. And I've got a couple of independent labels that are interested in hearing what you put down."

Danielle put an arm around him. "And we all thank you for your hard work, Uncle Steve," she said mockingly. "But we would thank you more if you would let us get on the bus and get some sleep."

"Your wish is my command, dear," he said

#

They traversed the length of Tennessee, played a couple of shows in Kentucky, and got down deep in the delta of Mississippi. Steve arranged for the band to see a collection of old Delta bluesmen playing in Greenville. Danielle was moved by the power of their performance, but was equally assured that she was not a blues musician. Eventually, her band mates were going to have to accept that or move on.

Between shows they travelled back and forth to Memphis, recording as many songs as they could. This was no elaborate affair. Their recordings were largely live with very few nuances added in.

True to his word, Steve resisted adding any additional shows, and by mid-November the bus rolled back toward Austin. Steve didn't make the trip with them. He took their recordings back to L.A. to see if he could drum up interest. Danielle didn't hold her breath, though. As long as she was being hamstrung, she doubted that anyone would be interested in them.

#

January 1995 found the band back on the road, working through West Texas, New Mexico, and up into Colorado and Wyoming. Steve wrangled some more dates further west. In Boise, Idaho, the band received such a welcome response that Danielle insisted that it become a regular stop.

After the Boise show, the band boarded the bus for a long ride to Eugene, Oregon. Their West Coast swing was almost over and everyone was looking forward to a return to Austin. When Steve boarded the bus, however, those plans were dashed. "I've added two more dates for us in LA, guys. I've lined up several record execs who have been hearing nothing but good things about you. We nail those two shows and I guarantee you we will hit Austin with a contract in hand."

Two weeks later they rolled into Los Angeles for two shows at a nightclub called The Snake Pit. They knew that there were record company executives in the audience and that this might be their only shot at a record deal. They were tired and on edge.

Backstage before the first night's show, Danielle tried to calm her nerves. Being so close to her goal was getting to her and her hands began to shake. Jim was also full of nerves, pacing relentlessly and chain smoking, while Al napped on a ratty couch behind them.

96

Jim saw Danielle's shaking hands and sneered. "Don't screw this up for us, kid. I haven't done all of this, come all this way, to screw up at the doorstep."

Danielle wanted to fire back, but this was no time for fighting. She realized that this was when she really needed their experience behind her. "Listen, I know that you and I don't really get along, but for tonight, can we try to help each other?"

Jim stopped pacing. "Will you listen to me?"

"Yes," Danielle answered.

"Okay, then do what I tell you. Keep it simple; don't go off the deep end with all the dancing around and the guitar tricks. Let your music do your talking for you. And don't be too much of a showoff. You're good, Danielle, really good. Just let your talent speak for itself."

It was the first time he had ever complimented her and it gave her an odd sense of accomplishment. Those few words of encouragement were all she needed to hear. She gave Jim a long, slow smile. "Don't worry about a thing," she said. "We're going to be fine."

After the show ended, Steve guided the three to a VIP room in the back of the club to meet with four middle aged white men in suits. Three of them were smoking, the fourth had some sort of liquor in his hand. Nothing at all set them apart from one another.

Steve went around the room shaking hands with them, and called them each by name. Danielle, Al, and Jim sat together on a couch on the other side of the room. She felt like she was about to go on trial, and she tried hard to hide her discomfort.

"Guys," Steve said to them, turning his back on the suits. "Let me introduce you. Over here," he said, pointing to the man on the far right, "Is Shane Wiseman of Atlantic Records. Then we have Sal Berrineti of CBS, Jay Hatfield of Capitol Records, and Mike Athey of Columbia." He then turned to face the suits. "Gentlemen, Danielle Regan and Texas Pride."

Mike Athey of Columbia, on the far left, was the shortest of the bunch. He waved his cigarette in the air. "Cut the crap, Redus. Let's just get this over with." He then turned his attention to her. "Listen, sweetie. Your act is cute and you can play a little bit. But nobody's going to buy a chick guitar player. Do yourself a favor...buy some new clothes, find a songwriter, and try your hand at adult contemporary. Nobody will ever take you seriously like this." With that he got up and hurried out of the room.

Danielle glared at him as he walked past, and he returned it with a smug smile and a wink. She wanted to hit him but she knew that she had to keep her cool. She gritted her teeth and managed a polite smile for the next suit in line.

Next was Sal from CBS. "Don't listen to him: he hasn't had a hit in years. I think you're great."

Danielle began to feel a surge of pride inside her. A surge that was quickly put out.

"But your music isn't going to fly. Now, we get you with a top flight choreographer, get you in some sexy outfits and some smoking dance moves, maybe we have something. You take six months to a year to work it out, and I'll be glad to give you another look."

She sat stunned by the idea that she would be a song and dance act. "I don't think so," she muttered.

"Have it your way, babe," he said, and walked out. "But that's your best bet. If you want to make it in this business, you've got to be willing to do what it takes."

Shane Wiseman of Atlantic didn't take long. He simply said not interested and walked out, leaving only Jay Hatfield of Capitol. He was a tall, distinguished looking man, clean shaven, with no signs of gray in his thick brown hair. He stubbed his cigarette and leaned forward in his chair.

"I think those guys are damn fools," he said in a voice that was soft but clear. "I think you are a great talent and you have a great sound. The crowd ate you up. The problem is, you're too late. Grunge has killed the whole guitar hero thing. If you had come along in '90 or '91, we could have put you out there as Stevie Ray's heir apparent. But now, it's all about grunge. I believe in you, and I'd sign you in a heartbeat, but I just don't think that there's a big enough audience out there for your type of music. My best advice to you is to keep playing the clubs and hope for a smaller, independent label to take a chance on you." He stood and straightened his navy blue suit. "I thank you for the performance, it was very entertaining. Good luck."

Dejected, the band sleepwalked through their second LA show and took the long bus ride home to Austin. No one spoke or ate or slept. Danielle stared out the window at the passing landscape, wondering where to go now. The thing that had made the grueling tour schedule bearable was the hope of a recording contract. Now, those hopes seemed dashed.

When they finally arrived, everyone scattered. Danielle began to wonder if she'd made the wrong decision by not following Adam to Atlanta. She had seen a billboard while in LA promoting the movie he had gone to shoot, *The Olympian*. Some people felt that it was going to be the hit of the summer. If she were the girlfriend of a Hollywood movie star, record labels would be dying to sign her.

With the record deal gone and her band headed for retirement, Danielle had nothing to do, so she went back to work at Randy's music store. Although Steve pressed her to look at musicians for a new band, she refused. Instead, she put Ole Red under her bed, no longer interested in playing.

Steve promised to keep at the phones and urged her to get back to playing. Randy and Teri tried to drag her out to the clubs at night, hoping that it would inspire her to pick up the guitar again. She again resisted. In a desperate attempt, Randy fired her from her job. Instead of going back to playing to make money, she got a job at a Hastings store in South Austin.

Her depression only deepened when *The Olympian* hit theaters in the summer. Suddenly, Adam's face was everywhere and every mention of him was like another shot at her heart. He attended the Hollywood premiere with a big time actress. They looked very happy together on TV.

By the middle of summer, she had saved up enough to move out of Randy's garage apartment into her own place closer to work. She began inquiring to the local colleges about grants and scholarships. She even toyed with the idea of returning to Chaparral, but there was nothing left for her there.

In early August Jim came to see her. He was dressed in his traditional polo shirt and khakis and looked well rested. She let him in reluctantly. He was clearly uncomfortable, as was she.

"What do you want?" she asked as Jim took a seat on her couch.

"Al and I have been talking, and we want to go back out."

"Oh, you do," Danielle half said, half asked. She sat on the arm of the couch with her feet in the seat next to Jim. "Why is that?"

He shifted in the seat so that he could face her. "Because we already screwed this up once, that's why," he said, his voice rising.

"And why should I play with a mean old man like you again?"

Jim took a deep breath to reign in his temper. "Listen, Al and I had a shot at the big time once, back in the '70s. We had a big spotlight show just like we had in LA but everybody got drunk off their ass right before the show and we made fools out of ourselves. When we sobered up and realized what had happened, we quit. He went on to be a teacher, I started my own business. We didn't play at all for seven years. When we went back, we were just weekend warriors, playing in dinky little bands just for the hell of it. We had both forgotten what it was like to be playing for something until you came along."

Danielle rubbed the back of her neck. "You think that we can do better?"

"You know we can. We were so close; it was in the palm of our hands. Just once, we'd like to know what it feels like to be the big boys. To have a record in the stores, to play in an arena. We gave up once; if we give up now, we'll never get another chance."

"I see," she said. "And I suppose that I should just quit my job and come running back, huh? It's all about you and Al and your shot at the big time. Maybe I don't want to go back out. What if I don't see the point?"

Jim stood up quickly, then took another deep breath. She could see that his temper was about to blow, but he was fighting it well. "I'm telling you that you don't want to wake up one day and realize that you're in your fifties and that you wasted the best years of your life. No one can make you come back, but I think that we deserve it. After all, we did put our lives and families on hold to support you. You could do the same for us."

"We'd have to start all over. Find a new manager, start in the ratty clubs again. I just don't want to go through all of that again."

"No, we don't," Jim said. He took her hands in his. "Steve is still in town…he never left. He's been sending copies of those recording sessions we did to every radio station he can think of. He says that he can get us gigs, he just needs a band to book."

She stood there, chewing her bottom lip, making a show of it. In her heart, though, there was no debate. She missed performing, and working in retail was about the worst thing she could imagine. "Fine. Let's give it another shot."

Despite the lengthy break, Danielle and the guys quickly rediscovered their groove and Steve put them back on the road, this time hitting only the spots where they had been very well received in the past. He had had the Memphis sessions pressed into a CD, which they titled *Good Texans*. At every stop, he set up a table and sold as many copies as he could, and he worked hard to get the band interviews with the local TV and radio stations.

The chemistry with the band was better than it had been before, and they played each show like it might be their last. By late September, Steve had managed to add several shows in the upper Midwest, taking the band to areas they had never hit before. The heartland loved them, but further to the east they met indifferent crowds. Steve double backed the band through Wisconsin, Iowa, and the Dakotas to find that many radio stations had begun playing their songs.

In January, they set off across the southeast, driving as far as the Florida Panhandle. As before, when they traveled back, they found audiences eager for more. Steve even managed to get the group into a recording studio in New Orleans, where they recorded five more original songs. They began making plans to press another homemade album.

They returned home in February 1996, ready for some rest. Steve wanted to see if he could book some dates along the Atlantic coast; the Eastern seaboard represented the last frontier for the band. He hoped that an East Coast presence could generate record company interest again.

On an uncomfortably cool February morning, Danielle went to meet Steve to discuss new dates and the possibility of having more CDs made. Only when she arrived, Steve wasn't alone. Sitting at the table with Steve was Jay Hatfield of Capitol Records.

She pulled out a chair and sat down suspiciously. "What's going on?"

Steve was grinning like a madman. "Mr. Hatfield here came to see me last night with a proposal."

"Really," Danielle said. Her interest was piqued now. "What kind of proposal would that be?"

"A modest one," Jay Hatfield responded. "I'm leaving Capitol for a new label, Generation Records. It's a small label, but well-funded. My directive is to field a roster of outstanding talent. The label's owners want this to be an outlet for talent, and are not so concerned with commercial success. I thought of you. You'll get a small advance to go into the studio and rerecord what you've already done. We'll shoot a couple of videos, see if we can get you some airplay and put you out on the road. From there we'll see what happens. If your album sells, we'll sweeten the deal for a second album; if not, then we're not out much."

"You thought of me? I don't know how to feel about that. Here you are, offering me a record deal while telling me that you don't think I'll sell. Kind of a mixed message. So why are you doing this?"

"Who cares why?" Steve interrupted. "You've got your contract. Album, video, tour, the whole bit. Don't look a gift horse in the mouth."

"I have never doubted your talent, Danielle," Hatfield responded. "But at Capitol, everything was about the bottom line. I had to judge any prospective act against how I thought they would perform at the cash register. That's the only reason I passed on you the first time. I believe in you, but I have doubts about your selling power. With Generation, I was told to forget sales and go for talent. I thought of you. If you agree to this, you'll be our first official act. If this label takes off, you'll be a trailblazer."

#

Recording the album proved to be a breeze. They booked time in Riverside Studios in Austin and Danielle and Steve produced the album themselves. It was recorded live in the studio and consisted mainly of the band's stage show minus the covers. Jim and Al's wives came in at the end to provide some background vocals, and many of the jam session musicians stopped by to lend a helping hand as needed.

Steve then took the album to California to play for Jay Hatfield while the band went out on a quick tour of the mid-south. Now with an album to promote, radio stations were more interested and the workload got heavier. To help, Steve hired an old associate named Gilbert Bell to be the band's road manager.

Gilbert was a hefty man with a thick brown beard, thick glasses, and a ton of tattoos. He had an easy going attitude and a lively sense of humor. He was also fiercely loyal and protective of his charges, and he took to the new band, especially Danielle. She asked only for professionalism and no one with drug or alcohol problems in the crew. He assured her that she would have it.

The band ripped through their dates in Texas and Louisiana, playing a high class of clubs but to the same enthusiastic fans that many passes in the area had earned them. In late April, the band finished their dates with a ragged show in Columbia, Missouri. They were planning to head home, but were summoned to Los Angeles instead, to attend a meeting at Generation Records.

There, the band's first album was unveiled. The album had been renamed *Original Texan*, and featured only Danielle on the cover. There was no mention of Texas Pride, in spite of the fact that they had always been billed in person.

"Wait a second," Danielle interrupted when the cover art was revealed. "That's not right. You left out the guys."

"It's not a mistake," Jay said calmly. "You're the star. You're the one we're selling. Their names and pictures appear on the inside of the liner notes. But you're the one on the cover, only you."

"Well, I don't like that. They're an equal part of this."

"They won't sell albums. You will. There's nothing you can do about it. It's all in the contract."

Behind her, Jim and Al stormed out. Danielle watched them go, then turned to Steve, feeling somewhat panicked. "Steve. Can't you do something?"

Steve spread his arms in a helpless gesture. "No, Dani. Those guys," he said, pointing at the door Jim and Al had just stormed out of, "Those guys are short timers anyway. This isn't their future. They're hurt because they wanted the glory, but once the checks come rolling in, they'll get over it. Don't let them get to you. This is about you."

"Well, it's still a shitty thing to do to them. They've worked hard too." She ran out of the room and chased Jim and Al down to the elevators. "I can't believe that they did that."

"Well, you finally did it, didn't you kid?" Jim asked in barely controlled anger. "You finally managed to sell us out completely."

"What are you talking about? I didn't know anything about this."

"He said it was in the contract, Dani," Al continued. "I thought we were all in this together. A real band, you know? Now we're just your backup players."

"You signed the contract too," Danielle said defensively. "I didn't read all of it, I just signed it. I didn't even think about something like this."

"Well, Miss Original Texan," Jim continued as the elevator doors opened. "Maybe you ought to pay more attention next time. Thanks for throwing us under the bus."

They stepped onto the elevator. Danielle started to follow, but Jim blocked her. "This one's full."

She stared at the closed elevator door, trying to sort out her emotions. Part of her was truly sad for what had happened. She never wanted to come off as arrogant or selfish. On the other hand, she *was* the star of the show and the others had never wanted the spotlight before. In a way, she felt like she deserved to stand apart from them.

Steve walked up behind her and put a reassuring hand on her back. "Don't worry about them, Dani. I think that they were just taken aback. I'll smooth everything over. The important thing to remember is that you have an album now. You're on your way."

"It doesn't do me a lot of good if my band hates me."

"They don't hate you," Steve said with a chuckle. "I'll handle it."

Steve did calm the band down, though they were still noticeably cool towards Danielle. Still, they managed to survive an additional three weeks in LA as they filmed videos for the three songs Hatfield had designated as singles. The first single, "So This Is Goodbye," was an up-tempo roadhouse rocker featuring Kim Wilson's harmonica work. The video featured Danielle leaving her boyfriend behind and eventually being picked up by the guys in a '59 Cadillac.

The second video, "Someday Baby," was another upbeat number. The video put the band in ZZ Top mode, helping a plain Jane win the boy of her dreams. However, the third video,

"Nobody's Children," showed a grittier side of the band. The song was a slow, lonely blues song. The video, shot in black and white, showed Danielle stepping through the homeless on L.A.'s skid row.

With the video shoots done, the band returned to Austin for some rest before heading out on their first national tour in June. They scattered once the bus got to Austin. Danielle wondered if they would be able to hold together well enough to finish the upcoming tour.

Just two weeks before the band departed, Danielle was summoned to the offices of the *Austin American Statesman*. She had been named one of 20 Young Austinites To Watch, a special insert the *Statesman* was going to run. She had been asked to come to the offices for a photo shoot.

She arrived and was quickly shown to the studio, where she found that she was not alone. A powerfully built young man with brown hair curling at his shoulders and solid two-day beard and smooth brown eyes was nervously tossing a baseball up in the air as he sat in a director's chair. He wore tight Levis, a starched white button up shirt, and black boots.

The makeup artist sat Danielle in a chair next to him and began to work on her. The young man turned to her. "How're you today?" His voice was deep and sexy, a hint of a familiar West Texas twang to it.

She slid her eyes to the right for a better look. "I'm fine. How are you?"

"Nervous," he answered, his voice dropping. "I'm not used to stuff like this."

She smiled as she looked away. She found it attractive that such a manly guy would admit to being nervous about something as easy as a photo shoot. "Why are you nervous? Never had your picture taken before?"

"This ain't my thing," he said, still tossing the baseball in the air.

"What is your thing?"

"Baseball. I play for the Horns. Scouts keep telling me that I will be the first pitcher taken in a couple of weeks. They say I'll be an instant millionaire. That's why I'm here."

"You must be pretty good then."

105

"I get by," he said, and he sounded totally sincere. She thought she saw him blush out of the corner of her eye.

"Don't get offended or anything," Danielle said after a minute. "But you don't strike me as the bad ass athlete type."

He chuckled; a nice, easygoing laugh that she found charming. It went along nicely with the rest of his manner. "I'm not," he said. "But when I get on the mound, I become a different person. I've got this real competitive streak in me. I get nasty on the field."

"So it's like a Clark Kent/Superman thing," Danielle prodded.

"Nah. I'm more of a Spiderman guy personally."

She laughed, irritating the make-up girl. "You're going to get me in trouble."

"That's all right," he responded. "If things get out of hand I've always got my costume on underneath."

Danielle laughed again. "What's your name?"

"Brett Walls," he answered.

"I'm Danielle Regan."

"Oh, I know who you are. Some teammates and I caught a show you did a while back. You were wearing this little black dress—"

"Oh my god. You saw that show?"

"Yes I did," he answered. "It was one of the best nights of my life. That was a damn nice show. Just wait until the guys find out that I actually got to meet you. They're going to be so jealous."

Danielle giggled. "Well, I'm glad that you enjoyed it, because I certainly didn't.

With her makeup finally done, Danielle eased out of the chair and stood to meet her new friend. When he stood she could tell that he was a good two inches taller than her. He offered his hand, and when she took it, his handshake was firm, but she knew that he was holding back. His skin was tough and calloused.

"Pleased to meet you, Brett."

"Pleased to meet you, Danielle." She felt that there was something more that he wanted to say, but he held back. So she decided to take the lead.

"When this is over would you like to go get a bite to eat?"

A big, somewhat goofy grin spread across his face. He did goofy well. "Yeah, I would."

They went to Nau's, where UT players were often treated to lunch. "The owner is a big UT fan, so she always takes care of the players. It's against NCAA rules though," Brett whispered to her. "So you have to be careful, because there are spies all around. There are tons of A&M and Baylor people here who would love to get us in trouble."

"I'm sure the NCAA isn't going to get mad over a free lunch," Danielle responded.

"Actually, they do. They nitpick everything. I mean, we wouldn't get hit hard, but it would look bad. This stuff goes on in every college town in the country, but some schools get watched more closely than others."

Danielle was incredulous. "They would get you in trouble for a five-dollar burger?"

"Yep," Brett said as he munched on said $5 burger. "No preferential treatment at all. But like I said, it happens everywhere. The main thing they're worried about is that those five dollar burgers might start coming with hundred-dollar lettuce on them."

"Ah, I see." Danielle leaned across the table and whispered. "Well, you don't have to worry about me. I'm not going to get you in trouble. I love the Horns."

"Hook 'em," he said, flashing the famous Hook 'Em Horns hand sign.

She gave the sign back with a giggle. Then she popped another fry in her mouth. "So what are you going to do with your millions?"

"I figure that I'll build myself a place back home, somewhere out in the country. Maybe start a little ranch."

"Where's home?"

"Up in the Panhandle," he said. "I've even got the site picked out. It's at the base of a big mesa, in a grove of trees. Someplace where I would have a nice view of the sunsets."

"Are Panhandle sunsets better than others?" she asked playfully.

His eyes lit up. "Absolutely. When we get a really good one, there are colors that don't even have names. You've got this big, wide open sky, so you can see it all with no clutter. It's beautiful."

She could see that Brett was no longer with her, but back home, watching one of those sunsets. She wished she had a strong connection to home. "It sounds great."

"It is. Maybe when we've both made our money, you can come up and see it for yourself."

"Well, I don't have millions waiting on me like you do, but I might take you up on your offer someday."

"Sounds like a plan." They were both nearly finished with their meals and it was almost time to go their separate ways. Danielle didn't want it to end.

"Hey, Brett, how would you like to go out Friday night? We could catch a movie or go play some pool."

"I'd love to," Brett answered. "But we're leaving for California on Wednesday. The tournament is starting. With any luck, we'll make it to Omaha for the College World Series, then there's the draft. It may be late June before I have time for anything."

"Damn. I'll be on tour by then." They sat in silence, staring at almost eaten burgers that they had both lost the appetite for.

"Well, it's too bad that we can't get together again," Brett finally said. "I had a great time today."

"Me too," Danielle answered sadly.

"Yeah. But we can write. Eventually our schedules have to clear up."

"Sure," she said, knowing in her heart that it would never happen.

Brett held up his thirty-two ounce Styrofoam cup. "In the meantime, here's hoping that we both have what it takes to make our dreams come true."

CHAPTER FIVE

The next few months were a whirlwind for Danielle. The album was a success, though not a blockbuster. It more than met the expectations of Generation Records, who extended the band for two more albums.

Reaction to the band was mixed. Rock fans, desperate for the next guitar god, took to the group instantly, and Danielle became an instant star and unintended sex symbol. Blues fans were tougher to convince. Critics outside of Texas almost universally thought the band was good, but that they were a novelty and once Danielle's newness wore off, they would be forgotten.

Critical uncertainty didn't stop the fans from embracing Danielle, though. She became an instant media darling, appearing on several talk shows and gracing countless magazine covers, including appearances on the covers of *Guitar Player* and *Texas Monthly* in the same month. *Texas Monthly* declared her to be the savior of Texas Blues.

Still, Danielle couldn't help but notice that almost as much attention was being paid to her beauty as was to her talent. While several cosmetic companies immediately approached her about endorsement deals, the one endorsement she really wanted, Fender, barely paid attention to her. She began to wonder if anyone was really taking her seriously.

The band finally stopped touring behind the album in mid-November 1996, against the advice of Steve, who felt that they needed to stay out there to stay in people's minds. Steve was always aware of how quickly the music industry could forget. Jim and Al demanded to spend the holidays with their families and Steve relented. Now, with time on her hands and more money than she knew what to do with, Danielle began writing songs for the next album. She was determined to make it even better than the first. She would make people pay attention to her talent.

#

Jim, Al, and Danielle reconvened on a blustery mid-January morning at a personality devoid building on South Congress that was bookended by a tattoo parlor on one side and a bail bondsman on the other. The crumbling building was furnished with a half dozen metal folding chairs and two desks salvaged from local thrift stores; one for Steve and one for his new secretary, Pamela. This, Steve advised them, was their new headquarters.

"We give you a top forty album and this is the best we get?" said Al, only half teasing. He and Jim were sitting side by side in folding chairs pushed up next to the window. "Some dump on the wrong side of the river?"

"This is just the first step," Steve answered. "You give me a number one album, a platinum album, and I'll put you in one of those fancy skyscrapers downtown. Until then, one top forty album means nothing."

"Well," Danielle started. "It's much better than working out of the North Austin Motel 6, isn't it, Steve?"

"Much better," he said with a smile. "Now, why I brought you here. We need to get back out on the road and get our name back on people's minds."

"I thought we were going to record a new album," Danielle said disapprovingly.

"We are, Dani, I promise you. I'm working on studio time right now. Until then, I want to get you on the road. You can test out the new material you've been working on."

Jim uncrossed his legs and began to shake his head. "Absolutely not. We have done everything you've asked us to do and more. Al and I have been talking a lot over the last couple of weeks and we've made a decision. It's time for you to write us our check and we'll be on our way. We're done."

Danielle looked from Jim to Steve, who had his hands tucked in his pockets and was sitting on the edge of his desk.

110

"Listen, I know that you guys are ready to get off the road, but now is a terrible time to stop. We're just starting to grab some momentum. The big payday is still out there."

Al, who had been balancing his chair on its back two legs, let the front legs fall back to the ground. "No, no, no. We go out now and then it'll be something else. Then another album and more shows and on and on. You've been doing this to us for years, Redus. We're done. That's all there is to it. Just write the check and we'll be on our way."

Danielle was becoming more agitated by the second. She was bouncing her legs up and down nervously. "Steve, what are they talking about?"

Steve held a finger up at her without looking at her. Instead, he addressed Jim and Al. "It's all a part of the game, gentlemen. You know how fickle the industry can be. We've got to keep pushing right now. I promise, nine more months. You're out by fall with more money in your pockets than you know what to do with."

"What are y'all talking about?" Danielle asked again, starting to get angry.

"Hey, sweetie, the men are talking business here…butt out," Jim snapped. To Steve he said, "Why is she even here?"

At that, Danielle shot up out of her seat, sending her chair skittering across the floor. "What am I doing here? What the fuck am I doing here? It's my fucking band, dipshit."

"You see," Al added, pointing at Danielle but talking to Steve. "You see what we have to deal with? All this hostility and this arrogance. This diva attitude. We just can't take it anymore."

"I am not a diva," Danielle growled.

"And, not to split hairs or anything," Jim said. "This is not your band. It's our band. We did you a favor and you have treated us, especially me, like a piece of shit on the bottom of your shoe. Then, to top it all off, you have the arrogance to try and claim our band as yours?"

Danielle stormed over until she was standing over him. "And who the hell got you where you are? Whose coattails have you been riding all this time? You came to me and begged me to go back out."

Al stood and put a hand on Danielle's arm and gently pulled her back from Jim. "It's all business, dear. That's all. Jim didn't go to you out of anything other than business. That's all. We're both too old to be on the road all the time, and we're definitely too old to be babysitting an insolent teenager."

"I'm not a teenager, thank you. I can't believe, after all I've done for you two—"

"You didn't do anything for us," Al continued, still guiding Danielle further away from Jim. "We did it for you. We supported you, gave you legitimacy. All you did was disrespect us at every turn. Now you're gonna pay up."

She pulled her arm free and whirled to face Steve. "What does he mean by that?"

Steve finally pushed up off of the desk and strolled toward Jim. "It's important for her career that she get back out on the road soon. I can't put together a band for her in enough time. I'll sweeten the pot if you'll go back out one more time. I'll start making calls about a new band immediately, but I need time."

Jim stood slowly and tucked his hands in the pockets of his slacks, mimicking Steve's posture. "Not our concern. Maybe if she had been nicer, we'd think about it. But Golden Girl over there thinks she's a big star, so let her carry the show on her own. Just write the check."

Danielle stomped over beside Steve. "What check? What is this?"

Steve looked at Danielle and shook his head. "I'll explain. Just let me finish this up."

Jim didn't give him the chance. "What he means is that he promised us both a big payday if we made nice with you and convinced you to get back in the game. That's why I went to you that day. We swallowed our pride and went back out with you, and now it's time we get paid." He turned again to Steve. "Write the check, Redus."

"Make that two checks," Al chirped as he settled back into his seat.

Steve sighed and turned, walked around the edge of his desk, and sat, then dug his checkbook out of a desk drawer. "You sure you can't do it a little longer? Six months, maybe? You could make another 35-40% on top of this."

"Write the checks, Steve," Al called. "I have an appointment with my investment broker in an hour."

Steve looked back down and finished writing the checks. He tore one off, wrote another, and then held one out in each hand. Jim and Al snapped them out of his fingers quickly. On their way towards the door, Jim couldn't resist turning back to Danielle with a smirk. He held the check high in two fingers. "Pleasure doing business with you."

With that, they turned and walked out. Danielle watched through the windows as they got into Jim's brand new Cadillac and drove away. Texas Pride was no more. Danielle looked over at Steve, still furious about what had happened. "What now, genius?"

Steve looked at her sadly for a minute, and then brightened up. "We put you on the road with a new band, a better band. A band that won't hold you back like they did. I'll start making some calls right now. I bet I can put an all-star lineup behind you."

"No," Danielle answered flatly. "I don't want an all-star band. I want a band that I have chemistry with."

"Well, I'll start calling some people. We'll find a band that you have some chemistry with. I just hope I can do it quickly, because I've got a great opportunity for you, but it's a time sensitive matter. I've got to be able to lock you in."

"Don't worry," Danielle answered, a smile slowly spreading across her face. "I know just who to call. You may have to make it worth their while, though."

"You name it," Steve said. "And I will make it happen."

#

That night, the assembled members of Reckless Passions sat backstage at Sliders and listened to Steve and Danielle pitch them the idea of becoming Danielle's backup band. In the months since Danielle had last talked to Ty, the band's fortunes had faltered. They were now reduced to playing the low rent clubs in the bad parts of town, and Danielle thought that she was throwing them a lifeline.

"So," Ty said, still soaked with sweat from a vigorous performance. "You want us to give up our identity to go on the road with Danielle?"

"Yes, but just temporarily," Steve answered.

"No," Danielle interjected. "You don't have to give up your identity. We would be billed as Danielle Regan and Reckless Passions. That way, you get exposure."

"Right." Steve backed her up, catching her drift. "We're going to be traveling the country. Everyone will know your name."

"Just for a tour," Ty asked.

"At least," Steve answered. "Although, Dani does need to get back into the studio."

"And I would prefer working with a band that I know as opposed to some studio hacks," she continued. "You get yourselves an album."

"Would our names appear on the album?" asked DeShon Welch. He was a big black man with long dreads and arms the size of tree trunks. He was an intimidating looking guy, and Steve's nervousness showed it.

"No," Steve answered shyly. "The label has made it clear that only Danielle's name will appear on the album. But you will all be credited in the liner notes, and you can be billed in live performances."

Danielle laughed at Steve's nerves. "Quit being a tough guy, DeShon. You'll get all the perks of being in a recording band, but you won't have the noose of celebrity hanging around your neck. It's the best of both worlds."

Garret Hardesty, the drummer, sat in a corner twirling his drumsticks. "Still, we don't get the recognition," he said. Garret was a skinny white kid with pale blond hair that he wore in a buzz.

"Recognition will come," Steve said. "Think about it. Who outside of Austin knows you now? In a few weeks you could be traveling around the country in a plush touring bus and staying at fine hotels."

"Yeah, right," DeShon chuckled. "I've seen her tour bus. It's older than hell."

"That's her tour bus, but the band you're going to be touring with is providing a brand new, state of the art bus. You'll be riding in luxury."

Danielle looked over at Steve. "You didn't mention another band."

"Just trust me on this, Danielle. It's a great opportunity."

"I don't know," Garrett said. "I think we're better off going our own way."

Danielle sighed. "That's fine. I'm not trying to bully you or bribe you. If you don't want to go, then don't. I just thought I could help some friends out."

Ty shot up out of his seat. "Who are we kidding? Nobody cares about us. We're playing crap ass clubs like this. What better chance are we ever going to have?" He looked at Danielle. "You're my friend and the best musician I've ever played with. I don't care what the rest of them do, but I'm in. Not just for now. As long as you want me. I'm tired of being the leader. You just tell me when and where to show up and I'm there."

Danielle smiled and got up to hug him. "Thank you."

DeShon got up and took them both in his arms. "You know we were just playing with you, girl. I'm in."

Garrett put down his drumsticks. "Let's see, a nationwide tour or playing Sliders for the rest of our lives? Come on, you know I'm in. I just had to make you work a little."

#

Steve put the new band through a week's worth of brutal rehearsals while he finalized the new tour. With a deal in place and the band beginning to whip into shape, he gathered the group together to reveal the new tour plans.

"So who is this the mystery band?" Danielle asked. "Is it Aerosmith?"

"Metallica," Garrett said. "Definitely Metallica."

"Naw, The Stones," Ty answered. "They're going out this year."

Steve let them shout out names, toying with them. Finally, he was ready to reveal his secret. "Ladies and gentlemen, this spring, you will be going on tour with...REACTOR!"

"Who the hell is Reactor?" Danielle snapped. "I thought you had some great deal for us."

"Reactor is a Scottish rock group that is coming to America."

"There ain't no such thing as a Scottish rock group," DeShon said. "What do they do, head bang with their bagpipes?"

"While they wear their skirts," Garrett continued. "With their sissy knee socks pulled all the way up."

Ty jumped in. "Hey guys, cut 'em some slack. There can be a Scottish rock group. What about U2?"

"They're Irish," Danielle answered.

"Is there a difference?"

"Irish dudes don't wear skirts," DeShon said. "They blow shit up."

Steve, frustrated, finally decided to step in. "Guys, guys, guys, get a grip will you? Just listen. Have you ever heard of Colin Nix?"

"Yeah, he played football for Auburn. I remember that dude," DeShon laughed.

"That was Patrick Nix, douche," Ty kidded. "Get your facts straight."

Danielle put a hand on DeShon's big shoulder, a bright smile on her face. "Colin Nix must be Stevie Nicks' third cousin by marriage, twice removed, by adoption and incredible circumstance."

"No," Steve said, starting to get upset. "Colin Nix is the biggest actor in British cinema right now. He's huge over there. He's like Tom Cruise in England."

"So what? What does he have to do with some sissy Scottish rock band?" Garrett asked impatiently.

"It's his band. He is this huge star over there, but he's tired of acting. He wants to be a musician, but nobody over there is taking him seriously. So he figured if he came over here, where nobody but the art house crowd knows him, he'll have a better chance."

"So we have to play second fiddle to a British actor on an ego trip," Ty said. "That's your great deal?"

"Listen to me. This guy is loaded and he's going all out. He's paying for everything…tour bus, five star hotels, the whole thing. And he specifically asked for you, Dani."

"Why?"

"Because he thinks that you are kindred spirits or something. What do I know? I don't care why he asked for you; the fact is he did. It's a great opportunity."

Danielle thought it over for a moment. "Is this guy legit?"

"He's got some talent," Steve answered. "He needs a lot of work. But opening for them will get you exposure, and honestly I think you'll kick the shit out of them every night. The tabloid press will eat it up. It's a win-win situation. Plus, it won't be as strenuous

116

as most tours because he doesn't want to be playing every night. There'll be lots of down time."

"Well, I guess it couldn't hurt," Danielle said uneasily. "I'm not sure it's a great idea, but we'll try it. It'll give the newbies a chance to get their feet wet."

"Newbies my ass," DeShon shot back.

Steve clapped his hands. "Great. I'll get you all copies of their CD so you can familiarize yourselves with their sound. The tour starts in New York in six weeks. Until then, I've gotten you guys some studio time here in town to keep you occupied."

Showing professionalism and a drive no one thought possible, the group managed to record an entire album in Austin while waiting for the Reactor tour to begin. Much like the first one, this album was recorded almost entirely live and used local musicians to add color at the end. However, the new band gave Danielle more room to breathe and the groove was noticeably better. Pleased with the lack of drama in the new band, Steve took the finished tapes to Generation as the group boarded a plane for New York to meet with Reactor.

Danielle was surprised by what she heard on the CD. She had expected a slightly wussified Brit rock band like Oasis, or a band with a heavy social consciousness like U2. Instead, they were a hard rock band with loud, aggressive guitars and very sexually suggestive lyrics. Lead singer Colin Nix didn't have a bad voice; she thought he sounded a little like Paul Rogers, but he needed some work.

Upon landing in New York, the group was met by a limo and whisked off to the Waldorf-Astoria, which would be where the band would camp while they waited for the first show in three days. From there, the two groups would share a massive, state of the art tour bus as they slowly meandered their way across the country.

Danielle settled into her room, not bothering to unpack her black duffel bag, but rather just digging through it for her trusty Longhorns nightshirt. After a long, hot shower, she was ready for bed, but with her mind still racing, she decided to play herself to sleep. Sitting on her bed with her legs stretched out in front of her, she absentmindedly strummed Ole Red until she finally slipped off to sleep.

She was awoken by someone beating on her door. Ole Red had slipped into her lap and her neck was stiff from the angle she had been sleeping. Drowsy, she had no idea how long she had been out as she stumbled to get to the door.

She opened the door without looking to see who it was, and found herself face to face with the English movie icon himself. Colin Nix was shorter than she had expected, noticeably shorter than she was. He had long, straight brown hair that bordered on light blond. His eyes were a milk chocolate brown and he had a scruffy beard. He was wearing a charcoal gray polo shirt—untucked and with no buttons done, showing a tuft of chest hair—faded blue jeans, and white tennis shoes.

When she opened the door, his face registered surprise for a moment, but he covered it quickly. "I'm sorry," he said smoothly as he turned his eyes away. "I didn't mean to disturb you."

"What?" Danielle ran a hand through her hair and tried to shake herself awake. Then she realized that she was wearing nothing but the nightshirt, which was long and loose but still showed plenty of leg. She felt herself blush, but tried to blow it off. "Don't worry about it. I've got the important stuff covered."

He gave her a quick once over. "Well, my compliments on the stuff you don't consider important." His speaking voice was deep and smooth, just like his singing voice, with just a hint of an upper class English accent. He stuck out his hand. "I just wanted to meet you. I'm a bit of a night owl, so I never considered that you would be asleep."

She gave him the slight hint of a smile and stepped to the side. "Well, come on in." She was keenly aware of how thick her own Southern accent was when she said it.

He responded with a grin full of brilliant white teeth. "Charming accent. I love it, that famous southern hospitality." As he entered the room, he saw Ole Red lying on the rumbled sheets. "Interesting sleeping companion. That's the sign of a dedicated artist. That's why I wanted you."

Danielle pushed the door closed gently. "I thought it was the sign of someone who needed to get out more."

He turned to face her. "A sense of humor too? I think I've stumbled upon the perfect woman."

She couldn't help but smile at his goofy line. She stepped past him carefully and sat on the edge of the bed. "I don't think I'd go that far, Mr. Nix."

"Please, just call me Colin." He pointed at the bed. "Do you mind?"

Danielle shrugged, trying to play it cool. "Go ahead."

He sat gingerly next to her, his hand brushing her knee as he did. She straightened her legs and he smirked. "Thank you for agreeing to this. I thought long and hard about who we should ask to be our opening act before I settled on you."

Danielle tucked her hands under her legs but she kept her eyes locked on his. "We're thankful for the opportunity. This," she said, her eyes sweeping across the room, "is a huge upgrade from my other tours. A girl could get used to this."

Colin chuckled. "Perspective. I live like this all of the time. It has its perks, but sometimes...."

She waited for him to finish the thought, but when he didn't, she pushed. "Sometimes what?"

He pushed himself up off the bed and walked to the window. He leaned against the wall and parted the heavy drapes with one hand, peering out over the New York skyline. "Sometimes I wish I were back in Scotland. Sometimes I miss the simple life."

"You miss the simple life?" Danielle stood and walked towards him, but kept a safe distance. "This is the epitome of a celebrity ego trip, dropping millions of dollars to come over here and play rock star for a summer."

Colin let the drapes drop out of his hands and looked at her with surprise that quickly turned to a smile. "Good point. I don't consider it playing, however." He turned toward her and hooked his thumbs into his pockets. "You don't know what it's like yet, being a big star. A *superstar*," he said with disgust. "It's so easy to be swallowed up by it. People willing to bend themselves to your slightest whim. Treating you like royalty, while at the same time demanding so much of you. They act like you owe them, and as long as you play nice, they will shower you with gifts and adulation." He crossed from one side of the window to the other while Danielle tracked him with her eyes.

119

"A few years ago, a rumor got started that I was going to come over here. That I was going to 'Go Hollywood,' he said, using his fingers to make quotation marks. "My fans were irate. They didn't want to lose me to Hollywood. I got death threats. Can you believe that? The sad thing was, it wasn't even true. I've never wanted to come to Hollywood. I find the fishbowl I'm in now small enough."

"Yet you come over here and throw your money around and act like a big shot. My manager tells me that the tour bus we're going to be on is the Taj Mahal on wheels."

"I have gotten spoiled to a certain degree of comfort, that's true. But I'm not very well known over here, and no one knows who Reactor is. This is my chance to roll back the clock, if you will. I understand that American rock'n'roll audiences can be hard to please. This should be a challenge."

"A challenge?" She smirked and turned away from him. "You know," she said, turning back around. "This is my life and I take it very seriously. There's nothing else I want to do, nothing I can fall back on. This isn't a game to me, and honestly I find it a little bit insulting that it is to you."

Colin stepped toward her and she instantly took a step back, which caused him to stop his own advance. "I'm sorry. I don't intend to insult you." He looked away for a moment, then looked back to her. "If it makes you feel better, I've been warned that your band will probably—what's the term the promoter used—blow us off the stage. My manager begged me to find a different act, one that wasn't as good. He's afraid that you'll embarrass me."

"And you chose us anyway?"

"Yes. Because I want you to embarrass me. I want to know what it's like to not be adored. And I want to know if I can do this. The only way I can do that is to put myself up against a legitimate American rock act. And when I couldn't get any of them, I got you."

Danielle was shocked by the comment, but before she could respond, Colin began laughing. "That was a joke. You were my first choice. But I do have to ask, what happened to your band? I thought you were a three piece."

"My old band quit on me. This is a new band."

He ran a nervous hand through his hair. "Is the prospect of playing with me that bad?"

"No," she said, releasing some of the tension that she had been feeling. "It was an internal thing. Don't worry, though. This band will be better. We will do fine. I promise that we will try not to embarrass you."

Colin moved forward cautiously and sat on the edge of the bed. "Don't worry about that. I did want to ask you, however, if you would mind joining me onstage. Just for a couple of songs in the middle of our set. I think it would be a nice thing for the audience."

"I can do that. I can probably pick up your songs pretty quick. I've been listening to your album for a while."

"No need," he said with a wave of his hand. "I thought we might do some classics. I love the Kinks, the Yardbirds, the Stones."

"I can do that, but no Beatles. I draw the line at the Beatles."

"Not a fan," he said, amused.

"No."

"Very well then," he answered. "No Beatles." There followed an uncomfortable silence between them. Colin stood and headed for the door, but turned before he got there. "Would you consider going to dinner with me tomorrow night?"

Danielle considered it for a moment. In her heart she wanted to, but she could feel the fear inside. "Maybe we should just keep things professional. At least for now."

"As you wish," he said with obvious disappointment. "I will see you tomorrow at rehearsal?"

"Sound check. And yes, I'll see you there."

#

The lower Manhattan nightclub that was the official launching pad for Reactor's American invasion was called Smoke and Mirrors. It reminded Danielle of the strip club where Alex Starr had first taught her to dance. Only this was no North Austin strip club. This was a top flight nightclub in New York City, and there was no shortage of music industry power brokers in the house.

Steve approached Danielle backstage as she peered out into the crowd. The rest of the guys were nervous. They had never played such a big stage to such a large crowd. Danielle was like a lioness on the hunt, chomping at the bit to get out there.

Steve came up behind her and began rubbing her shoulders. "It's just like we talked about, Dani. We've got a captive audience.

Go out there and smoke 'em. Hold nothing back." Danielle looked over her shoulder at him and he saw everything he needed to see. Then he nodded in the direction of the rest of the band. "You might want to say something to your band. They look like they are about to piss themselves."

She acknowledged him and walked over to them, huddled together in a corner. "Listen up, guys. Forget about where we are. This is no better than the clubs back home. Just follow my lead and do what you do. We're going to unleash some real, honest to goodness Texas blues, and these folks are gonna eat it up. Got it?" Their nervous stares didn't inspire confidence. "I didn't bring you guys here to fail. I wouldn't have done that. You can handle this."

Reactor was behind the eight ball from the start. Danielle and Reckless Passions soon found their stride and blasted the NYC crowd with their own brand of Texas blues rock. By the time Reactor took the stage, the crowd was thoroughly converted. Danielle stood offstage, watching as the band struggled through their set while the crowd hurled insults at them. Colin, with his rock star preening and the band's sexually charged lyrics, was an easy target.

He finally summoned her onstage. She stepped out to a roar of applause and then did her best not to upstage the band as they jammed on the Stones classics "Jumping Jack Flash" and "The Last Time." The band wasn't bad, but they lacked the cohesion that made Reckless Passions so good. She exited after the two songs and begged Steve to get her back to the hotel so that she wouldn't have to watch any more of the bloodshed.

Later that night, Colin again knocked on her door. He had already showered and his hair was still damp. When she opened the door he pointed a finger at her. "You held back tonight."

She shrugged and blinked to get her eyes adjusted to the sudden infusion of light. "I did my best."

"I don't want you to hold back," he said as he pushed by her and into her room. "I wanted you to come out there and make us look silly. We will never get better otherwise."

Colin plopped down on the foot of her bed. She stood over him. "They were tearing you apart out there."

"I know that," he answered harshly. "Why do you think that I wanted to start in New York? I wanted to get the worst out of the way. I figure that it will never be worse than it was tonight."

"You haven't played Philadelphia yet," she said seriously.

"Is Philadelphia worse?"

"You'll be begging for what you got tonight," she said with a laugh. "Philly fans are brutal and have a nasty habit of throwing stuff."

"What kind of stuff?" he said, a slight tremble in his voice. "Like rotten fruit and that sort of thing?"

"Like batteries."

"Batteries." He was getting worried. "Small batteries, I hope? Watch batteries maybe? I could handle that."

"They would throw car batteries if they could. Philly is a tough, tough town. They have a reputation for bad behavior."

"Maybe we should cancel that date."

She smiled gently and sat down beside him. "That wouldn't be a bad idea. I don't think you guys are ready for Philly. Hell, I'm not ready for Philly."

"Were we really that bad?"

Danielle patted him on the leg. "Y'all don't seem to have much chemistry. You all kind of do your own thing. When a band is really working right, all the pieces work together. It's kind of seamless."

"I noticed that when your band performed. It was like each of you knew what the other one was going to do before you did it. I don't know how to do that with my band."

"It just takes time," she said. "I've jammed with those guys for years. Then we rehearsed like crazy before we came out here. Even then, it took us a couple of songs to really get into a groove. That's what every rock band searches for. That perfect groove."

"I'm afraid that we may never develop that," he said solemnly.

Danielle put her arm around him. "There's no guarantee. The only advice that I can give you is to just keep plugging away. Hopefully, one night it will all click."

"Thank you," he said, and he stood to leave. "What do you think of us? Honestly?"

Danielle bit her lip for a moment as she pondered the question. She finally decided that honesty was the best policy. "I find it hard to take you seriously. All the tough guy lyrics and the sexual innuendo. It seems like a put on."

"It is," Colin answered. "Isn't that what American rock'n'roll is all about? Fighting and sex and drugs and all of that?"

"It's been done, time and time again. Besides, American audiences can spot a poser a mile away."

"What else can I do? I can't very well be taken seriously if I sing songs about growing up in the highlands and attending matches at Wimbledon, can I?"

"No," she laughed. "You can't."

"So what do I write about where I will be taken seriously?"

Danielle rubbed her eyes. "About common things. Things that everybody experiences. Love, loss, sadness, anger. You don't have to be specific."

"I don't know if I can do that."

Danielle sighed and guided him to the door. "I'm exhausted. I've got to get some sleep. Just chill out and when we hit the road in the morning, I will sit down with you and see if I can help you out, okay?"

He gave her a playful punch to the chin. "Will do."

#

Before the sun rose over New York City the next morning, Reckless Passions and Reactor boarded the mammoth, custom built tour bus that Garrett promptly dubbed Rockimus Prime. It was midnight blue and silver, longer and taller than most tour buses. Inside, bunks were built into the walls on either side, with plush single sized mattresses in each. The furniture was all gray leather, the carpet was luxurious, and the trim was all oak. Gilbert Bell, who Steve had insisted on being the tour manager, took Danielle on the grand tour.

"His highness has the entire back to himself. Full sized bedroom, king sized bed, full bathroom, fully stocked bar. The whole lot." Then he leaned in close, up on his tiptoes and whispered. "So if you need me during the show, you'll know where to find me."

Danielle took it all in with a sense of wonder. "Is this guy for real?"

Bell shook his head. "The first time I went out on the road I was as a roadie for a band named Saxon. You heard of them?"

124

Danielle shook her head.

"Well, it was cramped little vans, dingy roadside hotels, and cold fast food…and it was the best fucking time of my life. This," he said with disgust. "This isn't rock'n'roll. This is an actor playing a role. He says all the right things, but if he really wanted to know what it was like to be a rocker he'd do this shit in a station wagon."

Danielle laughed out loud. "If he did that, I wouldn't be here. I don't do station wagons. A girl has to have standards. But this," she took a slow look around. "This might do," she said with a fake British accent. "After all darling, I have a reputation to protect."

"Oh yes, tea and crumpets and the like," Bell responded, doing his best British butler routine. "Pip pip jolly ho. Excuse me, would you be a darling and please pass the Quaaludes and prostitutes? One penicillin or two?"

"My, Mr. Bell, what a salty mouth you have," she answered.

"Well, good to know that someone is having a good time." They both turned to see Colin standing in the doorway, watching them with a smirk. "I'm so glad that my generosity can be a source of humor for the two of you." He came up the rest of the way and pushed between the two of them on his way to the back. He stopped and turned back a few steps down the way. "And Gilbert, 'Ludes are sooo '70s. You really must update your tastes." He gave Danielle a quick wink and disappeared into the back.

Steve was next on board. "You should really be more careful. Some of these guys get their feelings hurt very easily. One wrong word and we'll be on the next Greyhound back home."

"Ah, don't worry 'bout it," Gilbert said with a meaty slap to Steve's back. "Colin's a fairly good guy with a good sense of humor. Besides, real rockers can always find a gig."

As the bus pulled out of NYC for the next gig in Baltimore, Danielle took advantage of the kitchen to cook her Scottish hosts a proper Southern breakfast. The members of the two bands ate at separate tables, not speaking to each other at all. Only Colin made any attempt to engage the members of Reckless Passions, who met him with polite distance.

Afterwards, Colin led Danielle to his room in the back of the bus. No bunks in the wall for Colin…he had a king sized bed with satin sheets and a huge TV, Nintendo, and a Bose stereo with surround sound speakers.

"So do you think that I'm just an actor playing a part?" He had an expectant look on his face. Danielle took her time, watching his reaction.

"That thought has crossed my mind. I can't really claim to know what your motives are. I think that at least part of you is taking this seriously, but I don't know how fully committed to this you are. You always have a day job to fall back on."

Colin thought it over. "I will give you that. But that's why you're here. I want you to help me make this real."

Danielle was strolling through his room, taking it all in. "I can't make it real for you. Only you can do that. I can help you make it better, but if this isn't something you're serious about, there's no point."

"Well, let's just see how it goes, then." He nodded towards the bed, where two shiny new acoustic guitars sat, one a sunburst Gibson, the other a blue Fender. "Take your pick."

She walked to the bed cautiously, examining the guitars but also keeping an eye on Colin. Finally, she sat on one end of the bed and took the Fender, wrapping her hand around the neck and strumming a couple of chords. "This one will do."

"Very good," he said with a smile. He sat on bed next to her and took the Gibson. They both sat, guitars at the ready, looking at each other. Danielle finally got impatient. "So play something."

Colin smiled back at her. "I thought you were going to help me write."

Danielle rolled her eyes. "You have to start somewhere. Don't you have some stray idea running around in your head?"

Colin, still smiling, shrugged. "I'm the poser, remember? Treat me like a schoolboy. Teach me. Guide me."

She tossed the guitar over her shoulder and shot up. "This was a bad idea. I shouldn't have done this. You can write songs fine without me."

Colin's smile never left his face and his blue eyes tingled with amusement. "I know I can. I thought you were flirting."

"I do not flirt when it comes to music. This isn't a joke to me, Mr. Nix, this is my life." She stormed towards the door. "Besides, I suck at flirting anyway."

"You do," he laughed. "But in its own way, it works. Please don't leave."

Danielle had paused at the door. She turned, eyes turned to the floor. "I'm such a dork. I'm sorry."

Colin came to her, knelt in front of her, and lifted her chin with his finger. "I love the way you are a dork. It's very cute."

"Cute?"

"Yes, cute. It's refreshing. So many of the women I meet try so hard. They all have fake boobs and bleached hair and no personality whatsoever. I like the fact that you don't put on airs. You are just you, and you don't care what anybody thinks about it. In that way, you remind me of someone I used to know."

"Someone that you loved?"

She saw a shadow sweep across his face at that moment, a flash of pain, quickly disguised. "Yes. But I don't care to talk about that. I want to talk about your abortive attempt at flirting."

"I told you, I don't flirt when it comes to music."

"I'm not sure you even know when you're flirting." He took her hands gently in his, and she noticed how smooth and soft his were. He stood slowly until he reached his full height. "Are you always so intense?"

"I don't really have a choice. My life hasn't been easy. Music is my only escape, so yeah, I take it seriously."

She realized that he was gently leading her back toward the bed. She could see the intent in his eyes. She had seen that look before, but she had to admit, it was disarming. He got back to the bed and sat down on the edge, but her eyes left his, drifting out through the big window at the back of the bus and to the cars flying by them on the interstate.

She took a deep breath. "Look. You're very charming, but I don't want to get mixed up in anything. I need to focus on my career and not get distracted."

"And I distract you."

"You intrigue me," she admitted. "I look at you and I know what you're thinking. I know why you brought me back here. I should be pissed, because you hardly know me. It's insulting to think I would just fall in bed with you. But there's something about you that makes me feel...."

Colin was focused entirely on her now. It was a serious side she hadn't seen in him yet. "Feel like what, Danielle?"

"Like I could fall for you very easily." As she said the words, a cold chill ran up her spine. She had already been down this road once.

"Why does that scare you?"

She jerked her hands away from his. Anger flared in her green eyes. "It doesn't," she said. She turned and stormed out of the room. As she left, she wondered if he knew that she was lying.

#

That night at the show in Baltimore, Danielle decided to let her fingers do the talking. When Colin summoned her onstage for their nightly jam, Danielle let loose with all the fire that she had. Reactor's rhythm section struggled to keep up, which just encouraged her to push it further. The crowd, not really into Reactor to begin with, loved it. Colin soaked up the barbs, preening for the crowd.

He came to her bunk later that night, but she pretended to be asleep. She just couldn't face him. She managed to avoid most interaction at all with him for days, and he soon quit trying.

Onstage, Reactor was improving nightly, and as they got better the crowds began to like them more and Colin began to get more serious. Reckless Passions was still overshadowing them every night, but the gap was closing. A rivalry began forming between the bands. Gilbert Bell was doing what he could to keep them apart, but he feared that a blow up was coming.

The blow up came in the middle of a cold night on the road to Chicago. Danielle woke up to the sounds of yelling and cheering coming from the kitchen. She flew out of bed to find Garrett and Reactor's bass player locked in each other's arms, stumbling around the kitchen, while the other band members surrounded them in a loose circle and cheered them on.

Danielle pushed her way past Ty and DeShon. "Stop it," she shouted. "Stop." But the two each worked a hand free and began throwing wild haymakers. Angry that they were ignoring her, she jumped in, trying to pry the two apart over the objections of the other members of Reactor. Still unable to break them up, she turned to DeShon and Ty. "Would you help, please?"

DeShon crossed his massive arms across his chest. "Nope. That bastard started this and Garrett's going to finish it." She looked at Ty, who looked at the floor. "Let 'em get it off their chest." Gilbert was leaning against the wall nursing a cold beer and watching with amusement. When he caught Danielle looking at him, he smirked back. "I been trying to keep them apart, but this is the only way they're ever going to learn."

Danielle rolled her eyes and went back to trying to break them up. She finally started to gain some separation when the bass player unleashed a vicious right hand that slammed into Danielle's left eye. The punch sent Danielle to her knees. Her vision blurred as her eyes began to water.

"Ah, hell no," she heard DeShon growl from behind her. "Now you're mine, fucker."

The other members of Reactor were ready to jump to the bass player's defense when Colin came bursting in, wearing nothing but a pair of red boxers and an open robe. "What the hell is going on in here?" He quickly surveyed the scene, breathing heavy, his face turning red. "The next one of my guys to move a muscle is on the next plane home."

Danielle made it to her feet, cupping her hand over her eye, which was stinging badly. She could hear Garrett panting at her side. She turned to him with daggers in her eyes. "I oughta fire your ass right now."

"I was just trying to—" he defended.

"I don't give a flying shit," she shot back. "This isn't high school. Show some goddamn professionalism." She turned to DeShon and Ty. "I won't put up with this again, is that clear? You wanna fight, take it somewhere else. In my band, you grow up or get out."

"We're not your band," DeShon fired back. "We're here as a favor to you." He pointed one of his big fingers at her. "You remember that. He was defending you. You didn't hear the shit they were saying about you."

Garrett, his hair wet with sweat, wiped at his brow. "Yeah, those fuckers were saying the worst things. I wasn't gonna stand for it."

She looked him over, her rage starting to die down. He had a couple of red marks on his face as well. "You don't need to do that. I don't care what they say about me."

Gilbert worked his way up to her, beer still in one hand, and investigated her eye.

"I'm fine," she said dismissively, trying to swat him away. "It just stunned me a bit."

Gilbert's anger was just beginning. "You're not fine. It's already turning black. You've got a show tomorrow night. I can't send you out there with a black eye. Steve is going to have my ass. I'm gonna go talk to Colin; I want that guy fired."

She reached out for his arm and turned him back. "Don't overreact." Over his shoulder, she could see Colin reading his own band the riot act. "It's being dealt with. Let's just get everybody back to bed."

Colin sauntered over, finally tying his robe. He gently touched her swollen eye. "That is quite a shiner you've got there. This is completely unacceptable. If you like, I'll fire him immediately."

She saw the bass player glaring at her from the other side of the kitchen. "Naw. Boys will be boys. I know better than to jump into the middle of a fight like that. I got what I deserved on that one."

"Well, let me just say, you can certainly take a punch."

"Lots of practice," she answered without thinking. She caught his reaction. "Don't ask."

"Well, at least come back to my room and let me tend to that. It's going to be a nasty bruise in the morning."

Danielle pushed his hand away. "I'm fine. I just need some sleep. I think everybody is going stir crazy."

Colin nodded in agreement. "Maybe it's time to get off the bus and give everyone some space. When we get to Chicago we should get everyone a hotel room for a couple of days."

"That's a good idea," Gilbert agreed.

"Sounds good," said Danielle. She patted Gilbert on the arm. "Let's get everybody back to bed, okay? Tell them that they've got a surprise waiting on them in Chicago."

He took a last tug on his beer and tossed the bottle in the trash, then shuffled off to corral his guys, but Colin caught Danielle. "You know, if you want to talk, I'm here for you. My mother was one."

130

Danielle was taken aback. "Your mother was one what?"

Colin leaned in and whispered. "A battered woman."

Danielle laughed out loud. "Shit, battered woman. You don't know the half of it. But that's not a chapter of my life I care to relive. So thank you for the offer, but—"

"It doesn't have to be about anything in particular," he said with a sad dog look on his face. "I would really like to sit down and talk to you. I feel I owe you an apology for the way I behaved the other night."

Danielle caught Gilbert looking on out of the corner of his eye. He shot her a sideways glance that needed no explanation. She reached out for Colin's arm and turned him towards his room. "Okay, fine, we'll talk." She guided Colin past Gilbert, thankful that he didn't say anything because the look in his eyes was enough.

They walked into Colin's room and he closed the door behind them. Danielle sat on the corner of the bed. The stinging in her eye was fading, replaced with a deeper, duller pain. She tried to cover it. "So what do you want to say?"

Colin pushed back a sheepish grin and ran his hands through his hair. She kind of liked the way it bounced right back. "I was an ass to you the other day. I have no excuses, and I won't insult you by trying to make any. I treated you like some groupie and I shouldn't have."

Danielle couldn't help but chuckle. "It's not that bad. You're hardly the first guy to make a move on me."

"Well, I still feel horrible. I'm afraid that it's just so easy, that sometimes I forget my manners."

She stood and gave him a playful punch on the arm. "Don't sweat it."

Danielle tried not to let it show, but there was a magic in the touch that hadn't been there before. The sudden sparkle in his eyes told her that he felt it too. She immediately regretted it and feared that he would try another awkward maneuver on her.

Instead, he reached up and gently touched her swelling eye. "That's just terrible," he whispered. "Such a beautiful face." He began tracing her features with one finger. "Those eyes. I could lose myself in those eyes. I could just fall into them and never stop."

Danielle lowered her eyes for a second, and when she looked back up, he was staring at her intently. There was no denying the pull now. She seemed unable to take a deep breath. "I don't know...." She was grasping for words now. "This is getting a little intense."

He scooted closer until he was almost on top of her. "I'm not afraid to get intense."

In that moment, she wanted nothing more than to kiss him, but she couldn't make herself take the leap. Their eyes danced with each other and then Danielle backed down, leaning back and creating separation between them.

"I can't. There's too much at stake right now. I can't get distracted."

"Danielle," he whispered. "You push yourself too hard. You have to give yourself time to live, to be a regular person, or this life will consume you. I've seen it happen. You're too special."

"There will be time," she answered calmly. "When I've really made it. Then I can slow down a little. Until then, I'm sorry, but I have to stay focused." She edged by him and headed for the door, but he caught her arm.

"You won't. You'll never stop pushing. Once you make it, you'll push twice as hard to stay on top. If you slip, you'll push three times harder to get back. People like you, they drive hard and they die young."

Danielle smiled and cupped his face in her hands. She liked the feel of his stubble on her palms. "I will be fine. Trust me. I've got this under control."

Colin took her hands in his and lowered them. "I used to go to school with someone just like you. He was determined to become the next great British actor. He wanted to get knighted and all of that. He pushed so hard that one day he just cracked. I never heard from him again. He was the best actor I ever worked with, but he never believed that he was good enough. And it drove him insane."

"Colin," she said, exasperated. "I appreciate the concern, but trust me. Okay?" She turned again, but Colin pulled back on her, spinning her around and into his arms. Before she could react, he was kissing her, and she soon melted into the kiss. They kissed passionately in the doorway until Danielle finally pried herself away.

"I've got to go."

Colin wouldn't release her. "Go to dinner with me when we get to Chicago. I promise that I won't bite."

Danielle gave him an innocent peck on the cheek and slid her wrists from his grasp. "Okay, I'll go."

#

When they got to Chicago, Colin sprang for two nights at the Four Seasons in order to give everyone some breathing room. It was a welcome break from the close quarters of the tour bus, which seemed to get smaller with each mile that passed under its wheels.

With no show until the next night, the members of both bands dispersed into the city to see what kind of trouble they could get into. Steve even flew in from Austin to meet them. With some time to kill before her date with Colin, she found her way to Steve's room.

Steve came to the door wearing a T-shirt and shorts, which was something she had never seen him in. He held the door open for her. "What do you need?"

"I just wanted to talk, if you're not busy."

"I'm never too busy for you, Dani." He held a small glass of liquor in one hand and he used that hand to point her to the couch. "Wow, look at you. Going out?"

She pushed her hair back behind her ears. "Yeah, I'm going out to dinner, but I'm kind of nervous."

Steve downed his drink in one shot and headed to the bar for a refill. "I'm surprised. I didn't really think that Colin was your type. I always figured you to go for a rough boy, a shit kicker or biker or something. A Texas boy, like that Adam kid that you used to date."

Danielle chuckled. "You mean that Adam kid that's busy boffing every starlet in Hollywood?" There was no hiding the hint of sadness in her voice.

Steve refilled his glass. "Yeah, like him. That kid surprised me. I never figured him for the playboy type."

Danielle shrugged her shoulders. "Hollywood changes people, I guess. Thank God Colin's not like that."

Steve sat down next to her and patted her knee like Grandpa used to do. "Colin hasn't gone Hollywood yet."

"I hadn't thought about that," Danielle answered. "Thanks for bringing that up though. I feel so much better now. I'm just a sea of tranquility."

"Sorry," he said as he took another drink. "To be honest, I have a hard time picturing you with anybody at all. You're too much of a loner. You keep people at a distance."

"I don't try to keep people at a distance. I don't like being a loner. It's just—"

"You don't like people being too close," he finished the thought for her. "Dani, you're not as tough to read as you like to think. I imagine that you have a good reason why you do it."

"Several." She stood and began pacing nervously in front of the couch. "I hate being like this." She stopped pacing and looked down at Steve, feeling like a teenage girl coming clean in front of her dad. "He kissed me on the bus. It was fantastic and all I wanted was more. But there's this voice in my head screaming to get away from him. I start seeing all these images…me pregnant in a trailer park somewhere, dying of AIDS in a hospital bed. Every bad thing that could possibly happen." She knelt in front of him. "Even things that aren't necessarily wrong. I could see myself being married to him, attending awards shows and such, but I'm just that. I'm Colin Nix's wife. I'm not Danielle Regan. I'm just an accessory."

Steve wrapped a thick arm around her neck and hugged her tight. "Dani, you're a great person with a great heart. You just need to trust in yourself, use your judgment." He let her go and she sat back on the carpet. "You've never been some starry-eyed kid. You have to trust yourself enough to let down your guard sometimes."

Danielle pushed herself up off the floor and straightened her skirt. "That's easier said than done, my friend."

That night, Colin took her to a Texas-style roadhouse because he wanted to give her a taste of home. It was fine with Danielle, who hated the idea of fancy restaurants anyway. They got a table in the back and he ordered a tall beer for himself and a Coke for her.

"I've got to admit, I'm surprised that you would bring me to a place like this. I kinda figured you for the fancy restaurant type of guy."

"Not when I come to America. I like the anonymity of being in America. When I'm back home, I have to go to places where the regular fans can't go. It's the only way I can have any peace."

"It's kind of weird that you're so big in Europe but not over here. Have you ever thought about coming over here to make movies?"

"No," he said definitely. "I don't want that. America is my get away. I love everything about America, especially the West. Cowboys and Indians and cattle drives and the Alamo. I love all of that. I would hate to lose my ability to travel America freely."

"If you don't want to lose your anonymity, why are you over here trying to be a rock star?"

Colin laughed. "I doubt that we will make it big over here."

Danielle was astonished and a little upset by the admission. "Then why do it? This is an awful lot of trouble and expense to go to if you're only playing make believe."

"Because it's fun," he said with a smile. "Because it's the closest I'll ever get to being a cowboy. It's like that Bon Jovi song. 'On a steel horse I ride....' You know? Rock stars are modern day cowboys."

"Bon Jovi doesn't know anything about cowboys," she said with a grin. "They're from Jersey."

"But they are rock stars. Don't you think that what we're doing is kind of like being a cowboy? Rolling from one town to the next, playing our songs and rolling out again. That's freedom."

"That's called a troubadour." Danielle took a deep breath and thought about it for a moment. "In a way I see what you're saying. But I don't always find it fun. If you do this for a living, it gets to be a grind."

Colin took a long drink of his beer and chuckled. "How could being a rock star not be fun?"

"Pressure," she answered right back. "We had to sell so many albums before our record company would extend our contract, and if the next one doesn't sell better, they might still drop us. There's pressure to be at your best every night because you don't want to shortchange your audience. There's pressure to look a certain way, act a certain way. I wish that I could play just for fun, but I can't."

Colin was watching her intently. "I had no idea that it was so different for you."

"Yeah, a lot of people don't. And I'm a woman, so it's even worse. A lot of people think that I'm some sort of novelty act. They don't respect me. And a lot of people can't see past my looks. It's a real pain in the ass sometimes."

Colin swallowed the bite he was working on and said simply, "Quit."

"Excuse me?"

"Quit," he said again. "Find some dashingly handsome actor who can take care of you and just live your life. There's no reason why you shouldn't be happy."

Danielle's thoughts drifted away from the table then. She thought back to Adam and a similar offer he had made. She looked out the window at the traffic rushing by on the freeway. "I had that chance once and passed on it."

Colin put his knife and fork down on the plate with a clatter. "With who?"

"Adam Quisenberry."

"From *The Olympian*? How did you meet him?"

A sad smile crossed Danielle's face. "I knew him when he was just a dorky college kid playing bongos on a street corner back in Austin. I almost gave all of this up to follow him to Hollywood."

"But you turned him down? Interesting."

"I knew that I could never live with myself if I quit. I have to make my own way; I'm not one to live off of others. I've been on my own too long to stop."

The waitress brought their steaks then and Danielle was glad for the break. The last thing she needed was to think more about Adam, who was off in Hollywood living it up with a different girl every night. She got enough of that from magazines and TV. She didn't want to think about him at all.

"I struck a nerve," Colin said uncomfortably. "I take it that you cared about him a lot."

She tried to shrug it off. "We were young and both had dreams to chase. His just came a lot easier than mine have. I chose music over him and he obviously never looked back. I can't say that I blame him, but sometimes I wonder what might have happened."

"I know exactly how you feel," he said, his voice soft as if he were afraid that someone would hear him. "She was what you might call a high school sweetheart. I went to London to pursue acting and she wouldn't come with me. She didn't want to leave Scotland. She was a small town girl…she had no need for big cities and fame and fortune and the like. She married a banker, and I guess they have a nice life together. I still wonder about her a lot."

That must have struck a nerve with him as well, because they finished their meal in silence.

CHAPTER SIX

Like a proper gentleman, Colin insisted on walking Danielle to her door at the end of the night. Once there, they stood facing each other, neither knowing what they wanted to do next. Finally, Danielle broke the silence.

"I'm sorry that I upset you tonight. I didn't mean to."

"How would you have upset me?"

"Talking about your ex and all."

Colin waved off her comment. "I brought it up. She's nothing but a memory now. This, you and me, the here and now, that's what I'm concerned about."

Danielle gave him a sweet smile. "Liar. I know that look. She may be a memory, but she is always at the front of your mind. Adam does the same thing to me. No matter how much I wish I didn't, I think about him all the time. I just don't want you to think that I'm trying to drag skeletons out of your closet."

He leaned up on his toes and gave her a sudden, quick kiss on the lips. "I keep my skeletons in the garage. My closets are too small." She couldn't contain her laugh, and it pleased him. "I hope that we can do this again soon."

"I do too," Danielle answered.

Colin then grabbed her softly around the wrist and pulled her into his arms quickly. He kissed her again, deeper and more passionately this time. Danielle resisted at first, but only for a moment before she let herself fall fully into his arms. The kiss didn't last as long as she would have liked before he was pushing her away. "I'll see you tomorrow night," he said with a teasing tone in his voice, and he walked away.

#

The next morning, Steve advised the group that they would not be continuing with Reactor to their next show in Detroit. Instead, they would stay behind to film videos for the first two singles off the next album. In the rush to get on the bus, Colin barely had time to say goodbye to Danielle before the separation.

The weather in Chicago turned gray when the group gathered to record the first video, for a song called "Alone in the Night." The weather was a perfect mirror for Danielle's mood, and her sadness was evident.

For the second video, "No Regrets," Steve surprised Danielle by recruiting legendary bluesman Buddy Guy to play a man looking back on his life. Danielle played the one who got away. For her scenes, Danielle was made up to look like a '40s era starlet, and the director commented that she was a vintage beauty. The comment stuck in her head.

After missing shows in Detroit and Madison, Wisconsin, Reckless Passions was able to rejoin Reactor in Lincoln, Nebraska. Colin and Danielle tried to hide their pleasure at the reunion, but no one was buying. One thing was clear, though...they were bringing the best out of each other every night on stage.

Back in Rockimus Prime and on the road after the Lincoln show, Danielle, just out of a shower and in nothing but a T-shirt and fleece shorts, hair still damp, was summoned to Colin's room by Gilbert. She walked in to see a candlelight dinner for two waiting for her and Colin, who was waiting for her in a pair of black slacks and a white dress shirt.

"Oh shit," she said, instantly embarrassed at being so dressed down.

Colin's smile was warm and bright in the flickering candlelight. "Don't. I love this look on you. No frills, no fuss."

She stood across from him with an unbelieving smile on her face. "Boy, you are really trying hard, aren't you?"

"Trying hard for what?"

"To get in my pants," she said coldly. She was watching him intently, curious to see his reaction.

Colin's smile faded and he half snarled at her. "Is that what you think I'm doing? That's what you think of me? You think all I care about is getting you into bed? I have to go a week without seeing you, and this is what I get?"

Danielle took two steps back, her hands up defensively. "Easy, tiger. I was playing with you. Don't be so defensive." Then she leaned forward, her eyes finding his. "Although, to be totally honest, some of your past actions could lead a girl to that conclusion."

He glared back at her for a moment, his brown eyes boiling with rage. There was something in the look that reminded her of her mother when she was ready to crack, and she felt her heart sink. Then, the moment passed and the goofy smile was back on his face. "Sorry, my mistake. I didn't realize that you were playing."

His embarrassment was clear, but Danielle still didn't like what she'd seen in his eyes. "You know, maybe I should just call it a night and we could do this some other time. I'm really beat tonight."

"No, no," Colin called, rising out of his seat to stop her from leaving. "Please stay. I apologize for losing my temper. That was totally unacceptable on my part. I hate the fact that you have reason to doubt me, or that you think that I might be playing you. I've been dealt that playboy reputation, and it has caused me problems more than once."

"I didn't mean to upset you," she said, settling into her seat. "It was just a joke." She didn't tell him that she had done it to gauge his reaction.

"I know, and I'm sorry. Totally my fault."

"Well, I've seen rage like that before, and it isn't pretty." She anticipated his follow up question and put a hand up to block it. "No, it's not something that I care to discuss with you, either. So don't even go there." She could tell that he didn't want to leave it alone, but the look on her face discouraged any further discussion.

#

The tour wound its way west through the mountains and down the West Coast. A week long break was scheduled once the bands hit L.A. before they played two nights at the famous Whiskey. Danielle, a student of rock history, was looking forward to playing there.

In the meantime, Colin decided that he was going to show Danielle a good time in the City of Angels. He took them both to a spa, which he enjoyed much more than she did, and he bought her a new, form fitting strapless blue dress that cost more than what she made in a year. It clearly made Colin happy to be able to fawn over her like this, but Danielle spent the day wishing that they were still going to steakhouses off the interstate.

That night, he took her to fancy Italian restaurant in Beverly Hills. The place was packed and the valet parking lot was full of very expensive foreign cars. Despite the fancy dress and the makeover, Danielle was keenly aware that he was taking her to a place where she was going to be far out of her element.

As they were about to enter, another couple was coming out and Danielle found herself face to face with Adam. He almost went past her without a second glance, but then he did a double take and stopped cold. On his arm was his latest flame/co-star, Lillian Fluery, a dark haired Canadian beauty who bore more than a passing resemblance to Danielle.

"Dani," he called out. "Is that really you?"

She gritted her teeth and turned around. "It's really me." Holding both arms out beside herself to give him a good look, she tugged on Colin's arm, pulling him closer. "And this is Colin."

Adam let out a long, slow whistle. "You certainly clean up nicely, don't you? I'm surprised though," he said, tucking his hands into the pockets of his suit. "I never thought you'd be caught dead in a classy place like this."

Colin, not amused, stepped between them. His voice got instantly deep. "Are you insinuating that she's not classy?" Danielle could feel his muscles bulging under her hands and saw the rage begin creeping into his eyes.

Adam saw it too and blew him off with a laugh and a pat on the shoulder. "Not at all, Bud. Dani and I go way back, and this isn't her type of place. She's more of a blue jeans and T-shirt kind of girl. That's all."

"Well," Colin growled. "Maybe she's stepped up in the world since you knew her."

Danielle found herself backing away slowly, wanting no part of the scene. They were definitely drawing attention as the paparazzi gathered outside began to shoot the scene, bathing them all in the flashbulbs. She looked over at Lillian, who was looking back at her with terror in her eyes.

Adam kept his hands in his pockets and stayed a safe distance from Colin, but his eyes were sparkling. He was loving the attention. "I wouldn't call dating a sissy ass poser like you a step up."

Colin balled his fists and stepped forward, ready to fight. "Let's find out who the poser is. I'd love to see how well you fare without your stunt double."

Adam gave him a toothy smile. "I don't use a stunt double, friend. Don't need one. I damn sure won't need one to kick your ass."

Danielle suddenly threw herself between the two of them, pushing them both back as she reached out and wrapped her arm around Adam's shorter and skinnier version of her. "Well, boys, why don't y'all tell us how it turns out? Lily and I will go watch a movie. Later boys."

She gently guided Lillian away, almost dragging her down the sidewalk. The girl was shaking like a leaf under Danielle's arm.

"That's not necessary," Adam said, his eyes never leaving Colin's. He began to slowly back away, making his way to his terrified girlfriend. When he was standing beside the two girls, he turned his attention to Danielle. "I don't want to embarrass your boy, Dani. You'd best take him inside. We'll be on our way. Unless, of course, you feel like trading up tonight."

Lillian's jaw dropped at the invitation, and Danielle knew that he would be going home alone tonight.

"Get lost before I knock your teeth out," Colin called out, a raging bull barely holding himself back.

"Oh, stop it," Danielle shot at him. "Who are you trying to impress anyway?" That caught him off guard and he lost some of his bravado.

"I'm not trying to impress anyone, but I won't let some redneck insult me."

"Redneck? Am I a redneck too?"

"Oh shit," Adam said with clear satisfaction. "Angus just fucked up. Now you're gonna get it."

Danielle looked over her shoulder. "Adam, shut up and take your little Pop-Tart home, would you? Her mother's probably wondering where she is."

"Clever, Dani," he responded. "Is that the best you've got?"

142

Danielle turned all the way around now. "Adam, you don't want to see the best I've got. Now shut up and get out of here before Mr. Matinee Idol gets his ass kicked by a girl. And you know that I can and I will."

Adam shrugged, but he was clearly in no mood to challenge her. "Okay, sweetie. But you really should reconsider your choice in men." He took Lillian by the hand and led her away.

Colin looked at her like a scolded child. "I was only trying to defend you. I wasn't going to let him get away with insulting you like that."

Danielle had to suppress the urge to scream. "He didn't insult me, Colin. He was telling the truth. This isn't my scene, and you know that. It's been nice, but it's not me, and if you have a problem with that then I'm wasting my time."

"I don't have a problem with that, Danielle," he protested. "Why can't I take you out on the town and show you off some? Is it so bad living the good life every now and then?"

"Define the good life, because I always thought that I did live the good life. There's nothing wrong with stepping out every now and then, but you can't get pissed off if people I know are surprised by it. And as far as Adam goes, he was goading you. He was trying to show you up in front of me, and you almost played right into it. I'm a big girl, Colin. I don't need you to fight my battles for me. I can fight them myself."

Colin put up his hands in surrender. "Fine. I get your point. I just thought that I was doing the right thing as your boyfriend."

She wrapped her arms around him and turned him back towards the restaurant. "Well, I'm not the typical girl, so you don't need to act like the typical boyfriend. Okay?"

Danielle awoke the next morning to Steve banging on the door of her hotel room. She took her time getting there, but when she opened it, he scampered in like a squirrel.

"What the hell went on last night?"

Danielle tried to rub the sleep out of her eyes. "What do you mean?"

He waved a newspaper in the air. "It's all over the news. You and Colin and that Adam kid in a screaming match on the sidewalk. Was there a fight? What's the deal?"

143

Danielle pushed by him and plopped back on the bed. "It was nothing. We were going into this restaurant and he was coming out. They both decided that they had to get their dicks out and measure up for their girls." She pulled the covers up over her head.

"Well goddamn it, next time tell them to throw down, because you're all over the news and the label has decided to step up the release of the album to try to catch the wave. They're all giddy over there."

She pushed the covers back away from her face. "Are you telling me that you want me to stage a public fight?"

"It wouldn't be the first time. That's the way the game is played, Dani. We've been out there on the road all this time, busting our asses, and one public pissing match just garnered you more publicity than all of it."

"Okay. Then how about I throw you out the window?"

Steve smiled at her. "That...would work really well, actually. I bet I could guarantee you a platinum album if you did. Of course, you'd be in prison, so I don't know if it would be worth it."

"It will be if you don't get out of here and let me get some sleep."

Steve swatted her on the leg. "All right. Get some sleep and we'll talk later. But be prepared. Things are going to start picking up steam with the album release coming."

"Yeah, yeah," she mumbled as she pulled the covers back up. "I'm thrilled."

The L.A. shows turned out to be huge as the tussle between Colin and Adam brought needed attention to the shows. The attention was even enough to get Reactor's album on the charts, if only for a week. Soon, they were rolling back out, first to San Diego and then back east to work across the southern U.S.

The release of Danielle's second album, *No Regrets...No Apologies* coincided with a show in Albuquerque, New Mexico. Colin agreed to move to the opening act for the night, giving Reckless Passions their first taste of being a headliner. The Albuquerque audience was already familiar with Danielle thanks to her constant touring, and they were especially boisterous on this night. The energetic crowd left some in Reactor's entourage to wonder why they never got the same reaction.

After the show, Danielle attended a release party for the album with Colin. They spent the night signing autographs and hobnobbing with studio executives. Both albums sold well, but it was impossible not to notice that Danielle's sold much better.

Just as Steve predicted, things got much more hectic with the release of the album. She was up before dawn every morning to make the rounds of local radio and TV stations. Her afternoons were filled with meet and greets and more interviews, and after the show, she had to turn in early in order to be able to drag herself out of bed the next morning to do it all over again. She even had to stop doing her guest spot during Reactor's set because it just became too much.

The work paid immediate dividends, though. *No Regrets...No Apologies* found an immediate audience, and the video for "Alone in the Night" entered into heavy rotation. The album quickly climbed into the Top 20, and the label pushed Steve to break them loose from Reactor and get them on the road as a headliner. But Danielle refused to back out of the deal.

After a show in Greenville, South Carolina, Colin decided to come to Danielle's hotel room instead of asking her to come to his. As soon as she opened the door, she could tell something was wrong. He tried to hide it, but there was worry written all over his face.

"What's wrong?" she asked as she took him by the arm and pulled him into her room.

Colin tried to play it off. "Nothing. Just thought I'd break the monotony by coming to your room for a change."

"Nice try," she responded. She led him to the bed and sat him down. She sat beside him, laying a hand on his thigh. "Now tell me what's bothering you. And don't try to tell me that it's nothing."

He wrapped his arms around her and pulled her in close. "I've been dying to see you. We've barely had any time together. I miss you."

Danielle pulled away from him. "You're not that good of an actor. What's going on? Tell me."

His forced smile faded from his face and he looked down at the floor. "I just...." He couldn't find the words. Danielle put a finger and pulled his face up, a move Grandpa had used on her before. She could see the pain in his eyes. "I got a letter."

"Oh no," she said. "Was it L?"

145

He cracked a weak smile. "I got a letter from Sarah."

"Who the fuck is Sarah?" she shot back. She began to feel fingers of jealously climbing up her spine.

"Sarah is the girl I told you about. The one I left behind."

Danielle nodded and snapped her fingers. "The one that married the banker. Yeah, I remember her. So what's the problem?"

He looked away again. Danielle waited for him to gather his thoughts. "She's divorced now. She's coming to New York and she wants to see me when we get back there."

Danielle's heart suddenly felt heavy, but she tried not to show it. "So? I have no problem with you having lunch with an old friend. I mean, you're with me now. Right?"

Colin's features softened and he put his hands on Danielle's face. "Right. But what if, when I see her, all of my old feelings return? What if I don't want her to be nothing more than an old friend?"

"Well then," she said, trying to quash the sick feeling welling inside her. "I'll have to kill her. It's no problem, you see? It all works out."

Colin laughed at that and gave her a quick peck on the forehead. "I wish it were that easy. I haven't seen her in so long, I just don't know."

Danielle was still trying to play it cool. "Maybe she's horribly scarred and deformed now."

"That's not funny."

"You're right, it's not. Listen, you love me, right?"

Colin looked shocked. "Of course I do. Haven't I made that clear?"

"Yes. I just wanted to be sure. So if you love me and I love you, then there's nothing to worry about. You go see your friend and then you come back to me. No worries."

Colin's look changed then, and Danielle didn't know why. "Did you just say that you love me?"

"Well, yeah. I thought I had made my feelings clear."

Colin ran a hand through her long, brown hair. "You've never actually said it before. To be honest, I didn't think that you were the type to ever say it."

Danielle was shocked. He was right, she had never told him. She wondered if she had even known it herself, or if it was even true.

"Well," she started, trying to cover her own surprise. "If I've never said it before, I'm saying it now."

Colin put his hand on the back of her neck and pulled her in closer. "I can't tell you what it means to me to hear you say that. I've told others, but no one has ever told me."

Danielle had a hard time catching her breath. "Not even Sarah?"

"Forget Sarah," he whispered, and kissed her with a fierce passion that she had never felt before. She let herself fall back on the bed and he was on top of her in an instant, his hands running all over her body. Soon, they shed their shirts.

At that point, Colin realized where they were heading. "Danielle," he whispered.

"I know, baby," she gasped back. "I'm ready."

He kissed her again and she closed her eyes and let go. For the first time that she could remember, there was no fear, no doubt. She was ready for what came next.

Until he quit kissing her and rolled off. Danielle pushed herself up on one elbow, still gasping for breath.

"What's wrong?"

Colin was laying on his back, staring up at the ceiling with unblinking eyes. "I want to do this. I really do. I want it badly."

Danielle swallowed hard and let out a long, slow breath. "Just not with me," she said, her voice trembling. She let herself fall onto her side.

He sat up and leaned over her, tracing the line of her jaw with a finger. "I'm sorry. I thought that she was in the past, but now she may not be. I don't want to lead you on. I just don't feel like this is right. I need to see her. I need to know for sure if there is anything left between us. If the old feelings aren't there, then I will know that it's you."

Danielle didn't know until that moment that you could actually feel your heart breaking. "I understand. You have to be sure that your past is your past." Her voice was cold now, emotionless as she tried to shut her feelings off.

"Right," he answered, sounding relieved.

"After this, you'll be mine for sure."

"Right," he said again.

Danielle continued to stare off into space. "Then maybe we should steer clear of each other. At least until after you meet her."

Colin stood and picked his shirt up off the floor where Danielle had thrown it. "That would probably be best. It's only a few days until we get to New York. Then I'll know. I promise." He let himself out.

Danielle lay on the bed, suppressing the urge to cry or scream. She wanted to hit something, to throw something. Sadness and anger fought a battle inside her and all she could do was lay there and feel it happen. She finally rolled over onto her back, and she saw Ole Red resting on its stand by her bed. She reached out, and let her fingers run over the strings. "At least there's one man in my life I can count on." For a split second, the tears started to come, but she fought them back. She wouldn't cry. Not over him.

The next morning, Danielle woke up to Gilbert banging on her door again. She had fallen asleep where she had been laying, still half undressed, her hair a tangled mess from a restless night of tossing and turning. She shuffled to the door and threw it open without checking.

"What the...?" Gilbert started before he really noticed her. "Dani, are you okay?"

She looked back at him with cold eyes. "Yeah. Why wouldn't I be?"

Gilbert pushed past her and found her shirt laying on the bed. "Put this on, please," he said, and threw it to her. She made no effort to catch it, and it hit her in the face and fell to the floor.

"What do you want?"

Gilbert tried to not look directly at her. "Reactor released us from our contract today and pulled out early this morning. We're done."

She looked back at him like a statue. "Oh well. Can we go home now?" Again, tears threatened to fall, but again she wouldn't let them.

Gilbert saw the pain, but chose not to push it. "Sure, Dani. We can go home now."

#

Steve charted a plane and the band flew home. No one was particularly sad that the tour was over. The tension between the two bands had never really gone away. Still, Danielle's hurt was evident and everyone gave her a wide berth.

When they arrived back in Austin, she left without saying goodbye to anyone, taking a cab back to her South Austin apartment. There, she took her phone off the hook and slept for two days.

On the third day she was unable to sleep any longer. She threw open her drapes to find that it was a rainy, miserable day outside. She stared out the window at the cars passing by on the rain soaked streets and decided that she'd had enough.

She dug her duffel bag out of the closet and quickly packed. She threw on a pair of shorts and a T-shirt, grabbed Ole Red, and headed out. She threw her stuff in the back seat and found the first road out of town. She had no idea where she was going, she just knew that she needed to get away.

#

When she didn't answer her door on the third day, a worried Steve insisted that her landlord open the door. He found the apartment a mess with clothes scattered everywhere. He raced back downstairs to find that her Camaro was gone.

Steve stomped back upstairs and looked at the empty apartment. He had to assure the landlord that rent would still be paid and to not evict her. Then he walked around the empty apartment, his mind racing.

The label was pressuring him to deliver another video and to get the band back out on the road. Now he had no star. So he did the best he could. He hired local actors and film crews to film storylines for two new songs, "No Apologies" and "For Salvation." He had the scenes spliced with concert footage of the band to produce two new videos without spending a lot of money on them.

Then he convinced the label that she had damaged her voice on the road, thus explaining why Reactor had dropped them. She needed to rest and would be unable to tour for the rest of the year. For the moment, they were appeased, but he knew that if he couldn't convince Danielle to come back soon, it might all be over.

#

Danielle drove aimlessly for days. First, she found herself on the Texas coast. She found a sleepy little town and hid out there. She swam in the ocean, tanned on the beach, and soaked up the Texas sun. But soon, she tired of the beach and moved on.

She went all the way to the Rio Grande and then turned north. She hadn't intended to, but she soon found herself headed back toward Chaparral. It had been four years since she'd put the town in her rearview mirror.

As she drew closer, she began to wonder if there was a reason why she had gravitated back there. Maybe she had done what she had needed to do. She had gone off to Austin and made a name for herself. Maybe it was time to come back, find a man, and settle down.

She shook the thought out of her head. She was only twenty-two and there was still a lot of life to live. She wasn't ready to settle down and she didn't want to come back here. Still, she thought about Grandma and Grandpa and Kel, and decided that she needed to go.

She rolled into town in the middle of a windy night, dust and tumbleweeds blowing across the highway in her headlights. She found a newly built Motel 6 on the outskirts of town and checked in. In the morning, she travelled to the cemetery. They were all there, trapped forever in their allotted spaces, now nothing more than tiny metal markers set into the ground. Any answers they might have held were lost to the west Texas wind.

She went on into town. Kel's old house was still there, but was now in a state of disrepair, the fence partially fallen, the yard choked with weeds and scattered toys. Oh well, it had never been the nicest place in town anyway.

She took her time driving through town. A lot had changed. Most of the old, family owned businesses had gone out of business, replaced by franchises. The swimming pool where she had worked as a life guard had been filled in with concrete and was now a skate park. She watched the kids on their skateboards and tried to remember what it used to be like, but failed.

She went by Grandma's and Grandpa's last, praying that it hadn't changed much. If this old town held any answers for her, it would be there. As she turned on to Roadrunner Trail her heart sank. She hoped that she wasn't seeing things right, but she was. The house was gone, along with most of the rest of the houses on the street. In its place was a fancy new brick building that was the administration building for the school district. Where Grandpa's garden used to be was the new bus barn.

Danielle was overcome by sadness. It was like her entire childhood had been bulldozed, leaving nothing but the bitter memories. She was quickly regretting this trip.

She spent a sleepless night thinking about it all. It was as if someone had completely wiped her childhood away. As night began to turn to day she began to think of it as a blessing instead of a tragedy. The past was gone and she didn't need to let it continue to drag her down. Peace and sleep finally came.

When she woke up later that afternoon, her mind was racing. New songs flooded into her brain so fast she couldn't write them down fast enough. She knew that she needed to get back home as soon as possible.

She hurriedly checked out, threw her things into the Camaro, and raced home. The entire way, she kept singing a song to herself over and over again. She was terrified that it would slip away from her if she didn't. *This song,* she thought to herself, *is going to be my masterpiece.*

She drug herself into Steve's office the next afternoon after having driven all night. She needed a shower and a change of clothes, but she felt great. Steve, on the other hand, was just short of a heart attack.

He rushed to her, hugged her tightly, and then pushed her back. "Goddamn you, Danielle. Do you know what kind of shit storm you left me in? I've been juggling so many different balls. I had to tell the label that you had lost your voice and that was why you couldn't go out."

Danielle just laughed and slapped him on the back. "Don't sweat it. I'm going to make this worthwhile for everyone. I need you to get the guys together and get me some studio time. I've got songs burning a hole in my pocket."

"What? I can't do that. You need to go out on the road. You need to promote the album. The label is losing their mind."

"I know you've been covering for me and I thank you. You're the best manager, and I know that I don't make things easy for you, but I need you to do this for me. I've got a vision and I promise you. *I promise you.* This next album is going to rewrite the rules. Okay?

And I need you to find me a piano player. And a backup singer, a woman with a higher range than mine, okay? We need to fill out our sound a little."

Steve took her in for a minute and then nodded. "Okay. I'll trust you on this. I'll make it happen, but you can't do this to me again. No more Houdini's."

Danielle smiled brightly and shook his hand. "Agreed."

CHAPTER SEVEN

Danielle was wearing a glamorous, off the shoulder black dress, diamond earrings, and necklace. Her hair was up and her make-up was perfect. She looked for all the world like a movie star. She was in the lobby of a swanky hotel, sitting on an upright trunk, as all around her, wealthy people swirled until it became nothing but a blur. When the scene cleared, she was still in her designer dress, but now she sat in a dirty alley. To her right there was a dumpster, and on the ground just beyond that, a bare female arm and leg lay motionless in a pool of blood, with a broken syringe inches away from the woman's hand. Danielle looked down at the sight, then up at the camera with a cold detachment. The song and the scene faded to nothing.

The lights in the screening room went up and Steve and Danielle exchanged satisfied glances. Jay Hatfield of Generation came up to her in a state of near disbelief. "Danielle," he said breathlessly, holding out his hand. She shook it. "I never thought that I'd say this, but I think you're about to become a huge star. That song, the video, the whole album, it's just going to blow everybody away. I underestimated you, but I won't let that happen again."

Danielle didn't try to hide her pleasure. "I just hope everybody shares your enthusiasm."

"They will, believe me. I'm putting our full marketing force behind this. By the end of the fall, you are going to be the biggest thing going, mark my words. You can't fail."

#

In the aftermath of Danielle's failed relationship with Colin Nix and the soul searching road trip that followed, Danielle had come back to Austin reenergized. The result was her third album, *Cathouse*. It was an album that would rewrite the rule book for the blues/rock genre. The album was tough, dark, and moody. The album title perfectly reflected the entire album; every song had the feeling of walking down a dark alley in the dead of night. Danger seemed to lurk behind every lyric, every riff.

The first single would be "Blessed Poison," an ode to the lifestyle that had killed her father and so many others. The theme of someone trapped by their own addiction, even when they knew it was costing them everything, was an especially haunting one for Danielle, who dedicated the song to the memory of Big Rick in the liner notes.

With *Cathouse*, Danielle was no longer the roadhouse guitar slinger recycling Stevie Ray riffs. She had now found her own voice. It was a gritty, edgy sound that dripped sex and danger.

She knew that a new album meant a new tour, a concept that didn't thrill her. She was tiring of life on the road. She had begun to think about buying a house and wanted to settle down. She was tired of feeling like she was constantly on the run.

While Steve put together tour dates, Danielle decided to have some fun. She headed up to Dallas for the weekend. She went to Six Flags and enjoyed behaving like a kid, in some ways for the first time. She rode rides until she was ready to puke, only to climb up on the next one as soon as she felt ready. After that, she went to a Rangers game and caught a foul ball. No one seemed to notice her at either place.

She had fun, but couldn't help but think that it would be more fun if she had someone to share it with. Her thoughts raced back, but they didn't go back to Colin. She thought about Adam and his look alike girlfriend, whom he was still seeing several months after the episode with Colin in L.A. She wondered, if she went to him would he leave Lillian for her? Lillian seemed like nothing more than a knockoff. Danielle knew that she couldn't do that. She longed for love, but she wouldn't throw someone else under the bus for it. Adam would just have to live in her memories.

The next day, she braved the fierce July heat for a trip to the Fort Worth Stockyards. She fully expected to pass through yet another tourist trap without notice. Yet almost from the moment that she got there, she noticed a man watching her intently. He was a tall man, easily 6'4" and powerfully built, with a nice bronze tan and dark brown hair that curled up at the base of his neck. He was clean shaven, with his baseball cap pulled down low and Ray Bans covering his eyes. He wore a T-shirt that was tight enough to show a chest full of muscles, and jean shorts that displayed strong, athletic legs. He was certainly a nice piece of eye candy, and he seemed pleased with what he saw as well.

He strolled over to her confidently and Danielle had to fight the urge to scurry off. He was there in an instant.

"Hi there," he said, his voice smooth and cool, with a hint of an accent she couldn't quite place. "Aren't you Danielle Regan?"

"Yes," she said hesitantly

He gave her a slightly lopsided grin and held out his hand. His hands were huge and rough; his grasp completely engulfed her hand. "I'm Dirk Crandall, pleased to meet you."

"A pleasure," she answered guardedly. He stood there, like he was waiting for her to realize something. He finally realized that she wasn't and continued.

"I play for the Stars. The Dallas Stars? The hockey team?"

"I know who the Stars are," she said with a tone. "But I don't recall you."

"I just got traded here at the deadline. This is the first chance I've had to really get to look around. During the season, things are too hectic."

"I can feel you there. I've been pretty busy lately too. This is my last chance to look around for a while. Last chance to feel normal before things get crazy for me."

Dirk waved her off. "Normal is boring. I lived the normal life for a long time. I don't ever want to live like a nobody again. That's what's great about living a life like ours, we don't have to be normal."

"I would kill to be normal. I've never known a normal life."

He reached out and grabbed her hand. "Maybe you just haven't lived the right kind of abnormal life. I bet I could show you things." A big smile broke out across his face. "All kinds of things. Things that would make you never want to be normal again. Why don't you come have lunch with me and I'll show you?"

Danielle was taken aback by the suddenness of his request, but there was something about his impulsive nature that she liked. He seemed to crackle with a sex appeal that was at once dangerous and irresistible. Her natural instincts told her to politely walk away, but she knew that she would never lose this loneliness if she was always afraid. "I guess we could do that. There's a great barbecue joint right around the corner."

"No," he said, drawing her in closer. He had a rugged smell that she liked. "I know a much better place. High class. Why don't you come with me and I'll show you?"

"I've got my own car."

He edged even closer. "Leave it here. I ride in style."

"I do too. And I have this thing about riding with other people. I don't like it."

He stepped back, but the smile never left his face. "Then I guess we'll take two cars. I just hope that you can keep up."

Dirk's car was a brand new Corvette with a custom metal flake purple paintjob and silver pinstripes. It was nice ride, but he drove like a maniac. He swerved in and out of I-20 traffic, never under ninety and with a couple of near misses. Despite his cockiness, Danielle, in her little Camaro, had no trouble keeping up with him. She knew that she was the superior driver, but that was hardly a good way to start a first date.

The restaurant he led her to was a French number in the Highland Park area of Dallas, and Danielle noticed how out of place her car looked in a lot full of Benzes and Porches. Inside, the maître de looked at the two of them in their shorts and tank tops with something worse than disgust until Dirk pulled a couple of big bills out of his pocket and waved them in front of him. They were quickly seated.

"Did you see that shit?" he asked when they sat down. "If we were just a couple of regular people stumbling in here, that guy wouldn't have looked twice at us. Give him a couple of hundreds and all of a sudden, he's real nice." He caught the eyes of a waitress and called her over with a snap of his fingers. He ordered a bottle of champagne and two entrees; Danielle didn't even know what he ordered. "You'll love it," he assured her. "One good thing about playing for Montreal, I learned a fair amount of French."

"I would have been fine with the barbecue joint."

"Nonsense. Places like that are under us. That's why they make places like this, for celebrities like you and I."

Danielle laughed. "I never considered myself a celebrity. I'm just a musician."

"You're too humble. You're a kick ass guitar player and the sexiest woman alive. You hold yourself back too much. I bet that there's a wild woman in there somewhere, just dying to get out. You got to let that bitch out."

"What you see is pretty much what you get. The life of a musician really isn't all that glamorous. It's really all just radio stations, arenas, and buses. Not much time for anything else."

He reached across the table and leaned over. "Honey, there's always time for anything else."

In an attempt to hide her smile, Danielle turned her head away and for the first time became aware that the restaurant featured live music in the form of a young girl in a formal black dress playing soft adult contemporary hits on a baby grand. She was a slight girl with dark red hair and a china doll complexion. She looked like a little girl, but she played with a finesse that drew Danielle's attention.

Danielle tore her eyes away from the girl and back to Dirk, but her ears remained focused on the girl in the black dress. Danielle managed to maintain a delicate balance through lunch, engaging Dirk in small talk while keeping one ear on the piano player. In the back of her mind, she had it all in that moment. Dirk was a nice piece of eye candy, with that rugged handsomeness that she found appealing, and the piano girl was providing the soundtrack.

Finally, as the waiter was bringing Baked Alaska, Danielle noticed that the music stopped, and she watched the girl duck into the ladies room. Danielle jumped up with a muttered excuse and followed the girl in.

Inside the marble and brass restroom, Danielle found the girl standing in front of the mirror splashing cold water in her face. There was a moment of terror in the girl's face when Danielle walked in. Danielle gave her a warm smile. "Are you okay?"

The girl visibly relaxed, letting her shoulders slump. "I'm fine, thank you," she said in a soft voice. "Just trying to stay awake. Six hours of easy listening after a morning full of classes and an all-night cram session doesn't work too well."

Danielle chuckled. "How old are you?"

The girl looked at her reflection in the mirror. "Nineteen going on a hundred."

Danielle leaned against the door frame and took her in. She seemed so frail, so tired. "So why do it? There's got to be easier ways to make money."

The girl's eyes slid over to Danielle. "Not one that lets me play piano. I'm doing the college girl thing for my parents. This is for me." She nodded past Danielle. "Playing the piano is my joy."

Danielle let a big smile cross her face, and for a second the girl recoiled. Danielle could only imagine what thoughts were going through her head. Danielle picked up a neatly folded linen towel off the counter. "You got any lipstick on you?"

With some trepidation, the girl reached into a matching handbag at her side and produced a tube. Danielle took it from her and scrawled a phone number on the towel in candy apple red. "Do yourself a favor. Call this number. The man's name is Steve. Tell him Danielle sent you. I assume that you can play something other than adult contemporary?"

"Of course," she answered, somewhat insulted. "What did you say your name was?"

"Danielle. And I've got a job for you if you want it."

The girl could barely contain the smile that broke across her face. "Okay."

Danielle turned and started out, but stopped part of the way through the door. "Do you sing?"

"Some," she said.

"Good. I'm serious. Call him. And go home and get some sleep."

Dirk was waiting anxiously for her when she got back to the table. "Everything come out okay?"

"Yes," Danielle said. "Everything is fine."

"I ate the dessert," he answered flatly. "I got bored. Sorry."

"It's okay. I was full anyway." Then she decided to change course. "Thanks for lunch and everything, but I need to get back to my hotel."

"I'll follow you there."

"That's really okay," Danielle answered. Dirk was nice to look at but he had the depth of a wading pool and she felt that she was wasting her time. It was time to bid the hulking hockey star a quick goodbye.

"Race ya," he said, a twinkle in his eye. Danielle thought about it for a second.

"You don't know where you're going."

"So tell me. Come on, the ride over here was the most fun I've had since I came to this hokey town. Let's do it."

She had to admit, the race across the Metroplex had been fun. "All right, let's do it."

Back at the hotel after another exhilarating dash through Dallas traffic, Danielle was flying high. She loved the thrill she felt behind the wheel, a thrill she hadn't felt in years. Dirk, being a gentleman, walked her right up to her door.

"Well," she said. "Thanks again for a nice day." She held out her hand.

Dirk took a look at her outstretched hand, smirked, and yanked her toward him. Before she knew what was happening Danielle was in his arms, their lips locked together. She felt like flames were licking at her from the inside. When she finally managed to tear herself away she gasped for breath. Dirk leaned in close and whispered in her ear. "Let's go out tonight. Doll yourself up and let's do it up right."

Danielle shook her head. "I didn't bring my doll up clothes. Sorry."

Dirk ran his hands up her bare arms. "So let's go buy you some." Danielle's mind was screaming no, but her mind wasn't making the decision any more.

That night, he met her at the hotel room door with a designer dress that was barely a dress at all. She was uncomfortable in it at first, but he was delighted by her in it. She hated how his constant compliments made her feel better about herself.

He took her to another upscale restaurant in the Las Calinas section of Irving. However, this place at least printed their menu in English so that she could read it. In the evening and around much older money, Dirk was more reserved. Danielle liked him that way much better. After dinner, he took her to see the Mustangs at Las

Colinas. They sat on a concrete bench and she rested her head on his strong shoulder as she watched the water cascading off the sculpture.

"So, Dirk, where are you from?" she asked innocently.

He looked over his shoulder at her like she was an alien. "Why do you want to know?"

Danielle smirked at him. "Making conversation. That's what people do when they're getting to know each other. Besides, I can't make out your accent."

"Oh," he said absentmindedly. "I'm from Banff. It's this little resort town in Western Canada."

"That's funny. You don't sound Canadian."

He squeezed her knee with one of his huge hands. "That's because I'm not French-Canadian. Western Canada is a lot like Texas, but with snow."

"Did you grow up with money?"

"God no," he answered. "My dad worked construction his whole life, and my older brothers followed him into it. I used to watch them come home every day, covered in grime and so tired they could barely walk. They'd complain of hurt knees and backs and everything else, but they'd trudge back out every morning. All they ever wanted out of life was a cold beer, a warm meal, and a soft bed. That was their entire life. I decided that I didn't want that kind of life. So I worked my ass off to get out of there. That's why I enjoy what I have now, because I know what it's like to have nothing."

Danielle lifted her head and looked into his face. He wouldn't turn to look at her. "You don't have to be a show off about it." She felt his arm tense up under her hands. "I don't come from money either. I've had to struggle and suffer, but I'm not ashamed of where I come from."

"I never said that I was ashamed," he snapped. "I just didn't want that life. I worked hard to get out and I am going to enjoy every bit of what I have. I'm not ashamed of that either."

"You have a right to enjoy yourself, but this afternoon you were showing off. It's not the most appealing thing. I've never liked people who like to shove their money in your face. I don't need designer dresses and fancy restaurants."

"I don't need those things," he answered. "I just want them. And I like to share the wealth."

"Well, I'm interested in you, not your money. I just want to hang out and get to know you. I'm more interested in the simple pleasures of life."

Dirk finally looked down at her and their eyes met. With one hand, he brought her face up to his and they kissed, a brief but fiery exchange, then he pulled away. "I don't know anything about those, so you'll have to show me."

#

For the next two weeks Danielle and Dirk spent all of their time together. They went swimming together at the hotel pool, where Danielle got her first up close look at his very athletic body. It was a view she had a hard time resisting. She took him on picnics in the park, and he taught her how to ice skate at the Stars' practice facility. She even helped him throw a cookout for his teammates who had stayed in Dallas for the summer, and made fast friends with many of them.

At night, they took long walks or went on drives, talking for hours on end. He began to press for a more physical relationship. She went as far as she felt comfortable, holding him back with incredible willpower. Still, she wasn't sure how long she could resist her new stud. She did know, late at night when he was gone, that she wasn't ready yet. She just wasn't sure why.

After three weeks in Dallas, Steve called. The tour dates were set and it was time to get back to work. The new tour would be their largest and longest, and they were now playing arenas, not clubs.

Danielle hated to say goodbye to Dirk, and he surprised her by offering to follow her to Austin. He had time to kill before spring training started, and he was anxious to get a taste of the Austin nightlife. With Dirk in tow, Danielle returned home, ready to work.

When the band reunited to begin rehearsals, Danielle was happy to see Trish Butler was in the fold as well. The china doll pianist from the Dallas restaurant looked a lot happier now. She tried to hide her nerves in a roomful of strangers, but Danielle could see through the tough façade. It was Ty that approached her first, however, and within minutes she started to relax.

The band rehearsed relentlessly, jamming away on the new songs for hours on end and giving Trish a chance to bone up on the back catalogue as well. Danielle and Steve were both pleased with the vocal harmonies between the two. The band's sound was rounding out.

Dirk, however, was bored. After having Danielle all to himself in Dallas, he was having a hard time getting her attention. Even when the day was over, Danielle talked non-stop about the new tour. He tried to convince Danielle to make it up to him by letting him stay at her place, but Danielle knew she couldn't trust him, or herself, in that situation.

Soon, rehearsal time was over. Steve had booked the band on a ten day publicity tour to drum up support for the new album. While Dirk headed back to Dallas, Danielle headed for New York.

Generation Records kicked off the festivities with a huge party to celebrate the release of "Blessed Poison," the first single. Danielle, dressed more like a movie star than a guitar slinger, politely posed for pictures with NYC's rich and famous. She patiently gave interviews with what seemed like every person in a hundred miles that owned a microphone.

The next morning, she drug herself out of bed early to make the media rounds. She performed "Blessed Poison" acoustically on *Today* and ended the night by doing a searing version with the full band on Letterman. In between, there were autograph signings and drop-ins at various radio stations.

The next day they moved on, first to Miami and then to Atlanta. It was more of the same. Appreciative fans and sycophantic celebrities all wanting to get close to Danielle. Steve could barely keep a smile off his face. "There's a storm brewing, Dani. This thing is going to explode."

It was in Chicago, however, that Danielle, with the best possible intentions, changed everything. During what was supposed to be some rare downtime at the hotel, she agreed to give a quick interview to a reporter from *People*. The interview started as a generic interview. She talked about the album and tour and showered praise on her bandmates.

Then the reporter uncorked a question Danielle hadn't prepared herself for.

"Despite all of your success, some in the media have criticized you for not exploiting your sexuality more. Is downplaying your obvious sex appeal something that you've done on purpose?"

Danielle's mind immediately drifted back to Brooke. She thought of the pressure that she herself had been under and that so many girls such as Brooke had succumbed to. She felt that she had a chance to make an impact on people's lives, and she went for it.

"My experiences with sex haven't been real positive. My mom spent her life throwing herself at every man in town because she thought sex and love were the same thing. My best friend growing up, sex ruined her life. On TV, they try to make it seem like this great experience, this beautiful moment. My best friend lost her virginity in a parking lot. So I came to realize that sex wasn't something to be taken lightly, and I made a promise to myself to make it mean something in my life."

The reporter seemed shocked, but she covered quickly. "Are you saying that you're still a virgin?"

"Yes, I am," Danielle answered defiantly. "And I'm not the least bit ashamed of it." Then she laughed. "Why are you so shocked? What does that say about me?"

The reporter was now beet red. She backtracked. "Nothing. It's just unusual. Rock music and sex are so connected."

"That's sad that it is such a surprise. I'm only twenty-two. You see what I mean? The media in our society has made sex too much of an issue."

The reporter regained her composure, and Danielle gave her a reassuring pat on the knee to let her know that it was okay. "Did you take some sort of vow? Are you waiting for marriage?"

Danielle shrugged. "I guess I'm just waiting to reach a point where I'm not afraid. I thought that I was there once, but it didn't work out. It's not a religious thing. I just don't want to be used. I want to know that whoever I'm with is there for me, all of me, and that I'm not some sort of conquest."

Once the interview was over, Steve rushed up to her. He had been sitting off to the side monitoring the conversation. He was as white as a ghost. "Do you know what you've just done?"

"I just sent a message to millions of girls that it's okay to wait and to not give in to pressure. It's a good thing."

"Yes," Steve agreed, but his mind was obviously running a hundred miles per hour. "You also just painted a huge bullseye on your chest. Do you know what's going to happen when that magazine hits the newsstands? You're going to be in everyone's sights. You've always complained that people focus more on your looks than your music. Now it's going to be ten times worse. The tabloids, the late night talk show hosts, you're going to be their number one target. Your every move is going to be watched and analyzed. Rumors are going to follow you around and people are going to be quick to jump on them. You're never going to have a moment's peace."

"Maybe so, but what should I do? How many young, impressionable girls are going to hear about this and feel that they've got an ally out there? Maybe these girls just need to know that they're not alone, that even celebrities like me feel that pressure, and if I can handle it, maybe it will help them handle it. If I can help make a positive change in someone's life, isn't that more important than all of this?"

Steve could only chuckle at his hard headed star. "You are a hell of a person, Dani. Life is never boring in your orbit. If you're sure about this, though, we might as well get out in front of it. Try to control the message some. Do some PSAs, some speaking engagements, stuff like that."

Danielle stood and wrapped her long arms around Steve's neck and pulled him in close to her. She locked her eyes on his. "My whole life has been a fight. This time I'm picking the battlefield, that's all. Just as long as I know that you've got my back, then I will be fine."

Steve hugged her tightly. "I've got your back and both sides."

The press tour ended before the magazine hit the street, but Danielle was already feeling the pressure she had put upon herself. Upon returning to Austin, Dirk met her and they went out for a night on the town. She took him to her favorite Mexican restaurant, and then they spent the rest of the night bar hopping on Sixth Street.

Dirk, bolstered by a night of heavy drinking, convinced Danielle to take him back to her apartment. He had his hands all over her before they could even get in the door. Once Danielle managed to get them inside, Dirk slammed the door shut and ripped his shirt off.

Danielle was going to protest, but he grabbed the back of her head and pulled her in for a fierce kiss.

Although he was rough, Danielle loved the passion that flowed out of him and into her. It was that type of passion that Danielle felt was missing in her life. She felt it when she played guitar, but she lived the rest of her life in a kind of limbo. She was too determined to pull back but too afraid to push too far. Dirk feared nothing and he was always up for whatever was next. She wished that she could be like that.

That passion was threatening to consume her now. He was working the buttons on her blouse, and she knew that if he succeeded in getting them off, she probably wouldn't be able to slow things down and she might not want to. As Dirk's hands explored her, Danielle's mind raced. Could she indulge the desire she was feeling and keep people from finding out?

The blouse came off, the thin fabric tearing in his hands. The passion was so intense now that his every movement bordered on violence. He pushed her down on the couch and pinned her there.

Was this really the way she wanted it? She thought about Colin and their near miss. He had been tender and loving. He had wanted to make love to her. What did Dirk want?

Now with Dirk pushing her down and pinning her, Danielle's control issues flared. She had been fighting hard to maintain some sort of control in this relationship. Now it was as tattered as the blouse that was lying on the floor.

She put her hands flat against his rock hard chest and pushed him up. She could barely breathe. "Wait a minute," she gasped. "Slow down."

Instead, he pushed back down. He buried his face in her neck and continued the seduction. "I can't slow down. You're so fucking hot. I have to have you right now."

"Dirk, hang on." She was nearing panic mode now. She felt like she was drowning. "Wait," she half yelled.

"I am waiting," he said breathlessly between kisses. "We should be in bed right now."

She began trying to inch towards the edge of the couch. She was desperate to get some sort of separation, but his arms still held her in a vice grip. Dirk's passion had passed from pleasurable to frightening.

"Come on, get off," she said. Again she tried to push him up. "Get off," she said, more forcefully this time.

Dirk finally lifted up. His breathing was ragged and his nostrils were flaring. "What is your deal? Why can't you just go along for the ride?"

"Because this isn't fun, Dirk. You're going way too fast."

He ran one meaty hand through her hair. "Just relax, I know what I'm doing. Just lay back and let me do all the work." He leaned back in for more, but she stopped him.

"That's not all of it. In a couple of days an interview that I gave is going to come out. One where I talk about not rushing into things and how I'm proud to still be a virgin. What happens if it comes out that I didn't even make it to publication?"

He pushed past her outstretched arms and nuzzled up to her. He whispered in her ear. "No one needs to know."

She continued to wiggle under his grasp. "Somebody will find out. Somebody always does. You'll tell one of your teammates, who will tell his wife and on and on. Then I'll look like a hypocrite to the whole world."

Dirk forced himself back up on his elbows. "So let me get this straight. You won't have sex with me because you don't want to look like a hypocrite? That's lame, Danielle. That's really lame."

She finally slid out from under him and sat up with her back against the arm of the couch. "That's not the only reason. You're just so aggressive. I love the way you just charge ahead in everything that you do, but I'm not like that. You just sweep me along and I have absolutely no control. Sometimes I wonder if you're even interested in me, or if it's just the sex."

The anger was boiling inside him now. "Danielle, if I wanted sex, I could get that whenever I wanted it. I've been holding out for you for weeks. I'm getting tired of waiting."

She looked him square in the eye and for the first time, he backed down from her. "Am I not worth waiting for?"

"That's not fair," he answered, looking down at the floor. "There's no way I can answer that question."

"Sure there is. Just tell me the truth. I'm a big girl, I can take it."

"Yes, you are." There was defeat in his voice. "But how long do you expect me to wait? It's been weeks."

"I've waited twenty-two years."

"It's not the same thing," he shot back. He was making fists with his hands, wadding up the fabric of the couch. "You don't know what you're missing."

Danielle shook her head in disbelief. She was thinking about Brooke again. "It can't be *that* good. I just don't believe it."

"It's better than good." His voice went soft and he edged across the couch towards her. He took her arm in his hand. "I could show you. It's the best thing ever. It's so beautiful, the closest you will ever get to heaven. Have you ever...?" He didn't finish the thought. The softness in his voice vanished and the rage came back into his eyes. "Of course not. This is you."

Danielle yanked her arm out of his slack grip. "What's that supposed to mean? Have I ever what?"

"Have you ever been completely outside of yourself? Like an out of body experience, where nothing else seems to exist?"

"I do know what that feels like. I feel that onstage sometimes."

Dirk saw an opening. He came near again. "It's like that, only from the inside out. I could do things to you—"

"I'm sure you could," Danielle interrupted. "But this isn't a good time. I'm about to go out on tour. We're barely going to see each other."

"Then we should do it before you leave." He sounded excited now, like a kid ready to go to Disneyland. "If we don't, it'll be too late. We'll be in training camp before you get back."

"There you go again," she responded. She pushed off the couch to get away from him. She walked to the sliding glass door that led to her balcony, then turned. "I don't want to 'do it.' I want it to mean something. You treat everything like a race."

Dirk swung his legs off the couch. "You do that to me. You make me crazy. I can't control myself when I'm around you."

"Well, I need you to find a way. I understand that it's hard. You make it hard on me too. Sometimes, I literally hurt. But once that article comes out, everybody is going to be watching me. I have to be careful."

Dirk was clearly disgusted. "You're more concerned with your image than anything else. You're just a goddamn tease."

"I'm not a tease," she screamed back at him.

"Yeah, you are." He got up and began stomping towards the door. "You always do this to me."

"God, you sound like a pouting child. Have you ever wondered why I'm so scared? Have you ever thought that I have reasons? No, you don't. Because at the end of the day, you don't care. All you want to do is get off."

He was at the door, but he stopped and turned. The hate on his face sent fear racing through her. If he decided that he wanted to take it, there was nothing she could do to stop him. She backed up a step."

"You're just a prude."

Danielle was afraid, but her pride was also hurt and she wouldn't back down from him. "You don't know shit about me, Dirk. You never cared to know. All I am, all I have ever been to you, is a challenge. I'm a fucking conquest."

"Some conquest," he snapped back.

"Well, don't let me keep you. If you want some that bad, I'm sure that you'll have no problem finding someone to give it up."

"You're right, I won't. Thanks for wasting my time. Fucking prude." He yanked the door open and slammed it shut behind him.

She watched the door to see if he came back, but after a few minutes she knew that he wasn't. She was an emotional wreck. She was angry and frustrated. Danielle began to tremble as she became fully aware of just how scared she had been, and was angry at herself for letting him scare her. Worst of all, she felt impotent in her anger, unable to find a way to process it.

She walked slowly to the bedroom. Ole Red sat waiting on his stand as always, ready to be her shoulder to cry on. She wrapped her hand around the neck and raised it up off its stand. She could see Kel, sitting in his recliner, scolding her for letting him get to her. Tears began to roll down her cheeks and she couldn't stop them. She didn't want to cry over him. She didn't want to admit that he had gotten to her that easily.

Then the anger overcame her sadness. She took Ole Red's neck in both hands and viciously swung it, screaming out in pain as she did, and brought it crashing to the floor. The neck shattered in her hands and the body broke away, only the strings keeping the guitar together. She held her hands up, watching the body swing from the stubborn strings, then she tossed the whole busted contraption aside. Kel would be pissed if he could see her, but what else was new? Every man in her life shit on her eventually.

#

"This guitar is beyond hope, Dani. What the hell did you do to it?" Ty was kneeling over the remains of Ole Red on Danielle's bedroom floor. "You've had this guitar for as long as I've known you. Why did you do this?"

Danielle sat cold and emotionless on the edge of her bed. She was studying the dozens of tiny scrapes and cuts her hands and arms had suffered on account of snapping strings and splintering wood. "I was tired of that old guitar. I want a new one."

"I would have bought him from you. Jesus, even the body is cracked up. Did you hit somebody with it?"

She glared at him, wishing now that she hadn't called him over. "I should have."

"Oh," Ty muttered. "He finally got to you, didn't he? We were wondering how long it was going to take."

"Who's we?"

"Everybody," Ty answered. "We've known all along that he was bad news. He was a major dick and he didn't deserve you. Honestly, no one even knows what the hell you saw in the guy."

"He didn't deserve me," she whispered. Her eyes drifted away from Ty as she replayed the entire affair over in her mind. Then she snapped back to the present. "Who does deserve me? You?"

Ty shot her a nasty look as he scooped up the broken pieces of what used to be Ole Red. "No, Dani. I've known for a long time that you don't look at me like that."

"Yeah, you're right. I don't. And I never will."

Ty stood up. "You're being such a bitch. I think you spent too much time around that asshole."

Danielle shot up off the bed and stuck a warning finger in Ty's face. "Don't you talk to me like that. I'll kick your ass out of this band so fast. Don't forget who the star of this show is."

Ty swatted her finger away. "You keep talking to me like that and I'll save you the trouble. Don't forget that it was you who came asking me for help when your old band got fed up with you. When those other guys left you high and dry I had your back, and this is how you treat me? You can shove it up your ass."

He turned to leave, Ole Red's corpse still in his arms. In her heart, Danielle knew that he was right. She was being awful to Ty, who had come at her request. She just couldn't bring herself to say it.

She watched him walk through the living room and to the front door. "Hey," she called out. He turned, still glaring at her. He waited impatiently for her. In that moment, Danielle could think of a million things she wanted to say. Yet she just stood there, watching him, until he finally lost patience and left. In the end, her silence spoke loudest.

#

Danielle's virginity declaration took what was supposed to be a small inside story and turned it into a cover story for *People*. The magazine came out just days before Danielle's tour started in Orlando, Florida. Just as Steve had predicted, it hit with the force of a nuclear bomb. Reporters mobbed the hotel where they were staying. Steve was forced to add extra security. The TV talk shows went nuts. Some were understandably crude, but others were actively supportive. A huge throng of fans formed in the hotel parking lot. Many of them were young girls who held up huge signs of thanks and encouragement.

Danielle sat by the window inside her room and stared down at the crowd. She knew that she should be pleased. Her words had made an impact and there was actually more support than she had anticipated. But she couldn't feel good about herself in any way. Ty still refused to talk to her. In fact, he would barely even acknowledge her. The rest of the band followed suit. Even Steve was keeping his distance.

She kept a tight lid on her emotions because she knew that if she didn't they would explode. Her every moment seemed to be an internal war. One moment she wanted to scream and hit things, the next she wanted to cry for days. The one overriding thought she had though, was that she had to be tough, she had to keep it together. She had to be in control. With Dirk, she had allowed herself to surrender that control and it had nearly cost her dearly.

Steve knocked on the door timidly, and when she opened it, he scooted past her quickly. He was careful not to look her in the eye. She hated that she had put everyone around her on eggshells. Steve carried a guitar case, which he gently laid on the bed.

"The media attention is crazy," he said as he fumbled with the latches on the case. "But you'll be glad to know that lots of people are in your corner." She pushed the door to her room closed easily and walked to the edge of the bed and sat down.

"That's good," she said flatly.

"Yeah," Steve answered just as flatly. "The whole tour has sold out. Requests for media credentials are through the roof. There are tons of interview requests, but I'm rejecting those until you're ready to talk again."

"Thanks," she said. She wanted to say more, to tell him what a great manager he was, but she couldn't force the words out of her mouth. After a few uncomfortable seconds of silence, he moved on, tapping the guitar case.

"Your friends at Fender finally came through. They sent this over earlier. They're ready to offer an endorsement deal. I'm looking over the contract now and I'll bring it to you when you're ready."

He finished popping the latches and lifted the lid. Inside, a brand new, sunburst Stratocaster waited for her. She ran her fingers gently over the guitar, admiring its beauty before she finally picked it up. It was lighter than Ole Red and the strings were lighter and smoother, but that was an easy change. They had included a custom guitar strap with her name in silver letters. That wasn't her style, but she'd use it tonight at least. It was a beautiful guitar, but it didn't feel the same. Ole Red had seemed to radiate power; this one didn't.

She slipped it over her head and played it for a moment. "It's beautiful. I'll have to send them a thank you note."

"Taken care of," Steve said confidently. He seemed to be relaxing some. "I'll bring the contract by later if you think you'll want to sign it."

What was he talking about? Of course she would want to sign it. She had wanted Fender since the beginning. The realization was setting in about how bad she was being. She just didn't feel like herself anymore and she hated it.

The drive to the Orlando Arena for the first concert was insane. Traffic crept along and fans and reporters alike walked along both sides of the street, taking pictures and holding up signs. Danielle stayed as far away from the windows as possible. Luckily, there was a secured entrance to the arena, so she didn't have to walk through the horde.

In the hours before the show began, she gave short interviews to local TV and radio only, avoiding the national media. Steve came in to remind her that VH1 was on hand to broadcast her first two songs live, a detail she had forgotten about.

She longed to get back onstage. She hoped that she could put everything behind her then. As show time loomed, the rest of the band congregated together. They were loose and ready to go, joking around with each other, until she walked in the room. The new girl, Trish, seemed intent on staying completely out of sight, and stuck close to Ty.

Finally, it was time. By the time the band began taking the stage, the crowd was roaring. Usually, this was when the adrenaline really began to run, but it wasn't working tonight. She almost dreaded it as each step brought her closer to the stage.

She took her new guitar onstage, original strings and all, and took her place. Over the PA system, the sound of a tornado siren cut through the crowd, and a moment later, Garrett began pounding out a beat on the bass drum. Danielle's fingers automatically found the opening chords to her first song, and as Garret began hitting the snare, she launched into her intro, the lights came up, and the crowd exploded. The roar nearly knocked her off her feet. It should have felt good. It didn't.

Everything was going like clockwork until Danielle launched into her solo on the second song, "You're My Weakness." The song reminded her of Dirk, and she attacked the solo with unusual vigor. She ravaged the neck of the guitar, attacking the strings, bending them violently as the storm of the emotions bottled up inside of her came pouring out through her music. The VH1 cameras were capturing every moment, beaming it to millions of viewers as Danielle officially claimed her spot among the elite guitarists of all time. The solo was almost over when she went for one last bend.

It was too much. The thin strings couldn't take the pressure and one snapped, recoiling with terrible force. Danielle felt the broken string arc across her cheek and for a split second, she remembered her mother slapping her with a broken record. Instantly blood began flowing from the gash. The anger rose again. In one fluid motion, she lifted the guitar over her head and tossed it aside, sending it skidding off the stage. Just off stage to her left Ty had three guitars waiting on a rack, each one tuned for a specific song. She stormed over and yanked a black Les Paul off the rack, slipped the strap over her head, and picked up right where she'd left off, launching into yet another solo while blood poured out of the cut on her cheek. The band had been teetering on the verge of stopping, but now they started back up and finished strong.

The rest of the night, she played the black Les Paul and bled. She refused to stop or even slow down. There was little audience interaction, no prancing around or showboating. Her playing was so aggressive that her fingers were beginning to bleed by the end of the night.

As the band rolled out the next morning for their next show, Steve read a review from the *Orlando Sentinel* that described her performance as savage and brutal. "She blew through Orlando like a hurricane, shredding every song and eardrum in her path. She was passionate to the point it bordered on madness. She was unwavering and unrepentant, tossing aside simple distractions such as broken strings and bloody cuts like they were gnats. Her performance perfectly echoes the mood of her new album, dark and dangerous. This is a performer who has just begun to hit her stride...."

That night in Gainesville, Danielle arrived at the arena to find that Steve and the crew had raided every pawn shop in town and bought an army of guitars, then labeled each one with giant stickers that read Handle With Care. Everyone thought it was funny, even Danielle. She just couldn't bring herself to laugh.

The incident had a backlash, though. Fender withdrew their endorsement deal. The suits had not been pleased at her treatment of their gift. She sent the guitar back in response.

The tour rolled through the Atlantic seaboard and back across the upper Midwest. The reviews continued to be positive and the album continued to sell, dominating the charts. In East Rutherford,

New Jersey, Danielle added a twist. She began performing a new song written in solitude called "I Walk Alone." She played it solo, on a darkened stage, and the pain and isolation in her words were apparent to everyone.

The media continued to focus their attention on her sexuality, only now it was becoming antagonistic. Dirk had gone public, repeating his accusations that she was a tease. She was the daily butt of jokes on drive time radio, and the National Organization of Women condemned her proclamation as "a dangerous step backwards in the evolution of women."

Just as Steve predicted, fans showed up at every show with signs offering their services to her. Crazed fans were ejected by security on a constant basis, and a parade of famous men started sniffing around, all wanting to meet her.

Through it all, though, the fan mail poured in. It became the only enjoyable part of her day. Parents and kids, Christian organizations, and parents groups all applauded and defended her. She tried to respond to them all, especially the kids.

There was no break in the tour for the holidays so the band spent Thanksgiving together in a hotel in Indianapolis. Steve rented out one of the conference rooms and had a special dinner catered. Danielle, though, had so alienated herself that she spent Thanksgiving in her room eating pizza. The chasm seemed enormous.

They spent Christmas in Denver. Again, Steve rented a room and threw a lavish party. He bought everyone leather jackets and claimed Danielle had picked them out, but everyone knew better. Again, she didn't make an appearance.

Instead, she sat in her room in the dark with the blinds open. She stared off at the peaks of the Rockies and wondered what was wrong with her. She no longer felt anger or sadness. She only felt emptiness.

When a knock sounded on her door, she made her way slowly to answer it. Trish was standing on the other side, wearing a long green and red dress and with her hair pulled back. She stood there, clearly nervous, with her hands behind her back.

"What?" Danielle asked. It sounded more harsh than she had intended.

Trish fumbled for a moment. "I…just wanted to come wish you a Merry Christmas. I just can't stand the thought of anybody being alone at Christmas."

"Thank you for the thought."

Trish pulled her hands out from behind her back. "I brought you some pie from the party. It's pecan. I don't know if you like it."

Danielle took the slice of pie, which was on a Styrofoam plate and covered in Saran Wrap. She had barely spoken to the girl since the day she'd hired her, yet Trish was completely terrified of her. The realization of just how far she was pushing everyone away hit her then. She looked again at the girl; barely out of high school and here she was, hundreds of miles from home on Christmas and shaking like a beaten dog.

Danielle stepped aside. "Would you mind coming in for a minute?"

Trish seemed both relieved and horrified at the same time, but she did come in and stood just inside the door with her hands clasped in front of her. "I just want to tell you," Trish said cautiously. "That I appreciate what you said in your interview. It took a lot of guts to come out like that. I know it couldn't have been easy."

Danielle shrugged. "It was just the truth."

"Yes, but it means a lot." Trish walked past Danielle and sat down on her bed. "I was fifteen when I lost my virginity. I was trying to prove my love for him. Then he went and told all his friends at school that I was easy. I spent the rest of my high school years trying to keep the guys off me. I gave up trying to date my senior year because every guy I went out with thought he was going to get lucky. It was the biggest mistake of my life and I've always wished I could do it over. So if some other fifteen-year-old has the courage to say no, then you've done a great thing."

Danielle stood near the window and peeled the Saran Wrap off the pie. "Thanks," she said, and then took a bite.

"Do you regret it?" Trish asked.

Danielle thought about it for a moment, then shrugged. "Sometimes, maybe. I don't know. It's not one of my biggest regrets. Still, I've done something I can't take back. I can't put the genie back in the box, you know? Nothing will ever be the same. I wonder sometimes if I screwed up."

"Um," Trish answered. "Because everybody says that you haven't been the same since."

Danielle took another bite. "It's not that. Believe me, it has nothing to do with that."

"Oh. Well is it me? I know that I'm the new guy and all. If I'm screwing things up in some way, I could leave. I don't want to be a problem."

"Jesus, no. It's not you. I love what you bring to the band. So don't worry about that, okay?"

Trish nodded her head. "Well, I guess I'll go now. Merry Christmas, Ms. Regan." She started for the door and Danielle watched her go. Just as she was about to leave the room, Danielle blurted out.

"I feel like a prisoner."

Trish, one foot out the door, stopped and looked back over her shoulder. "What?"

Danielle had no idea what made her say it, but now the gate was opened, she couldn't stop it. "I feel like I'm trapped within myself. I want to cry, I want to scream, but I can't. It's like something is locked up inside me. I hate it. I hate that you've been with us for months and I barely know you, have hardly even talked to you. I can't stand it that my band hates me and my manager won't talk to me. I can't even enjoy myself on stage anymore. It's like every time I start to feel, something shuts down."

"When did it start?" Trish asked as she closed the door.

Danielle took a deep breath and walked over to her bed, put the pie down on the nightstand, and sat on the bed with her back against the headboard. "I got very angry when Dirk and I broke up. I think that I was mad at myself more than anything. I took it out on Ty, and since then, I just haven't felt normal."

"Did he do something to you?"

Danielle smirked. "Yeah, he did things to me, all right. Things that nobody else has done to me. Not necessarily in a bad way. I felt things with him. But the whole time I was with him, my mind and heart kept telling me that he was all wrong and that I should cut the guy loose, but I couldn't."

"Did you have sex with him?" she asked, but Danielle could tell by the sound of her voice that she was afraid of the answer.

"No. But it wasn't for lack of wanting to, or the lack of him trying. I had to make myself hold back, because I knew it would be wrong. He wasn't the right one."

Trish was clearly relieved. "It seems to me that you've been holding back for a long time. Maybe that's the problem…you can't decide what you hold back anymore. You're holding on too tight."

Danielle sighed. "Maybe you're right. But what do I do about it? Now I'm all out there with that stupid interview I gave. Everyone's watching me. I can't get away with anything."

"If you don't mind my saying so, I think you should just relax and trust in the people around you. Everybody down there loves you and they would protect you. They don't like seeing you like this. You don't have to be so tough all of the time."

Danielle looked at the girl in the pale moonlight that poured in through the window and envied her. She was still so innocent in so many ways. Sometimes, Danielle felt so much older than she really was. She wondered if she had ever been so innocent.

"You know," Trish continued. "I used to go watch you a lot. I was so jealous because you were up there, having fun and making a living playing music. I wanted to be like you. Now when I watch you, you're not having fun. I think anyone who doesn't have fun doing this is missing out."

"Yeah, I know," Danielle said. She was surprised that she didn't get angry. With anyone else she probably would have been. "But how do I let go? I've been holding myself together so long, I don't know how."

"I don't know, but a good place to start might be to go downstairs and hang out with your friends."

It was impossible not to notice the change in the atmosphere when Danielle entered the party. It was obvious that everyone was on eggshells. She wanted to bolt, but Trish held on to her firmly. The girl was stronger than she looked.

Steve was the first to approach her. He offered her a Coke, which she gladly took and immediately chugged. Trish looked at her curiously. "Some people drink coffee, some smoke. I drink Coke."

"Okay," Trish responded and guided her deeper into the room. Danielle saw where she was being taken. Ty sat at a long table with the rest of the band, eyeing Danielle suspiciously. She knew what she had to do, and pulled away from Trish's grasp.

"Hey guys, mind if I sit?" Everyone moved over and Danielle took a seat. "Look, I know that I've been a bitch. I've got some issues, but they're mine and I've been taking it out on you guys, and I'm sorry. You've always done right by me and I've screwed you guys over. I'm not looking for you to forgive me; just know that I am aware of how I've been and that I'm sorry about it."

She stood and pushed away from the table.

Ty spoke first. "Everybody has the right to be a bitch sometimes. The key is whether or not you're a big enough person to admit to it when you are."

Danielle smiled at him, and realized that she couldn't remember the last time she had smiled. "Well, they're gonna have to invent a new word for what I've been, because bitch just won't cut it."

"That's the damn truth," DeShon agreed. "But you have humbled yourself at our feet, so you may rise and go forth, my child." He even went so far as to make the sign of the cross in the air like a real priest. "Say five Hail Marys and ten I'll Never Do It Agains and we will be square."

"Well, thank you, Your Holiness. I'm assuming you were an altar boy when you were a kid."

"Yeah, that's me," he answered with a big, toothy grin. "I was Gangsta Catholic. Actually, I just liked the robes and the 'special time' with the priests."

Ty punched her on the arm. "See, we're cool. You've just gotta relax. You're way too intense sometimes."

"And to come to us for approval before you starting dating again. That guy was a royal asshole," Garrett added.

"That guy was a jerk," Trish agreed as she sat down next to Ty. "You know, he once asked me if I would go down on him while you were in the bathroom? He told me that I could find out how stardom tasted."

"Why didn't you tell me that? I would have kicked his ass."

"Because I didn't want you to get mad at me and fire me. So I just turned and walked away. You haven't exactly been the most approachable person."

"Jesus. I have been a bitch. Was Dirk really that bad?"

Garrett rolled his eyes. "Dude was always walking around like Billy Badass. 'I play hockey. I make millions. Look at me.' Honestly, none of us could believe that you didn't see through him."

Danielle looked at the faces of her bandmates, her friends, her family, and smiled. "Well, he's old news now. So let's say that we put this whole thing behind us and get back to business."

Danielle and Reckless Passions rang in 1998 in Salt Lake City, and she took special time during the show to thank the band for their support. She also addressed for the first time her very public virginity. She implored everyone to do what their hearts and minds told them to and not be bullied or pressured. She used the speech as a segue into her song "Shamed Into Love," which was based upon Brooke's attempt to find love through pregnancy. She got a standing ovation.

In L.A. a few days later, Generation Records threw a party for the band to celebrate *Cathouse* going platinum. It was a swanky affair with plenty of Hollywood stars. Among them were Adam and his new girlfriend, a Brazilian swimsuit model. Although he steered clear of Danielle, Hollywood gossip reporters wrote that the two kept constant watch on each other during the night.

Danielle got a huge reception as the band cut across the Bible Belt and the Deep South. Then it was back home to Texas, where the band would wrap up the tour with a special "Texas Edition," which featured a revised set list and longer performances.

By the spring of 1998, the band had exhausted themselves on the road. They turned down an opportunity to tour Australia and voted unanimously to take some needed time off instead.

The success of *Cathouse* had also driven up sales of the first two albums. For the first time, Danielle had substantial money coming in. She decided that she had outgrown her little apartment in South Austin and began looking for a real home. However, when she couldn't find one that suited her, she decided to build one, and she knew just the place.

1998 was also the end of the line for her little Camaro, which was impossible to keep running. With money in the bank, she found a new ride. This one was a fully restored, 1968 Camaro SS convertible, black with silver pinstripes. She dubbed the car "Black Beauty," and it became the true love of her life.

While the rest of the group disbanded, Danielle continued to work. She began speaking to many youth and Christian groups and took an active role in local charities. She quickly became a highly sought after speaker.

To help finance the construction of Danielle's house, Steve managed to land her endorsement deals with Coke and Levis, and even convinced Fender to give her another chance. In very short order, he was making Danielle a wealthy woman.

Then one morning Steve called her and she knew instantly that something was up. He was evasive until Danielle finally got upset and ordered him to tell her what was wrong. The news left Danielle's emotions in a tailspin. Adam was back in town, and he wanted to see her.

CHAPTER EIGHT

Danielle agreed to meet Adam at a neutral site, a coffee shop just off of Lamar Street not far from downtown. She planned to arrive first, but he had already grabbed a table by the window. He was in a clean phase, freshly shaven with short hair…a good look for him. Then again, she thought any look was good for him.

She sat down across from him and he pushed a tall Styrofoam cup over to her. "You know that I don't drink coffee," she scolded.

He gave her his five hundred megawatt matinee idol smile. "Try it, you'll like it. It's more like hot chocolate than coffee."

Danielle was appalled. "It's a hundred and two outside. Why in the hell would I want to drink hot chocolate?"

Adam shook his head and laughed. "Same old Dani. You are simply not capable of rolling with it."

"When people ask me to 'roll with it,' they usually have other things in mind."

"I just wanted some coffee. Is that so wrong?"

She rolled her eyes but took a sip anyway. It did taste a lot like hot chocolate, which might have been good if it wasn't so hot outside. "It's okay," she answered politely. "Now why am I here?"

Adam leaned over the table and smiled at her. "Because you can't resist my call."

"Oh, please."

"Okay, so maybe that's not it," he said, and leaned back in his chair. "I wanted to see you, because I have a proposition."

"I'm not that kind of girl," she smirked.

"Very funny. I'm serious about this. I'm making a new movie and this one is very close to my heart. I'm not just starring in it, I also wrote it and I'm directing it."

"Good for you," she responded. "I remember when all you wanted to do was make movies, not star in them."

"I know," he said with a touch of sadness in his voice. It passed quickly. "I'm trying to get back to that. So I want you to be my co-star."

"What?" Danielle half laughed, half yelled. Everyone else turned to look at them, and immediately tourists started reaching for cameras. Danielle rolled her eyes and looked back at Adam. "I'm not an actor. You know that."

"You could be, if you ever tried. I've seen your videos and interviews. The camera loves you, just like I knew it did back then. You wouldn't even have to stretch. The character that you'd be playing is basically you."

"What do you mean by that?"

Adam again leaned in closer and lowered his voice. "I wrote this movie about us. The character I want you to play has been scarred by a troubled past and she has a hard time letting go of the pain. I play a free spirit who's never really been in love. We meet on vacation in a sleepy California coastal town and have a brief romance before our lives take us in separate directions, and we both learn valuable lessons about ourselves. I call it 'Marina Del Rey' after the George Strait song."

"Never heard it."

Adam was appalled. "You've never heard 'Marina Del Rey'? What rock have you been living under? How could you have never heard that song?"

"I don't listen to country. You know that."

"You should start. There's a lot of good country out there. I tell you what, I'll bring you a CD. Give it a listen and see what you think."

"Adam, I'm not going to make a movie with you. I appreciate the offer, really. But I think you need a professional for this. I'm not an actress."

Adam couldn't hide the disappointment on his face. "Are you sure? I believe that you can do it. All you have to do is let go...." He trailed off and they locked eyes. "Okay, so maybe you can't. But you have to admit that we have chemistry. The most important thing in a romantic movie is the chemistry. I could help you through the rest."

"Chemistry? Is that what they're calling it these days?" Then she patted Adam on the arm. "I'm serious though. I'm not cut out for acting."

She stood up to leave, but he grabbed her wrist. They hadn't touched in so long, but in an instant she knew that all the old feelings were still there. "Wait. Sit. Please." She eased back into her chair. "If you won't be in the movie with me, would you at least do a couple of songs for the movie? I really want you to be a part of this."

Danielle took a long look into his eyes and relived in the space of a breath every moment of their lives together, both good and bad. "I'm sure I could do that for you. We're on a break right now. How many do you want?"

Adam instantly cheered up. "Great. Tell you what, let me run a copy of the script over, and that CD I was telling you about. Give it a read and a listen, and just do whatever you're inspired to do. I'll be around for a while, so we can stay in touch."

Danielle was curious. "How do you mean, 'be around'? Like living down here?"

"Yeah. I bought a place outside of San Marcos. A converted ranch in this grove of oak trees. It's a beautiful place. Very spacious."

"So you're leaving L.A.?" Her heart started beating faster in her chest.

"Not totally," he said. "I mean, I make movies. I have to stay connected, maintain a presence. But I do want a place to get away. When I first thought about it, I came down here to buy that land. You remember the land out by Lake Travis that I took you to?"

Danielle nodded and bit her lip. "Uh huh. I really liked that place."

"Yeah, me too. Unfortunately, someone else bought it. Anyway, I found that place out west of San Marcos. It's almost perfect, close enough to the action but far enough away to have some privacy. How about you? Where are you living now?"

She smiled sadly. "I'm still at the same little apartment off of Riverside."

"You're still living there? Shouldn't someone like you being living in a bigger place? A safer place with better security?"

"I will soon. I'm having a place built. I actually can't wait to move in."

"Really? That's great Dani. It's time you move up some, reap some of the benefits of your success. Where's it at?"

Danielle licked her lips and looked away to try and hide her smile. Adam caught on quickly.

"That's your place they're building out there? On my land?"

"No. On *my* land. I got it first."

Adam was genuinely angry. "I was going to build our dream house out there."

"For who? You and that Brazilian bimbo you've been strutting around with?"

"I can't believe you stole my land. I found that land. You wouldn't have known about it if I hadn't taken you out there."

"Well you did, so tough luck. You know what they say. All's fair in love and real estate."

Adam recovered quickly. "So you got the land. How's the love part treating you?"

Danielle couldn't tell if it was intended as a shot, but she wasn't going to let him get to her. "That's nonya."

"What the hell is nonya?"

"Nonya business," she said with a smile. "I'll be waiting on that script." She stood and headed for the door.

"You didn't drink your coffee," he called out to her.

She turned around just before she walked out the door. "You drink it. You need it more than I do."

Adam brought the script and the CD by like he'd promised, but Danielle pretended to be gone so he left it at the door. That night, she put on the CD and began reading. The movie was a total departure for Adam, who had made his name as an action star. This one was an old fashioned romance, and Danielle had serious doubts about how audiences would accept him in such a role.

On the other hand, she did agree that the main characters bore a remarkable resemblance to Adam and herself and the George Strait song it was named after fit the movie well. Reading the script, she had all kinds of ideas in her head, and not all of them involved writing songs.

The next day she paid Steve a visit in the offices of Reckless Roads Inc., the management company he and Danielle had started to manage the band's business. Gone was the seedy SoCo location. They were now in one of the new high rises going up all over downtown Austin.

Steve's receptionist showed Danielle into his office. He sat in a leather business chair, looking down on the sprawling downtown scene. He turned when Danielle came in, a huge smile on his face. "I told you that I'd get you here, didn't I?"

Danielle laughed. "You did everything you told me you would do. We're a long way from Randy's kitchen now."

Steve came out from behind his desk and put his big arm around her. "We're not here because of me. We're here because of you. You believed in me and you are one hell of a fine musician. You got us here." He guided her into the chair on the other side of his desk. "So why are you here?"

"Do you think I'd be a hell of a talented actress?" she asked with a coy smile.

Steve watched her curiously as he took his own seat. "Actress? Where did you get that idea?"

"Adam. That was why he wanted to meet with me. He wrote a movie based on us, and he wants me to play me."

Steve suddenly seemed very uncomfortable. "I honestly don't know about that. Have you ever acted before?"

"I act like I give a crap every time your lips move." Steve flipped her off in response. "No, I haven't," she said through her laughter. "I never even thought about it until I read the script. Now I'm kind of intrigued. I'm thinking about it. I mean, we're not doing anything for a while. It might be fun."

"If you really want to, let me know and I'll make it happen. Personally, I'd stick to writing songs for the damn thing."

"I already told him that I would do that."

Steve sat back and stared at the wall behind her. "Do you think his offer is on the up and up? This could all just be an excuse to get back into your life. He butters you up and figures that you'll fall back into his arms in due time."

Danielle waited for his gaze to drift from the wall back to her. "You think he'd do that? That is a lot of trouble to go to for a girl."

"You're a girl people will go to a lot of trouble for. Besides, right now all he's got is a script. Every two bit hack in Hollywood walks around with a script in his back pocket. Hell, we don't even know for sure that he wrote it. He could have bought it off one of his screenwriter friends."

"Maybe," she said. "It seemed legit though. Besides, aren't I worth the trouble?"

"Yes," he said. "At least until people get to know you."

Danielle was only half shocked by the comment. "That was mean. How dare you speak to your star client that way?"

"I'm sorry, what did you say? I was only acting like I was listening to you."

Danielle shook her head. "You suck. But honestly, what do you think? Check this out." Danielle stood up, scooped up a yellow notepad, and began fanning herself with it. "I do declare," she started in an exaggerated Deep South accent, "That it is hot out here and I think I will go take a swim in the ocean. I hope some studly, misguided loser doesn't stumble upon me out here in the water."

Steve sat forward and was watching her intently. "Dani," he said with all seriousness. "Stick to singing."

Danielle looked at him seriously for a moment, then fell back down in her chair, laughing hysterically. "You're right. I'm no actress, but I do have some ideas for songs. I'll need to get the guys together and get some studio time."

"Most of the guys are gone, but Trish is still around. She's taking summer classes at Southwest Texas. I can give her a call. Do you want me to do some fishing and find out how serious Boy Wonder is about this movie of his?"

"Yeah," Danielle said. "I'm curious. I'll start writing some songs."

"Perfect. You do your thing and I'll do mine."

Danielle worked up some rough versions of several new songs and decided that it was as good an excuse as any to visit Adam at his new ranch house. His home was located on a huge tract of land northwest of San Marcos. The house itself was far off the main road and down in a depression so that it couldn't be seen from the main road. It had a massive, well-watered lawn and a dozen large oak trees providing plenty of shade for the intense summer heat, as well as another layer of camouflage. The house was well lit, with a dozen motion activated spotlights escorting her all the way to the house.

Danielle nervously knocked on the front door. She knew in her heart that she wasn't really there to give him the tape, but she didn't want to be obvious about wanting to see him again. Her nerves kicked up even more when he didn't immediately answer and she had to knock again.

She finally heard the sound of locks being turned and tried to straighten herself out the best she could. The door swung open with Danielle in mid spiffing, and she tried hard to hide it as Adam stepped out. He didn't try to hide the smile on his face when he saw her. Over his shoulder, she could see flickering lights on the wall and she could hear soft music playing inside.

"Well, look who graces my doorstep on this fine summer evening," he said. "Get in here." He opened the door wider and she stepped through. As he pulled the door shut behind her, she turned and held out the tape, trying to keep her hands from shaking.

"These are some demos for the songs I've been working on. I thought you might want to give them a listen and see what you think."

He took them from her quickly. "Sure thing. Although I'm sure that they will be perfect. I trust you."

She glanced at the light flickering on the wall. Candlelight. She wondered if he had seen her coming and thrown this together.

Adam took her gently by the arm. "Come here for a minute, will you?"

"Sure," she answered, letting him lead her out of the living room and into the dining room. There was a short dinner table with two candles burning, two place settings, and one floral centerpiece. Adam's seat was at the head of the table, and just to his right sat a gorgeous Hispanic woman wearing a very tight, very low cut dress, and having plenty of accoutrements to fill it out with. Her black hair was long and free and her dark eyes twinkled in the candlelight. She looked up at Danielle with daggers in those eyes.

"Danielle," Adam started, either not noticing or not caring about the dirty look the Latina shot at her. "This is Adrianna. She's a model. She's from Peru, not Brazil, by the way." He turned to the other woman and said something that Danielle assumed was an introduction.

"I didn't know you spoke Spanish."

"I'm learning," he answered. "Would you like to join us for dinner?"

Danielle didn't need to field another one of those nasty looks from the Peruvian beauty to know the answer to that question. "No, I need to get back. I just wanted your feedback on those songs. I'll let you get back to your dinner."

She slid out of his grip and started quickly for the door. Adam was right behind her. "Danielle, wait."

She stopped and spun quickly, and Adam, who was chasing her, nearly bowled her over.

"What?" she snapped.

"You didn't come out here to give me half-finished versions of your songs."

"Didn't I?" she said coldly.

"You know, all I asked you to do was be in a movie. I never said anything else."

"I never said you did," she shot back.

"Then why are you here?"

She looked deep into his eyes, hoping to find an answer in there somewhere. When she didn't, she just turned and started for the door again. She had it open when he reached over her shoulder and gently pushed it closed. He stood directly behind her and leaned in to whisper in her ear.

"All you ever have to do is say the word and I'll come running. The ball's in your court."

She pushed back on him with her elbow and he let the door go. Danielle hurried outside and quickly found her way back to the road. She wanted to be mad at him for leading her on, but she was really just mad at herself. Still, she couldn't get his last statement out of her head. If she wanted him, would he really come that easily? Did she want him to?

When the rest of the band reconvened at the end of the summer, Danielle had a backlog of songs and was desperate to get back into the studio. Steve shoehorned her into a three day window at Contour

Studios, a small recording studio on the east side of Austin. She originally intended to record a couple of songs for Adam's movie. Instead, she recorded an entire album, each new idea seeming to blossom into a full-fledged song almost instantly. She wasn't sure if he would use everything, but she felt most confident in her first two attempts at a ballad, "The Leap" and "There Comes A Time." On the last day of recording, she and Trish recorded a haunting duet of the song that inspired it all, George Strait's "Marina Del Rey."

She sent the finished tapes to Adam in California, where he was filming, with a brief personal note, then turned her attention on the next Reckless Passions album. She was firing on all cylinders now. She promised the label she'd have them a finished record in six weeks, and she did it in four. Generation was ecstatic, and promised to have the album out quickly.

Danielle could barely contain her excitement over the new album. She gave an in depth interview on an area radio station, where she gave the audience a sneak peek.

"This one's going to sound a lot different," she told him. "There's a lot of ear candy on this one. We experimented a lot more. The theme is a lot like *Cathouse* though. The point being that you can put all the glitz and glamour you want on something, but underneath it all, there's still this darkness. Seedy is seedy. That's why we called it *Stripclub*. That's what strip clubs do. They put all this glass and chrome and lights around, but when you get down to it, it's still seedy, just like some low end dive. It's all in the presentation." She finished the interview by playing a couple of acoustic songs off the new album.

She even got risky when it came time to shoot the video for the first single, "Tremble." She called up Alex Starr, who was still plying her trade as an exotic dancer, to star in the video. Alex was shot doing her best work in as little clothing as possible. Danielle then took the stage, guitar in hand, and replicated many of Alex's moves. When the footage was spliced together, it was by far the sexiest video she had shot. The band and crew played the part of the leering audience.

She was proud of the video, but Generation balked. Danielle's girl next door image had proven to have a powerful pull to a more conservative demographic. The image of America's sweetheart slithering across the stage next to a stripper was a little too much for them. Despite her best efforts, the label wouldn't budge and the video was scrapped.

They shot a new version that featured Alex playing an aggressive bad girl who attempted to seduce a straight arrow while his friends all tried to warn him off. Danielle refused to appear in the reshoot as a protest. It was Alex who smoothed things over, though, when she convinced Danielle that she much preferred the second version, as it gave her a chance to show what she could do with her clothes on.

The album was set for a November release, with a tour to begin in January. To drum up support, the group hit the road for the usual promo appearances. She hadn't done herself any favors with the sexual tone of the album. The public was still infatuated with Danielle's own sexuality, and she spent most of the time answering questions about her continued chastity.

Danielle's new house was done just before Thanksgiving, and to celebrate she threw a party for the entire Reckless Passions organization. Randy and Teri Holder helped her put on a feast of smoked meats and sides for a true Hill Country Thanksgiving. It was everything she could have imagined, the warm and inviting home that she had almost had once, many years ago.

In the mornings, she awoke to the sun rising over Lake Travis and went jogging. Everything was coming together now. She spent her nights working out new songs in her basement recording studio. However, when she wasn't busy, it was hard to ignore how big and empty the house felt when she was alone.

Reckless Passions' 1999 *Stripclub* Tour kicked off on the West Coast in late January. Adam was waiting backstage at the Great Western Forum in L.A, minus his Peruvian girlfriend. He rewarded them for a great show by treating the entire crew to dinner, making lifelong fans in the process.

He used his influence as one of Hollywood's A List to reserve Malibu's exclusive Oenida Steakhouse for the night. Adam never blinked as Danielle's crew devoured an ungodly amount of food and liquor.

While he was distracted entertaining the rest of the group, Danielle tried to slip away unnoticed. She wanted to get back to the hotel and as far away from Adam as she could. Instead, he caught her in the parking lot.

"You never called," he said from behind her.

Danielle glanced once over her shoulder and then away. "Excuse me?"

Adam grabbed her arm gently and turned her around. "I told you that all you had to do was call and I would come running. You never called."

"And I never will," she shot back. "I'm not the type to steal another girl's boyfriend."

He pulled her closer. She could smell his cologne and it brought the old memories flooding back. "It's not stealing if he comes willingly."

"I guess whatever helps you sleep at night. The reality of the situation is a little different, but I guess you've spent so much time out here that you can't tell the difference anymore. Besides, what if we're together and some other woman calls?"

"Wouldn't happen."

"And how am I supposed to believe that? What makes me so special?"

"Love," he answered, drawing her even closer. She hated being so close because all she wanted was to get closer. Every second in his presence was breaking down her walls. She could feel herself being torn in two.

"You wouldn't know anything about love," she growled. "How many women have you been with? You go through women like they're disposable."

"There's a reason for that," he said softly.

"I'm sure there is, Adam. I'm sure you have justified all kinds of reasons. But I'm not disposable."

Adam let go of her arm and instead ran his fingers through her hair. "I never said you were. All those other girls I've gone through aren't you. And I'll tell you something else. I've treated every woman I've been with like a princess. I've never laid a hand on a woman in anger, and I've never cheated on anyone."

"Well, let's just give you a damn Nobel Prize then. You still churn through them. If you're such a great boyfriend, why can't you keep a girl?"

Adam's gaze shifted to somewhere over her shoulder and his grip loosened. She could tell that there was something that he wanted to say at that moment. Then she saw the taxi she had called pull up to the curb.

She quickly pulled away from him. The move jerked him back into reality. "Wait," he called. "Don't go."

Danielle was already stepping into the cab. "I won't be a notch on your bedpost, Adam." He called out again, but she had already closed the door. She forced herself to stare straight ahead and not look back, and prayed that someday, walking away from him wouldn't be so hard.

The tour rolled out of L.A. and across the Southwest. Controversy erupted later as the tour began to work its way up the Eastern Seaboard after the video for the album's second single, "Wrecked," hit the airwaves. The song was easily the hardest song she had done to date and showed yet another side of Danielle's rapidly expanding musical vocabulary.

For the video, she was made up as a Goth princess and chained to two stone pillars in a dark wood. As the video played, villagers tormented her with fire, threw stones at her, and cut her with knives. In the end, the pillars collapsed and she fell to the ground. She weakly looked into the camera to deliver the last line as the villagers were seen closing in for the kill.

The dark mood of the song and the violence of the video stunned many of her fans, but it drew rave reviews from critics who hated her goody two shoes image. However, she got a rash of angry fan mail, which put her in a nasty mood. Those close to her could tell that she was heading for a major meltdown.

The tour pulled into Philadelphia, a notoriously tough town and one Danielle was never particularly fond of. The problems started immediately. Equipment problems kept them from doing their usual sound check. The Philly crowd greeted Danielle with a swarm of crude signs and suggestions. Once the show began, one fan in particular began to taunt her from the foot of the stage. He was hairy and overweight, and kept up a steady verbal assault on her. He was so loud that they could hear him on the tapes of the show later.

She did her best to ignore him, but he was clearly getting to her and he knew it. The Philly crowd began to smell blood in the water and upped the ante. At last, she bent over to the offender and loudly told him to "shut the fuck up." This drew the ire of the crowd, who began to boo and hurl things at the stage. Ty took a battery to the side of the head, and that was the last straw.

Danielle quit playing and stepped to the microphone, where she delivered a profanity laced rant on their behavior. The crowd responded with a shower of beer and hot dogs and whatever else could be thrown toward the stage. The band ran for cover, but Danielle defiantly stood and delivered a double barreled middle finger salute. As she finally left the stage, she took off her guitar and hurled it like a spear at the man who had started it all. The guitar hit the barricade he was standing behind and shattered, causing a swarm of fans to go after the souvenir.

While the band made a quick getaway from the City of Brotherly Love, Steve issued a quick press release to explain the situation. Danielle swore that she would never set foot there again. Soon word spread and amateur video popped up showing the whole incident. Again, Danielle was the target of criticism for her actions. She would later tell a reporter for a Columbus, OH television station, "You have fifteen thousand people throwing D cells at your head and see how polite you are."

Entertainment Weekly ran an article called "Cracking Up?" where the reporter insinuated that Danielle was folding under the pressure to retain her girl next door image. "She opened Pandora's Box, completely unprepared for what would follow. Now she's discovering that she has zero margin for error and she can't handle it. Events that barely would have warranted a mention a year ago are now major infractions, and she is finding out just how hard the life of a willing role model can be."

Steve answered with an editorial in the magazine the next week where he defended Danielle. "The problem," he wrote, "is that Danielle is an artist, and her voice is being stifled because people can't differentiate between Danielle the artist and Danielle the person."

The controversies may have been a source of stress for Danielle, but they were a godsend for the label. The attention attracted by The Virgin Behaving Badly drove album sales through the roof. Surprisingly, *Stripclub* would outsell *Cathouse* and generated a renewed interest in her first two albums. In a matter of weeks, Danielle went from having one platinum album to four, and had solidified her status as one of rock's elite stars.

Not all of the tour stops were as hostile as Philadelphia. In Boise, the crowd was so pleased that she had come back that the show sold out a half an hour after tickets went on sale. Cheering fans lined both sides of the highway as the bus pulled into town. The mayor even presented Danielle the key to the city. Before their performance, the crowd chanted "Dani, Dani" and "Philly Sucks." The band responded with a marathon three hour show that would go down as one of their finest moments.

Everyone was ready to go home, but the label ordered videos for two more songs, "I Walk Alone" and "Fallin' Out of Love Again." So the group boarded the bus for L.A., intent on getting done as quickly as possible. The video for "I Walk Alone" was shot in black and white and played on the Philadelphia incident. One reviewer would later write, "The sadness in Danielle's eyes is no act. Even more so than the song itself, the look in her eyes tells the story of a young woman who's carrying the weight of the world on her shoulders and is weary from the strain."

When the group arrived at the studio to shoot the video for "Fallin' Out of Love Again," Danielle got a surprise. Adam was waiting for her.

"What are you doing here?"

"We've got business to discuss," he said with a smile.

"Then talk to Steve. That's his department." She looked around for him, but he was nowhere to be found.

"I already did, darlin'. This was his idea. He felt that you would be more receptive in a more professional setting. I thought a candle light dinner was more appropriate, but he said something about you roasting my chestnuts, so we agreed on this."

"I'm so glad that you find this funny. You have all the empathy of a flea. What business do we have to discuss?"

"Videos. For the soundtrack to my movie, remember? We need a couple of videos, and since that's what you're here for anyway —"

"More? Jesus Christ, when is it ever gonna end?"

"Such is the life, right?" He was making no effort to hide his pleasure. "We're aiming for a Thanksgiving release, but I want to start airing videos early to try to drum up interest. I want to do two, "The Leap" and "Marina Del Rey." I promise to be fast. I already have the concepts, I just need the artist."

"Nobody has said a word about this to me," she said.

"Listen, I just need a couple of extra days. I don't even need the band for the video to "Marina Del Rey," I just need you. Now, personal things aside, I know that you've always prided yourself on being professional, so let's just treat this like business, okay?"

"Why don't you just use the actress from the movie, or use some clips?"

"Because you're the performer and the audience wants to see the performer. I'm just asking for a couple of extra days. Come on, for old time's sake?"

Danielle turned away from him because she knew she couldn't look at him and say no. It didn't help, she still couldn't. "Fine. But you owe me for this."

He stood and gave her a gentle kiss on the lips. "Will you take my heart as repayment?"

She licked her lips, looking for something to say. "You normally offer something lower, don't you?"

He seemed honestly offended by the comment, but he covered it up quickly. "Not for you, sweetie. You deserve more than that."

#

That day, the band shot the video for "Fallin' Out of Love Again." The video showed the band members standing in a long line, each performing their part. At the end, it was revealed that they were standing outside a decrepit old building with a large neon sign that said LOVE, but the building was boarded up with a large CLOSED sign on the door. It was a cheesy concept, but they just wanted to get it over with.

The next day, they reported to yet another set to film yet another video. Danielle was heavily made up and had donned a white-blonde wig. Then she was dressed in an extravagant wedding dress. Each band member and Adam were put into a room with floor to ceiling mirrors for walls. As "The Leap" played over a loudspeaker, each person was instructed to do whatever they felt like, but to try to display some kind of loneliness.

195

Danielle's box was heavily lit with white light. The light, the mirrors, the hair, and the dress combined to give her scenes a "washed out" appearance. While watching a playback later, Ty remarked that she looked like "a creepy angel." From that point on, "The Leap" was referred to as "The Creepy Angel."

When the video was finished, it was revealed that the boxes were all connected. They were all trying to reach each other, but were unable to see past themselves to see anything else. Adam would go on to win several awards for the video.

After filming was finished, the rest of the group headed out, but Danielle had to stay. However, the video for "Marina Del Rey" was much easier. All she had to do was stroll down the beach lip synching the song. In a yellow bikini. Danielle, who was notoriously insecure about her body, had to be coaxed into the outfit. It took all of Adam's best sweet talking, but he convinced her to do it. She repeated her walk several times to make sure they had plenty of good footage. In the video, Adam and Danielle walk towards each other, but once they get there, they both keep walking on past.

Once Adam felt that he had enough footage, he pulled her into the surf and splashed her. Danielle returned the favor and they played in the water, all the tension between them melting away, at least for a moment. She had no idea that they were still filming. When asked about the shoot later, Adam revealed, "You have to find a way to get Danielle out of her own head. If you can do that, there's this wonderful, beautiful spirit there, just dying to get out. But it's very hard to get to that place."

He had managed to get to that place, and Danielle finally let her old hard feelings go. That night, he took her out to dinner and doted on her the whole time. They laughed and talked about old times, but he remained the gentleman and didn't push for a good night kiss.

The next day, she boarded the plane for home, anxious to sleep in her own bed but somewhat reluctant to leave. As the plane started down the runway, she thought about the words to "Marina Del Rey." "As the plane is touching down/tears touch my eyes, for I have found/my heart has stayed/in Marina Del Rey." As her plane made its way towards Texas, she wondered if her heart had stayed as well.

CHAPTER NINE

In the fall of 1999, Danielle Regan released her fifth studio album, *Vintage Beauty*. After the massive success of *Cathouse* and *Stripclub*, Generation Records was eager to cash in on Danielle's massive popularity. Danielle was inspired to take the band in a new direction after yet another person remarked that she looked like a '40s movie star.

Vintage Beauty was a complete change of direction from her previous albums. The band used '50s era instruments, and Steve found them a studio in Rhode Island that still recorded using throwback equipment. The end result was an album that sounded like a stroll through the annals of rock history.

When *Vintage Beauty* was completed and delivered to Generation Records in early October, Jay Hatfield had reservations. He wasn't crazy about the idea of a retro record following the colossal successes of her last two albums. Steve convinced him that with Christmas coming the vibe was right, and it made sense to get the album in stores before the holidays.

The album's first single, "When She Passes By," debuted over Thanksgiving weekend. The song could have come straight off the Chess Records label, complete with a soulful sax intro and some classic Chicago-style blues guitar. The song was a radical departure from the traditional Reckless Passions sound, but it struck a chord with audiences and would soon become the band's first Top Five single.

The video for the song helped drive the single's success. The band was depicted as the house band at a USO show during World War II. The band played in the background while a young cigarette girl tried to keep her soldier boyfriend's attention. However, he was continually distracted by a beautiful mystery girl, played by Danielle.

Danielle threw a lavish Christmas party that year for the band and their support staff. Since moving into her new home by the lake, Danielle had taken to throwing frequent parties. Filling the house with people helped her forget how large and lonely the house was when she was alone.

Once the party broke up, she cleaned up and turned out the lights, leaving only the Christmas tree and a few candles to light the room. She collapsed on her couch, worn out from the busy day, and stared absently into the lights on the tree. Her mind was racing, pouring over the events of her life. She was looking for that moment where things might have gone differently.

After a while, she noticed a small present still laying under tree. She slid onto the floor and crawled over to the tree on hands and knees. The present was elegantly wrapped and unlabeled.

She opened it to find a vanilla jewelry box inside. Inside the box was a simple, classic diamond ring.

"I was beginning to wonder if you were ever going to see that," said a voice from behind her. She whirled quickly as Adam stepped out of the shadows of a side room. He was wearing a dark gray suit and was starting to grow his hair long again. "Your piano player snuck me in. This was all her idea. But the ring was mine."

She took another look at the ring, then snapped the box shut. She tossed it to him. "Keep it."

Adam caught the toss and smiled sadly as he stepped further into the room. He put the ring down on a table and tucked both hands into his pockets. "This isn't a joke, Dani. I'm not playing a game. I'm dead serious here. I'm tired of playing games. I'm tired of getting jealous every time I hear that you're dating someone new. We should be together, and I think you know that."

Danielle stood and dusted herself off. "So you want me to stay home while you bounce from starlet to starlet out in Hollywood? No thanks."

"It's not like that. Don't tell me that you haven't noticed yet. Everybody else in the world has noticed it."

"Noticed what?" she asked incredulously.

Adam smirked and looked away with a chuckle. "How every girl I date looks like you." His gaze came back to her. "Think about it. Tall, dark, curvy, exotic. I've spent the last several years of my life trying to replace you, but I can't. I don't jump from girl to girl because I get bored like you think I do. I do it because none of them are you."

His admission hit her with stunning force. Her limbs began to feel weak and the room started to spin. Adam was at her side in an instant, and the touch of his hand on her arm sent a wave of warmth pulsing through her. She threw her arms around him and held on for dear life. They stood there like that in the light of the Christmas tree and neither said a word. They didn't have to.

She woke up to find her face buried in Adam's chest. They had collapsed on the couch and finally fell asleep. Adam was fiddling with a strand of her hair and twirling it around his fingers. She could hear his heartbeat in her ears. She wanted nothing more than to freeze that moment before one of them screwed it up. She finally tilted her head to look up at him, and was greeted with that million megawatt smile.

"I've been waiting for you to wake up."

"Why?" she whispered.

He took her left hand and slipped the ring on her finger. She looked at it again, more closely this time. He had done well; it was classy and elegant, but understated. She smiled as she watched the light dance off the diamond. She felt like she was on the verge of completing her life.

He'll never be true.

She shook the thought out of her head. This was different, she told herself. Now she knew why he jumped from girl to girl. Now it all made sense. If he had her, he wouldn't need to stray. She snuggled up closer to him and tried desperately to convince herself that it was true.

On New Year's Eve, Adam took Danielle to his ranch outside San Marcos for the candlelight dinner she had thought she was going to get a year and a half earlier. He cooked while she showered. When she stepped out, he had left a brilliant red dress out for her.

When she came to the table, it took Adam one look to tell him what Danielle had already known. "Red's not your color."

She looked down at herself and agreed. "No, it's not. But it's a beautiful dress anyway."

He stood before her and put his hands on her hips. "Maybe I should take you out of it."

She put her hands on his chest and pushed away just a little. "Maybe you need to slow down," she said with a flirty smile.

"Maybe," he said with a smile of his own. "Let's eat."

After their meal he took her out on his patio, where he danced with her under the stars. The night was chilly, but not cold, and the cool air felt good on her face. It was shaping up to be a perfect, romantic evening.

Too perfect.

As she could have predicted, dancing led to kissing, and that led them inside. Her thoughts raced back to their teenage days when making out was the best thing in the world. This wasn't then, and she knew he wasn't planning on stopping there.

He was guiding her toward the bedroom and she was doing nothing to stop him. She wanted nothing more than to enjoy every moment. But her mind was racing.

How many girls has he taken to that bed? How many times has he played this game?

At his bedroom door, she stopped him.

"What's wrong?" he asked breathlessly.

"You're going too fast."

"We're engaged," he answered. She could hear a hint of anger in his voice.

"For a week," she shot back. "We've done nothing but orbit each other for years. I think I need more than a week."

Adam pushed away and ran his hands through his hair. "God, you are so...."

"So what?" she asked. Now her blood was beginning to boil too. "What am I Adam? Other than not as easy as what you're used to? Am I a tease?"

"You're so damn scared. Why can't you just let go? Quit thinking so much and just live, Dani."

"Okay, fine. You want me to let go? You want me in that bed tonight? Give me a date."

He seemed confused. "What date?"

"A wedding date?"

"Jesus Christ, Danielle. We just got engaged. Why can't you just enjoy it?

Danielle just smirked at him. "So to recap this. A week is plenty of time to get into bed, but not to set a wedding date. Are you even serious about getting married, or is this just a game to you?"

"Of course I'm serious. I wouldn't have asked if I wasn't. I'm just not in a huge hurry."

Danielle just nodded and pushed past him. "For what I want you're not in a huge hurry. But when it comes to what you want, it has to be now."

Adam let out a sigh of resignation. "Okay, so maybe I jumped the gun a little bit. I'm sorry. You make me crazy when I'm around you. I want you so bad that I hate to wait."

Danielle straightened herself out. "I'm sorry if I led you on. I want you too. But I need something from you first."

He took her gently in his arms and ran his fingers through her hair. "Tell me what you need and I'll give it to you."

"Assurance. That I'm the only one. That you're really ready for this. You know me, Adam. I don't do things half-assed. If we're going to get married, I intend for it to be forever. Can you convince me that it's what you want?"

"Forever's a long time, Dani."

Danielle laughed. "That's a cop out. Jesus, you could have just lied to me and said yes, pulled a date out of your ass, and we'd be in bed right now."

"You'd see right through me if I did that," Adam answered. "Honestly, I'm scared of getting married. Both of my parents were divorced multiple times, so I'm reluctant to make promises that I may not be able to keep. I need a long engagement so I can get used to this."

"That's fine," she answered coldly. "I need time too. I need time and I need assurances you can't give to me right now. So I'll make you a deal. You get what you want when I get the other ring on my finger. Deal?"

Adam smirked. "A ring doesn't guarantee fidelity. It doesn't guarantee forever. Believe me on that."

"No, but it'll mean something to me. And hopefully it would make it harder for you to stray. A proposal is nothing, but actually taking the vows is something else. Anybody can make a girl a promise. You walk me down the aisle and then I'll know you're serious."

"That's the only way you'll sleep with me?"

Danielle gave him her flirty smile. "Don't you want the wedding night to mean something?"

Adam looked frustrated, but he knew that he was losing this fight. "It would anyway, Danielle. I can't believe that this is the only way to make you trust me."

Danielle wrapped her arms around his neck. "I reserve the right to change my mind. But for right now, this is what I need."

Adam gave her a gentle kiss on the forehead. "Okay then. I'll be a good boy for now."

"Don't worry," she said. "You'll have all the time in the world to be a bad boy later."

It was as if their agreement only served to spur on Danielle's desires. It seemed that the very sight of Adam was enough to fan the flames. To make matters worse, they began staying at each other's houses. The knowledge that he was just down the hall drove her crazy. It was the most perverse form of torture, but maybe that's what they both needed to drive away their demons.

One morning after spending the night at Adam's ranch, she woke up to hear him rummaging around outside. Curious to see what he was up to, she hurried outside without bothering to switch out of her nightshirt. She found him out front, packing up his newest ride, a loaded F350 dually.

Danielle was almost afraid to ask, but she did any way. "Going somewhere?"

Adam, who was busy tying a tarp over the top of the truck bed, looked over his shoulder and smiled at her. "Heading to Cali. I gotta start shooting a new movie soon, and I like to get out there early and get settled in." He caught Danielle's reaction before she realized she'd had one, and left the tarp to come to her. He brushed a strand of hair out of her eyes. "I've been having so much fun here with you that it snuck up on me. And I'm not used to having to consult with anybody. Usually I just pack up and go."

Danielle shrugged. "It's fine. We'll both have to make some adjustments. How long are you going to be gone?"

"Six to ten weeks. Just depends on the director. I've never worked with this guy before so I don't know how he works. Some guys are real fast and some guys take forever. I'll be back as soon as I can."

"Six weeks," she repeated. "I'll be going back out on tour by then. We're not going to see each other for months."

"Not necessarily," Adam said. "I've been thinking about that. I don't want to go so long without seeing you either, so I was thinking about buying an RV and following you guys around once I'm done shooting."

Danielle pulled away from him and went to go finish tying down his tarp. "You don't have to do that. We've got a big fancy bus now. You could ride along. I'm sure the others wouldn't mind."

Adam came up behind her, wrapped his arms around her waist, and buried his face in her neck. "No thanks. I'd like to have my own space. But I could be part of your convoy."

Danielle finished with her knot and wiggled around to face him. "I'd feel bad about not travelling with the guys. I think it's important for band togetherness that I stay with them."

"So ride your bus. It's not like we could do anything on the road...." He let the comment hang in the air, giving her an opportunity to come up with some things that they could do on the road. She didn't bite. "We'll still be with each other when we stop, but we also get a chance to have some space. It's a win-win."

"Sounds like a plan, stud. But I still hate to be without you between now and then. I've got some time left…why don't I follow you out there? I could stay for a couple of weeks before I have to come back for rehearsals."

Adam's face brightened at the suggestion. Danielle wondered if that wasn't his hope all along. "Why don't you just ride with me? There's plenty of room in the truck, and I could use the company. It's a long drive to California."

Danielle thought about for a minute, but the very idea made her uncomfortable. She finally shook her head no. "I think I'd rather follow you."

"You still don't like riding with other people, do you?"

"Nope," she said. "That's why I have my own car, so that I don't have to ride with other people. Besides, I come up with some of my best stuff while I drive."

"Well, I guess we could keep in contact with our cell phones while we're on the road."

Danielle laughed. "You know that I don't have a cell phone. I can't stand those things. I'm too old fashioned, I guess."

"Well, at least that explains why you haven't given me your number," Adam smirked. "But good god, Danielle, how could you not have a cell phone yet? I know eleven year olds that have cell phones."

Danielle punched him playfully in the arm. "I prefer the freedom of not having one. When I want to get lost, I want to get lost. Giving people the ability to call me no matter where I am defeats the purpose."

Adam let her go and went back to loading up his truck. "Have it your way. But if you get lost on the road I won't be able to come back for you."

She started back inside to get dressed, but stopped and turned around. "I won't get lost. Me and my Black Beauty never get lost."

Adam turned around. "You really trust that old thing out on the highway?"

"I trust it more than I trust you," she said with a smile.

In California Danielle spent her days on set and was amazed at how much went into making a movie. With Adam busy most of the day, she wandered around, helping in whatever ways she could and hanging out with the cast and crew. She even gave one of Adam's co-stars guitar lessons in her down time.

At night Adam did his best to show her the life of a Hollywood movie star. Every night they dined at some elite restaurant and rubbed elbows with other celebrities. He showered her with expensive dresses and jewelry beyond anything that Colin had ever attempted to give her.

The problem with going where the celebrities went was that the paparazzi followed. It didn't take long for the tabloids to pick up on them as a couple. Soon after that, someone caught the ring on her finger. Soon they were being followed everywhere they went, and

Danielle began to feel claustrophobic. She loved being with Adam, but the attention was getting to be too much.

Chapter Ten

Danielle was never more relieved to get back out on the road than she was for the *Vintage Beauty* tour. Away from Hollywood and back with her people, life returned to its normal, hectic ways. There were subtle differences in that the media was paying even more attention now, but Gilbert did a good job of keeping the press off her. She felt like she had so much more room to breathe.

Fan reaction was mixed and seemed to divide along gender lines. Most of Danielle's female fans greeted her with excitement and the fan mail was largely positive. Her male fans were more upset, which Steve explained as disappointment that they weren't the ones putting the ring on her finger. There was, however, a deluge of fan mail from all walks of life encouraging her to wait for marriage to consummate her relationship.

The primary question in the media was whether or not she already had. Tiring of the question early on, she picked out a favored writer from *Texas Monthly* and granted an exclusive interview in which she discussed her relationship in depth. She disclosed that they had both agreed to wait. She hoped that the declaration would be enough to silence the questions and return the focus to her tour.

They had been on the road for over five weeks before Adam and his new RV caught up to the band in Minnesota. Steve arranged for Adam to be given full access and he would join the band's convoy on the road.

His presence on the tour was noticed as soon as he arrived, and it started a new round of questions from the entertainment media. They were questions that Danielle and Adam ignored, although it was hard for Adam not to play up to the media. He lived in a world where you had to engage the press, while Danielle had made a habit of keeping them at arm's length. So Adam became Danielle's press secretary by default. Once again she found a way to hide in his shadow. There were some perks to dating a Hollywood A-lister.

Another perk that Danielle found was that the band and crew loved him. That hadn't always been the case with her other boyfriends, each of whom had run afoul of her little family in one way or another. He was always around, joking, playing pranks, buying dinner, and throwing back a few beers at the end of the night. He used his contacts to obtain advanced copies of upcoming movies for private screenings on off nights. His presence helped make it the most enjoyable tour yet.

However, Adam still wanted to lavish gifts and attention on her, a habit that was starting to get annoying. She tried to be as gracious as she could, but she had no use for many of the incredibly expensive gifts he kept giving her. Still, she knew it was only a matter of time before she reached a breaking point.

Adam was conspicuously absent from their show at the Key Arena in Seattle. Danielle didn't think much of it until the ride back from the show. The band was scheduled for a few much needed days off, and she was anxious to see him. However, when they arrived back at the hotel she found that he had been in her room. He had left candles burning, a red rose on her bed, and a box, which she knew contained yet another designer dress.

On top of the box was an envelope, and inside were instructions to clean up, doll up, and then to meet him at a specific restaurant. All she really wanted to do was grab a sandwich and a Coke and go to bed, but she knew that he was out there waiting, so she reluctantly complied with his instructions.

Gilbert managed to get her a car and sneak her out a back door past all the waiting fans and paparazzi. Soon she was standing in front of a trendy seafood restaurant on the waterfront. He had reserved a table for two on the patio in the back. There a plate of fresh lobster already waiting for her.

Adam grinned like an ape when he saw her approach, but the smile quickly faded. "You didn't have to rush," he said.

"I didn't."

"Oh," he said, surprised. "You don't look like you put much effort into it tonight. You look...haggard."

Danielle plopped down in the chair opposite him and took a big gulp of champagne. "Oh well, let's see. I've played twenty-nine concerts in the last thirty-four nights. I've been living on a tour bus for three and a half months. I just got through playing a two and half hour concert, and instead of taking advantage of the last break in this tour by going to bed and sleeping as late as I want, I had to get cleaned up and rush all the way over here to be with you. Gee, I wonder why I would look haggard."

"Okay," he said defensively. "I get you. I'm sorry. I didn't mean to upset you."

"I know you didn't," she sighed as she ran her hands through her hair.

"Is there a problem?"

She glared up and him. "Yes, there is. I'm not one of your little Hollywood starlet playthings, Adam. You don't have to wine me and dine me. I'd be perfectly happy with room service and a movie."

"You mean the dinner or the gifts?"

"All of it. Baby, I don't need the fancy clothes and flashy gifts. I'm not into all that stuff, and I thought that you'd know that. I want you, the real you."

Adam had a bite part of the way up to his mouth, but then he dropped his fork and angrily wiped his mouth with his napkin. "You're the only woman in the world who would get mad about me pampering her. The only goddamn one."

"I don't need to be pampered, Adam. I can take care of myself. I've been doing it most of my life. All of this that you do, every night, is overkill. Once in a while is fine, but not every damn night."

"Unbelievable. Danielle, I just don't know what you want half the time. Do you?"

"Do I what?"

"Know what you want?"

Danielle looked away, watching the lights reflecting off the water. "I don't know, Adam. Maybe I'd like to know that my fiancé knows me. That would be nice. You used to. But that was before you turned into Johnny Hollywood."

Adam smirked at her. "I know you better than anybody. I know you better than you know yourself."

"I don't think you do. I'm still the girl that used to buy you breakfast at Denny's when you didn't have a dime to your name. I'm the same girl who used to play street corners for loose change. I haven't changed. You have. If you want some Malibu Barbie to play sugar daddy for then you're barking up the wrong tree. It's not me, and I'm sick of trying to fit into your world." She pushed away from the table. "Enjoy the lobster." She stormed off and he made no effort to stop her.

Danielle was awoken by a light tapping at her door. She rolled over and looked at the alarm clock on the nightstand. She threw off her covers and stomped to the door. She didn't bother to look through the peephole…she knew that Gilbert kept the floor secure.

She opened the door and the light from the hallway flooded into the room. All she could see was a silhouette in the doorway. A silhouette that reached for her and drew her in close.

"I'm sorry, baby," Adam whispered in her ear. He ran his fingers through her hair. "I lost sight of who I was marrying. That's my fault. I just needed a reminder. I've been in Hollywood too long, I think."

She pulled back and looked up into his face, but she couldn't make out his features. "I'm still the same old Dani."

"I know." He gave her a gentle kiss on the forehead. "You know what I'd love to do right now?"

"What?"

"I'd like to go lie down on that bed over there and watch you sleep in my arms."

She smiled at him and wrapped her arms around him as tight as she could. "I'd love that."

She slept most of the next day, but when she woke up Adam was still there. He was fast asleep as well, his arms still wrapped around her. She loved the closeness they shared then, the feel of his arms around her waist and the smell of him. She snuggled up tighter and went back to sleep until she could sleep no more.

When she finally woke up for good he was awake and watching her. He greeted her with a genuine smile, not one of his put on movie star smiles. "I could get used to this."

"I could too. But right now I could really go for some breakfast. There's a Denny's not far from here. Interested?" She smiled back.

"That sounds great." He started running his hands up and down her arms. "Could you do me one little favor? From now on, when something's bothering you, do you think that you could just talk to me instead of blowing up like that?"

Danielle giggled. "I'll try, but I make no promises. I've got to keep you on your toes, after all."

After the days off, the tour rolled on through the Western U.S., including the band's first trip to Hawaii. Danielle felt much better about the relationship now that she had confronted him. He was losing the chip on his shoulder.

They had taken to sleeping together, causing Danielle to give serious second thoughts to their vow. Then that tidbit found its way into the media and caused a big blowup. Danielle had to explain how they could sleep together and not have sex. The tone of her fan mail turned ugly. She found herself wishing more and more that she had just kept her damn mouth shut all those years ago.

In Denver the band wrapped up the main part of their tour with a monster show that neared three hours. All that was left was the now traditional Texas Tour, where the band would saturate their home state, hitting all the small cities around the state in a blues inspired blitzkrieg. Steve worked a couple of extra off days into the schedule to let them rest up before the finishing kick began.

Adam decided the time was perfect to throw a party, and secured a hotel ballroom to do just that. He was the life of the party and showed that, when the mood struck him, he could drink even road hardened roadies under the table.

When they finally left for Danielle's room it was clear what was on his mind and his hands. He was more aggressive than she was used to, and she attributed it to a night of heavy drinking. She was willing to commit. She only needed one thing.

When they got in the door, he slammed it shut with a kick and pinned her against the wall. "Come on," he whispered as he kissed her neck. "Don't make me wait any longer."

She was enjoying his kisses and his touch. She wanted nothing more than to give in to the passion and let him have his way. "Just give me a date," she whispered breathlessly.

He quit kissing her and backed away. "Are you kidding me?"

Danielle's eyes snapped open and she gasped for breath. "Just a time frame. Something. Six months, a year. I just want an idea."

Adam rolled his eyes and backed away. "Goddamn, Dani. Would you please just let it go?"

She could see where this was going. "All I want to know is that at some point you actually plan on walking me down the aisle. That's all I'm asking for."

Adam appeared ready to hit something, and Danielle couldn't help edging away from him. "I've already promised to marry you. That's what that ring is for. I don't know when yet. I'm not ready for that."

"This ring?" Danielle held up her left hand. "This ring is starting to look a lot like an empty promise."

"It's not an empty promise," he snarled.

She took a deep breath to stifle the fear that was welling inside her, and walked slowly up to him. She wrapped her arms around his neck and looked deep into his eyes, looking for some sort of read. "Just a time frame. Two years. Three years. When will you be ready? Lie to me. Just give me something and I'm yours."

Instead, he put his hands on her waist and pushed her back hard. "Why do I have to be the one who gives in first? Why can't you give in first for a change? Why does it always have to be your way?"

"Oh my God," Danielle cried out in disbelief. "You've got to be kidding me."

Adam went to the door and yanked it open. "No, I'm not kidding. I need to know that you're in this 100% before I can give you that. You won't put yourself on the line, so why should I?"

Danielle laughed. "You need to know that I'm in this 100%? You can't even commit enough to lie about being committed. I want your heart. Until I know that I have it, you can't have me."

"You've got it," he said softly.

She walked to the door and held it open wider. Their eyes met in challenge. "Apparently not, and I don't even think that you're all that interested in mine. Not my heart any way. I think you need to sleep in your own bed tonight."

"I don't have a room. Steve didn't think I needed one."

"Good thing you have an RV then." She put a palm flat against his chest and pushed him out into the hall. She was about to slam it shut when the elevator door dinged and Steve came bursting out of it.

"Dani, thank God. We've got a major issue on our hands."

Dani's gaze went from Steve to Adam, who seemed to sober up instantly. He shrugged and she looked back to Steve. "What now?"

Steve held up a VHS tape. "This."

"You forgot to return your copy of the *Muppet Movie* on time? I think you'll be fine." Steve put it in her hand and she read the label. "Dani Does Dallas? What the hell is this?"

"Your old boyfriend Dirk has sold your sex tape, and it's raunchy."

"What?" Adam called out over Steve's shoulder. "What was all that shit about waiting until marriage?"

"It's not me, dipshit," she shot back. "I need to see this."

They all walked to Steve's room, where he had already reviewed the tape. "This is an advanced copy," he explained as he loaded the VCR. "The official release is next week. The press will be getting word of it any minute, I'm sure."

"Just show me the video," she said impatiently. She was sitting on the edge of his bed, one leg bouncing wildly with nerves as she chewed on a fingernail. Adam leaned against the door frame pouting.

Soon ex-NHL star Dirk Crandall appeared on the screen. He introduced himself and then pointed to a nude girl on the bed who, at first glance, could have been Danielle. She had the long dark hair and the body style was right.

Danielle was leaning in close, trying to take in every detail. "That is so not me," she said angrily.

"It's close enough. The basics are right. He makes sure that you never get a good look at her face."

Danielle shook her head as she watched the action unfold on the screen. It was raunchy, just as Steve had promised.

"This is bullshit," Adam spat. "I can't even get a hand up your skirt, and he gets that?"

Danielle turned to Adam with a look that could have wilted a lesser man. "Why don't you go fuck yourself then? I don't recall asking you to come along." She turned back to the screen. "That girl is wearing stiletto heels and is probably a good inch shorter than me," she said, pointing to the screen. "And her boobs are way too big."

"That doesn't really help us. No one has ever seen yours."

Adam snorted. "As uptight as she is, she's probably never seen them either."

Danielle again shot him a nasty look. "Get. The fuck. Out."

"Hey, it's looking like this is as close as I'm ever going to get. I have to live vicariously through this asshole if I want to fuck my own fiancée."

Danielle shot to her feet. "I'll fuck you up if you want."

Steve pushed up off the bed and got between Adam and Danielle. "Why don't you go to bed, okay? You are really not helping." Then he came back to Danielle's side. "We need to find a way to refute this, because no one can compare your bodies."

Danielle sneered at the TV. "The camera work is shaky, the lighting is terrible, and you never get a good look at this girl. How could anyone with half a brain take this seriously?"

"You're talking about entertainment journalism. You couldn't put half a brain together with the whole lot of them. All he has to say is that you asked for it this way to protect your reputation. We need something he can't explain away."

They turned their attention back to the screen again, watching in silence for several minutes. She sat on the floor, her face inches away from the screen. Then Danielle snapped her fingers. "There! Pause it. Is there a way you could blow up that frame into a still picture, really big, lots of detail?"

"Yeah. It'd take some time. Couldn't do anything until the morning. Why?"

She smiled big at him. "You think we'll have an audience tomorrow?"

"Guaranteed. Why?"

She patted him on the arm as she stood to leave. "Don't worry about it. I've got everything under control. Just get me a big picture of that frame right there...focus on the girl."

The next morning, she woke up and could hear the commotion outside. She took her time, took a long hot shower, and picked out her clothes carefully. Per her instructions, Steve had gathered a large contingent of journalists and paparazzi in the hallway not far from her room, held back by a barricade of beefy security guards.

Steve called her later in the morning to confirm that he had the picture she wanted. He brought it to her and she saw what she wanted to see.

She handed it back to him. "Take this out there, but keep it out of sight. Let my audience know that I will be out there in just a minute with my official response to Dirk's video."

"Do you want to clue me in on what you've got up your sleeve?"

"Nothing. That's the whole point. Just give me two minutes and I'll come out and make an official announcement."

Two minutes later, Danielle emerged and flashbulbs began going off. She slowly sauntered up to the gathering, wearing a black Dallas Stars jersey that hung to her knees. She gave a smile and a wave. Steve and Adam stood side by side and watched, both wondering what she was up to.

"How are y'all doing today?" she said, exaggerating her Texas twang. "Something sure has got you boys all fired up."

The questions came fast and furious from the gathered media, but Danielle wasn't listening She knew what they were asking about. "Now, I know that a former acquaintance of mine has made a little tape. I know that he claims that I'm the co-star in his little tape. I don't know if you boys have seen it yet, but I watched it last night and it was hilarious. I laughed my ass off. I had no idea that a guy so big could pack such a small punch."

The crowd laughed and her smile got bigger.

"Now I watched that tape real close after I quit laughing so hard. You may have noticed that the girl in the video doesn't show her face, and I sure don't blame her. If I were that bad of an actress I'd hide my face too." More laughter.

"The thing is, fellas, that I knew it wasn't me. If I was going to make a sex tape it sure wouldn't be with a light hitter like that. I know that he claims it is me, but I can promise you it's not. For one, that girl is much better endowed than I am, but y'all wouldn't really know that." She reached out and took the picture from Steve's hands and flipped it around. "If you look careful, you can clearly see that this girl has an appendectomy scar, and a fairly nasty one at that."

214

She tossed the picture on the floor and in one fluid motion, pulled the jersey off and stood in front of the cameras in nothing but a sheer white bra and panties. "Now, you tell me if you see any scars."

She stood and posed, and let everyone get a good look before she slid back into the jersey. "Thanks boys," she called. She strolled past a stunned Adam and Steve and with a cocky smirk. "You think he'll like that show?"

#

Danielle's pseudo strip tease was all over the news for days, and more than overshadowed the release of the discredited sex tape. Extensive comparisons were done between the girl in the video and the nearly nude Danielle, and side by side they didn't look that alike at all.

With Dirk's claims discredited and Danielle's shots at his manhood replayed all over the spectrum, the former hockey star faded from view. The adult film company that had bought the video sued him for fraud, but Danielle declined to pursue any further action against him. She was satisfied with public humiliation.

A week after the tour ended, Adam surprised Danielle with an impromptu vacation to Cabo San Lucas. She was hesitant to go, but he promised her that he would give her a wedding date if she did. They blew off steam and rebuilt their strained relationship. They lived on the beach during the day and in the clubs at night. Both felt recharged by the trip.

Returning home brought Danielle back to cold reality. Pictures of the two of them frolicking on the beach were all over the tabloids and the Internet. *People* ran a story wondering if the All-American girl was growing up or beginning to crack under the constant scrutiny that her personal life was under.

She read the article with disgust and threw the magazine in the trash. "You see what happens? I go play on the beach and now I'm a slut." She ran a nervous hand through her hair. "It doesn't matter what I do. Half the country thinks I'm a prude for still being a virgin, and the other half thinks I'm a whore because I might not be anymore. What the hell do people want from me?"

Adam was lying on the floor in their living room doing sit-ups, but he stopped to look at her. "You need to quit worrying about what other people think of you. I know when you came out in that

215

interview that you wanted to be a role model, but I don't think it's worth putting yourself through all of this emotional turmoil."

"I just wanted to do something good. God knows that the only role models I had growing up were negative ones."

He got up off the floor and gave her a quick kiss on the top of the head as he went to the kitchen for a beer. "You don't have to shoulder the weight of the world. I think that you've been a damn fine role model. You made yourself a star. You're the best guitar player in the world. You don't do drugs, you don't get in trouble with the law. You give to charity. You're a good person, and that's all that should matter."

Danielle pushed herself up off the couch and went to Adam, taking the bottle out of his hand and taking a long drink. "It shouldn't," she agreed. "But it does. It's easy to sit there and say it shouldn't matter, but you don't read the fan mail that I get. What I'm doing really does make an impact with some people. I get letters from parents who are so glad that there's someone out there trying to do things right. There are teens who are under incredible peer pressure. Religious groups that are using me as an example to their youth groups. They've all invested so much hope in me. The thought of letting those people down just makes me sick."

Adam took a big drink, then put the beer down and took Danielle in his arms. "You are the most incredible woman. Is this why you're so hesitant?"

She snuggled up closer to him. "Some of it. I mean, we started sleeping in the same room and the press knew about it in two days. I don't know how to keep anything secret from them. If I can't keep it secret, I can't risk it. Besides, every experience I've had with sex has led to pain. That's not a real ringing endorsement. I have enough pain without it."

Adam chuckled. "You keep this whole morality thing up and they're going to kick you out of the celebrities club."

"Boo hoo," she mocked. "Hey, didn't you tell me that if I went on vacation with you, you'd give me a time frame?"

Adam was suddenly uncomfortable. He reached around her for his beer. "I did. I'm thinking about that. I'm looking at projects that I've got lined up. I don't know what plans you have. So I'm trying to arrive at a time."

"Will this time arrive before I turn eighty?"

Adam grinned at her. "Maybe. Just don't rush me. I'm working on it, I promise you. You'll get your time."

"Okay," she answered. "Just remember what's waiting for you."

#

In September Trish and Ty were set to marry. Instead of having individual bachelor/bachelorette parties, they decided to take their best friends out for a night on the town. Adam and Danielle hopped from bar to bar on 6th Street, dancing and drinking into the early hours of the morning.

As the party was winding down and last call approached, Danielle noticed that she had gotten separated from Adam. She found him sitting at a bar talking up a tall blonde cowgirl, whose hands were getting a little too adventurous. Danielle came up behind him and began rubbing his back.

"Baby, it's time to go. Everybody's tired."

Adam shrugged her off. "Not me. I've got plenty left in me. It's not even last call yet."

The blonde shot her a nasty look and Danielle returned it. "Well, I'm tired. We can go home and you can drink as long as you want."

"He doesn't want to leave, sweetie," Blondie mouthed off. "I think he made that pretty clear. So why don't you get lost?"

Danielle stepped out from behind Adam. "I've got a ring on my finger that says that you need to mind your own business."

Blondie looked Danielle up and down and didn't look impressed. "From what I've been hearing, your man needs a woman who can spread her legs once in a while, and that ain't you."

Danielle was making a fist at her side. "How about I spread your face for you instead?"

Blondie shot up off her bar stool. "Bring it, bitch," she challenged. They locked eyes and it was taking every ounce of Danielle's self-control to keep from hitting her.

The longer she delayed, the cockier Blondie got. She finally looked past her to Adam. "She's not gonna do anything. Let's go back to my place." She reached for Adam's hand.

Danielle swatted her hands away. Blondie responded by slapping Danielle in the face hard enough to bring tears to her eyes. Danielle punched her in the face and then the two became tangled and fell to the floor. Friends of the two combatants pulled them apart before any more damage could be done.

Angry, Danielle turned to Adam, who was watching the entire thing in amusement. "I'm going home. You do whatever the hell you want. I don't care."

"I'm coming, I'm coming," he slurred as he struggled up off his barstool. "You didn't have to beat the poor girl up. She was just being friendly."

"Oh, don't insult me. I know better than that. You would have gone home with her."

"No, I wouldn't have. I was just enjoying the attention."

"Well dear, I hope you got what you were after. Now you can enjoy the walk home, because I don't want you in my car right now."

The next day, Adam was barely sober enough to attend the wedding. Danielle, as the maid of honor, watched him with disgust as he tried to stay awake during the ceremony. He seemed to be completely horrified just being this close to a wedding.

She kept her distance from him at the reception, during which Adam hit the bar heavily. At one point, she did overhear Adam refer to Ty as "that poor bastard" while talking to Garrett at the bar. Danielle realized that her time frame was looking more like a rumor.

After that, Danielle began to work harder on writing songs for a new album, even though she had promised Trish and Ty that no work would start until 2001. Adam had to leave to do some advance publicity for his newest movie, and Danielle was glad to be rid of him. It gave her a chance to think about where she was going. It was becoming all too apparent that Adam would never want to get married, and the more she pressured him about it the more he drank.

She didn't know what to do. In her heart, if she couldn't marry him she didn't want him around. She loved Adam and wanted to be with him, but her old fears about his fidelity were boiling to the surface. On the other hand, she didn't want to be alone. She had gotten used to having someone in her life.

#

Adam returned in mid-October but Danielle buried herself in her writing and steered clear of him. Adam responded by drinking out on the patio. Danielle could see him from the living room as he drank, and she found herself wishing that he would just fall off. It was a horrible thing to think, but she could think of no better way out.

By midnight he was well past drunk. Danielle kept her head down and her guitar plugged in to drown out any noise. He finally stumbled back into the house. "Let's go to bed, Dani. Let's go right now."

She barely looked up at him. "You go on. I'll be up there in a little bit."

"No," he shouted. He stomped up and turned over the table where her notebook was sitting. He stood over her, fuming, and glared down at her. "Turn that goddamn thing off and come upstairs now."

Danielle felt fear rising inside her and knew that she couldn't let it go. "Don't boss me in my own house, please."

"This is our house," he shouted back. "We're together now. This was my land and you stole it."

"You're drunk, Adam. Go to bed and sleep it off." She couldn't even bring herself to look at him. He didn't look like the same person anymore; the alcohol and the rage and the fear had changed him. She went back to playing the guitar.

He reached down and tore the guitar out of her hands, the strap burning the back of her neck as he ripped the guitar away. Then he turned and smashed the guitar on the floor, over and over until it was in pieces. Then he tossed the shattered neck aside. "Now come upstairs. Or do you want it right here?"

She looked at the busted remains of her guitar, then looked up into Adam's eyes. He looked like a monster to her now. She fought hard to keep her emotions in control, keenly aware of how precarious her situation was. "Why don't you go take care of that yourself and leave me alone?"

With a growl, he reached out and slapped her so hard that she fell across the couch. He was on top of her instantly. "You're mine, and you're gonna quit holding out on me and give me what I want."

Danielle wriggled and fought, her hands groping for anything that she could use to get him away. He was so big and strong now that he would easily overpower her if she didn't get free. He was tearing away her clothes like a beast. Finally, she worked her way to the edge of the couch and then dropped off, but he fell right on top of her. Still grasping, her hand found a jagged piece of the broken guitar neck. She swung and felt the wood smack into the side of Adam's head. It was enough to catch him off guard, and she finally had enough room to scurry out from under him.

Adam recovered from the blow and lunged for her. She kicked at him, hitting him once on the shoulder before another kick hit him in his nose and caused blood to squirt onto the floor.

"Bitch," he called out, and began to crawl after her like a panther. She saw the body of her guitar lying nearby and crawled over to it, then threw it at him as hard as she could. It hit him and bounced off, but she now had enough time to jump to her feet. She kicked him once more, this time square and hard in the side of the head, and he went down.

Danielle had always feared a crazed fan getting into her house and had designed it for just such an occurrence. It came in handy now. She quickly stepped past Adam and raced for the stairs. She could hear him behind her, raging like a wounded beast, spitting out curses at her. She just needed a few more seconds....

She flew up the stairs, turned the corner quickly, and made a beeline for her bedroom. He was stomping up the stairs after her. She reached her bedroom and slammed the heavy oak doors shut, locked the doorknobs first, then engaged two more locks, one at the top and one that went into the floor. She was barricaded, at least for the moment. But she didn't know how long the doors would hold out if he was determined to break them down.

She went to her nightstand, which had a specially built compartment in the back that Adam didn't know about. She opened it now and took out the fully loaded revolver she kept in there. She had never imagined that she would need it to protect her from her own fiancé.

Adam reached the doors and began banging on them. He made a terrible racket and the doors gave some, but held. Eventually, the banging stopped. When he had gone silent for several minutes, she quietly unlocked the door, gun in her right hand. She cracked the door and found him passed out in the hallway. The alcohol and the fatigue had finally taken him down.

She didn't know how much time she would have, so she moved quickly. She tucked the gun in the waistband of her jeans and stepped quietly past him. She went down the stairs and then down into her studio. There she made a desperate phone call and waited.

It was mid-morning when Adam finally woke up, groaning loudly. He called out for Danielle but she didn't answer. She was sitting in a recliner downstairs. Behind her, Gilbert Bell and two of his biggest roadies stood and watched carefully. In her lap, the cocked and loaded revolver sat under her hand.

He stumbled down the stairs, clearly confused. He smiled at first, then his expression soured. "What the fuck is going on here?"

Danielle tossed him the keys to his pickup. "It's loaded and has a full tank of gas. Get in and get out. Don't look back."

He held the key ring in his hands, staring at it as he tried to figure out what was going on. Then he saw that Danielle had attached her engagement ring to it. "Dani, this is crazy."

"The lady said hit the road," Gilbert growled behind her. "She won't ask you twice. You really don't want us to escort you out."

Adam had the deer in the headlights look now. "Dani," he appealed. Then he noticed the gun in her lap. "You're serious."

"As a heart attack," she answered coldly. "You went too far last night. I never want to see you again."

Adam leaned against the bannister for support. "Dani, I made a mistake. I was drunk and I didn't know what I was doing. You have to forgive me." He seemed to be on the edge of tears.

"Last night was unforgivable."

"Dani," he stammered. "You want a date? How about now? Tonight, tomorrow. You tell me and I'm there. You wanted a time frame."

"Shut up, Adam. It's been over for a while now. I didn't want to acknowledge it, but I knew it. Last night was just the finishing touch. You never wanted to marry me...you don't want to get married at all. You would have been miserable if you had. You were stringing me along. There's nothing you can say or do that will change my mind. Now get out before things get nasty."

He wanted to argue, but the sight of the three hulking men behind her and the gun in her lap convinced him otherwise. His shoulders slumped as the reality set it. With his tail firmly between his legs, Adam shuffled toward the door, opened it, and stepped through it, giving her one last longing look as he closed the door.

Danielle and Gilbert stood side-by-side by the living room window and watched him go. When he was finally out of sight, Gilbert put his strong hand on her back. "My boys and I will have all your locks changed in an hour, and I've got a friend who'll be by this afternoon to install a new security system for you. You don't worry about a thing. He'll never get in again."

She let out a ragged breath and uncocked her gun. "Thank you," she said, her eyes still tracking the road although he was long gone. "I know y'all will do fine. If you don't mind, though, I'm going to go lie down."

Gilbert smiled sadly at her. "You do that. I know that you're exhausted. I won't leave until the fort is secured."

Danielle trudged away and started back up the stairs toward her bedroom.

"Miss," Gilbert called out. Danielle turned around. "He wasn't good enough for you anyway."

"Thanks." She knew that he was right, but that didn't make it any easier.

CHAPTER ELEVEN

Danielle spent a week in solitude following Adam's exile. She answered no phone calls and never left the house. Finally, she decided that she'd had enough of the same four walls. She packed a bag and threw it in the back of Black Beauty and set off on a road trip.

On the way out of town she mailed Steve a letter. She didn't want to talk to him personally and give him the chance to talk her down. She wasn't running, she told him. She just needed a change of scenery.

She headed southeast to Houston and then hopped over to New Orleans. From there she worked her away across the Sunbelt, then up the Atlantic coast. She stopped her northern advance right where Lee had, at Gettysburg. Then she started working her way back down south and headed west. She had just about convinced herself that she was ready to go home.

Then she hit Nashville.

She rolled in late on a rainy night in March, feeling physically and emotionally exhausted. She hadn't played or sang a note in weeks. Now, however, she was beginning to feel the slow burn deep in her soul. Her spirit ached to return to playing; it longed for music, an indulgence she hadn't allowed herself at all during her trip.

She spent the first day in a hotel room off of I-40 catching up on her sleep and watching TV. Late that night, burdened by guilt, she picked up the phone and called Steve's house.

She soon heard his gruff voice on the other line. "Where the hell are you?"

Danielle was taken aback by his anger. "How did you even know it was me?"

"The phone has a more annoying ring when you call."

She detected an edge of drowsiness in his voice. She had woken him. Well, she'd be pissed off too, so she decided to turn to humor. "You'd have felt stupid if I had been some poor Mormon calling to tell you the joy of the Lord."

He chuckled at that. "No, actually, I think I feel worse doing it to you. Besides, Mormons don't call. They knock on the door."

"What if it had been your momma callin' to check on you?"

He groaned. "My mother calls at a decent hour. What do you want, Danielle?"

She sat quietly for a moment as she thought about that one. She was sitting in bed, back against the headboard and legs stretched out in front of her. The remains of chicken salad on a room service cart were pushed up against one wall, and a half empty of glass of sweet tea sat on the nightstand next to her phone. "I just wanted to hear a friendly voice. But I misdialed and got you instead."

"Yeah right," he answered. Then after a pregnant pause, he guessed, "Lonely?"

"Yeah. I think I've been out here too long. I'll be coming home soon."

"Will you be ready to record when you get here?" His voice took on a sudden edge of hope and the drowsiness was gone in an instant. "Should I tell the guys to start getting ready?"

"Absolutely," she said, sounding more eager than she felt. "Definitely tell them to start getting ready. I'm going to spend a few days here, get the lay of the land, try to get some inspiration. Then I'll head home."

Steve made a noise into the phone and she heard him fumbling around for something. "Where exactly is here? I don't recognize the area code you're calling from."

"You've got caller ID now?"

"Helps protect me from late night calls from Mormons. Where are you?"

"Nashville."

"Nashville," he said with disgust.

Danielle for some reason felt nervous, and she began twisting her fingers in the curls of the phone cord. "Yeah, Nashville. You know, Music City? The Grand Ole Opry? I'm sure that you've heard of it."

"I've heard of it. I'm just wondering what you're doing in the national capital of Hicksville." There was no disguising the disgust in his voice now. Danielle well knew that Steve had a deep and thorough hatred of country music.

"You know, from what I've seen so far, it's not that bad. The place I'm staying in has indoor plumbing and air conditioning, and I noticed a disturbing lack of male rape on the street corners. I've yet to see a single sheep or chicken wandering about aimlessly, and the people I've talked to have all had a full set of teeth and speak perfect English."

"You're a real riot, Dani."

"The point is it's not as bad as you think. I want to spend some time here and soak up the local music scene, maybe get some ideas. We've already perfected the blues/rock thing. Now maybe we can mix in a little country flavor and make the ultimate American music sound. Just let me do my thing a little while longer."

"All right, fine," he said in resignation. "You're just going to do it anyway."

"That's right, I am. Tell the guys to start gathering up whatever they've been working on and clearing up their schedules. It's about time to get back to work."

There was another pause on the other end of the line before Steve spoke again. "You sound genuinely excited. I haven't heard you sound this wound up about anything in quite a while."

Danielle hadn't thought about it, but he was right. "I guess I am. Huh. Feels good."

"Sounds good," Steve countered. "It always scares me to death when you go into one of your depressions. I'm afraid one of these days you'll never pull out of it."

A chill ran down her spine. She had thought the same thing on more than one occasion. "You worry too much," she said, trying to sound flippant about it. "Gather the guys. I'll call later. Goodnight."

Danielle hung up quickly. She picked up her glass and took a long, slow drink of tea as she stared out of the window at the

Nashville skyline. She wondered what it was about this city that seemed to be drawing her in, holding her. Danielle couldn't put her finger on it, but she felt that she needed to be here.

Over the next two weeks Danielle made herself a regular. Every night she was in the clubs, taking in different varieties of country music. During the day, she hit the music stores and watched more than one impromptu jam session break out. The spontaneity of it reminded her of the old Friday night music jams back at Randy's place. She bought herself an acoustic guitar and a Telecaster hollow body, and began working on some new material in front of the window late at night, using the Nashville lights to fire her imagination. This place wasn't Austin, but things were happening here. It was a vibe she was trying to tap into, but was finding little success.

The next time she called Steve she waited for business hours and caught him in the office. He was thriving in that controlled mix of chaos that he kept percolating around him. She could hear it in his voice.

"I want to record the next album down here."

Steve choked. "By down here, please tell me that you're calling me from a pay phone in the lobby."

"Not quite," she said quietly. He had a manner of speaking to her at times that reminded her of her father. "Look, I'm loving the energy here. But I just can't seem to capture it. The songs I'm writing aren't sounding right."

"How are they sounding?"

"Like me."

Steve was quiet for a few seconds. "I'm pretty sure that's what the label wants. I think that they'd be happy with that."

"That's not what I mean. They sound too much like me. You know that I don't want to do *Cathouse* 2. I'm looking for something fresh."

"You think that you'll get it down there?"

"Yes."

"Dani," he said paternally. "You know that your band is a dyed-in-the-wool rock band, right? That you are the world's foremost blues guitar player. I don't see how you're going to do a country album with that mix."

226

"I don't want to do a country album," she fired back. "I want to do an American album. A perfect blend of rock, blues, and country. Something a little bit me, a little bit them, and a little bit Nashville. I need help getting it right. This is some tricky alchemy I'm trying to do here, Steve."

He sighed into the phone and waited two heartbeats. "What do you have in mind?"

"I think I'm going to need to work with a producer here, someone who knows how to capture the sound. There are some people down here who are really close to what I'm after, but they don't have the same edge we have. I feel like there's this great combination, this powerful sound that I'm supposed to grab, but it keeps slipping through my fingers."

"So my assignment, if I choose to accept it, is to find someone who can help you do this." He often asked questions in ways that weren't really questions.

"Yes, that's what I want. And price is no object. I need to do this album."

Steve cleared his throat and Danielle could hear him drumming his fingers on his desk, a nervous habit. "I'm starting to worry about you, Dani. You don't normally talk like this. Are you okay? Maybe you should come home."

"No," she snapped. "I know what I'm doing. Ever since I pulled into town I've felt this…thing. I'm supposed to be here. Something has brought me here and something is holding me. I know that sounds like some sort of metaphysical crap, but it's true. I'm asking you to help me nail this down, Steve."

There was a long silence on the other end of the line. She knew that he was carefully sizing up his next answer. She didn't want to give him the chance.

"Listen, you know that country is huge now. You know how guys like Garth Brooks have been crossing over onto the pop charts. I'm sure that you've noticed the chart positions and the album sales. This is a chance for us to grab a hold of that and create something even better. Imagine an album like *Cathouse*, but on both the rock and country charts. Think of the album sales alone. Think of that huge, untapped audience out there. They've been primed and now they're ready for the real thing. They've never seen anything like me."

The businessman in him couldn't resist, just like she knew he couldn't. "Give me a good callback number and sit by the phone. I'm going to work my contacts and see what I can do. This is going to be a challenge."

"Steve, you don't have challenges. You just have obstacles that you haven't overcome yet. That's why you're the best manager in the business." She gave him the direct number to her room and hung up.

Nearly three hours later her phone rang. She had fallen asleep in bed watching afternoon TV, because sleep was definitely a better alternative than afternoon TV. She snapped awake quickly and lunged for the phone. "Yeah."

"Fell asleep, huh? What about all that Nashville magic you've been yammering on about?"

"Beaten into submission by talk shows and infomercials. What do you got for me?"

"Okay," he said hesitantly. "Have you ever heard of Moonshine Mike?"

"Moonshine Mike," she answered with a laugh. "What the hell is that?"

"Well, all of that country/pop crossover business you were blabbering about? He's responsible for about half of it. Real name is Michael Stratford. He comes from money, graduated top of his class from Duke with a degree in business. He was on his way to Wall Street when he dropped out of sight. Pops up in Nashville claiming to be a music producer. Uses his own money to fund his first few projects, convinces some up and coming talent to give him a shot and boom. Instant success. Everything he's touched has turned to gold. The guy can pick talent out of a garbage can."

"Sounds like my guy."

"Maybe," he said with hesitation.

Danielle was curious. "Why maybe?"

"Because with quick success comes a price. He's got a reputation for being a hardass in the studio and a bit of an eccentric, and very much a diva. Putting the two of you together could be a bad mix. You know how you feel about divas."

Danielle chewed on that a minute and then spit it out. "No worries. You also know that I'm a consummate professional in the studio. I'm sure he is too. We'll work together. I'm sure he'll annoy me some but I can deal with it in the short term. You're sure he's the best bet?"

"All of the people I've talked to say he is. He's probably drooling all over himself over the possibility of working with an established artist like you, especially someone outside of his mainstream. You could give him access to a whole new level of artist."

"Well then, let's set something up."

"I already have," Steve said. "He wants to meet for lunch tomorrow. There's this restaurant where he eats lunch every day...French trained chef and the whole nine yards. I'm catching the 7:15 flight out. Can you pick me up?"

"Of course I can," she answered.

"Dani, I'm begging you, play it cool with this guy. He can be very unpredictable."

She was waiting anxiously when Steve's flight arrived. He stepped off the plane with a single carry on. When she hugged him, he dropped his bag and returned the hug. "I really wish you'd quit running off like this."

She stepped back and gave him a playful smile. "This is my magic. It's how I work. Don't mess with the mojo."

Steve shook his head. "Where is all this magic shit come from all of the sudden? Are you on drugs?"

"Who knows?" she said as she fell in step beside him. They waited for his bag to appear at baggage claim and then she escorted him to her car. He sighed when he saw it.

"I hate this rolling death trap of yours."

She put her finger to his lips to shush him. "Don't talk about my baby that way. This isn't a death trap. This is one of the finest specimens Detroit ever produced. She runs like a top. Like a nasty, demonic top bent on consuming any car that gets in her way."

"Says you," he said as he sat down and fastened the lap belt across him. "Just get me to the hotel in one piece please."

"Sure thing," she said, doing her best to hide her devilish grin from him. She wasn't sure if his instructions included breaking posted speed limits by a considerable amount or weaving in and out of traffic like a lunatic, but she did it anyway and took a sadistic delight in his tense, white knuckle responses and occasional gasps of fear. She thought to herself that she was a sick bitch sometimes, but it was all in good fun and Steve needed to loosen up.

He had to set some sort of record for the least amount of time to disembark from a parked vehicle once they made it to the hotel. Danielle laughed at him. "Come on, admit it. That was fun."

"Not remotely."

"Exhilarating? Thrilling?"

"Nauseating."

"Just like a good roller coaster, then. Mission accomplished," she said, very proud of herself.

She checked him in and showed him to his room, and he quickly bid her goodnight. Before he did he handed her a black folder. "Info on Moonshine Mike. Read it. He likes it when people reference his previous work. It's like a validation of his talent."

Danielle took it and gave him a playful peck on the check. "Will do. I hope you enjoyed your ride." He slammed the door in her face.

The next day broke overcast with a smell of rain in the air. Steve was up early. His suit was immaculate as always, and he was much more composed than the night before. Danielle, on the other hand, just threw on her most comfortable pair of jeans, a shear gray blouse, and a pair of ankle high black boots, and threw her hair back into a quick ponytail.

On the way down the elevator to the car she made a point of straightening his tie, even though they both knew that it was arrow straight already. "Can't have you looking all sloppy for our meeting with Whiskey Will."

"It's Moonshine Mike. I know that you're goofing around, but this guy isn't known for having a great sense of humor. Be professional."

She took a step back and gave him a scolding look. "I am professional," she said sharply, and it was no joke. "I know how to conduct myself in a business meeting. Give me some credit."

The restaurant was a small, white stucco building lodged into a tiny lot downtown. It was the type of place that didn't advertise its presence because they didn't want the riff raff wandering in. All the fixtures were real brass, the doors were oak, and the floor was marble. Everything was clean and stiff, including the wait staff. As the hostess led them through the crowd, Danielle noticed the patrons eating miniscule portions off square plates.

Moonshine Mike had his own small, round table by a window, and he sat with his back to the door and the window to his right. In front of him was a square bowl full of some sort of soup, fresh enough that steam was still coming off of it, and he was sipping milk out of a crystal wine glass.

He was not at all what Danielle was expecting. He was rail thin, his hair was black and curly and looked unwashed. On his head he wore a battered velvet top hat, and he hid his eyes behind round, John Lennon-style sunglasses. His mannerisms were extremely effeminate.

He invited them to sit, but there were no other chairs provided so Danielle stole chairs from the surrounding tables. Steve sat directly on Mike's left and Danielle sat across from him. She sat up prim and proper like her grandmother had taught her to, hands folded discreetly in her lap, and began.

"Thank you for meeting with me today. I'm excited about what we can accomplish together—"

He put up a delicate hand. "Let me stop you right there." He made a show of removing his glasses and setting them down on the table, revealing soft brown eyes. He looked up into her eyes. "Let me explain something to you, dear. I am country music. I have made my name taking low rent wannabes with marginal talent and making them something more. I find the country in them and I cultivate it. What I do is art, but it is art in the name of country music, the true gospel. Hank Williams was Jesus incarnate. I know this as fact."

"That's why I'm excited—"

He slammed his dainty palms down on the table. "Do not interrupt me." Danielle saw heads turn all over the restaurant. "I have dedicated my life to country music. I have thrown off the constraints of my previous life and given myself to the gospel. My life's mission is to spread its glory throughout the land. I am an apostle. I am not given to interlopers coming into my town to play make believe. The gospel is not something to be played with. It is not a crayon to be used to spice up your tired and overblown excuse for music. You may have used your pretty face and the smattering of ability you possess to win over the mindless hordes, but you are not worthy of the gospel. You will never be worthy and you are wholly undeserving of it. I only brought you here today so that I could tell you that to your face. Now get away from me and take your soulless music out of my town, you insufferable little tramp."

He slowly put his glasses back on and smirked at her. Danielle sat across from him in stunned silence while Steve quickly pushed away from the table, intent on getting her out of there before she blew.

"Do I need to use smaller words? Get. Out."

Steve reached out for her arm, but he was too late. She reached out and flipped the square bowl of soup over, spilling it in his lap. Then she lunged across the table and grabbed him by the lapels.

"Let me tell you something, you mangy little fuck," she said, her voice a near growl. Again, heads turned to watch the scene unfold. "I've got a wall full of gold and platinum records that I earned. I didn't sit back like an arrogant little bitch and tell someone else which buttons to push. My fingers have bled for my music. My heart has broken. Have you ever done that? You, with your faggy little top hat and glasses? You're a fucking fake. You're the no talent hack. I shit out more talent in a day than you'll ever have, and you insult me? I ought to rip your fucking heart out through your throat, you miserable shit."

Steve managed to pull her off him, but she took a fistful of his shirt with her. She was a mad dog now, nearly foaming at the mouth and shouting a stream of obscenities while the rest of the crowd watched in stunned silence. Steve still struggled to drag her away. She latched on onto Mike's arm, her fingernails digging into his skin, and pulled herself right up next to his ear.

"I tell you what, you puke. I'm gonna record this album, and it's gonna beat the shit out of anything you've ever recorded. I'm gonna come back here and I'm gonna play your precious Opry, and I'm gonna fucking slay it when I do. I hope you wither and die while you watch it, you dickhole. And if you don't, I'm gonna come right back here to this table and I'm gonna piss in your milk."

She was losing her grip as Steve's strength overcame her rage. So as a last act of defiance, she grabbed his milk and threw it in his face, glass and all. Steve maneuvered between them and was pushing her towards the door. "Remember my face, fucker. You're gonna be seeing it again."

She continued her rant as Steve drug her out of the building. She saw the faces looking at her in shock, some laughing at her. As he got her to the door she saw a man who looked incredibly out of place, wearing a beat to shit cowboy hat and dirty Carhatt jacket. He was laughing at the scene.

"Fuck you," she screamed at him. "Fuck all y'all."

Steve finally managed to get her outside and pushed her around the side of the building. She was still rabid and raging. "Who the hell does he think he is?"

"Danielle, calm down. Now." Steve didn't often order her. "I told you that he was unpredictable. I told you that it might be a bad idea."

"You were right. This whole idea was just stupid."

"So...back to Austin," Steve asked hopefully.

"Absolutely. Fuck Nashville."

Steve packed quickly and booked the next available flight out. Danielle, though, crashed once the adrenaline wore off and lay down instead. After a short nap she got up and packed her bags. It was getting late and she didn't feel like hitting the road yet, so instead she jumped in the car for one last night out.

She found herself in a dingy little club called Honey White's to see a young singer/songwriter whose posters she had been seeing all over town. The club was well off of Music Row in a building that looked more like a shack. She was expecting to see the stage surrounded by chicken wire with sawdust all over the floor. However, it was actually fairly clean, though cramped and without air conditioning. She ordered a Coke and sat back to enjoy the show.

There wasn't much to enjoy. The performer came out with no band, just an acoustic guitar. She could tell by the way he spoke that he was from back east, but when he sang he did so with an affected Southern twang. The songs were so stereotypically redneck that she wondered if he was serious or if he was just making fun of the whole thing.

"He sucks, doesn't he?"

Danielle looked up to find a muscular cowboy standing beside her table holding a Coors longneck. In the poor light she could barely make out his features, but she knew that he looked good in his Western shirt, starched Wranglers, and brown cowboy hat.

"I don't know that I would say that."

He laughed. It was a hearty laugh. "I would. And I'm bein' kind. I think you would too. I've been watching you wince and squirm for about a half hour."

Danielle grimaced. "It's that obvious, huh?"

"Yeah it is. I can tell a music lover when I see one. Mind if I sit?"

Danielle used her foot to push a chair out from the table. "Free country. Suit yourself."

He pulled the chair out further with his boot and sat down on her right side. He held out a big hand and she took it. His skin was rough and his grip strong. She felt callouses on his fingers. "Kyle Greer. Nice to meet you."

Now that he was down on her level, she got a better look at him. He had long, dishwater blond hair and hazel eyes. He hadn't shaved in a couple of days, and the scruffy look was good on him. She smiled. "Danielle Regan."

If he recognized the name he didn't show it. Instead, he leaned in closer and pointed to the stage. "This guy is a New Yorker." Danielle was trying to focus on his words, but the smell of his cologne was distracting her, in a good way. "He's bad on purpose. He thinks that all of us hicks down here are too dumb to know that he's making fun of us."

"I was wondering if he was serious."

"Nah. He couldn't cut it as a comedian so he decided to try this instead. He pretends to be one of us and then he makes funs of us. It doesn't play too well, but he likes the heckling. Thing is, the word's out now so nobody really reacts anymore."

Danielle took a sip and managed to tear her eyes off of the stranger long enough to look back at the stage. "I think he's an ass."

The man laughed again. "And I bet that you'd tell him, too."

"What do you mean by that?"

Kyle Greer had a nice smile, one that lit up the dark bar. "Well, you weren't shy about telling ole Moonshine Mike what you thought about him."

Danielle was suddenly horrified. "You were there?"

234

"Yeah," he said, still amused. "You looked right at me right before that big bald fella drug ya out the door."

Danielle buried her face in her hands. "Oh my god. I'm sorry." She forced herself to look up at him. "That was not my proudest moment."

Kyle patted her on the shoulder. "Don't be. Moonshine's had that one comin' for a while now. No one around here will tell him off. I'm just glad I got to see it. That was a thing of beauty."

"Well I'm glad I could provide you with some free entertainment."

"If you don't mind my asking, why were you meeting with Moonshine Mike anyway? Someone like you doesn't need help from that windbag."

Danielle sighed. "So you do know who I am."

"Of course. Word's been out for a while. Let's be honest here, darlin'. There's not too many places a woman like you can go and not be noticed. Beauty like yours is going to stand out."

"Great, and here I was thinking that I was being all inconspicuous."

"Don't worry. Nobody will mess with you down here. But the question remains. Why did you want to work with Moonshine Mike?"

Danielle took another drink and looked away. "I had this stupid idea about combining our sound with a Nashville twist and trying to make the ultimate American album. I wanted someone who knew the scene down here to help me. It was a bad idea."

"Actually, it's not. A lot of the best young artists have been mixing in more of a rock sound for a while now." He looked her over like he was sizing her up. "You, nobody's seen anything quite like you down here. I can definitely see what you're goin' for. Moonshine Mike's not what you need."

"And you know what I need?"

"Yeah," he said sheepishly. "You need me."

Danielle threw her head back and laughed. Then she patted his knee. "That was very nice. Very smooth. Thank you for that." She stood to leave. "I can't wait to put this damn town in my rearview mirror."

She started out but Kyle caught her at the door. "Come on, Ms. Regan. Just hear me out. You've been kickin' around down here for weeks...I can't believe that you'd just abandon ship now."

She stepped out into the cool night air. "I think that I've had enough Nashville to last me a lifetime. When strangers start propositioning me in bars, it's definitely time to go."

Kyle caught her arm and spun her around. The neon light above the door cast a colored aura around him. "I can get you the sound you want. It's not a stupid idea, you just didn't know who to turn to."

"And it just happens to be you and you just happened to find me here. I'm not stupid...I can smell a set up."

"It doesn't have to be me. There are a number of producers around here that could help you. People who really know what they're doin'. I'd like to be that guy, but if not, I could point you in the right direction. I just don't want you to base your entire opinion of Nashville and country music on that blowhard Moonshine Mike."

"So you're the guy I need to see, huh?"

Kyle tucked his hands in his jeans pockets. "I'd like to be. I could do it. I need someone to give me a chance. Just a chance." He pulled out his wallet and took out a card and handed it across. "Meet with me. Give me a chance. Tomorrow afternoon. I'll have something for you that will change your mind. We could meet in the lobby of your hotel."

"I'm not telling you where I'm staying." His desperation reminded her of her meeting with Steve so long ago. He too, had just been looking for someone to give him a chance. "I tell you what. I'll give you a chance to change my mind. Give me a time and a place."

Kyle smiled and turned the card over and pulled a pen out of his pocket. He quickly wrote on the back of the card, then handed it over. "Meet me here at two."

She took the card without looking at it. "Fine. You've got one chance to convince me. Just a word of warning. My bags will be packed. If you don't convince me, I'm hitting the road and I'll never come back here again. Better give me your best shot."

He tipped his hat at her. "I promise I will."

Danielle went back to the hotel and called Steve, who has just settling in for the night. She gave him what little info she had on Kyle

Greer and he promised he would see what he could find out about the stranger.

Danielle tried to wind down by writing some songs, but it wasn't working. Her mind kept alternating between rage at Moonshine Mike and curiosity about Kyle. There was something intimately likable about him, but she knew better than to trust her own judgment about people, especially men.

The next morning, Steve woke her up with a way too early call. She groped for the phone, found it, and groaned into it.

"I got some info on that guy you called me about. Ready?"

"Yeah," she grumbled.

"Well, there's not a lot to report. He showed up down there in the early '90s. He tried to make it on his own and never did. He's done tons of session work, some with some artists you'd recognize. Now he works for one of those songwriting houses you read about in *Rolling Stone*."

Danielle was starting to wake up now. She forced herself to sit up. "The ones in the office buildings where they check in every day and get assigned partners and they just write all day?"

"Exactly. He's had several songs appear on albums, but no hits. I talked to lots of people who've worked with him. They all said pretty much the same thing. He's reliable, professional, and easy going. He seems to lack the edge necessary to really get ahead, though. Nobody doubts his talent, and he would make a good producer. They just doubt that he really wants it bad enough."

She chewed on her bottom lip as she thought about it. He certainly seemed to want it bad enough yesterday.

"Danielle, what are you thinking? I thought we had agreed to call this off and you'd come back home. I'm getting the feeling that you're second thinking that."

"Maybe. I met this guy last night. He thinks that he can do what I'm looking for. I think he might have the goods."

"I know that you may not want it, Danielle, but I'm going to tell you what I think. I think that you're dying to show up Moonshine Mike and doing it with some nobody like this would really get his goat. That, and I think you're smitten with this guy. That's a bad combination in my opinion."

"Well, you're not wrong. About wanting to get at Moonshine Mike. I don't know where you came up with that other part though. I'm going to meet with him this afternoon and I want to see what he has for me. If he falls on his face, I'm gone. If not...."

"Danielle, please just stop this and come home. I don't know why you're so set on doing this down there. I could find you someone better. Someone with a track record."

"Steve, do you remember when I first took you on, back when nobody else would? I get that same feeling from him. I really feel like I need to give this guy a chance. Let me meet with him today, then we'll talk."

"Fine. You do what you feel you have to. Stay in contact. But please be careful...after what happened with Adam I'm worried about you."

"This has nothing to do with Adam. It's just business. I know my instincts suck when it comes to love, but my business instincts are usually right on."

"It's more than that, Danielle, and I think you know it." He hung up quickly and Danielle felt like she had just gotten in trouble. She tried to laugh it off. He was being overprotective of her. It was just business.

The address Kyle had given her was for a rundown studio in a rough looking part of town. The paint was cracked and faded, the parking lot overrun with weeds and deserted except for a beat up red and silver pickup. She parked next to it and cautiously made her way to the door.

She found the door unlocked and slid right in. The lighting was going out and flickering. Inside was a receptionist desk with two long halls on either side. She peered down the left hall and saw nothing. She looked down the right and saw a door with a red light on above it. She guessed that was where he was hiding.

She walked slowly down the hall, half expecting some ridiculous slasher film monster to jump out of the shadows. She stood in front of the door with the red light, started to knock, then stopped, and before she could decide whether to knock or run, Kyle opened it from the other side.

"I was wondering when you'd get here. Come on in. I know it's a dump, but I can get in any time I want for free, so you can't really beat that deal."

She stepped past him and into a control room that looked eerily similar to the one they had used for *Vintage Beauty*. However, she didn't think that the equipment in here was outdated by design.

"How do you get free studio time?" she asked as she slowly lowered herself into an office chair that had seen better days.

Kyle pushed the door closed and took a similarly rough looking seat next to her. "I help the landlord with the maintenance." She must have made a face because he blushed. "I just started a couple of month ago. It's a work in progress. When I started, not one of these studios was operable. Now I've got three out of the six workin'. The equipment's older than sin, but we're just takin' what we can get. We want to make this place somewhere for people to go cut demos who don't have a lot of money."

"Wow. That's really cool. Are you always so charitable?"

He grinned sheepishly. "Nah. But I've been there and it's hard. People in the industry want to hear demos, but it's hard to come up with the money. The good places will cost you an arm and a leg. We're just tryin' to make it a little easier. The place still has a long ways to go, though."

Their eyes met and an awkward silence followed. He finally broke the contact. "Well, I won't waste any more of your time. What I've done is taken one of your CDs and tried to remix some of your songs with a more country feel. It's a little difficult considerin' that I have to work with the existing track as is, but what I mainly tried to do was include some different instrumentations and change the mix slightly. I also redid some of your guitar parts, using a more standard Nashville tuning. I'm not quite sure what it is you use."

She shrugged. "It changes from song to song and guitar to guitar. Whatever sounds right for the part. So I'm curious. Let me hear what you've got."

He pushed a button and the beginning strains of "Open All Night" filled the air, though instead of her soulful blues intro, there was a steel guitar and fiddle. Her voice came on next. The original song was there, but it was almost unrecognizable. The rhythm tracks were buried far down in the mix, as were the guitars. Her vocals were front and center and she was suddenly a little embarrassed. Had she been hiding her voice all along? The song ended and he killed the tape. "Want to hear another?"

She paused, then shook her head. "No. Could you play that back, but bring the drum and bass up some more?"

"Sure." He played the song again and began to fiddle with the mix. As the song played, Danielle would instruct him, up with this, lower with that. They listened to it several times before she really liked what she heard.

"What do you think now?" Kyle had a horrible poker face; she could read the hope in his eyes.

"It's good, all things considered. To be honest, we'd need to redo the whole arrangement to make it work right, but like you said, you're limited in what you can do. Let me hear another."

He nodded, hit another button, and "Blessed Poison" came on. She immediately reached over and killed the song. "Not that one." Their eyes locked again. "You can fiddle with any of my songs you want, but not that one. That one's special to me and I love it just the way it is. Do you have another?"

Kyle nodded. At first he looked terrified, but she thought that he finally got it. "Yeah, I do."

They went through several more songs and they soon began to read each other's thoughts and make changes before the other even asked. They were clicking, and it was sounding good. When they were done, Danielle leaned back and was almost thrown to the floor by the broken chair, but Kyle reached out and grabbed her arm. "I wouldn't do that. Don't really have the budget for good chairs right now."

"Thanks," she said slowly. "Well. I'm impressed enough to keep working. Next test. I know that you're a professional songwriter. I'd like to try and write a song with you. Are you game?"

"Sure thing. Let me get my stuff."

"No. Not right now. All my gear is back at the hotel. I've got your card, I'll give you a call. Okay?"

Kyle smiled, a nice warm smile. "That sounds great."

There was only one Kyle Greer listed in the White Pages, and it didn't take long for Danielle to find his house, a decaying A frame in a neighborhood not far from the studio. The tiny house had a cracked driveway leading to a detached garage in back, and a chain link fence to keep in an overgrown and weed ridden yard. The exterior was brown brick with faded brown trim, and a skinny cement porch covered in brown Astroturf. She saw the same Chevy truck sitting in the driveway and she pulled in behind it. There was a light on behind a pulled blind in one of the front windows.

She put the car in park and reached over the back seat for her acoustic guitar before getting out. She headed for the door and was about to reach out and knock when the door flew open.

"I said I'm...." Kyle stopped midsentence. He was wearing a black Lynyrd Skynyrd T-shirt with a ripped sleeve and a pair of Budweiser boxers. He had the door knob in one hand and a half eaten rib slathered in BBQ sauce in the other. There were a couple of smears of BBQ sauce on his face. "Shit," he muttered under his breath. Danielle tried to hide her smile and he tucked the hand with the rib behind his back. "Ms. Regan, I'm sorry. I wasn't expecting company."

"I know," she giggled. "I wanted to catch you unaware, see what you were like when you weren't prepared. I was hoping we could hang out a little, maybe try to write a song. But if you're busy...."

"No, not at all. I was just eating dinner."

"And saving some for later, from the looks of it."

"Ah," he moaned. He let go of the doorknob and used the bottom of his shirt to wipe his face. He had a nice, flat stomach; not ripped like Adam was, but toned. When he was done, he opened the screen door for her. "Come on it. Just give me a minute to straighten up."

He stepped aside and Danielle stepped in. The first thing she noticed was a huge Confederate flag hanging on the wall over a beat up couch. The kitchen was a straight walk through the living room, and she could see his dining room table with the rest of his dinner waiting. To the left were two rooms with doors closed, bedrooms she assumed. The place had last been decorated sometime in the '70s. The carpet was yellow shag, the walls were covered with cheap wood paneling, and there was a huge grate on the floor where the furnace must be. Besides the couch, he had an imitation leather recliner with a tear in one arm, and a short coffee table that looked ready for the trash heap. It was covered with magazines. She heard before she saw the TV, which was set against the front wall. He was watching baseball.

She stepped far enough inside to see that he was watching the Braves and the Astros. "Braves fan?"

Kyle pushed the front door shut and edged past her. "Huh? Oh, no, not really. Just somethin' to have on. I'm not much of a sports fan. Not unless you count huntin' and fishin' as sports."

"I don't," she answered matter-of-factly. "Those are hobbies, not sports."

"Yeah, I kind of agree. Let me just get this put away and we can talk."

Danielle laid her guitar gently in his recliner. "Don't worry about it. Finish your dinner. I've got all night. Besides, I'm a Texas girl…I know better than to let good barbecue get cold."

He had been busy trying to clean up, but now he stopped and smiled at her. "You're sure that you don't mind?"

"Nah, go ahead."

Kyle sat down in a metal frame chair with black and white Naugahyde covering. Three more were spread around the table, which she noticed was just a foldable card table. He ate off a paper plate using plastic utensils. There was a bottle of Coors on the table next to his plate. He took a drink as she sat down to his right.

"I thought that you were a Bud man."

"Hell no," he said as he put the bottle down. "Bud tastes like piss."

"Doesn't it all?" she answered with a grin.

"No," he answered, sounding almost offended by the comment. "What makes you think that? There are some excellent beers out there. Bud just isn't one of them."

Danielle shrugged. "What makes me think it tastes like piss? Because all of the beers that I ever drank tasted like piss, that's why."

"No, not that. What makes you think that I'm a Bud man?" Danielle chuckled and nodded in the direction of his lap. He looked down and took a second to realize what she was getting at. "Oh. These are the last evidence of an old girlfriend. She liked to do stuff like that. I drive a Chevy, so she always bought me Ford stuff. You know the type."

242

Danielle shook her head. "Not really."

Kyle shrugged. "There are plates on the counter if you want some of this. I buy family style and milk it for several days."

"I ate before I came over, so go ahead and knock yourself out."

He made a grunting noise and went back to his rib. If he was self-conscious about the way he was eating he didn't show it. After a few minutes of nothing but the sound of his chewing Danielle decided to make some small talk. "So are you from here originally?"

Kyle wiped his mouth with a napkin this time. "No. My dad was in the air force so we moved around a lot. I was pretty much a drifter in my early years. Settled here about...." He paused and looked skyward for a moment. "Almost eight years now." Then he looked around his meager home. "Got a lot to show for it, huh?"

Danielle tried to shrug off the comment. "Seems comfortable enough."

"Yeah, comfortable. That's my problem."

Danielle put her elbows on the table and rested her chin in one palm. "What do you mean by that?"

He swallowed a bite of potato salad and shrugged. "I get comfortable and I stop pushin' myself. It was very hard for me to approach you earlier. But I've got to be more assertive. Time's tickin' away and I've got nothing to show for it."

"What, are you dying or something?"

"No more than you are." He registered the shock on her face and covered quickly. "I mean, time is tickin' on us all. Forty is a lot closer than it used to be and this is not where I pictured myself."

"But if you're comfortable, doesn't that mean that you're happy?"

"I thought so," Kyle answered. "Leighanne thought differently."

"Girlfriend?"

"Fiancée. Well, former fiancée. I thought that she was the love of my life. She was always riding me to push harder, work harder. Hell, I was happy to have a steady roof over my head. She wanted more and I couldn't give it to her. So she found someone who could." Danielle watched him intently, but he wasn't giving away anything. "You know who Cale Trickett is?"

"He's a singer, isn't he?"

243

"One of the hottest voices in Nashville. She's his old lady now."

Danielle bit her tongue. She had always hated people who referred to their girlfriends as old lady. It seemed trashy to her. She looked up to see him watching her.

"She was a climber. She thought I was a rising star. Once she saw that I wasn't, she was long gone. She never loved me, certainly not the way I loved her."

"Ah, a sensitive man," she teased. "Under all of this sloppy exterior. So are you doing this for her? Trying to show her that you finally made something of yourself?"

"Hell no. I'm past her. But it got me to thinkin' that it was time to make a move. You see some people around this town and they're still bangin' away, playin' ratty little clubs or street corners. They're still chasing that dream, but it's passed them by. I don't want to be that guy." Then he pointed his rib at her. "In fact, I won't be that guy. When she left me and I sobered up—because I spent about a month completely shitfaced—I gave myself a year to make somethin' of myself. To at least get a start. If nothin' happens, then I'm gone. I'm gonna pack up my stuff and hit the road."

"That's a lonely life. I've done the drifter bit. It gets old pretty fast."

He shook his head. "But you weren't really driftin'. You had somethin' to come home to. I don't. I could just float until somethin' strikes my fancy. Go anywhere, do anything. Total freedom."

Danielle leaned back and tilted her chair until only the back two legs were on the ground. "Sounds nice. Why not do it now?"

"Because reality is never as nice as the idea. Besides, I'm too old to be livin' a Steppenwolf song for the rest of my life."

"How much time you got left?"

He looked her dead in the eyes. "Three weeks."

"Shit," she muttered.

"Yeah, no kiddin'. You're my last hope. And though I've never been big on the whole destiny bit, it does strike me that you happened into town and across my path at the absolute right time. And that you tried to hire that dickhead Moonshine Mike instead any one of the dozen producers who could have given you want you wanted without the diva bullshit."

244

Danielle laughed. "That wasn't my best call." After that, the conversation waned and she watched him finish eating and stow away his leftovers. The fridge had plenty of leftovers from other places, lots of Coors longnecks, and a six pack of canned Cokes. She took one out and held it up for him to see. "Mind if I drink one?"

"Sure. You can have a beer if you want."

"No thanks," she said as she pushed the refrigerator door shut. "This doesn't taste like piss."

He chuckled and led her back into the living room. She picked her guitar up and took a seat on the couch while he picked up the remote and muted the TV. "I keep my gear in the other room. Be right back." Kyle ducked into a room on his right and came back a few minutes later with his own guitar in one hand and a tape recorder in the other. "I got a four track, too. If we really get somethin' rollin', I'll break it out. I just like to start with this to get the raw ideas down."

"I use a sixteen track at home." She saw the jealous look on his face. "I've got a home studio in my basement. I usually have an album 70% completed before I even step foot in a real studio, so this is a whole new experience for me."

"You're one of those people," he said as he hooked up the recorder and checked the cassette. "The type that can pull a song out of their ass and have a masterpiece in ten minutes."

"I guess," Danielle answered sheepishly. "I have my moments. I wrote 'Blessed Poison' in my head while I was driving across West Texas. Didn't have a damn thing on me, not even a pen and paper to write anything down. I just had to keep singing it to myself, hour after hour, until I got home and could get something down on tape."

"I hate people like you," he said, but she knew he didn't mean it personally. "I've been writing for years and I haven't had an experience like that." He sat down next to her with his guitar. He started strumming slowly, warming up his fingers. She did the same, but much faster. He didn't seem impressed and continued running through some warm up exercises. She soon realized that she was playing a complimentary pattern to his and smiled.

"What?"

"We're already connecting," she said. "Listen." Kyle sat and listened as they played and a smile crossed his face as well. "You might not want to start packing yet."

The sun was up over the horizon by the time Danielle emerged. The night had been promising. They had several rough ideas on tape. She was feeling even more inspired, but was completely out of gas. Kyle had offered to let her sleep at his place while he went off to work, but she declined.

Danielle knocked on his door at precisely ten o'clock, expecting him to be half naked and mostly asleep. Instead he was bright eyed and bushy tailed, this time wearing some black athletic shorts and a red T shirt from the 1962 Winter National drag races. He smiled as he held the door open for her.

"I figured that you'd be dead to the world," she said as she carried her gear in. This time she had brought her electric guitar and amp with her.

"I knocked off work about four and came home and slept. I don't need much sleep to recharge my batteries."

Danielle smelled the wonderful aroma of chargrilled beef as she put her instruments down. On his kitchen table were two actual plates, each with a bacon cheeseburger on it, and a Coors for himself and a bottle of Coke for her. She made a sound that might have been a purr.

"Cooked them myself," Kyle said with pride. "I read an interview once where you said that your favorite food in the world is a bacon cheeseburger."

"I don't remember that interview. I'm sure I said it though, because it's true."

"Well, sit down and eat. I love a girl who will eat real food. Leighanne was one of those prissy girls that only ate salads and drank mineral water."

Danielle sat down and opened her Coke. "She sounds like a princess. I can't believe that she'd be your type."

"She gave great...." He stopped himself and looked up, embarrassed. Danielle held her Coke inches from her lips, frozen in expectation. "She was very passionate."

"Uh huh," she said. "So how does one work in an office building writing songs? I never pictured songwriting as a nine to five job."

"In Nashville it is. I don't like it that much, and I'm not that good at it. I'm better working like we did last night. But some of those people, they come in and boom, they've got four songs written just like that."

"Yeah, but don't y'all just have a spinner or something? Song ideas: My mom, My dog, My truck...."

"I've worked with people who can write a song about anything. You can literally pull an idea out of your ass and they'll have you a song in a half hour. Those are the ones who pull the big money. It makes me sick."

"So how is it that you've been doing this for years and never had a hit? I mean, writing a country song isn't that hard. It's not like there's that much of a difference. I've heard some really corny country songs."

"If it's so easy then why are you asking me to help you? It's harder than it looks. There are thousands of us, tens of thousands of songs. Who's to say why no A&R man has ever chosen one of my songs to be a single?"

"Okay, sorry," Danielle answered defensively. "I was just asking."

Kyle was not backing down though. "You came to me asking to help you write songs because 'the vibe isn't right,' and then you sit there and say it's not hard? How am I supposed to take that? How come I've never had a hit? Maybe because I'm not as lucky as you are. Or as good looking. Or as talented." His voice trailed off.

Danielle pushed away from the table and stood up. "You've got a point. I think I'll go now." She walked quickly to retrieve her gear. Kyle remained seated.

She raced back to the hotel, her mind so hung up on the events of the evening that she didn't even remember the drive back. She left her gear in the car and ran into the hotel and up the stairs to her eighth floor room, trying to outrun the embarrassment and hurt that she felt. When she finally got to her room, she threw herself down on the bed and cried herself to sleep.

The phone began ringing a little after eight. The first time it woke her up. The next three times it kept her from going back to sleep. When sleep was finally out of the question, she began packing and worked right through the next five calls.

Finally, with all of her stuff packed and the final inspection of her room complete, the phone rang for a tenth time. Annoyed and ready to fight, she stormed to the phone and yanked it up. Before she could answer, the voice on the other end said, "I hold them back. I hold my best songs back."

Danielle's immediate rage abated. "What?"

"I screwed up last night."

"No shit," she shot back. The rage was boiling back up to the surface now. "I get that the question came off rude, but what kind of an asshole do you have to be? I don't let people talk to me like that, ever. My mother talked to me like that right up until the day I nearly strangled her. She's the last person who will ever do it. So yeah, you screwed up. But you put me in my place, so you can feel good about that at least." She slammed the receiver down and glared at it, daring it to ring again.

It did.

She picked up. "I'm askin' for another chance with you," Kyle said immediately. "Your manager warned me that you weren't big on second chances. I'd like to change your mind."

"Why should I? And when did you talk to Steve?"

"This morning. He called to discuss the financial arrangement. When I told him what happened last night, he gave me your number. I get the idea that he's hopin' that you go home now. I don't think that he likes me."

"He hates all things country music. And he thinks that this is a stupid idea. At this point, I can't say that I'm really feeling much southern hospitality."

"Listen, yesterday was a bad day for me. I'd really like a chance to make it up to you. That's not who I am. Just give me today. Let me come pick you up and take you out for the day, show you my Nashville. No music talk, no work, let's just get to know each other. At the end of the day, if you're still pissed at me, I'll pack your bags myself."

"They're already packed and by the door." She paused for a minute. She still felt the pull to stay. "One chance. I'll pick you up. You have to convince me to stay."

"I'll be ready when you get here." he said hopefully, and hung up. Danielle hung her phone up gently and stared at it.

"What are you doing, Danielle?" She didn't have an answer for herself. She stifled the urge to go ahead and leave…she had told him she'd give him the day. She threw her packed bags on her bed, changed clothes, and left. The entire time, she kept asking herself why.

Kyle was out the door the second she pulled into the driveway. He wore his boots, starched blue jeans, a blue plaid shirt, and a denim baseball hat with a Peterbuilt logo stitched onto it. He slid casually into the passenger seat.

"Thank you," he said sincerely.

"Yeah, whatever. Where am I going?"

He directed her to a hole in the wall diner where they ordered pulled pork sandwiches and sweet tea. He guided her to a booth by the window. Once they were settled in, Kyle began.

"Okay, so about last night. First, I was way out of line jumpin' on you like that. I felt bad because you're right. That's not the way music should be made. I never wanted to punch a time clock, but here I am, that's exactly what I do. I took my anger at myself out on you because you reminded me of my failures. I was too embarrassed to stop you from leaving, which I should have done. I'm not tryin' to excuse it either. There is no excuse. I just want you to understand."

"Understood." Danielle kept her face emotionless. She had learned that a stone face could get you places.

"Good. I quit that job at the songwriting house. As soon as you left I called my boss and pulled a Johnny Paycheck on him."

"A what?"

"Johnny Paycheck. Take this job and shove it?" Danielle had no idea. Kyle shrugged it off. "It's a song from the '70s. The point is, I want to get back to the real reasons that I got into makin' music. I need you to do that. My career is stalled, and if you bail on me now I'm screwed."

"That's not really my problem. I feel for you, but we all follow our own path. I had to make my own hard choices. I could have quit, almost did a couple of times. I could have taken the easy way, but I never did."

"I understand that. But you were willin' to give me a chance before. Why I don't know, but you were. I'm just askin' to keep that chance. Don't let my bein' a douche last night change your mind."

Danielle ran her fingertip along the rim of her tea glass. "Did you ever consider that maybe this isn't the life for you?"

Kyle lowered his eyes, looking defeated. "Yeah, maybe you're right. I just thought that maybe...."

Danielle had blown up at more than one undeserving person over the years. She had to like the way he owned up to everything. "I tell you what. I'll forget last night and we'll go on. But this is your one and only get out of jail free card. For life. Don't waste it."

"For life?" Kyle asked, eyebrows raised.

"Yeah. I might want to keep working with you. So it's for life."

Kyle stared at her, trying to read more into her words. Danielle wasn't giving anything away. Then the waitress brought their food and the moment passed.

Kyle led Danielle through a day long tour of the city. He showed her historic sites as well as personal landmarks, such as the theater where he played his first gig and the studio where he did his first session. George Strait signed an autograph here, and he filled in on Faith Hill's band there. She realized that his love of music was legitimate; she could see it by the way his face lit up with ever memory he shared.

She kept her personal information to herself. Instead, she engaged him, letting him talk and taking in the info. By the time they ate chicken fried steak dinners at a roadhouse outside of town, she felt that she knew him fairly well.

Kyle's dad was an air force lifer, a mechanic who prided himself on his duty and his patriotism, but who was largely disinterested with fatherly duties. He wasn't abusive, Kyle stressed, he was a great guy who preferred not to be bothered with paternal responsibility. That fell on his mom, a loving mother hen type who supported her kids and husband with her whole heart, but never questioned her traditional role and never dared challenge his father on anything. He had older siblings who had scattered and rarely contacted him.

His best friend growing up was a cousin on his mother's side who died in a car accident as a teen. Other than that, Kyle was a loner who made friends easily but never let anyone get too close. He admitted a weakness for girls, especially blondes, and that he fell in love easily and therefore easily got his heart broken. He was a romantic who tried to hide the fact behind a tough guy exterior.

Any time Kyle pressed for personal info on Danielle, she changed the subject. She had no desire to drag out old skeletons for public viewing. She had also been burned by wearing her heart on her sleeve, and wasn't about to make the same mistake.

When she dropped him off at his house she thought that he was going to go for a goodnight kiss, but he passed, leaving Danielle both relieved and upset. On the way to the hotel, she berated herself. She was letting this man worm his way into her heart, and she had to stop it. He was, she reminded herself, a slacker; a hack with no direction, ambition, or drive. She knew that he was nothing but trouble, but her heart was seeing something different.

The next day, they met for breakfast before going back to his place to work on material. With their issues behind them, they began belting out songs at a breakneck pace. Kyle began to assert himself more. He guided her through the songwriting process in a new way. He helped her sharpen her lyrics and make the tunes more melodic and radio friendly, and introduced her to Nashville tuning on her guitar.

After they had written several songs, Kyle disappeared into the back for several minutes. When he came back, he had a different guitar, a beat to hell black and white Kay acoustic that looked like it had been rescued from a dumpster. He sat on the floor at Danielle's feet and began playing a slow tune.

Danielle sat and watched as he began singing. His voice was gruff but she loved the emotion as he sang of a lost love. It was clear that the person he was singing about had truly meant something to him, the pain was too evident. It was a beautiful song. As he finished, his eyes were wet with tears that he would not let fall.

"That's beautiful," Danielle said softly. "What's it called?"

"Sometimes It Fades." People have been telling me that it's a guaranteed Top 5 hit if I gave it to the right person, but I never wanted to. It's the best thing I've ever written." Their eyes locked. "I want you to have it."

Danielle was taken aback. "I can't. That's your song. You should sing it."

"Shit," he said. "I'm never going to do anything with it. You heard me sing. I'm fine for a honky tonk crowd, but I'll never get a record deal."

Danielle put her guitar aside and slid off the couch and onto the floor next to him. "I bet I could get you a deal. There's an audience for good music out there, and your voice is actually very sexy. Lots of us like that rough edge. Two calls and I can get you something."

"I don't want it. You're the performer, and I think that you'd do it justice. I won't let anyone else sing it. Either you do it or I take it to my grave."

"Kyle," she scolded. "Don't be like that. You might like the spotlight if you gave it a chance."

"No. This is how it goes. I had hoped you'd appreciate this." He stood up with a grunt. "I had hoped that you'd get it." He took the guitar with him to the back.

Danielle watched him go, then stood and slipped into her guitar strap. It took just a few moments to find the right starting place, and then she started playing the song. This time, she drew it out, filling the places in between with sorrowful runs. He peeked around the corner as she began to solo. He was standing in front of her by the time she finished. She locked her smoldering green eyes on him. "That's how I would do it. Still want me to sing it?"

Kyle smiled. "You put some steel guitar and a fiddle on that and you've got yourself a certified country hit on your hands."

"I don't know how to play those things."

Kyle smiled wider. "I do."

Ty and Trish were the first band members to drift into town. By the time they arrived, Danielle and Kyle had written an album's worth of new material on their own. Still, seeing her two best friends gave her heart a lift. She couldn't wait to introduce them to Kyle.

Kyle took them to a country and western bar with a pine dance floor that circled a roughly built stage. There was a band playing when they got there, and a few couples were twirling around the floor under the glow of the neon lights of the beer signs on the wall. They took a table near the bar. "The band is just made up of whoever jumps up on stage," Kyle explained. "Throughout the night people will jump in and out and the music will change according to who's playing and who's leading. Pretty much anything goes."

"Anybody can jump up on stage?" Trish asked, almost insulted. "What if they suck?"

"Then they get booed off. The crowd knows what they like and what they don't. They won't put up with crap."

Ty and Danielle traded glances. "Like Sixth Street on a Friday night," she said with a smile.

Ty was reading her thoughts. "I think that we should just sit and watch, Dani."

"No," she said with an impish grin. "Let's show Nashville what Austin can do. Come on." She took him by the hand and led him to the foot of the stage, where they waited for a break. Then they jumped up. Danielle tapped a cowboy with a Telecaster and asked if she could cut in. He handed over the ax while Ty took another one and they each took a second to tune up. She gave the other musicians a few notes and they started playing "Blessed Poison."

Danielle and Ty played off of each other just like they always had, and at the instrumental section of the song they engaged in a dueling guitar bit. Not to be outdone, one of the fiddle players jumped right in with them and traded some runs of his own. The crowd was eating it up as the rest of the band changed the tune. Danielle recognized it as a George Strait song…thanks to Adam for that one. A pretty little blonde grabbed the mike and started singing in a high, but nice voice. Danielle and Ty fell right in.

Danielle could see Kyle and Trish at their table, both drinking Coors and watching them intently. Danielle stuck her tongue out at them and she and Ty changed the song again, this time to Stevie Ray's "Change It." Again, the backing band fell in with them. The seesaw game continued, Danielle and Ty each taking turns with some sizzling guitar runs only to have the band swing it back around again. Finally, they flew up the white flag and exited the stage to applause.

"How long has it been since you had that much fun onstage?" a giddy Danielle asked Ty as they walked back to the table.

"It reminded me of Randy's. You remember how much fun that used to be?"

"Yeah," she answered, and they both fell silent.

"Y'all are good," Kyle said as he tipped his beer. "I grant you that. I can tell that you've played together for a long time."

Danielle squeezed Ty's arm. "This guy's like a brother to me. I don't know what I'd do with him. Without both of them," she said, nodding at Trish.

Kyle smiled. "This one has been clueing me in on some of your adventures. You are apparently a bit of a firecracker."

Danielle took a swig from Kyle's bottle and grimaced. "Jesus, how do you drink this stuff?" She waved the waitress over and ordered a Coke. "I've had my moments." She admitted. "But you've already seen that side of me."

"Is it true that a stripper taught you how to dance?"

Danielle felt herself blush. "Yes. She taught me how to perform. I kind of made up my own moves after a while. But Mick Jagger, I'm not."

Kyle stood quickly and grabbed her hand. "Well, let's see how good you dance. Ever two step?"

"No," she said as he drug her to the dance floor.

"Well, I'm no stripper, but I can show you." He led her to floor and instructed her on the finer points of the two step. She struggled at first, stumbling around and embarrassing herself. Kyle wouldn't let her quit. The band saw what was going on and kept playing good two stepping songs. Other dancers shouted out tips and she began to get the hang of it. Once she finally finished a song without a major mistake the crowd applauded again.

As another song started up and they began another dance, Danielle risked a hard look at this new man in her life. She studied his features as they twirled; his soft blue eyes, rugged good looks, and ramrod straight posture. She smelled his cologne mixing with the smell of the wood, beer, and sweat, and for a fleeting moment, the thought entered her head.

I'm falling in love with this guy.

Garrett arrived the next day, drum kit in tow, ready to play. DeShon was delayed, though, and he wanted them to start without him. Garrett felt that DeShon was avoiding it, wanting no part of the whole project. Danielle was disappointed but accepted it.

Steve booked them some rehearsal space and the group gathered to begin hashing out new material. Kyle came along and brought several of his friends and a bevy of new instruments, things she had never thought of using before. Kyle and Danielle played the rest of the band their new songs. Suggestions were made and things began to evolve.

DeShon arrived a week later and Danielle thought that the hulking black man might have intimidated her new friends, but only for a bit. He seemed moody and disinterested. Garrett assured her he would warm to the project, but she had doubts.

For Danielle, recording had always been her favorite part of the job. She loved the creative process, the search to find each song's perfect sound. She took it seriously, but also enjoyed it and it had always come relatively easy.

This time was an exception. The chemistry between Kyle's people and the band wasn't happening. Even after the weeks of rehearsal, the sound wasn't coming together the way she wanted it. Kyle sat in the booth as each recording inevitably went south and the two kept exchanging worried glances.

Danielle had promised Steve that if this didn't happen quickly she would abandon the project, but it wasn't in her nature to give up. After a series of disappointing takes, Danielle called for a break.

Kyle met her in the hallway and drug her by the arm into a janitor's closet. "Your bass player is screwing everything up."

Danielle was offended. "Excuse me. We're all professionals here. So if you're insinuating that DeShon is intentionally screwing things up—"

"That's damn straight what I'm saying. I've been watching him. He's glaring at my people, glaring at me, rolling his eyes. He's sabotaging it. He's playing off the beat. Now I listened to everything you've ever recorded before we started this project because I wanted to know your sound. Either you've had to do a lot of post recording work to cover his flaws or he is blowing this, because this isn't how he plays. If I were you, I'd have a little talk with him."

Danielle wanted to be mad, to defend DeShon, but she had been secretly thinking the same thing. He hadn't seemed to want anything to do with the project. In fact, he hadn't been the same since the sessions for *Vintage Beauty*. "Okay, I'll go talk to him."

Danielle found DeShon outside, smoking a cigarette by himself behind the building. "Hey big guy," she called. "What's going on?"

DeShon glanced over his shoulder, then looked away. "Nothing."

"Yeah, no kidding. We're spinning our wheels here."

"Yep." He blew a slow lungful of smoke into the air.

She stood at his side, an arm's length away, staring at the side of his face. "Is there something going on?"

He grunted in response.

"I'd like to think that there's something going on, because I know that you're a damn great bass player. Way too good to be making the sloppy mistakes that you've been making so far. I'd hate to think that you're intentionally trying to ruin this."

He let out another long stream of smoke. "Think what you want."

Danielle paused a minute to think, then she walked around in front of DeShon. "What I think is this. I think I can go back in that studio and have Kyle play bass and get a track down in half an hour. And if I do that, and if I'm right, then that means you're sandbagging me. I don't think I can tolerate that."

DeShon raised an eyebrow. "You firing me? Because I can go any time you want me to."

Danielle put her hands on her hips. "Do you want to be fired? Because I really don't want to do that. You're an integral part of this band and you're my friend. At least you used to be. Something has changed and I would sure like to know what."

DeShon threw his cigarette on the pavement at his feet and rubbed it out with his toe. "Look around. You drug me into hillbilly heaven and you want to know what's wrong? This is what's wrong. This isn't us. I don't know why you want to start playing shitkicker music, but if this is what you want, then leave me out of it. I keep looking over my shoulder, waiting for the white hoods to come take me away."

"Oh, spare me," she shot back. "This isn't the sixties, for God's sake. We play the south all the time. You should know better than that. And where exactly did this crap come from? You've never tried to use your color as a cop out before."

He took an angry step toward her. For a moment, she almost threw her hands up to defend herself. Instead, she stifled the urge and stood her ground.

"I'm not copping out. You're the one who changed. You drug us to New England to record the whitest album possible, now you've got us doing hillbilly music. If anybody's turning racist, it's you. We used to play the blues, now we play this shit."

"Oh, Jesus," she muttered. "You too, huh? My last bass player pulled this shit on me. Maybe I'm not satisfied to just be a blues guitarist. Maybe I want more, that I want to stretch out. All I'm trying to do is keep our sound fresh. I'm looking for new ideas so that we don't wind up recording the same album every time. If that makes me a racist, then I guess I am. Doesn't take much these days, does it?"

"What's that supposed to mean?"

She stepped right up to him, her chest bumping his, and she craned her neck so that she could look him in the eyes. "It means that I don't appreciate your insinuation. It means that all I'm trying to do is keep challenging myself. All that matters to me is the music, and you know that. Or at least I thought that you did. I don't know where this bullshit is coming from, but it needs to stop. Now I'm going back inside to get back to work. You get your shit together and get back in there and do your job, or get lost and I'll find somebody else."

"You think you can replace me that easily?"

"No. I know that I can't replace you. That's why I'm so pissed. You're the best. But if you're gonna be a pussy and question every move I make then you'll leave me no choice. It's up to you what happens next, not me." She stormed off, but paused at the door. "You've got ten minutes. Smoke another cigarette and make your decision. At eleven minutes, we start recording and you're out."

She stepped back inside and waited for the door to shut behind her. Then she let out a primal scream and turned and started to hit the wall, but stopped herself. She couldn't afford to break her hand, so she kicked it instead, but not too hard. Kyle and Ty both came walking down the hall to check on her. She shook her head at them.

"He's on some victim/racist trip. Says I'm playing too white and not playing the blues anymore."

Kyle started to answer, but Ty put up a hand to stop him. "Let me talk to Dani a second." He took her by the arm and pulled her aside. "DeShon's been hanging out with some new dudes, playing in some side bands during the down times. They've been giving him shit about playing with you. It's been getting to him. You know DeShon, he comes off so tough and so cool, but he's sensitive to stuff.

Just cut him a little slack. He'll come around. He needs to know who his real friends are."

"Yeah, well it may be too late for that," she answered. "I told him that he has ten minutes to get his crap together or he's gone."

"Ah shit."

Ten minutes turned into fifteen before Danielle gave up. She assembled the rest of the band and returned to the studio. They were just about to start back up when DeShon came in. He smiled weakly at Danielle and held up a hand with a bare wrist and said, "My watch is broken."

Danielle smiled as DeShon picked up his bass. "Okay, now let's make some music."

Recording started to get easier and slowly the album came together. Every night Kyle and Danielle went back to his house to review the day's progress and hang out, but the temperature had cooled considerably. Danielle began to rationalize it, telling herself that it was for the best. He obviously had more important things on his plate than romance, and she certainly wasn't ready to leave her life behind. She accepted the reality of the situation.

Time was growing short. The album was more or less done with the exception of some last minute touches. They both figured that it would be done in two or three more days. Danielle sent the rest of the band home, though everybody decided to get together for one last dinner.

They went to Moonshine Mike's favorite restaurant and Danielle was disappointed to find out that he hadn't been back there since their altercation. She wanted to rub it in a little, to let him know she was still there. It was a small loss.

Dinner was nice but she noticed that Trish and Ty were watching her all night. They picked up the vibe as well. When it was over, Danielle didn't even bother to say goodnight to Kyle. Instead she took Ty and Trish back to the hotel and quickly bid them goodnight. A little later, Trish knocked on the door.

Danielle, wearing a tattered Fender T shirt and gray shorts, opened the door and Trish slid in. "So what's wrong?" Trish looked around as she asked and noticed that Danielle was already packed and ready to go.

"Nothing's wrong. In fact, I'm excited," Danielle said as she stepped past Trish and plopped down on the couch. Trish sat down beside her. "I think that the album is going great. I think it will be a hit. I'm ready to get back to Austin and get this thing rolling."

"That's not what I'm talking about and you know it. I mean with Kyle. That first night we were in town you looked like you were in heaven out on that dance floor with him. Now things are icy between you. Did you have a fight?"

"No. Everything is fine. I think you read too much into it. We've been getting along, he's a nice guy. There's just nothing there. It's strictly business."

"Bull," Trish shot back. She never cussed. "That night wasn't business. I know you too well. You were feeling something."

"Maybe I was," Danielle admitted. "But it doesn't matter. This is his big opportunity. He needs to be here. I can't be. I'm tired of Nashville. I'm ready to get back to living my life, which means leaving him behind. So what's the point?"

Trish was chewing on her thumbnail and thinking. "Oh. So you're shutting down because you don't want to get hurt again."

Danielle pushed up off the couch. "Don't start with me, please. We're going in different directions. I should pine for someone I can't have? That's not what I want. It's just not meant to be."

"You don't know that, because you won't even give it a chance. These things can be worked out. Does he even know how you feel about him?"

"He should."

"You haven't told him?"

"Hell no," Danielle answered. "I'm not going to put myself out there like that. I can't give him that kind of leverage on me."

"Pride," Trish said with a roll of her eyes.

"Smart," Danielle responded. "Besides, I don't know how he feels about me either."

"Well, somebody needs to take a chance and put it out there before it's too late. He could be the one for you, Danielle. He brings something out in you that no one, not even Adam, ever has. Don't waste it."

259

"It's not going to be me that puts it out there. I've been down that road before. No, if he wants me, he's going to have to make the first move."

Trish sighed and stood up. "I'm afraid that you're making a big mistake here, sis."

Danielle shrugged. "Wouldn't be the first one."

Ty and Trish left the next morning, leaving Danielle alone. She spent the day in the control room with Kyle, recording punch ins and listening to mixes. Late in the afternoon, they wrapped it up. They agreed that the next day, Danielle would go in to the studio and do her final overdubs and then it would be done.

They sat through a quiet dinner together. Danielle could sense that he had things he wanted to say, but he refused to say them. She wondered if he knew that she did too. A few times she started to say something, but she choked it back.

Kyle invited her back to his place. The humidity in the air was thick and heavy...a storm was brewing. "Best not," she said. She pointed at the clouds building back to the west. "Wouldn't want to get caught driving home in that."

Kyle waved her off. "It'll be hours before that gets here, if it even does. Could veer off or peter out. Just come over for a little bit. Come on, it's our last night together."

"Fine."

They walked in and Danielle took her familiar spot on his couch beneath the giant flag. Kyle kicked off his boots and went to the kitchen for a beer and a Coke. She took her drink with a thin smile and took a sip.

Kyle set his beer down on the coffee table without tasting it. He leaned forward and rested his elbows on his knees. He was angled toward her but looking at the floor. "I want to thank you for the opportunity you've given me. I'll always be in your debt."

"You're welcome," she said coldly. "Thank you for your hard work."

He finally forced himself to look at her, and she met his gaze halfway. "I...don't know...." Danielle waited patiently for him to finish. "I think...I think that I can get some guys to go out on the road with you. I'll make some calls, talk to some guys and see what I can do."

Danielle slumped back and took another drink. "We'd appreciate it." She was kicking herself for agreeing to come and trying to think of a graceful way out.

"I hate this," he finally said. "We get along so well, and then...." Danielle didn't finish the thought for him. "Could we just hang out tonight and talk and have fun like we did? I don't want you to go with things like this."

"Sure," she said. He found a baseball game on TV and popped some popcorn in the microwave and they watched, making small talk and cracking jokes. Neither of them said what was really on their minds.

In the seventh inning, the rain began to beat against his window. "That's my cue. If I'm going to get back across town before that storm hits in force, I need to go now."

"Please don't." She looked back expectantly. "The roads get slick and people get stupid, and you don't know the town that well. Stay."

"I think I can handle a little rain. I'll see you at the studio tomorrow morning." She pulled away from him and opened the front door. The rain was pouring in sheets so thick she could barely see her car in the driveway.

Kyle came up behind her and put his hands on her shoulders. "It's nasty out there. Stay. I'd feel a lot better." Danielle turned to face him and he smiled. "I'll be a perfect gentleman, I swear."

She stayed. They finished the game and then caught an old action movie on one of the cable channels before Danielle ran out of steam. He gave her an old T-shirt to sleep in and she took the bed. She was asleep the second her head hit the pillow.

She awoke sometime in the night and felt him beside her. One arm was thrown across her stomach and she could feel his breath on the back of her neck. She moved her arms and felt that the blankets were still wrapped around her tightly. He was sleeping on top of the covers. A thick beam of moonlight broke through a broken slat on his blinds, drenching the room in a pale glow. She felt warm and safe in his arms, and she snuggled up closer to him and drifted back to sleep.

In the morning, the smell of bacon and eggs woke her up. He had been the perfect gentleman as promised. She yawned and stretched, trying to wake up, when Kyle came in with a plate. He set it on the nightstand, leaned over, and gave the stretching Danielle a quick, innocent kiss on the lips. "I don't want you to go, Danielle. I love you."

She was caught off-guard, half asleep and taken aback. She smiled against her will. "I wish I could stay." That wasn't the answer he was looking for and he started to pull away, but she wrapped her arms around his neck and held him. "I can't...say certain things. But I've been dreading this day. I've wanted to tell you."

"I have too," he whispered back. He leaned in and gave her a deeper, more passionate kiss. She felt her willpower slipping away. Her mind let go of the fear and the doubt. But all too soon, he pulled away. "They're waiting for us at the studio," he said sadly. "I'll let you get dressed."

Kyle insisted that she go to the studio on her own, saying that he had something to do on the way. She began scolding herself in the car. She had opened up, and he had pulled away from her. Typical. By the time he got there, she had already begun recording her parts with the engineer. He took over, giving her gentle instructions on how to improve on each pass. They were back to the same coolly professional relationship that they had been bouncing in and out of the entire time.

She set her focus on the music, trying as best she could to block him out. The work went quickly. When they were done, Kyle met her in the hallway with a smile. "I think that we've got it locked down. I'll finish the mixes tomorrow and your boss told me to overnight the masters to him. We're all done."

"I guess we are." She held out her hand and he took it gently. "Thank you very much, Mr. Greer. I need to be going now. I'd like to at least make it back to Little Rock tonight." Danielle didn't give him a chance to stop her or say anything else; she simply pushed past him and to her car. She waited the whole time to feel his strong hands stopping her...she both dreaded and craved it. But he never did.

She packed her car quickly, and ran through the suite one last time to make sure she didn't leave anything behind. She kept waiting for a knock on the door that never came. Convinced that it was over, she quickly went to the desk to check out.

Kyle was sitting in his truck, parked two spaces down from her. When he saw her coming he jumped out. "You didn't give me a chance...."

She again passed by him to her car. Just get in, she thought. Drive away and get it over with. She started to open the door, but he pushed it closed.

"Listen to me," he said urgently.

"Why?" she answered, but it sounded more like a plea in her ears. "What's the point? We're done. This is done. You have your life here, which is probably about to get a lot busier. I've got my life back home and I miss it. The only reason I stayed this long was for you."

Kyle took her face in his hands. "I know. I've tried everything I could to keep you here. The only place that I really want to be is with you. I knew that already, but sleeping with you in my arms last night...."

"So what do we do?" She felt tears welling in her eyes and willed them to stop. She wouldn't cry for him.

"I don't know. I know that you have to go, you have responsibilities. I have them here."

"Come with me," Danielle pleaded. "Austin is a music town too."

"I'd have to start all over. I'd have to make new friends, new connections." It was an excuse and they both knew it.

"Come on the road with me."

Kyle shook his head. "I can't. I just can't." He let go of her and walked back to the truck, opened the door, took something out, then came back. He handed it to her. It was the Confederate flag that had hung on his wall, folded into a neat triangle. "I want you to have this. I want you to think about me when you look at it. I fell in love with you under this flag, and I hope that you feel the same. Maybe someday things will be different."

She took it from him. A few tears broke loose and more threatened to follow. He kissed her again, but this time, it was a goodbye kiss. He trudged back to his truck and pulled away.

Danielle watched him go, wiping tears from her eyes. When he was out of sight, she opened the door and tossed the flag on the passenger seat.

The drive to Little Rock was interstate all the way, but it seemed grueling. She kept glancing at the flag and thinking about what he had said. Then the idea came to her. She thought of a way to tell him the things that she never could force herself to say.

It was a stupid idea, she told herself. You're going to get yourself in trouble. It'll cost you. She knew it all was true, but she didn't give a damn. She would pay tribute to Kyle the only way she could.

CHAPTER TWELVE

No one quite knew what to expect when they crowded into the conference room of the band's downtown Austin headquarters. Since leaving Nashville, Danielle had been incredibly secretive, only promising that she was going to deliver greatness. So as Steve and the band gathered, they were curious and a little worried. Everyone was keenly aware of how closely Danielle always seemed to be to falling off the edge.

Joining them were Jay Hatfield and Rico Cardenas of Generation Records. After years of being Danielle's A&R rep, Hatfield was moving up in the organization and Rico was his successor. Steve had clued them in on what to expect. They each had their doubts about Danielle's sudden interest in country music.

Danielle was hiding in an unused suite one floor above them as she got ready to present the finished album and the artwork she had commissioned at her own expense. She was ready for battle on a corporate playing field, dressed in an expensive navy blue business suit, hair pulled back. To an outsider she looked like anything but a world class rock star.

Once she was sure everyone was in place, she picked up the leather satchel that she had put everything in and marched quickly to the elevators. The doors opened and she stepped out into the lobby. She knew the names and the faces of every person who worked for her and was friendly with them, but she didn't return smiles or say hello to anyone on her way to the conference room. She was all business now.

She stopped outside the double doors to the conference room and listened. She could hear them all making small talk inside. With a deep breath, she pushed open the doors and strode into the room as confidently as possible. When she reached the head of the table she laid her satchel down. A large easel had been placed just off to the side. She pulled it over beside her.

"Thank you all for coming. I'm very excited to present our latest album and artwork for you. I want to take just a moment to explain the secrecy. I started this project thinking this would be just another album, but it became so much more than that. I pushed harder than ever, expected more of myself than I ever have. I dug deeper. This is the most personal collection of songs I've ever written, so it's very important to me that this is exactly how I want it. Over the last few weeks, I've gone back and remastered the entire album, so the mixes are slightly different from what they were when we left Nashville, and I also commissioned the artwork myself."

She turned her attention to Jay Hatfield, who was sitting to her right and towards the back of the room. He was sitting casually, dress shirt unbuttoned at the top, tie thrown off, cradling his chin in one hand. She could read in his face his curiosity, his doubt, and his excitement. Their relationship had always been cool, but she sensed in these few moments that it was about to swing dramatically, one way or another.

"Mr. Hatfield, this thing is ready to go. All you have to do is press 'em and ship 'em." He nodded but said nothing. "So," she said with a deep breath, "I present to you, *Southern Hospitality*."

She unzipped the satchel, took out the artwork, and hung it on the easel, a thin piece of cloth taped over it. She glanced over her shoulder to make sure she had everyone's attention, then removed the cloth. The title, *Southern Hospitality*, was written in cursive script in the top left corner in red, white, and blue, but it was the picture beneath it that made everyone gasp. It was Danielle, clearly nude, wrapped in the Confederate battle flag that Kyle had presented to her on the last day. She was holding the flag so that it covered up what needed to be covered and not much else. Her hair was slightly disheveled and she looked up at the camera with a seductive grin.

Jay smirked, but Rico Cardenas, his right hand man, stood up and shouted, "No way, no way." Across the table, DeShon slammed his fists down on the oak table and threw himself out of his chair. He shot her a go to hell look, shook his head, and stormed out, slamming the door behind him. The rest of the band chattered nervously. Steve buried his face in his hands.

Danielle stood straight and tall at the center of the room and cleared her throat. "Let me clarify. This is the album, this is the cover. There is no room for compromise, no negotiations. This is what I want."

"That's the most racist thing I've ever seen," Rico shouted, pointing at the image. "I can't sell that."

"You don't have to sell it," she responded with eerie calm. "The music will sell it. You just have to distribute it. And if this is the most racist thing that you've ever seen, then you haven't seen much. Racy, definitely, but not racist."

"The flag! The flag!"

"Who gives a shit about the flag?" she responded. "I'm sitting there 90% naked, and you're worried about a flag?"

Jay let it carry on a little longer, then stood and whistled for everyone to shut up. "Dani, you're smart. You know what people think about that flag. Even with the sexy picture, that's all people are going to see."

"I know that. They need to get over it. That flag hung on Kyle Greer's wall. He gave it to me when I left because that was all he had to give. When I wrap myself in that flag, it's because I can't wrap myself in him. That's what it stands for."

"It doesn't matter—" he started.

"It does matter. I'll make it matter. This album is all about him and me. We fell in love on his couch, under that flag. That is the image I want. That picture says everything about what the album is. Like I said, there's no compromise here."

Jay held up his hands. "I understand and I totally get what you're saying. For the record, I love it. I think it's sexy and it's ballsy, and just from what Steve has told me about the album, I agree that it captures the essence of the music. I don't dispute that. What you need to see is the business side of this. The backlash that we, the label, will get if we put this out. The negative publicity. It will be a nightmare."

Danielle walked around the table, taking her hair down as she did. When she was right in front of him, she smiled. "I'm not afraid of the fight. You know that. I'll take the heat. I'll be right out front on this. I'll make myself the target. I've done it before. But I need to know that you, my label, has my back on this. Yes, it will be some negative publicity. There'll be protests and boycotts and some stores won't carry it."

Jay nodded and Rico chirped. "Yes, exactly. It's ruin."

She put her hand on the back of his chair. "It's not ruin." She was still looking Jay in the eye. "You know what negative publicity does. People will be dying to get their hands on it. Boycotts just fuel interest. We'll be on all the news channels. They'll play snippets of songs and videos. This thing will explode. People will threaten and there will be some short term problems, but that will fade. You know how short people's attention spans are. You just have to weather the storm."

"She's right," Steve grunted from behind her. "If you weather the initial surge, it's a goldmine. The album's damn good. She's going to blow the country market wide open for you. You've just got to have the courage to stand up to the criticism."

Danielle smiled and waited for Jay's decision. He looked to the door. "I don't think that your band is on board."

"I'll take care of them. Are you on board?"

Rico was still chattering, but she knew that she had Jay. "I'm sticking my neck out for you. If you weren't our top selling artist I wouldn't. But five straight platinum albums are hard to argue against."

Rico shot up out of his chair. "You've got to be kidding me."

"I'll take point on this one," Jay said. "You won't have anything to do with it. I'm not afraid of the fight either."

Rico packed up his stuff and left. Danielle put the album on for Steve, Jay, and the rest of the band to listen to. Then she stepped out into the hall and found DeShon pacing angrily. She pulled the door closed, let out a breath, unbuttoned her jacket, and ran her hands through her hair. "That wasn't so bad."

DeShon stopped pacing and glared at her. "How could you do this? What happened to you? I thought that you were better than this."

"Better than what?" she shot back. "What has your panties in a bunch?"

"Don't act like you don't know. I knew when you drug us down there that you'd changed."

"So you're hung up on the flag too? Really?"

"You're damn right I am. I've always hated the goddamn hicks running around waving that flag like it was something to be proud of, and now you're doing it."

"If you had stayed in there and listened to me I would have explained it."

DeShon was having none of it. "I don't give a shit what your explanation is. I know all about your boyfriend. He's just another ignorant hick that you're putting ahead of us. I'm tired of you and all of your stupid boyfriends. I'm tired of being expected to be your safety net. I thought we were friends, but today, you made it clear that we're just your workers."

"That's not true. Come on. We've known each other forever. You know that I don't think of you like a worker."

DeShon's stance softened a little. "Listen. You don't get how hard it is. I was fine when it was just some kidding around. When I had to go down to Crackerville for you, they let me have it. Now I'm supposed to go back to my friends and show them this? You know what kind of shit they'll give me? They already think I'm an Uncle Tom."

Danielle approached him slowly. "Then tell them to fuck off. Real friends wouldn't do that to you. You don't owe those guys anything. Just because you're black doesn't mean that you have to take their shit. You've earned what you have, and you shouldn't have to apologize for it."

DeShon stepped past her and further down the hall. "It's not that easy man. I don't expect you to get it. Forget them, what about you? You always talk about us as a family, but did we get any say in this? You call us when you need us and then you send us on our way. We don't get a say. We don't get songwriting credits or producer credits. It's all you. Your name on the marquee, your picture on the cover. Did you stop to think for one moment about the situation that you were putting me in? It's not just my friends, it's everybody. I put up with that picture, if I stick my name on that, then I'm ruined. I'll be a traitor to my whole race."

"Do you honestly believe that?"

"It doesn't matter what I believe. It's how I will be perceived. You know how this works, America's Virgin. You know how people paint you with a wide brush."

They stood there, sizing each other up in the hallway as silent moments passed. Danielle finally spoke first. "I didn't think about that. I'm sorry. And yes, I do know how people define you. In most cases, I would do something about it. But this album, this one album, I won't budge on."

"You never budge."

"You're right. I can try to be better going forward. But this one is too important to me. I have to see this through. I'd like you to come with us because I don't want to lose you, as a friend or a bandmate. But I understand if you can't do it."

"There's no way," he said, shaking his head. "I can't put my name on that album. I just can't do it. The heat would be too much."

"Okay. What about this. We remove your name from the album completely, no mention of you at all. You never played on it. Then we release a statement that you have left the band to pursue other projects. That way you save face. Then, after the buzz has died down, you can quietly slide back in and we'll work on a new deal where everyone gets an equal say going forward. Deal?"

DeShon thought it over for a long minute. She knew that in his heart he was a loyal guy, and she could only imagine how torn he must have been. "Take my name off, release the statement. As for coming back, we'll just have to see. That's a year from now, I don't know where I'll be. I've got some other opportunities."

"Okay, fine. Will you at least talk to me about it, though?"

"We'll talk after the tour. Until then, don't come around. I'll probably leave town anyway. Maybe go up to New York for a while." He turned to leave and she watched him until the elevator doors shut behind him. He never once turned around. She knew then that he was gone and wouldn't be coming back.

Danielle stepped back into the conference room where the others were still listening to the final mix. Steve and Jay Hatfield were in deep conversation but smiling ear to ear. Garrett, Ty, and Trish looked up at her with an unspoken question in their eyes.

"He's gone. He says that he can't be a part of this. We're going to release a statement saying that he left so that he won't have trouble with his friends. It's just the four of us now."

Garrett pushed away from the table. "Three. I'm out. That's not my shit," he said, stabbing his finger at the stereo. "I've ridden this roller coaster long enough. If you're going to let DeShon walk over a stupid picture, then you've said all you need to say about how much we mean to you."

"It's about more than that," she snapped back.

"I know what it's about. We've been talking about it for a long time now. About your selfishness and your disrespect. It's over for me. I'm sticking by my friend."

"If that's what you feel like you have to do."

"It is." He pushed by her and strode out the door. She looked down at Trish and Ty, who were holding hands and watching the exchange fearfully.

"Are y'all going to leave too? It's okay if you do, no hard feelings. I'm used to it by now."

"Are you just going to let them walk like that?" Ty asked in disbelief.

"I tried to talk DeShon out of it, but I get where he's coming from. It wasn't going to happen. I don't give a shit about Garrett. He's your friend, not mine. I would have fired him years ago if it weren't for you and DeShon. I don't want to lose you two. You're my best friends. But I'm not going to grovel."

Ty's eyes went from Danielle to the door and then back. Beside him, Trish tightened her grip on his hand and Danielle could see that she was about to lose her entire band. Trish spoke up. "I'll stick with you. I can't say that I'm in total agreement with your choices, but I get what you're doing."

"Yeah," Ty whispered. "We'll stay with you. I mean, hell, you and I go back longer than those guys do."

"Thank you," she whispered. "I promise, once this album cycle is over, I'll do a better job including you. We'll become an actual band. Songwriting credit and the whole nine yards."

Steve walked over to them. "It sounds even better now. What did you do?"

Danielle shrugged. "I just fiddled with the mixes. I listened to it again and I thought it was too country…I couldn't hear us in there. So I brought us out a little more."

"Good job. Where's DeShon and Garrett?"

"They quit," Ty answered with a sigh. "So we're going to need a whole new rhythm section."

Steve worked quickly to put a new rhythm section in place as preparations kicked into high gear for the upcoming tour. Still, Steve kept reminding Danielle of the upcoming storm she was about to unleash. She had the feeling that Steve was holding out hope that she would change her mind about the cover.

The label kept a lid on the album art as long as they could, but a week before *Southern Hospitality* dropped, a photo leaked. The outrage was immediate. Danielle spent hours on the phone assuring everyone at the label that it would work out if they were patient. She didn't tell them that she was spoiling for the fight.

In an effort to head off the storm, Steve arranged for Danielle to do a one-on-one interview with respected entertainment reporter, Angie Jones. Jones had been desperately seeking an exclusive with Danielle since her virgin interview, and Steve felt that giving her the interview would curry some favor with the TV veteran. Danielle was all too willing.

They met at a seaside hotel in Galveston and took advantage of the gorgeous weather and shot the interview on the deck with the Gulf of Mexico as the backdrop. Angie Jones swept onto the set two hours and fifteen minutes late, her big hair with a fresh coat of black color in it, and she wore a designer dress with the diamond jewelry to match. She was the exact Hollywood phony that Danielle had always made a point to avoid.

She greeted Danielle with an air kiss to each cheek and then motioned for her to sit in one of the white deck chairs that had been arranged for them. They then waited another fifteen minutes for the crew to get the scene lit to her satisfaction.

Angie didn't say a word to Danielle until she motioned her producer to begin rolling, then she quickly turned her attention. "Hello, Danielle. Thank you for taking the time to talk to me about your newest album, *Southern Hospitality*." She leaned over and patted Danielle on the knee. "I've been wanting to sit down with you like this for a long time."

Danielle smiled pleasantly. "I'm the dream maker."

"Yes, you are." Angie answered with a smile. "I'd say that you've been the subject of a great number of dreams over the years." Her smile faded as she got ready to get serious. "So tell me Danielle, how is that chastity belt of yours?"

"Still locked. How's your divorce coming?"

"Too slow," Angie responded with a laugh, but there was an exchange of glares between the two that let it be known that battle lines had been drawn. "That vow of yours has to be a heavy cross to bear. You've had a few very public breakdowns over the years. Would you say that your virginity has been the driving factor behind those?"

Danielle smirked. "I've struggled with a lot of things, but that isn't one of them. It's easy when you know what you want and why. I'd say my biggest struggle, the thing that I really have a hard time with, is dealing with other people's crap. You know how that goes."

"Indeed I do," Angie responded. "Still, for a woman your age to still be a virgin. It seems…unhealthy."

"Treating your body like a human petri dish is unhealthy too, but there are certain people who do it. I'm comfortable with my choices."

"You haven't always behaved like you're comfortable," Angie said, a hint of challenge in her voice.

"I have a tendency to react before I think. That's just me."

"You threw a guitar at an audience member at one of your concerts."

Danielle shrugged. "The guy was being…a jerk, for lack of a better term. That wasn't my proudest moment, but if my actions made that guy think twice before acting like a pig, then I would say it was worth it."

"You don't sound like you're sorry about it."

Danielle stared back at her coldly. "I'm not. I wish I'd have hit the fat bastard." Off set, Steve buried his face in his hands. Danielle saw the move and tried hard to suppress her smile.

Angie was stunned for a moment, but rallied quickly. "This new album of yours certainly has people up in arms."

"No," Danielle corrected. "Nobody's talking about the album. Everybody's upset about the cover photo, which is silly."

Angie tried to act startled. "You think that it's silly? Do you even understand why people are upset about the cover? Do you realize why it is so offensive?"

Danielle chuckled. "Offensive? Really? Let me ask you something. If the cover was exactly the same, except that I was wrapped in a sheet instead, would it still be offensive? Would we even be having this discussion right now?"

"Probably not," Angie relented.

"Exactly, but nothing has really changed. You know, I have gone into the music stores and I have seen album covers that are so much worse than this, and nobody even cared. All you have to do is say 'it's my art' and you get a free pass. It doesn't even have anything to do with the music, it's just an excuse to be provocative."

"Aren't you claiming that this album cover is your art?"

Danielle smiled bigger. "Not at all. It's just the cover. But it does present a very concise visual image of the music on the album, and the bigger story of how the album came to be. That picture and the title represent a whole chapter of my life in a very succinct way. Which is why I fought so hard with my label for it. In the interest of full disclosure, no one but me wanted this cover. Two members of my band quit over it. The label threatened not to put it out. Even my manager has tried to get me to change it."

"Yet you have refused. Why? In one move, you went from being a role model to millions to being labeled a racist. Is it really worth it?"

Danielle shrugged in response. "It's worth it to put out the album that I want with the cover that I want. I've compromised on things before because at the end of the day I realized that it wasn't that big of a deal. This is very important to me. That picture represents more than just a collection of songs. It represents a turning point in my life. Some people want to bully me. I don't bully. Some people want to claim that they can look into my heart and make pronouncements about me. If that were true then we wouldn't be having this discussion right now, because when people looked into my heart they'd see the reasons why I chose this cover. Then they'd see that it has nothing to do with race or political correctness or anything else. It's all personal."

Angie was beginning to get visibly uncomfortable. Danielle reasoned that Angie had expected her to cave once the heat was turned on. She was unprepared for Danielle to stand strong, and now the veteran reporter was off guard.

"Still," Angie continued. "Do you not understand the historical subtext here?"

"I understand it perfectly. I get why some people view the Confederate flag the way that they do. That's perfectly fine, that's their right. Just don't tell me that I have to look at it the same way, because I don't. It's a flag, a piece of cloth, and it only carries the value that you assign to it. I don't expect others to see it the same way I do, I'm just asking for people to quit cramming their political views down my throat."

"I don't think that anyone is trying to deny you your freedom of expression, Danielle. But you're talking about a symbol of hatred and intolerance here."

Danielle laughed out loud. "Intolerance? Are people being tolerant of me right now? That's the biggest joke in the world. People don't really care if you're intolerant, you just have to make sure that you hate the right people. The whole enlightened Hollywood scene is a total lie. They don't even try to hide their hate, because they know that no one will call them on it. Just don't step out of line like I have."

"Don't you feel bad about this at all? You've risked losing millions of fans over this picture. Over this stupid flag. Your entire career can be ruined. I can't believe that it is worth that risk."

Danielle's smile faded for the first time and her eyes became cloudy. "Yes," she said quietly. "It absolutely is. You see, there's a story behind that picture, and there's someone very important behind the story. Someone that I needed to say things to. I didn't have the courage to say them at the time, so this was the only way I could say to him what I needed to say. This picture, this whole album, is all about him and me. All the extraneous garbage that people keep throwing on me has nothing to do with it. That's what I keep trying to get people to understand, if they would just step down off of their high horses for a minute."

"But certainly there was a better way," Angie responded. "A phone call perhaps? Maybe a letter?"

Danielle laughed again. "Oh, there was probably a better way had I really thought about it. But it's not really my style to do things the easy way." Then her smile faded again and she became pensive. "It's probably also a way to punish myself. A public flogging for failing to do what I should have done back in Nashville."

Angie's demeanor changed now. She was almost sympathetic with her next question. "Do you punish yourself often?"

Danielle didn't bat an eye. "All the time, Angie. All the time."

The interview did help blunt the controversy a little, and it even opened a brief public discussion about Hollywood hypocrisy. However, the effect didn't last long and did little to stop the more progressive voices in the media from eviscerating her at every turn. The criticism was indeed brutal, as everyone had feared it would be.

Despite the controversy, when the album and its debut single, "Sometimes It Fades," actually dropped, they hit with the force of a nuclear bomb. The album smashed sales records, especially on the country charts where she had the fastest selling "debut" in history. "Sometimes It Fades" became her first Number One hit, and at one point held down the top spot on the Pop, Rock, Country, and Blues charts at the same time.

The breakout success of the album eased pressure from the label. Money had a tendency to do that. However, public defense of their star was flaccid at best, and the overall position of the label was to shift everything onto Danielle under the guise of "artistic freedom."

Ultimately many of her concert dates were cancelled, making this tour her smallest to date. Still, each event would bring out thousands of demonstrators outside the arena carrying signs that decried her as a racist and a poor role model. Danielle did her best to hide it, but it was evident to those closest to her that it hurt.

Each night, at each show, Danielle looked around anxiously, hoping that Kyle would show up backstage. She scanned the crowds hoping to see him out there. She was doing all of this for him. Had she wounded him so much that he wouldn't even see her? Didn't he get the message, or did he just not care?

The tragedy of 9/11 helped douse a lot of the fires that were still burning under Danielle's feet. Suddenly a silly album cover just wasn't that important. She still got the cold shoulder from the rest of the entertainment industry. Despite her best efforts, she was not allowed to participate in any of the events to raise money for the victim's families or to pay tribute to the fallen. She thought about writing a special song, but the label politely declined. The heat was off and they were happy to let the entire incident slip slowly from consciousness. Jay Hatfield even flew out to meet her before a show in Louisville, Kentucky to tell her that it was now the perfect time to "lay low and come back strong in two years, when all this would be a distant memory."

The tour wound up with a show in Shreveport, Louisiana. Her early enthusiasm for the tour had waned with each stop. By the time the tour wrapped up there was no jamming on stage and very little audience interaction. She played her songs as they were on the albums, did one brief encore, and jumped on the bus. All she wanted to do was end it.

The rest of the band returned to their hotel for the night and to prepare for the trip home the next day. Danielle couldn't wait that long so she rented a car and drove back to Austin. She needed time to think.

As the miles disappeared under her wheels, she thought back on the whole drama. She had been so cocksure when she first came back and had done exactly what she promised she would do by weathering the storm. Yet she had underestimated the toll it would take on her. If her message had gotten through at all it had generated no response from Kyle.

Somewhere along the way she came to grips with the fact that she had once again run a good man out of her life thanks to her fear. She thought of Adam and his fear of commitment, and realized that she suffered from the same affliction. She thought of her father, lying dead somewhere, and her mother, who had left her behind to follow a pedophile. She thought of poor Brooke and how she had been shunned, and of Kel and his friend. All of those things had instilled a deep seeded fear that she just couldn't shake.

Yet Kyle was different and she realized that it had scared her worse than she realized. She had nothing to hang her hat on. He had no career to put in front of her. He wasn't a womanizer, never gave her any reason to feel pushed or threatened.

Danielle drove through the night and into the day. By the time the Austin skyline rose to meet her, the sun was on its way down again. She was physically weary and emotionally spent. She negotiated her way home as much by instinct and muscle memory as she did by sight.

The last miles seemed to drag on endlessly, but Danielle finally made it. She pulled into the circular drive in front instead of pulling into the garage, parked the car, and had to force herself up to avoid falling asleep in the driver's seat. She didn't bother to grab her bags. All she wanted to do was sleep forever. She unlocked the door, pushed it open, and then kicked it shut behind her and began peeling off her clothes as she sleepily made her way toward the bedroom.

A knock on the door stopped her. Danielle turned and trudged back to the front door and threw it open without bothering to look out first. Kyle stood grinning on the other side. He smiled, started to say something, then looked down to see her in her underwear and looked up with an even bigger grin. "If this is how Texans answer the door, I'm all in."

Danielle smiled weakly. "Ha, ha. I'm going to bed. "

"Hot damn, I shoulda moved here sooner."

He took a step forward as Danielle tried to close the door. She shook her head. "I know that I'm dreaming this." Then his words hit her. "Wait. What do you mean move here?"

"I'm movin' here. Got all my shit packed up in a horse trailer. I've been stayin' at a Days Inn down the road waitin' for you to get back." He took another step forward and took her hands in his. It seemed like forever since she'd last seen him. She couldn't remember if he had looked this good the last time, but then again, the last time she was busy breaking his heart.

"What about your career taking off and all of that?"

He shook his head slowly. "It doesn't mean anything. My heart is where you are. It took me a while, too long, to realize that you were all that mattered. When you left, you took my reasons for stayin'."

Danielle looked deep into his eyes and tried to hide the emotions raging inside of her. Her every instinct cried for her to run to him, to leap into his arms, but she couldn't do it. She could barely move at all.

"The biggest mistake I've ever made was watchin' you drive out of my life. I've spent months kickin' myself for lettin' you go. I'd almost convinced myself that we never had anything. Then all the stuff with the cover and the flag, and I got it. I knew that you were hurtin', just like me, and you made yourself a target so that you could keep feelin' that pain. But I got it, Danielle. I got what you were sayin'."

Danielle felt weak, her mind racing. All of the things that she had rehearsed saying to him died on her tongue. She could do nothing to but stare into his eyes until she felt the tears begin to break loose and run down her cheeks. She was powerless to stop them. Instead, she just let herself collapse into his arms and he squeezed her tight.

Kyle pushed further into the room without letting go, kicking the door shut behind him. They held each other there for the longest time, and when they finally broke the embrace, her raging emotions were no more. She had no more questions. She had what she was looking for. "I'm so sorry," she whispered. "I never wanted to hurt you."

"Don't worry about it," he answered. "I needed to hurt. I need to feel somethin'. I hadn't done that in a long time. It's good to hurt sometimes."

"I'm tired of hurting," she said back, almost whimpering.

"You won't. Not anymore. I'm here now. I've got a plan. I'll find a place to stay, put a band together, and find myself a nice, steady gig somewhere. I'll make a life here, just like I did in Nashville."

Danielle wrapped her arms around his neck. "There's so much I want to say, I just can't find the words right now."

"You look beat."

"I'm exhausted. This whole ordeal has just drained me."

He broke away from her. "Then you go to bed. I'll swing back by tomorrow sometime and we'll talk.

"You don't have to do that. I've got plenty of room here. There's a guest bedroom right across from mine. You can stay here and we can talk in the morning."

Kyle smiled at her. "Whatever you say. Sure beats the Days Inn."

She took him gently by the hand and led him up the stairs. She stopped him at the door of the guest bedroom. "My room is right there," she said, pointing to her own bedroom door. "If you need anything."

"Sure thing," he said, and leaned over to give her a peck on the cheek. "Goodnight, angel."

Danielle turned and headed for her room. Although she was exhausted she didn't want to leave Kyle's side. It had been so long since she'd seen him. She never wanted him to be out of her sight again.

Then his hand was on her shoulder, turning her around gently. "I need something." He leaned in and kissed her again. She had kissed a lot. Colin's kisses had sent shockwaves through her. Dirk's had been steamy. Adam's had been the best, but no one had ever kissed her the way Kyle did at that moment. She had been desperately missing his touch, longing for his kiss, for months.

He finally broke the kiss. "You're shaking."

"I'm scared," she muttered breathlessly.

Kyle smiled. "You don't have anything to be scared of. I won't hurt you."

Danielle pulled him closer. "That's not what I'm scared of."

He wanted to ask her more, but she didn't give him the chance. She reached behind her until her hands found the doorknob. She twisted it open and then pushed the door open with her heel. Kyle realized what she meant and started to protest.

Danielle kissed him again. "Don't talk," she said. "Don't think." She wasn't sure if she was telling him or herself. It didn't matter now. "Just make love to me."

Kyle pulled her as close to him as he could and kissed her with even more passion than the first time. He backed her into the bedroom, reached out with his free hand, and pushed the door closed.

#

Danielle woke up some time in the night and snuck away from Kyle, leaving him sleeping peacefully in her bed. She wrapped a blanket around herself and tiptoed down the stairs and out onto the patio. She sat down and watched as the sun slowly rose over Lake Travis. For the first time in a long time, she truly felt alive.

Kyle appeared a short time later, still naked, and sat down behind her, wrapping his arms around her. "Are you all right?"

"Yeah, I'm fine," she said softly.

He ran his hands up and down her exposed arms. "You seem a little sad. Do you regret it?"

"I don't regret it at all. Things have changed now. I've changed, and it will take me a little bit to adjust. That's all."

"I'm sorry."

"Don't be. It has nothing to do with you. I've felt this before. It's like graduating high school. An old part of my life is over and a new one is starting. While I'm excited for what's to come, I'm a little sad for what is gone."

Kyle chuckled. "Are you comparing having sex to graduating high school?"

She smiled and elbowed him gently in the ribs. "No. It's about crossing thresholds. Just like childhood ended at graduation, a part of my life ended last night. A pretty big part. I walked in my door last night and I was a virgin, and now I'm not. I crossed a threshold. But I was a virgin for so long, I became defined by it. Now it's gone. It makes me a little sad. Give me a few hours and it'll pass."

"Is passing thresholds a problem for you?'"

"No."

"Because I was thinking about crossing another one."

Danielle looked over her shoulder at him. "What are you talking about?"

Instead of telling her, he began gently kissing her neck and shoulders, edging the blanket down out of his way with his fingers. She closed her eyes and let him do what he wanted until she could stand it no more. She turned to face him…she wanted his lips on hers.

In between kisses, he finally managed to say "Would you marry me?"

Danielle stopped and looked him in the eye. There was no fear, no indecision. All her old demons were gone now, banished in the cold light of dawn. This was a new day and a new Danielle. Her smile was so big she felt like her face might break. "Absolutely."

She came in for another kiss, but he pushed her back. "Soon. I don't want to wait."

Danielle nodded her head slightly, still maneuvering for a kiss. "I hate long engagements anyway," she whispered. Then she overpowered his attempts to hold her back. She wouldn't even let him take her back to bed. It didn't matter if someone might see them out here. Danielle had finally found the love she had been looking for. She would hide no more.

Trish and Ty were the first to know, then Steve, Randy, and Teri. Word soon spread among the network of friends and acquaintances. It didn't take long for the word to hit the press. Danielle Regan was engaged again, and this time, she made no attempt to deny rumors that she was off the board in more ways than one.

The crush of media attention was difficult for Kyle to handle. Suddenly, every time he went out of the house he was blinded with flashbulbs and hounded with questions. Danielle told him to ignore it and he tried, but it was a hard thing to do.

Kyle got another surprise when he watched Danielle go through a huge pile of fan mail. It was something that she did regularly, but he had never seen it. As she sat in the living room floor and sorted the letters into four piles around her, he drank a beer and watched curiously.

"What are the piles for?"

"I divide them by content." She put a hand on the first pile. "These are from kids. These are positive letters from adults or organizations. These are the hate letters, and those are the death threats."

"Death threats?" He walked over to the pile and picked one up. His face turned green as he started reading. Then he wadded it up and threw it down. "That's demented."

"I get a healthy dose of those, especially when I've done something to get on the news. Most of them are just weirdos. Sometimes, though, you get one where someone mentions something you did that lets you know that they were close. Those are scary. Anyway, Steve keeps a file of all the bad ones just in case something ever happened to me."

"Doesn't it bother you?"

"At first it did, yeah. I cried the first time I got one. I just couldn't figure out what I had done to make someone want to kill me. Over time, you figure out that most of these people are either jacking with you or they have some sort of mental problem or they're just venting. You eventually learn how to pick out the real serious ones, and I go straight to the cops when I get one. These here are pretty standard though. Word is out that I'm not a virgin anymore, and a lot of guys are pissed because they wanted to be the first. It'll pass."

Kyle took a long drink and looked back down at the pile. "I don't know how you do it."

"Like I said, you get used to it. It's a part of the job."

They decided on an April wedding. The governor offered them the use of the Capitol grounds, but they decided on a small wedding at her home instead. Both were more interested in making it official than having a big ceremony.

In the meantime, the two wrote new songs at breakneck speed. When a friend and writer for the *Austin Chronicle* caught her grocery shopping, she spilled the beans, promising a new album would be out soon. It made the pages of the *Chronicle* and stirred up a hornet's nest of interest.

When the story hit the papers, it was a shock to Steve. He had no idea that they were working on a new album. He called her in a near panic.

"Steve, calm down," Danielle assured him. "When we get married, we're going on a long honeymoon, and I honestly can't tell you when I'll want to work again. So we thought that it would be a good idea to put something out beforehand. The label can put it out while I'm taking a break. It'll be ready by the end of March."

"What is this about being totally different? What are you going to do now?"

Danielle could only laugh. "Trust me, okay? There are no rebel flags or anything this time around. You'll have it in your hands soon."

Steve was reluctant, but he knew his headstrong star already had everything planned out. "Okay. But no rebel flags. You promised."

They finished the album by Danielle's self-imposed March 31 deadline. Steve decided to throw them a party to celebrate both the completion of the new album and their coming marriage. He rented the ballroom of the Westlake Country Club well outside of Austin and away from prying eyes.

It was the first time that Kyle had ever seen Danielle all dolled up. "You look stunning," he said when she come down the stairs. "But you know what? I think I like you in jeans better."

"Good," she answered. "Because this is a rare occurrence."

"Speaking of rare occurrences," Kyle began. "Why don't we make it two for two tonight?"

Danielle got an uneasy feeling. "What are you thinking about?"

"I was thinking that we could take my truck. Both of us. Together."

It was exactly what she was afraid he was going to ask. The one thing that had driven him nuts about her was her insistence on driving everywhere they went. "Well, we're going to a pretty ritzy place, and I spent all day cleaning up Black Beauty, so why don't we take it tonight and you can drive some other night?"

"When?" he asked, just a little annoyed.

"Some other time."

"Why won't you let me drive? "

"Because I love to drive. It relaxes me."

Kyle shook his head. "I like to drive too. So we can take your car, but I'll drive. How about that?"

Danielle laughed dismissively. "Nobody drives that car but me. That's my baby. It's like my first husband. I tell you what. Let me drive tonight, and tomorrow we can go out and you can drive to your heart's content. What do you say?"

"And you'll go with me?"

"Of course I will. I'm not a total control freak." She caught Kyle's smirk at her. "I said that I'm not a *total* control freak. Just, like, 90%. Come on."

The Westlake Country Club was many miles outside of town down the Capitol of Texas highway, and it was well worth the drive. Surrounded by the majestic hills of Central Texas, the grounds were well manicured and the interior was all money. The furniture, the dishes, and even the food was top notch. Steve made sure that no expense was spared to celebrate his star's coming wedding.

"It almost feels like a farewell party," Danielle confided to him during a quiet moment.

"Maybe it is," Steve answered. "You said it yourself, you don't know when you'll be ready to work again. You don't have to anymore. Maybe you'll decide that married life is all you need. You have some kids and you don't play anymore. If that's the case, I just wanted you to understand how much I appreciate you for your talent and your faith in me."

Danielle gave him a peck on the cheek. "That was a long time ago. We sure have been through the ringer since then. I couldn't have done it without you."

"It was all worth it. I hope that you enjoy your life, wherever it takes you from here."

After dinner, the couple received gifts from all of those in attendance. Then it was time for the second reason for the party. Steve unveiled the new album, recorded completely between Danielle and Kyle with no other outside input. As the crowd mingled and danced it became clear that this was a radically different Danielle. There were no guitar pyrotechnics or monster riffs. Instead, the album was moody and sexy. It was a testament to the sensual side of herself that she had only recently discovered.

She accepted congratulations all around as she weaved through the crowd. She finally found Kyle, chatting up Trish and Ty about the new album. "What we wanted to do was make an album that you could make love to, over and over again, all night long."

Danielle snuck up behind him. "And you can. It's been tested." She gave her friends a wink. "Repeatedly." She then turned her attention to her fiancé. "I think it's time to go. It's getting late."

As they left, Danielle looked up into the night sky. Out here, away from the city lights, she thought she could see every star in the sky. "Baby, I don't think life can get any better."

"Sure it can," he said, pulling her in close. "Wait until we get married. We'll have a couple of kids and we can both be the parents that we wished we'd had growing up. We can travel whenever and wherever we want to. No punching time clocks. No answering to anybody. We're just getting started."

They stopped at the back bumper of the Camaro. "Well, I'm starting something else first."

Kyle was confused. "What do you mean?"

She tossed him the car keys. "Letting go. She's all yours, Captain."

Kyle couldn't hide his delight. He started the car and revved the engine. Then he let the top down. "Are you sure about this?"

"Yes, so hurry before I change my mind. I'm going crazy over here already."

"Yes, dear," he said sarcastically. Soon, they were flying down the highway, the cool March wind biting into their skin.

"How do you do this?" Danielle asked.

"Do what?"

"Sit over here. It's just not right. Everything looks different over here."

Kyle laughed at her. "Welcome to my world. It sucks to be the passenger, doesn't it?"

"Yes it does," she answered back. "But at least the view is nice."

He looked to see her staring at him. "You know, every time I look at you, you seem more beautiful."

Danielle laughed. "That's just because you're under my spell now. You're bewitched. Resistance is futile."

"You're damn right I am," Kyle responded. "And I always will be. I love you, angel."

Danielle smiled back at him. Illuminated in the glow of the passing headlights, he was even more handsome than before. Her mind drifted away to thoughts of the future. To kids and dogs and white picket fences. Steve was right. She wasn't coming back. It was time to say goodbye to Danielle Regan, guitar goddess. She was soon to be Danielle Greer, wife and mother. It was time to cross another threshold. She smiled at the thought.

And then the world went black.

CHAPTER THIRTEEN

The news filtered out slowly. First reports indicated only a major traffic accident on the Capitol of Texas highway. Local news teams arrived almost as soon as the first responders did. Live shots only showed two twisted hunks of smoking metal.

It was early on that Saturday morning before rumors began to swirl that there was someone of note in the car. In Austin, that could have meant a politician, an athlete, an actor...or a musician. Around Breckenridge Hospital a crowd of curious onlookers began to gather.

Local news crews continued reporting as the darkness gave way to daylight. The first official announcement came at 9:12 am. Sean Alec Moore, a forty-five-year-old bank teller from Wisconsin, had died as a result of injuries sustained in the crash. Moore had been driving a Dodge Ram pickup at a high rate of speed when he crossed four lanes of traffic and struck the second car, which they only listed as a sports car, on the left quarter panel. Moore had been ejected from his vehicle at impact. It was not indicated if he had been under the influence.

At 10:30, Steve was rousted out of a deep sleep by a heavy knock on his door. A state trooper was there to inform him of the accident. Danielle had listed him as her next of kin.

Steve dressed hurriedly and raced to the hospital. A reporter for Austin's KVUE recognized him as he scurried past barricades and into the hospital. She was the first to go on air and make it official. Danielle Regan was the person of note. A dark cloud descended upon Austin. The city had already lost one favorite son when Stevie Ray had died. Was it about to lose another?

As dusk fell, the crowd turned into a candlelight vigil. Cars drove by, windows down, blaring Danielle's music from their stereos. Local radio stations put her on heavy rotation.

By this time, the national media had begun to descend upon the scene. Pictures of the twisted remains of Danielle's beloved Black Beauty began appearing online. A security detail had to be posted at the salvage yard to protect against memorabilia hunters.

Sunday morning, rumors spread that a second person had died as a result of the crash. Fans waited nervously for the reports to be confirmed. A macabre cheer went up from the masses as it was confirmed that Kyle Greer, a 34-year-old songwriter and Danielle's fiancé, had succumbed. Steve and the rest of Danielle's extended family watched the scene from behind hospital windows, and wondered how you could cheer someone's death.

The waiting game continued to play out. Every so often, reports would begin that Danielle had died, forcing the hospital to publicly deny them. While old friends made it to Danielle's bedside, old acquaintances made their way in front of the cameras. Dirk Crandall popped up, talking about how he was the true love of Danielle's life and pitching the idea of a tell-all book. A couple of former roadies talked about life on the road with her and painted her as a demanding and overbearing diva. One crazy old lady popped up claiming to be her mother. It was a circus.

Inside, it was an agonizing wait. The entire band came back, as well as many of the crew and supporting staff behind Danielle's organization. Randy and Teri Holder were among the first there and they refused to leave, despite their own health issues. Adam hopped the first flight back. No one mentioned how things had ended between them; no one doubted how deeply he loved her. Steve was in command, putting his managerial skills to use as he stayed on top of Danielle's condition and the dissemination of that information to the press.

Jay Hatfield flew in to inform Steve that the label, sensing perhaps a final opportunity to cash in, was rushing out the new album. Steve didn't feel quite right about it, but after all the heat they'd taken for *Southern Hospitality*, the label felt she owed them one. The new album, titled *Between the Sheets*, was expected to hit stores in weeks.

They all waited and hoped and tried to build each other up. DeShon forgave the flag flap. Randy prayed to Big Rick to forgive him for failing to keep his little girl safe. Steve refused to hear any of it. She was too strong, too tough to die, he told them. She was going to emerge from this stronger than ever. Secretly, he was making funeral arrangements. Everyone waited, for better or for worse, for Danielle.

#

There was no white light. There was no tunnel. There were no loved ones, long since gone, to guide the way home. At first, there was nothing but darkness.

Then came the pain. Agonizing, awful pain, a constant agony. Then there were sensations. Of being wet, of being sticky, of being cold. Of flying, or maybe swimming? There were images that made no sense, swirling collages of light and color that were frightening and meaningless at the same time. There were sounds that roared like a thousand voices screaming out at once, each with a different thing to say. There was fear and pain and then the darkness returned.

She was cold. It was the first coherent thought she had. Very cold. And it was dark. Her body felt heavy, like all of her limbs had been weighted down. She couldn't move. She could hear sounds all around her, but could make no sense of them. She could not open her eyes, she could not speak. Her brain didn't seem to work right.

Panic began to set in. The sounds got louder and harsher. Then the darkness returned and the pain went away. The cycle repeated over and over again. Time had no meaning. There was only cold and pain and panic, the rise of voices, and then the darkness.

Then it changed. Danielle found that she could flex her fingers and wiggle her toes. She still couldn't speak because there was something in her throat. She began to separate the noises, the beeps and whirs of machinery from the hushed tones of voices. She couldn't make out the words, but she knew that people were talking to her.

The darkness, the bottomless pit that swallowed all the sensations, came less and less often. Each time she emerged from it, things seemed to be sharper. She was making more sense of things.

When the light finally came, it didn't trickle in slowly. It overwhelmed her. An instant pain shot through her eyes and her brain. The thing in her mouth kept her quiet, but her arms and hands moved to block the light. The light was the last thing she had seen before this all happened. The light scared her.

Then came recognition. There were faces, doctors and nurses, machines, her arms, and her hands. There were other faces…not doctors, but friends. They had no names, their words made no sense, but she knew that they were friends. Slowly, so slowly, the world was beginning to make sense again.

It was dark the next time Danielle opened her eyes. The tube in her mouth was gone, but her throat was sore and dry. She tried to sit up, but she was strapped down. She started to thrash…she wanted up, she wanted out. Pain began to creep into her consciousness, but she welcomed it. She was alive. Sometimes you needed to hurt. Who had said that?

Steve was at her side in an instant. "Calm down. You're all right now." He began to rub her head, whispering the words in her ear. He looked over her shoulder to make sure that none of the hospital staff was watching, then he released the straps that held her. She sat up quickly, too quickly. Dizziness overcame her and she slid back down.

"Take it easy," Steve implored. "It takes a while to come back from the dead."

Danielle edged her way back up the bed. She tried to speak but her voice was just a hoarse croak. Steve quickly poured her some water in a Styrofoam cup. She gulped it down greedily. Despite Steve's warnings, she gulped down two more.

She still couldn't speak. "You'll get your voice back. You've been on a respirator for two weeks. It'll take some time."

Unable to ask questions, she made a questioning motion with her hands.

"How much do you remember?"

Danielle shook her head. Nothing.

Steve took a deep breath and shifted in his seat. He was stalling. "This is the deal. You're in Breckenridge Hospital. You've been unconscious for the better part of two weeks. You were actually comatose for three days. You suffered a major concussion, ruptured your spleen, broke three ribs, and suffered a compound fracture of your left leg. Other than that, you look like you've gone twelve rounds with Mike Tyson, but you will be fine. Your injuries will heal."

She sat silently, processing the information. Then she looked back to him and struggled to say one word. "Kyle?"

Steve squirmed in his seat. Then he looked her dead in the eye. She needed to know. "Baby, he never knew what hit him. The guy plowed right into the driver's side. They did everything they could, but...."

Danielle, devastated, slumped back down in the bed. She wanted to scream but didn't have the voice. She didn't have the tears to cry. So she sat there and wondered if she could will herself to die.

"There's something else you should know. This won't be easy for you to hear." Her eyes came up to meet his. "This was no accident. It was an assassination. The guy who hit you, targeted you. The cops are keeping it quiet for now. He was a fan."

Danielle's grief turned to anger. A fan? Steve looked at her and knew that he needed to tell the rest quickly.

"The cops went up to this guy's house up in Wisconsin. He left a suicide note. He thought that you were saving yourself for him and that you were supposed to be together. When that didn't happen, he lost it. He quit his job, sold everything he owned, and bought that monstrosity of a pickup he was driving. He followed you and when he had a chance, he drove into you as fast he could. He wasn't drunk, he didn't fall asleep. It was intentional. The only thing that saved you was that he turned a little too late. Instead of a true head on, he plowed into the driver's side and Kyle took the brunt of the collision. If he had hit you guys square, at the speed he was going...."

Danielle wished for all the world that he had. Once again, death had sought her out, stealing away that which was most precious to her, and left her behind. All the anger that she thought she had put behind her came roaring back, yet now she had no outlet for it. Suddenly, the sound of the monitors she was hooked up to seemed deafening, like they were mocking her. So she ripped the leads off of herself. She tore the IV out of her arm. She tore at her bandages and her gown and anything else her fingers could get at. Steve could do nothing to soothe her, to control her rage. Nurses ran in to restrain her, and finally, someone gave her a shot....

Danielle went home a week later. She was still bruised, though they were fading fast. The cuts were just narrow red lines now. Her midsection was still tender and sore from the operation that had removed her ruptured spleen, and her leg was in a cast and would be for quite some time.

By now, the initial shock had worn off and reality had set in. Months to recover from her injuries, more months to rehab her leg. The doctor had warned her that future back and neck problems were likely. Her leg would probably always hurt, and she might even limp. Without her spleen, she would be more susceptible to infection.

Danielle sat in her recliner and looked around the house. It was just as they had left it that night. All around her were reminders of Kyle. She was both comforted and saddened by them. She gathered his clothes up off the floor. They still smelled faintly of him. She collapsed on the bed, holding them tightly to her face, and cried herself to sleep.

After a couple more weeks, Trish managed to coax Danielle out of the house. The bruises and cuts were all gone and her midsection was healing. Even her broken ribs were better, which made everything so much easier. All that was left were the light scars from the cuts and the huge cast on her leg.

Trish took her driving around the city, and everywhere they went people honked and waved. When they went out to lunch the owner of the restaurant tore up their ticket, and fans frequently came by just to wish her well. A couple of times some photographers started taking pictures, only to have bystanders run them off. Austin had been spared the pain of losing another child, and the city was now fiercely protecting her.

She requested that Trish let her off on 6th Street. Danielle worked her way slowly down the street on her crutches. It was daytime and the vibe was different, but it was still 6th. If she closed her eyes, she could still imagine that she was eighteen, sitting on a corner with a guitar and a dream and nothing else. The people would watch and listen and then throw some money in her guitar case. It didn't seem like that long ago.

She was standing on a corner daydreaming when she felt a pat on her arm. A young girl stood there nervously chewing on her lip and holding a CD in her hands. She managed a shy smile. "Could you sign this for me, please?"

"Sure," Danielle answered. She took the CD and a Sharpie and prepared to sign it, and then took a double take. It was her picture on the cover; she recognized the infamous rebel flag picture immediately. Only someone had digitally edited the photo, removed the detail from the flag, airbrushed her and put a blue tinge on everything. The CD was titled *Between The Sheets*. Confused, she looked at the back cover. It was the CD that she and Kyle had just finished. She had no idea that it had been released. She politely signed it for the girl and then quickly worked her way back to Trish's car. She needed to go see Steve.

"We were powerless to stop it, Dani." Steve explained as they sat in his office. "I had already forwarded the masters to Jay. When they realized that you might not make it, they rushed the album out. Once we gave them the tapes, it was out of our hands. Jay said that you owed the label that after all the heat from the last album."

"So those bastards were making money off me while I was laying there dying?"

"Unfortunately. I think that they might have been hoping that you would. Either way, it's probably going to wind up being your biggest hit. It's flying off shelves. The single is already your biggest one."

"What single?" she asked angrily.

"'Sometimes It Fades.' They had it out to stations within hours of your accident. The single officially came out a few days later. It's been a monster. They've got plans to release at least four more. It's what they do."

"Son of a bitch," she grunted. "After all I've done for them."

Steve came around from behind the desk and sat on the edge. "I'm sorry. I know it seems kind of heartless and classless, but for them, it's just business. There's not much room for sentiment."

Danielle sat there for a moment, thinking. Then she grabbed her crutches and struggled to her feet. "I guess it was going to come out anyway. It doesn't really matter in the grand scheme of things." She got to the door and stopped. "Nothing matters anymore."

Over the next few weeks, Danielle received many visitors at the house. She was polite but withdrawn. She rarely strayed from the house. Despite the best efforts of her friends to get her out or to establish a routine, she resisted. She spent most of her time in bed, dreaming about what might have been. On occasion, the rage would overtake her and she would react by tearing the house apart, breaking things and punching holes in the wall. Her friends feared that she was going insane.

One night, a thunderstorm blew through Austin. Danielle stood at the patio door, balancing on her crutches and watching the lightning play across the sky. It was as if God himself was mocking her. She looked around her home at all of the things that she had amassed over her career. She thought of gold and platinum records and awards. She thought of all the money and the fame. It all seemed worthless to her.

The storm inside her was equal to the one outside. Danielle took one of her crutches and smashed the patio door, watching with satisfaction as the glass tumbled to the ground. Then she threw the crutches aside and hobbled out onto the patio. A cold rain pummeled her as the lightning flashed and the thunder roared at her.

"Fuck you," she screamed at the sky. She stood there, waiting for the lightning bolt, waiting for God's vengeance. "Quit playing with me. Just do it." Still, no lightning, no heavenly response to her cries. "You coward. You want somebody. I'm right here. Take me."

She stood and waited and taunted. It went on until the lightning stopped completely and the cold rain became nothing but a gentle sprinkle. "You chickenshit," she growled, and finally hobbled back inside the house.

She tore through the house room by room until she found herself at the basement door. She tore it open and nearly fell going to down the stairs. Her home studio was where she and Kyle had written so many songs together. They had almost lived down here, writing songs and making love and sleeping and doing it all over again. This had been their sanctuary.

Danielle looked at the room, trying to decide what to destroy first, and spied his guitar, standing silently on a stand. She limped over to it and yanked it up. She held it high, ready to bring it smashing down on the hard floor.

She thought of the songs that he had written on that guitar and of Ole Red and how she had destroyed it in a fit of rage as well. Instead, she collapsed in a heap on the floor. His guitar twanged as it hit the ground.

When Danielle finally decided to get up, she reached out for support and her fingers grazed the strings on his guitar. She looked at it through wet, red eyes. The wood had cracked and buckled where it had hit, but the neck was still in one piece. She pulled it into her and sat up. She scooted back against the wall and began to play

Kyle had only loved two things in his life. Danielle and music. Now, music was all that was left. Music had brought them together. Music had galvanized their relationship; it was everything to them. Now, music was all she had left. She played and played, throughout the night and into the day. She ignored the knocks on the door and the phone calls. She surfaced only to eat. At some point, she began to record.

Steve barely recognized her when Danielle walked into his office. Her always long hair had been cut boyishly short and dyed a bright red. She was pale and wearing a lot of makeup, which was entirely out of character for her. Only her height and her noticeable limp gave her away. She plopped a box down on the corner of his desk and handed him two disks.

"What is this?"

Danielle plopped down in a chair. "That's my last song. I even shot a video for it. Give it to the label and let them do their thing with it. That's the last thing they get out of me. Batten down the hatches, because the video is going to piss some people off. The box is stuff that I want you to have. Do what you want with it. Keep it, sell it, burn it. It's yours."

"Danielle…," Steve started.

"Don't. I've thought this over a lot. It's time for a new adventure. I've sold everything I own. I'm making a new start. Tell the guys goodbye for me."

"Dani, wait," Steve called. She turned and looked into his eyes. He knew that look. It was the same one she had shown him in the clubs just before a show. It was the look of a lion on the prowl. "You'll still have checks coming in, royalties...."

"You handle the business here. I've made you my POA. It's in the box. Whatever decisions you make from here, you have my blessing. Do what you gotta do. I want to get lost."

Steve was fighting hard to keep from breaking down. "You know that you're the daughter that I never had."

"I know," she said quietly.

Steve walked up to her and kissed her gently on the cheek. "Take care of yourself, Danielle."

"I will."

When she was gone, he slipped in the DVD and hit play. The song was called "Just A Whisper." The video was set in an old church with broken windows and overturned pews. There were dozens of lit candles around her. She was wearing a short black dress, her hair was dyed jet black, and she was made up to appear almost white. She looked like a vampire.

The song started slowly and began to build. He was struck by how well she sang on the track. People had always focused on her playing, but she was actually an extremely good singer. The guitar work was intricate and complex, the tune was haunting.

As the song began to build to its climax, Danielle sent a candelabra crashing to the ground, igniting the church. There was a clear shot of a crucifix on the wall burning. She stepped out of the burning building with her guitar, a red and white Strat that looked a lot like Ole Red. She walked down the street, the church still flaming in the background, as rain began to fall.

As the song started to ride out, she came across a car accident on the road. There were two body bags on the pavement. She dropped her guitar on the first one with a glare, then laid down next to the second one. She curled up next to it and closed her eyes. As the song faded out, the screen went black and the word Farewell came up.

Steve shook his head and laughed. Yes, this was going to cause him a lot of grief. Yet, he would fight and he would make sure the video aired, just as it was. Let the people bitch and moan. Danielle might be gone, but she would have the last word.

#

There were many roads out of Austin. She chose Highway 183, headed northwest. It was the same road her mother had taken out of Austin when she was eight. Only she wasn't headed back to Chaparral. There was nothing left for her there. She would turn somewhere along the line. It didn't matter where. All she needed was a starting point, a direction. The rest she would leave to the road and to the wind.

Danielle did not, as she had done as a child, look back as Austin slowly vanished in her rearview mirror. She did not mourn. She was choosing to leave this time. She was leaving all of her ghosts and her demons there as well. She left her father, and her beloved Kyle. She left her friends and her career. Danielle Regan was, for all intents and purposes, dead.

It was early spring of 2003 and a sultry, twenty-eight-year-old redhead named Renae Tucker left Austin for parts unknown. She had nothing but a suitcase full of clothes, money in her pocket, and no history to speak of. She was a blank canvas, with an entire world in front of her.

Before You Go...

HELP AN AUTHOR
write a review
THANK YOU!

Share your voice and help guide other readers to these wonderful books. Even if it's only a line or two your reviews help readers discover the author's books so they can continue creating stories that you'll love. Login to your favorite retailer and leave a review. Thank you.

About the Author

Donny Hunt has worked as a reporter, sportscaster and photographer. He lives in Amarillo Texas with his wife and four children. Blessed Poison is his first novel.